VICTORIA MARY SACKVILLE-WEST

(1892–1962) was born at Knole in Sevenoaks, Kent. Her parents were first cousins, her father being the third Baron Sackville and her mother the illegitimate daughter of Lionel Sackville-West and the Spanish dancer Pepita. Knole was to be an abiding passion throughout her life, the inspiration of much of her writing, and the source of great sorrow when, as a woman, she was unable to inherit it on her father's death. Vita was educated at home, except for three years spent at a school in London where she came to know Violet Keppel (later Trefusis) with whom, from 1918–21, she was to have a passionate affair.

In 1910 Vita met Harold Nicolson, the young diplomat whom she married three years later. In 1915 they bought a cottage two miles from Knole where they planned their first garden; three years later Vita Sackville-West's first novel, *Heritage*, was published. A distinguished novelist, poet, short-story writer, biographer, travel writer, critic, historian and gardener, her novels include *The Edwardians* (1930), *All Passion Spent* (1931) and *Seducers in Ecuador* (1942); of her poetry, *The Land* (1926) was awarded the Hawthornden Prize and *The Garden* (1946) won the Heinemann Prize.

During the 1920s her close and influential friendship with Virginia Woolf was at its height, culminating in the publication of Virginia Woolf's novel *Orlando* (1928), a celebration of her friend. In 1930 Harold and Vita bought Sissinghurst Castle in Kent, where they created their famous garden. A Fellow of the Royal Society of Literature and a JP for Kent, Vita Sackville-West was made a Companion of Honour in 1948. She died at Sissinghurst, after an operation for cancer, at the age of seventy.

Virago publishes *The Edwardians*, *All Passion Spent*, *Family History* (1932) and *No Signposts in the Sea* (1961). *Seducers in Ecuador* and *The Heir* (1922) will be published in 1987.

FAMILY HISTORY

VITA SACKVILLE-WEST

WITH A NEW INTRODUCTION BY
VICTORIA GLENDINNING

PENGUIN BOOKS – VIRAGO PRESS

Penguin Books
Viking Penguin Inc., 40 West 23rd Street,
New York, New York 10010, U.S.A.
Penguin Books Ltd, Harmondsworth,
Middlesex, England
Penguin Books Australia Ltd, Ringwood,
Victoria, Australia
Penguin Books Canada Limited, 2801 John Street,
Markham, Ontario, Canada L3R 1B4
Penguin Books (N.Z.) Ltd, 182–190 Wairau Road,
Auckland 10, New Zealand

First published in Great Britain by The Hogarth Press 1932
First published in the United States of America by Doubleday & Company, Inc. 1932
This edition first published in Great Britain by Virago Press Ltd. 1986
Published in Penguin Books 1987

Portions of this book first appeared in *Harper's Bazaar*

Printed in Great Britain
by Cox & Wyman Ltd. of Reading, Berkshire
Set in Baskerville

INTRODUCTION

Vita Sackville-West began writing this novel in May 1931, just four days after the publication of *All Passion Spent* which, like *The Edwardians* the year before that, was very successful and brought her increased fame and a lot of money. She finished *Family History* in thirteen months, and although it did well—6,000 copies were sold before publication day in October 1932—it was not a bestseller on the scale of the previous two, and has been largely neglected since. Her husband Harold Nicolson, when he read it in proof, privately considered it "very competent and moving but not exactly her type of thought". Later he revised his opinion, writing in his diary: "Read *Family History* in train and weep copiously."

It was dedicated by Vita Sackville-West "To My Mother", only for the reason that the temperamental Lady Sackville had just made a terrible scene because Vita had dedicated her poem "Sissinghurst" to Virginia Woolf and not to her. There is one extraordinary feature of *Family History*, elucidated by Vita in her Foreword. She attempts in this novel to introduce a spelling reform, writing "that" as "thatt" when it is used as a pronoun, to distinguish it from its other grammatical functions, as in, for example, "I fear that thatt will irritate my readers." It irritated even her, she writes, when she was reading over her manuscript; not surprisingly, no one followed her lead, and happily she dropped the idea.

My own feeling about the book has changed. In the biography *Vita* I wrote of it rather dismissively as "this not very distinguished novel". *Family History* was written at a time when her own personal life and her husband's professional life were both in a state of confusion. Submerged by biographical minutiae, I saw it principally as a love story illustrative of Vita's own impatient attitude towards lovers who became too possessive and dependent. That is of course what it is, but as fiction it is much more interesting and complex. Reading it again, one can see how Vita detached herself imaginatively from the purely personal, and also how the love story serves as the occasion for expressing the author's perceptions of what the class structure of England was, and how it was changing.

The love story itself concerns Evelyn Jarrold, a pretty widow nearing forty, and a young man, Miles Vane-Merrick, who is fifteen years her junior. The age gap makes any relationship between them less likely to last and more socially uneasy, even reprehensible in conventional terms: Evelyn, however much in love she may be, will not consider marrying Miles. (The age gap was perhaps Vita's way of "translating" the hazards of lesbian love into heterosexual terms.) Both of them, we are told, have strong personalities and tyrannical natures, so if things go wrong there is no chance that either will give in; thus a crash is inevitable. But "even the most passionate lover of truth shuts his eyes to truth in the early stages of love", and these two love one another passionately.

The story, and our understanding of its implications, unfold in a series of "Portraits". We learn that Evelyn Jarrold has soft and expensive clothes, a soft and expensive life, and too much time on her hands. She is "jealously possessive" by nature, and has a very close relationship with her teenage son Dan—who is an idealised portrait of Vita's elder son Ben, as she told him at the time. Vita identified strongly with seventeen-year-old Ben, but did not have this physically demonstrative relationship with him; there is a hint of incestuous desire in the scene where young Dan dances with his mother and feels her yield, and feels too "the softness of her woman's body in her silken clothes, and knew how much Miles must have loved her, and how much she must have loved Miles". Evelyn is even jealous of the devotion of her niece; she must have everyone half in love with her. "Doesn't everyone like to be loved? . . . One never gets enough love."

She could well be a monster, but is not by virtue of the fact that she is indeed lovable, a woman who is "apparently a model of the domestic virtues and who yet suggested all the chic of *Vogue* and all the passion of Shakespeare". The reader, like Dan, can understand how much Miles must have loved her.

The "Portrait of Miles Vane-Merrick" reveals him as a peculiarly middle-aged twenty-five-year-old in spite of his glamorous good looks—maybe because the author projected a good deal of her forty-year-old self on to him. He is a busy chap—an idealistic socialist, in the middle of writing "a stiff book on the economic situation" (this is the time of the great Depression), he becomes an M.P. He is also a landowner and a dedicated country squire. The descriptions of his castle in Kent, from the moment when he drives Evelyn and her son "off the main road, down a rough little lane between hedges", are descriptions of Vita's Sissinghurst—the tower, the archway, the courtyard, the orchard, the moat, the cottage with mullioned windows, the way it all consists of "isolated buildings" linked by ancient brick walls.

In 1931–32 Sissinghurst was not as visitors see it today. The archway under the tower had only just been unblocked, planning and planting were still piecemeal and sketchy, and the Nicolsons were only just finishing clearing the site of nettles and rubbish; Miles's castle seems to Evelyn "an encampment". Vita indeed camped there often during the time she was writing *Family History*; the family did not move in until April 1932. She was often alone there with a friend or lover, and they would stand at night, like Miles and Evelyn in the novel, on the roof of the tower "leaning their elbows on the parapet, and looking out in silence over the fields, the woods, the hop-gardens, and the lake down in the hollow from which a faint mist was rising". In conveying Miles's proud and passionate feelings about his castle, Vita had only to transcribe her own growing attachment to Sissinghurst.

Nowhere in the novel does Vita Sackville-West quote Byron's famous lines

> Man's love is of man's life a thing apart,
> 'Tis woman's whole existence.

But that is what this love story is about. Byron's formulation has a complacent air; in Vita's book, the message is a dreadful warning to both the man and the woman. Nor do I think she was postulating this state of affairs as the norm between the sexes. It was simply the situation between this particular man and this particular woman. The fact that Vita found her lovers rather too ready to make her their "whole existence", while she needed to compartmentalise her life, explains her choice of theme but does not exhaust its fictional possibilities.

Evelyn, staying with Miles, is dismayed by the fact that he unfeelingly keeps to his working day; he in turn finds that her "vanity and passion" disrupt his life. She realises that "he was a full man and she was an empty woman". Miles adores her when she is gay and easy-going; he loves her, but "she represented his diversion, not his whole life". He is maddened when she is "difficult and strenuous and jealous". The crux is this:

Love and the woman were insufficient for an active mind. Love and the man, however, were all-too-sufficient for a starved heart and unoccupied mind.

What each learns from this predicament, and how it is all resolved, the reader will find out for herself or himself. The author is careful to keep the balance of sympathy swinging between the two: it is easy to understand Miles's exasperation with idle, possessive, demanding Evelyn. And yet his friend Viola says, "I am sorry for any woman who loves Miles", and he himself wonders whether "he has a heart at all":

Love as Evelyn understood it was an entire absorption of one lover into the other. He wanted to retain his individuality, his activity, his time-table. He wanted to lead his own life, parallel with the life of love, separate, independent.

If Evelyn is spoilt, trivial, conventional, unanalytical, limited in her interests, as she is, what is one to make of a man like Miles who "likes women to be idle and decorative" (so long as they keep out of his way when he is busy) and who says that while he likes intelligence he "hates clever women"? If some women became mindlessly dependent pets, and ended up with no function and no weapon except love itself, whose fault was it, I should like to know?

The clash between their expectations is in part a function of the generation gap between them. It is possible, we infer, that Miles might sustain a better, if less erotic, relationship with an educated girl of his own age who had a life of her own. This brings us to a broader and perhaps more interesting theme of *Family History*: the collision of values and

attitudes to work, sex and social behaviour in a society that
Vita, in the early 1930s, saw as changing radically. (Collision
is the master metaphor of this novel, made graphic by a
tragedy on the railway line glimpsed by Evelyn on her first
visit to Miles's castle.)

Vita Sackville-West is not primarily interested in the
working classes, represented here by Miles's devoted
retainers and Evelyn's servant. If Evelyn is self-conscious
about her employees' disapproval of her, it is because her
roots are middle class. Please note: many people today use
"middle class" pejoratively, to mean bourgeois and
therefore over-privileged. Formerly, "middle class" was
used equally pejoratively but by the upper classes, including
such as Vita, to mean bourgeois and therefore not out of the
top drawer, even a bit "common". The reasons for this shift
of perspective lie in social changes that Vita did not even
envisage; but that is another day's story.

Evelyn, whose father is a country solicitor, "passes"
among the landed aristocracy by virtue of her wealth,
beauty, and graceful manners. She is rigidly conventional
and class-conscious, relying on the rites and ceremonies of
polite society to sustain her own place in it and keep others
out. She feels mystified and threatened by Miles's friendly
acceptance of his clever, working-class political agent, and
she is surprised by Miles's own casual ways: he has no
chauffeur, and he does not change for dinner. As a born
member of the territorial aristocracy and an intellectual, the
implication is he can afford to break the rules.

The old aristocracy is seen at play at the ball at Chevron
House. Readers of *The Edwardians*, Vita's romantic-ironic
novel based on her own Edwardian girlhood, will recognise
the Duchess, twenty years on—"somewhat wrinkled and
withered" now—and Lady Roehampton, with whom the
young Duke had had an affair; he is absent, still unmarried,

"proverbially inaccessible" and travelling somewhere in Asia. (So he escaped after all.) Apart from him, the younger generation are a degenerate lot. "The standard of looks was amazing"—but there are no brains and no ideas in those beautiful well-bred young heads. Decadence has set in.

So much for old wealth. New wealth is represented by Evelyn's in-laws, the Jarrolds. Old Mr Jarrold is an industrial magnate who came up the hard way, without education, raising himself by his own bootstraps. He has provided his family with 200 acres of Surrey and a "square, red, ornate and comfortable house". Mr Jarrold is as "solid as an old bull in a field", unlike his more refined but useless sons, who have not had to work for their living and "imagine themselves the aristocracy of the future". This, by 1930, was quite possible since "new families quickly merged with the genuine article". But the younger Jarrolds are "rotten fruit", as irresponsible and lazy as the guests at the Chevron House ball.

Old Mr Jarrold says it takes three generations of prosperity to make a real English gentleman. Dan Jarrold, Evelyn's son, is the third generation; he is at Eton, he could be "the genuine article" and fulfil his grandfather's conventional ambitions. But Dan is "interested in ideas", admiring the maverick Miles Vane-Merrick to the point of idolatry. He will be a rebel—like Miles, like the young Duke in *The Edwardians*, and like subversive Leonard Anquetil, also from *The Edwardians*, who has married the Duke's sister Viola.

Vita Sackville-West brings Viola and Leonard Anquetil, now the parents of a grown daughter, into *Family History* to suggest the life of ideas and radical thinking that was flourishing independently of the philistinism of most high society. As we read about the Anquetils' progressive, articulate household, it is hard not to recognise some version

of the Bloomsbury group, which Vita knew through
Virginia and Leonard Woolf (who published *Family History*
at the Hogarth Press). Vita was never altogether comfortable
in Bloomsbury, though she loved Virginia; and her unease is
reflected and magnified in conservative Evelyn's reactions to
these clever friends of Miles's. Evelyn recognises that "this
was a different England"; she is impressed by the frankness
and "reality" of the Anquetils' conversation, but shocked by
the subjects that they discuss. She is startled too by their lack
of ritual deference to women and, yet again, by the fact that
no one changes for dinner. "Evening dress was a formula, a
safeguard, like good manners; it was part of all those things
which greased the wheels of life." The Anquetils, like Miles,
have the confidence to dispense with all that.

But the Anquetils are not the author's favourite
characters. Vita Sackville-West seems as enamoured of
Miles Vane-Merrick as is her fictional Evelyn, and Miles
propounds his social philosophy with some eloquence. He is
not "modern", even for 1932; he is a "reversion to type", a
Renaissance man or an Elizabethan Englishman: adventurous, cultivated, intellectually curious, a citizen of the
world. On the question of class he is for the traditional
hierarchical system, in spite of his socialism. He believes in
the "dignity" of the labourer and in being proud of "what
you really are". His ideal seems to be a sort of romantic
feudalism: "He loved the people, though he loathed and
hated democracy."

There is precious little protein in this for the 1980s. But it is
as well to remember that before the Second World War
social class was an inescapable and self-evident fact of life,
like the weather, and something that could not easily be
disregarded even by free spirits. Miles's *ancien régime* style of
thinking mirrors Vita Sackville-West's precisely: she called
herself a "pre-1792 Tory". Many of her friends would have

shared her opinions, while taking a less benevolent, or paternalistic, view of the working class. Vita was not a radical, nor an original thinker in any profound sense; she was as trapped in the class into which she was born as any farm labourer. She herself was to seem appallingly reactionary to her son Ben as he grew older. The traditional upper classes had a lot to lose by the spread of democracy, including much that had gratified not only themselves but their dependent inferiors. It becomes easier to understand if one thinks of the parallel history of feminism: men, and complacently dependent women too, had everything to lose, apparently, from change, and even the "nicest" men, in the context of feminism, might have echoed Miles's comment on the class system: "Instinct makes me reactionary, reason makes me progressive."

Family History, then, is not a socially subversive novel but a period piece. This realisation is reinforced by the details of life, taken for granted in these pages, which half a century later acquire a new dimension as social history. It takes a great effort of the imagination, for a start, for us to credit how disturbing it was for Evelyn to meet all these people who did not "change for dinner". I find it interesting too to think about the extent to which having servants must have inhibited personal life: Evelyn is embarrassed by their noticing the bright blue envelopes which arrive almost daily from Miles. (This is taken, indirectly, from life: Vita's own very noticeable bright blue envelopes were arriving almost daily at this time at a house in Chelsea—two at a time, since she was writing to two young women, one of them called Evelyn, who were living together, and it caused not just embarrassment but trouble.)

Then there are the greyish-yellow fogs, a hazard to health, so thick that "women had earrings torn from their ears" by invisible assailants. The Clean Air Acts after the Second

World War put a stop to those pea-soupers. The last pages of
this book describe the progress of a terminal illness. In the
1920s and thirties, only the poor went into hospital. Even in
cases of grave illness, the well-off were looked after at home
by day-nurses and night-nurses, as recounted in detail here.
There is a period flavour too in the assumption that "chill
deadly air" can bring on infection or inflammation, in the
frequent visits of the physicians, and in the remedies they
prescribe: chloral for sleeping, and "piqûres" of morphia
where we would say "injections". Fifteen years later, the
patient would have been given the new antibiotics, and need
not have died at all.

Why did Vita Sackville-West launch herself into this
thirty-page sickroom marathon? Already in the novel she
had described one deathbed—that of someone who was "a
product of the Victorian age". In this infinitely more
protracted second one she was perhaps essaying a "modern"
version of a nineteenth-century deathbed scene in order to
mark the belated passing of the sexual and social attitudes of
the Victorian age. She pulls out all the stops, and we are
affected by it, even against our will, though the writing of
this section is not above criticism: you may feel that the
nurse's private thoughts are conveyed in a carelessly
repetitive way.

But the final pages pack an emotional charge it is
impossible to withstand. Is it a happy ending or an unhappy
one? I guarantee that like Harold Nicolson, who was reading
Family History on the train between Staplehurst (the station
for Sissinghurst) and Charing Cross on 23 October 1932,
most readers will "weep copiously".

Victoria Glendinning, London, 1986

FOREWORD

In this novel I have spelt the word 'that' in two different ways: either with one 't' or with two, in order to differentiate between the conjunction and the demonstrative adjective and demonstrative or relative pronoun. I fear that this innovation may irritate many readers. It has irritated me, in reading over my own manuscript, for the unfamiliar is always irritating until it has taken its place as the familiar.

I am no friend to phonetic spelling. I prefer to think that foreigners to our language must struggle with their own difficulties in the matter of such words as plough, cough, thorough, through, though, rough; words which, spelt in the same way, are pronounced quite differently. Or with such words as Hugh, hew, hue, you, ewe, knew, gnu, view, lieu, queue; words which, spelt differently, are pronounced in the same way. I prefer to think that even the English young, like the foreigner, must grapple with the task. I should like to see the decimal system introduced into England, to save the English young many hours which might be better employed than in wrestling with our extraordinary and obsolete calculations in pounds, shillings, and pence; rods, poles, and perches. But I should not like to see the English language wholly shorn of its very peculiar peculiarities.

Nevertheless, I do believe that in the interests of clarity, the addition of the extra 't' should abolish for ever the confusion of thatt ambiguous little word.

CONTENTS

PART I

PORTRAIT OF THE JARROLDS

M-m-m, my dear," said old Mr. Jarrold, taking his daughter-in-law for the hundred-and-twentieth time round his Museum, "thatt's the first bit of coal brought up from the pits at Orlestone. Look at it. Thatt's what sent Dan to Eton. Thatt's what made a gentleman of Dan. A dirty lump, I daresay, but worth more than all those cowrie-shells I brought back from Java. M-m-m."

Mr. Jarrold was such a dear old man that Evelyn Jarrold, his daughter-in-law, looked willingly for the hundred-and-twentieth time at the first bit of coal from Orlestone, and indeed at all the other miscellaneous exhibits in the Museum. Mr. Jarrold always seemed to forget that she had been round the Museum before, and seized upon her whenever she came to luncheon at the Park Lane house, to take her round the Museum afterwards. Although he referred continually to his grandson Dan, his advanced age apparently allowed him to ignore the fact that Dan's mother was no stranger to the house, to the family, or to the Museum. He might still treat her as a visitor and as an attractive woman; might still exercise his somewhat senile gallantry. "M-m-m, my dear," he said, taking her arm, leading her from show-case to show-case.

She looked dutifully at his collection, disguising her boredom because she was naturally kind-hearted and liked to please the old man. Rather dusty, she thought, and lacking in life; but they preserved some kind of existence so long as Mr. Jarrold remained alive to croon his saga over them. Lumps of coal; cowrie-shells; the practical and the romantic. She knew the order of value in which he placed them. Yet he had gone once to Java, in his yacht; but his yacht had been but the outcome of his dirty lumps of coal; he had owned a yacht, because other rich men owned yachts; and the unexpected sorrow of his life,—greater even than the sorrow of his eldest son's death in 1916,—had been his rejection from the Royal Yacht Squadron. He had been obliged to go round the world flying the blue instead of the white ensign. Evelyn experienced some indignation on his behalf whenever she remembered his humiliation.

"M-m-m, my dear," he murmured, like an old and sleepy bee.

Still, he had done well for himself and his family in the world; so well, that a baronetcy was confidently expected before the year was out. He was prominent among industrial magnates, and his charity was both lavish and discriminating. Mr. Jarrold alone affected to pooh-pooh the suggestion of the baronetcy. Honours and success had clearly waited in store for the Jarrolds from the first. Evelyn Wilson, as the daughter of a country solicitor, had been congratulated on her good fortune when she became engaged to the eldest Jarrold son so far back as 1913. It was unfortunate, of course, that her husband should have been killed in the war, but at any rate her son remained as the heir. Neither her friends nor her father saw any reason to revise their congratulations.

The Museum was certainly dark and dusty, curiously housed in the Park Lane family mansion. The show-cases

extended round the dark well of a hall, and round the
upper galleries of thatt hall, fenced off from the well by
balustrades of mouchara-bieh. Mr. Jarrold took a pride
in the Eastern touch provided by those pierced and
fretted balustrades. They testified that he, also, was
acquainted with the Orient. They testified that he, also,
was a man of taste, a traveller, a man of culture. Anybody
who knew Mr. Jarrold knew, naturally, that he did not
give a fig for culture, except in so far as his fortune could
provide it as an adjunct, an extra, a subject alternately for
boast or for derision, whether typified by his own travels
or by his grandson's classical education at Eton. Both ex-
periences resolved themselves into the same category for
Mr. Jarrold: a gentleman's luxury, quite separate from
practical life. He enjoyed turning his grandson on, after
dinner, to repeat a dozen lines from the *Aeneid;* such an
accompaniment seemed to improve the quality of his port.
"Come on, Dan," he would say; "*Tu regere imperio populos
Romane memento,*—how does it go?" And then he would
beat time to the magnificent rhythm with a fork, and
would derive satisfaction from the fact that he had a
grandson who—thanks to him—could quote Virgil. But
his electric gramophone, which wound itself up and
changed its own records, and was also a wireless, gave him
the same sort of pleasure. Culture, for him, was something
rather expensive, and of no practical use at all.

Still, he was a dear old man, and Evelyn followed him
willingly as he mumbled round his Museum.

It had all been assembled by himself personally; no
exhibit went back further than his own generation, or,
one might say, further than the Jarrold family itself. Mr.
Jarrold was practically the creator of the family. Only in

his generation had the Jarrolds clambered definitely out of
the clay. Mr. Jarrold could point to the lump of coal
which had sent his sons to St. Paul's and his grandson to
Eton; he could point to the model of the first shunting-
station at the pit-head. He was very much the founder of
a dynasty as he took visitors round these show-cases. It
was only when he came to the evidences of his travels
that he became a little confused, a little shame-faced.
Here, he evidently felt, the unnecessary impinged upon
the sensible. The presence of the unnecessary could be
explained away only by the fact that men with fortunes
such as William Jarrold's could afford to own yachts.
Yachts took such men, in their rare holidays, to strange,
un-English places from which it was almost obligatory to
bring back queer, un-English objects, if only to show how
great the difference between English people and natives
was. Mr. Jarrold muddled all this up vaguely with culture.
It induced in him a confused state of mind. Pride became
blurred by apology. Apology became overlaid by pride.
It was fine to have a grandson who could quote Virgil,
though the quotation of Virgil was also a little shameful;
something to be treated with a mixture of derision and
pride. It was fine to have travelled on one's own yacht to
the East, though a little shameful to have troubled to
assemble works of art,—as Mr. Jarrold considered his
mouchara-bieh balustrades to be,—from the East. Works
of art were all right so long as they were expensive enough.
But Mr. Jarrold could never quite apply thatt justification
to his collection of curios.

They were his weakness; he loved them. He kept the
master-key of the show-cases on his watch-chain.

His watch-chain was almost an emblem of civic dignity.

It crossed his stomach in great gold links, and disappeared into a waistcoat pocket at either end. Mr. Jarrold's clothes were a trifle old-fashioned, for his tailor had been forbidden to vary their cut for the past forty years. Black clothes in London, with a morning coat and a grey stripe in the trousers; dark grey tweed of a peculiarly unbending thickness in the country. When he went out, whether in London or the country, he donned a square black hat, midway between a topper and a bowler. Evelyn said that in London he looked like a nineteenth-century statesman, and in the country like a nineteenth-century squire. The mutton-chop whiskers, fringing his rubicund old face, and the broad tie invariably pushed through a ring, produced this effect. His short, thick-set hands, covered with freckles and fine red hairs, were the hands of a practical man accustomed to power and authority. He had never known a day's illness in his life, and now in his seventy-fifth year his faculties remained undiminished. His constant mumble which might have been taken as a sign of old age, was, in fact, nothing more than a nervous habit of which he himself was scarcely conscious, and was thoroughly belied by the piercing glance of his small grey eye. Thatt eye declared that William Jarrold, coal-owner and iron-master, would see through all nonsense and would stand none of it, either from his family or his employees. His sons had winced before it, his subordinates had trembled, and his wife had always known her place. It was a favourite saying of his, that a man should be master in his own house.

But he was not in the least grim, and he had always liked a pretty woman, though he had been wise enough not to marry one. He liked his daughter-in-law Evelyn.

His gaiety increased noticeably whenever she came to the house. Evelyn liked him too; she almost loved him. They were the best of friends. She took trouble to please him, chaffing him affectionately, creating little private jokes between them, so that he purred like an old tom-cat and chaffed her in return. "Ah, my dear, you waste your time on an old fellow like me." For all his chaff, however, she knew that his views on life were severe. His upper middle-class morality was absolutely rigid. A second marriage he would have tolerated, since it was not reasonably to be expected that her life should have to come to an end on the day Tommy was killed in Flanders, but any less reputable affair he would condemn out of hand. He took it for granted that Evelyn, like all the other members of his family, knew exactly how far she ought to go. He had no doubt that she had accepted a certain amount of admiration between the ages of twenty-four, when Tommy was killed, and thirty-nine, which she now must be. Thatt was natural. He had paid her a good many compliments himself, and younger men must have paid her many more. But of her virtue he was unquestioningly convinced. And if anyone in his presence expressed a wonder at her continued celibacy, he explained it by saying that she lived for the boy.

"When does Dan come back, my dear?"

"On the twentieth, Papa."

All his children called him Papa. Evelyn had brought herself to it with difficulty.

"And you're both coming down to Newlands for Christmas?"

"But of course. If you'll have us."

"Don't you always come for Christmas? Well, then.

Besides, what should I do without you? And I want you
to talk to Evan."

"What's the matter with Evan, Papa?"

"Drinks too much," said Mr. Jarrold shortly.

"Evan?"

"Evan. Suppose he thinks I can't see. I can, though.
I can see when a bottle of brandy, half full at the end of
dinner, is empty by breakfast. Damn good brandy too,—
much too good to get drunk on."

"You mean?"

"I mean that he sneaks down to the dining-room and
finishes it after I've gone to bed. Thatt's what I mean.
M-m-m."

"Why don't you tell Paterson to put away the drinks
after you leave the dining-room?"

"Sensible as usual, my dear,—I like your sense—but
Paterson would see through it. I can't give my own son
away to Paterson. Difficult enough to give him away to
you."

Evelyn had known for years that Evan drank.

"Very well, Papa, I'll talk to him."

"I haven't told his mother," said Mr. Jarrold, shooting
a sudden glance at her.

"No, of course not, Papa; much better not."

"Don't you think so?" said Mr. Jarrold, delighted and
relieved by this confirmation. "Only distress her,—what?
—and do no good to Evan. Tommy never drank, did he?"

"No!" said Evelyn, suddenly laughing, and for some
reason she pressed the old man's arm affectionately to her
side; "Tommy had every virtue and no vices." Mr. Jarrold
must never know anything about Tommy's mean little
vices. Tommy was a 'good fellow' in his father's eyes.

"Dull dog, Tommy," rose to Mr. Jarrold's tongue, but
he suppressed it, remembering that Tommy was dead and
had been Evelyn's husband. "I can't think where Evan
gets it from," he grumbled; "I never drank as a young
man; at least, no more than was natural. A binge every
now and then; but I never soaked. Evan soaks."

"Have you said anything to him yourself, Papa?"

"No fear!" said Mr. Jarrold emphatically. "Why, if a
man of my age said anything of the sort to a man of his
age, he'd drink two bottles of brandy instead of one. I've
lived long enough to know thatt. No; I'll give him a
chance first. M-m-m. You talk to him, my dear, and if he
takes no notice of what you say I'll weigh in. I'll bring up
all the big guns too. 'Tell him I'll cut him off with a shill-
ing. 'Tell him I won't regard him as my son. 'Won't have
drunkards directing my business when I'm gone. 'Won't
have drunkards looking after Dan's interests. Not safe.
As soon trust the Rolls to a drunken chauffeur. But I won't
speak to him myself till everything else has failed."

"I shall probably fail, Papa."

"Certain to. Hopeless job I'm giving you. Shan't blame
you if you do. The hand that rocks the cradle can't cork
the bottle. M-m-m. All the same, Evan likes you. Likes
you too much, I sometimes think. There's just a chance,
he might listen. Try."

"I'll try, Papa," said Evelyn, who had already tried.

"That's right. Tackle the hopeless job, and you may
bring it off. I have, sometimes. Tackled the hopeless job.
Not often. Only on big issues. Evan isn't a big issue."

"Poor Evan, Papa!"

"Nonsense. Don't sentimentalise. He ought to have
more guts. Everybody has temptations. Had them myself.

Didn't give way. Not thatt sort, though. Poor Evan,—rubbish. Tell him to take a pull on himself. Tell him to remember the business. He wants a share in it, doesn't he? Well, he won't get it unless he takes a pull. Not a pull at the bottle, mind. Another sort of pull. M-m-m. At his socks."

Evelyn found the subject embarrassing; it gave her a feeling of dishonesty to pretend surprise at Mr. Jarrold's confidences, when she herself could have told him far more about Evan than he was ever likely to know.

"Don't let us think about it any more now," she said; "I promise you that I'll see what I can do at Christmas. Show me some more of your treasures. I don't believe I have ever seen everything in the Museum. And I shall have to be going in a few minutes."

"Appointment?"

"Only with a dressmaker," said Evelyn smiling.

"Ah, thatt's good," said Mr. Jarrold, faintly stirred by this suggestion of feminine mysteries; "have lots of pretty frocks for Christmas. You always look nice, my dear. Those furs,—very becoming to you. And nice scent too. Like women to use scent. Suitable. Always say that women are the flowers of life, and flowers ought to smell good. Most of the new ones don't though."

"Did Mrs. Jarrold tell you thatt, Papa?"

"I've got a nose of my own, haven't I? Improved varieties—pooh. They've improved all the smell out of them. Give me cabbage roses every time, and nice soft clothes for women. Muslin, thatt's what I like, and pretty colours."

"I can't wear muslin in December, I'm afraid, Papa."

"Oh, you're all right," said Mr. Jarrold, looking at her

approvingly; "you look soft, and warm,—the way women ought to look, and as though you hadn't a bone in your body. Healthy, though. Most women nowadays look as though they hadn't room to keep their lungs in."

"You'll soon be telling me that I'm fat," said Evelyn.

"Slender, slender," said Mr. Jarrold; "not sickly, I meant, and not as hard as a board. Just right. We might get some skating at Christmas."

She was accustomed to his abrupt changes of subject.

"I hope so," she replied, glowing; "I love skating, and so does Dan."

"Spoil his hunting, though," said Mr. Jarrold.

"I don't know that thatt would break his heart," said Evelyn cautiously. She felt her own heart beginning to beat faster. Here was the opening she had been waiting for, and much as she disliked the prospect she must avail herself of it. She had promised Dan. Dan, who was frightened of his grandfather, had persuaded himself that his mother would make everything all right, and though Evelyn had sighed over his weakness when she saw how easily he shifted his difficulties on to her, she had resolved not to fail him.

"Nonsense," said Mr. Jarrold; "every proper boy would break his heart if his hunting was spoilt in his Christmas holidays. Dash it, not every boy has hunters like Dan. Most boys have to come out on an old tub of a pony on two days of the week. But no one could ever say I didn't mount my grandson properly."

He was quite angry, quite indignant. He took his hand away from Evelyn's arm, and walked away by himself, staring into a show-case full of grinning Javanese masks, his hands clasped behind his back, muttering to himself.

"Of course they couldn't," said Evelyn, inclined to laugh although she foresaw that she was in for a bad quarter of an hour; "you've always given Dan the best hunters of any boy in England. He was asking after them only the other day,—St. Andrew's Day. I went down to Eton, and almost the first thing he said was, How's Silver Star?"

"Glad to hear it," said Mr. Jarrold grimly, without turning round.

He was not in the least mollified. She could see thatt, by the nervous, angry way he kept clasping and unclasping his fingers. Childish old creature! she thought. He had deliberately chosen to be affronted in his pride, just as a pretext for losing his temper. In a moment she would give him something to lose his temper about, in sober earnest. Perhaps he would even forbid her to come to Newlands with Dan for Christmas. Thatt would be a relief. These family gatherings, taken so much as a matter of course, were sometimes almost more than she could bear. She would go with Dan to the South of France. . . .

"Papa, don't be so cross. The boy loves riding, you know, and he could ride even if he couldn't hunt."

"Is thatt all he wants?" said Mr. Jarrold, swinging round on her. He looked so savage that she really quailed. "To go ambling round the park instead of going across country? Perhaps he'd like Wilkins to take him on a leading-rein? Perhaps he'd like me to buy him a donkey? The boy's a coward, Evelyn. I've always known it, but I wouldn't face it. My grandson, a coward! But, by God, I won't have it. He *shall* hunt. All gentlemen hunt, don't they? when they can afford it, which most of them can't. No one shall say that Jarrold's grandson isn't a gentleman, or that his grandfather can't afford to mount him. Hunt he shall, and I don't care if he breaks his neck doing it."

"He isn't a coward," said Evelyn in a low voice. She was trying to control the trembling which had seized upon her, determined to go through with this ordeal now that it had started. "He's a sensitive boy, he loves animals, and he doesn't like cruelty. Thatt's all. You had to know it sooner or later. I promised him I would tell you that he means to give up hunting."

"Didn't dare tell me himself, what? Gets his mother to do it for him! A moral coward as well as a physical one. Very pretty! And what's all this rubbish about cruelty? The poor fox, I suppose? Doesn't he want to shoot either, may I ask?"

"No, Papa, since you ask, he doesn't."

"I see. This is what comes of trying to make a gentleman of my grandson,—my eldest grandson, mark you; my heir. I offer him the best hunters and the best shooting in England, but he'd rather have his nose in a book. Why, my sons are better gentlemen than he is. Tommy was a sportsman, whatever you may say. He hadn't an idea in his head, but he could get his horse over a fence as cleanly as anybody. Geoffrey, too, lazy beggar though he is. And young Robin, too,—now, there's a good boy, a real boy. Dan and Evan are the duds. Nice things you've been telling me, Evelyn!"

"You're very hard on Dan," said Evelyn, nettled at hearing her son called a dud; "everybody can't be cut on the same pattern. You admit yourself that Tommy hadn't an idea in his head. ("Tommy was a damned good fellow," interjected Mr. Jarrold.) Dan's head is full of

ideas, he's an intelligent boy, and he thinks for himself.
Isn't thatt something?"

"Something, but not much," said Mr. Jarrold, calming
down a little. "It's not natural for a boy of his age to
think for himself. Dangerous. Not natural for an English
boy, I mean. Don't know about foreigners. Anyway, they
wear socks till they're fourteen. French boys do. I've seen
them. And bowl hoops."

Evelyn laughed; she couldn't help it.

"Oh, you may laugh. You say everybody can't be cut
on the same pattern. Why not? We've evolved the best
pàttern in the world, so why not stick to it? Besides, we've
got more than one pattern. I'm not a gentleman myself,—
never pretended to be, I'm a successful business man. I've
got my place in the world too. But once I've done the job,
I don't see why my sons and grandsons shouldn't reap the
benefit. They say it takes three generations to make a
gentleman. Well, Dan's got his three generations behind
him."

"I don't see why you should expect him to be an empty-
headed ninny," said Evelyn, less alarmed now that she
was annoyed, and now that Mr. Jarrold's first rage had
passed.

"Obstinate, aren't you? M-m-m. Stick up for your
young. Quite right. But see here, Evelyn, what's come
over Dan? You insisted on taking him off to Italy or somewhere in the summer, so I haven't really seen him since
Easter. He was sound enough then. Has he been getting
into a bad set at Eton?"

"So far as I can make out, he hasn't any friends at
Eton."

"All wrong, all wrong," muttered Mr. Jarrold. He was not angry now; only puzzled and distressed. Evelyn wondered how far she dared go. Perhaps it was wiser to prepare the old man's mind before the Christmas holidays.

"You see, Papa. Dan is growing up. A year makes a lot of difference at thatt age. Remember, Dan is seventeen now."

"Only a phase, I dare say," said Mr. Jarrold more hopefully. He looked tired; his burst of anger had tired him.

"Perhaps, Papa. So you mustn't get too much annoyed with him if you hear him saying things you don't agree with."

"Not a Socialist, is he?" barked Mr. Jarrold, preparing to lose his temper again.

"I don't think he takes much interest in politics," Evelyn said evasively. She decided that she had given the old man enough shocks for the present.

"Or a pacifist? nothing like thatt? Couldn't stand thatt. Religious, is he?"

"Not very," said Evelyn, with a smile.

"Don't care about thatt, so long as he goes to church at Newlands. He must go on Christmas Day and every Sunday. Must keep up appearances for the sake of the village."

"I'm sure he'll do thatt, Papa," said Evelyn, not feeling sure at all.

"Well, well . . ." grumbled Mr. Jarrold. "This hunting business bothers me, all the same. Quite sure he isn't a coward? How are his games?"

"I'm afraid I didn't ask."

"He ought to have told you. If he was keen, he would have told you without asking. Bad sign. Bad sign."

"He got his Trials Prize last half, you know. And he's in the First Hundred."

"Don't care. Who ever went to Eton to be educated? Manners and character,—thatt's what you go to Eton for. Learn to be a man of the world. Learn to control yourself, and so to control others."

Mr. Jarrold, she might have retorted, had never learnt to control himself and yet had controlled others with conspicuous success. Like many a greater man, he had given way to his feelings and his bouts of temper whenever he felt inclined. He had never absorbed the English gospel of repression, ardently as he might preach it now for the benefit of his sons or his grandson. But then, he had never been to an English public school. He had never even come under the heritage of Dr. Arnold's influence. He had knocked his way upward through life, getting crudely to the top, meeting his fellow men in the ordinary, un-gentlemanly rough-and-tumble of competition. He had dispensed with both manners and classical education. Nor had games entered much into his life. He had never had time. He had originated in a different class and a different age. Evelyn could not see that he was any the worse for thatt.

"Doesn't it all rather depend," she said, "on what we want Dan to do when he grows up?"

"Dan needn't do anything," said Mr. Jarrold proudly. "He can go into the Guards." He spoke without irony. "He'll be a peer before he's twenty-five. He can fill up his time in the House of Lords."

"Papa, what do you mean?"

"I've let the cat out of the bag, it seems," said Mr. Jarrold, cocking his head at her, his temper completely restored. He was charmingly naïf at that moment, and Evelyn forgave him all his trespasses.

"Really, Papa? New Year's Honours?"

Mr. Jarrold nodded.

"Does Mrs. Jarrold know?"

"Haven't told her. Haven't told Evan or Geoffrey or Catherine. Didn't mean to tell *you*. Meant to let you all see it in *The Times*. Surprise."

"Well, Papa, I won't give you away." She put her arms round him and kissed him. She was sure that he had let her into his secret to make up for having been so cross about Dan. Dear old man. During the brief moment of her kiss he savoured the slight, warm scent that hid within her furs.

"Trust you, Evelyn."

"You can. I'm so glad. You don't know how glad I am. For you."

She spoke truthfully. She was glad for the old man's sake, and, because she came from the middle class herself, for the sake of her son. Aristocracy held a glamour for her. She was glad that Mr. Jarrold should be rewarded, because such a reward would please him; and she was glad to think that her son would eventually take his place in the House of Lords. Her father would be pleased, too, pottering in retirement among his water-colours at Biggleswade. "My grandson," he would say, "Lord. . . ."

"What name have you decided on?" she asked.

"Can't make up my mind. Thought you might help. Newlands sounds a bit too new, somehow. Silly business. Wouldn't accept it, but for Dan. And now you tell me

Dan won't hunt, or shoot,—demmit, he'll go vegetarian and teetotal next. Crank. Hate cranks."

"What about Orlestone as a name?" she said, edging him off the dangerous subject. Orlestone was in the district of the Jarrold coal-pits.

"Orlestone. Not bad. Thought of it myself."

"Well, you can tell us for certain on New Year's Day, Papa."

"Mind you look surprised," said Mr. Jarrold.

"But of course! Mrs. Jarrold mightn't like it, if she thought I had known before she did."

"Stuff,—she minds nothing except the slugs eating the esquilogias."

"The what, Papa?"

"Esquilogias. One of those flowers she's always poring over."

"Aquilegias, you mean, Papa,—or eschscholtzias."

"Cross between the two. Anyhow, something that makes me feel left out in the cold. When she talks about them to one of those gardening friends of hers. She had a man down the other day, who'd discovered seventy new kinds of lily in Manchuria."

"Dear me, Papa."

"Well, I may have got it wrong. He'd discovered something somewhere, and there were seventy kinds of it. They discussed each kind in detail. I went to sleep."

He was in a good mood now, pleased that Evelyn should know his secret, gratified that she should have received it with suitable delight. Because the revelation had made him shy, he turned it off with a joke. Quite enough emotion had been displayed when she kissed him. They understood one another very well.

"Dear Papa, I'm afraid I must be going now."

"Got your car? Want a taxi?"

"Neither. I shall walk."

"Cold day," said Mr. Jarrold warningly.

"I've got a fur coat."

"Quite right to walk when you can," said Mr. Jarrold, accompanying her down the polished gallery of the Museum; "keeps your complexion fresh." He stumped along beside her. "You won't tell anybody, Evelyn, eh?"

"Word of honour, Papa."

"M-m. I'll take thatt."

At the top of the stairs they met Geoffrey Jarrold coming up with an unknown young man.

"Hullo, Papa. I was looking for you. Hullo, Evelyn. This is Miles Vane-Merrick, Papa. He wants to talk to you about conditions among industrial workers. I told him I was sure you couldn't be bothered."

"M-m-m," said Mr. Jarrold. Vane-Merrick's name was well known to him as a rising young M.P.,—an aristocrat in the ranks of the I.L.P. Vane-Merrick might be worth talking to. "Come along," said Mr. Jarrold; "Evelyn's just going,—got an appointment with a dressmaker. My daughter-in-law, Mr. Vane-Merrick."

They smiled conventionally and nodded to one another. Evelyn saw a fair young man with an extraordinarily gay, frank, and alert expression. Vane-Merrick saw a dark, slim woman dressed in green velvet and sables, a bunch of violets pinned into her furs. He was struck even then by her look of passionate reserve. It was not so much her obvious loveliness and elegance that attracted him, as the secret her whole being withheld. Their glances crossed for an instant. She went on her way, elegantly, down the polished staircase, exchanging remarks with her father-in-law who insisted on escorting her.

A biting wind caught Evelyn as she emerged from the security of the Jarrolds' house into the roar of London. She shivered, and turned up her fur collar, putting down her nose against the wind. The scarlet buses thundered past her, going down Park Lane. They reminded her of the days when she had been obliged to travel in buses; when she had taken her place among the waiting groups on the kerb, getting in the way of hurrying passers-by, being pushed aside by competitive boarders of the bus; days when the harsh cry of the conductor's voice came accompanied by an out-stretched, barring arm, "Outside only!" like the cry of fate, condemning one forever to the outside seat, in the rain, in the cold, though a bus was ostensibly the most democratic of conveyances. To-day, even buses had changed. Their outsides offered as much shelter as their insides. Moreover, one could smoke on the top. Life was undergoing the process of being levelled up for everyone. Evelyn Jarrold felt less sympathy for bus-boarders than Evelyn Wilson had felt twenty years ago. Perhaps thatt was because Evelyn Jarrold had entered into the preserves of the capitalists. She now registered a definite annoyance when taxis delayed the free passage of her motor through Hyde Park, and was apt to recall the days when the Park was closed to all but privately-owned vehicles. Her grievance against buses and the conductor with his strident voice had diminished noticeably since she herself had owned her private car or had been able to hail a taxi whenever she stood in need of one.

Perversely, despite the wind and the general unpleasant-

ness of the December weather, she preferred to walk.
One could afford to walk, when one was lapped in sables,
and could hail a taxi whenever weather-conditions became
intolerable. The icy wind, whipping, biting, brought a
certain exhilaration. Discomforts that one need not necessarily endure, always do induce a certain exhilaration.
Hence the perennial charm of picnics.

Evelyn struggled up Park Lane against the wind. Life
was easy and pleasant for her,—too easy, too pleasant,—
and she welcomed the wind as something that would
buffet her from without. People were too much inclined
as a rule to consider her wishes; to make much of her, to
spoil her; the Jarrolds adored her, and her many friends
were a great deal fonder of her than she of them. It was all
too soft and comfortable. It made her sometimes a little
impatient and uneasy. In material ways, too, she was
fortunate; at the dressmaker's where she was going she
would order anything she wanted, and she knew that she
would want a great deal, being easily tempted in such
feminine ways. She would be unable to resist the pretty
tissues, the furs and flowers; indeed there was no reason
why she should resist them. She would have a lot of things
sent home on approval, strewing them all over her room
and wandering amongst them, while Privett, her dour
maid who had been with her ever since her marriage,
looked on disapprovingly, saying only, when consulted,
that she had got enough clothes already. But she would
eventually charm a smile even out of Privett.

Madame Louise the head saleswoman at Rivers and
Roberts came forward with a pleased smirk to welcome
Mrs. Jarrold. She reserved thatt smirk for customers
whom it was a pleasure to dress, those customers who

would always do credit to the firm. Customers of the other sort were greeted only with a hard and supercilious stare, as much as to enquire what their business might be with Rivers and Roberts. But Mrs. Tommy Jarrold was a favourite, no doubt about it. Even the mannequins smiled, and the great Mr. Rivers himself came out from behind a curtain when he heard that Mrs. Jarrold was in the shop. He was very small and finicky, with long expressive hands and tiny little feet in patent-leather shoes; when he flittered beside Madame Louise, who was large and tightly encased in black satin, her grey hair cropped and brushed back so that she looked almost like an eighteenth-century gentleman, one expected her to pick up Mr. Rivers and spank him. Evelyn often wondered amusedly at their exact relationship. They were colleagues, deferring to one another's opinion, but did they loathe one another secretly? Did the most terrible scenes take place behind thatt curtain, in Mr. Rivers' sanctum? scenes from which they emerged, bland and smiling, when the arrival of an American duchess was announced to them by a scared assistant? However they might behave in private, in public they were a formidable combination. A glance from them was enough to make a stout millionairess feel like a disgrace upon the earth.

They implied by their manner that it was a matter of complete indifference to them whether they sold their goods or not. In fact, their manner suggested, they would rather not sell them at all, such trafficking being beneath their dignity. They were artists, creators, who if they received a cheque would scarcely know what to do with it. If any client committed the solecism of asking a price, they raised their eyebrows and summoned some inferior being to give the answer, during which time they discreetly turned away to save themselves the pain of overhearing so sordid a discussion. It was always assumed that anybody who entered Rivers and Roberts' must be above such small considerations. The whole atmosphere of the establishment breathed such an assumption.

For the display of their creations they employed a number of young women of surpassing beauty, whom Madame Louise treated with quasi-paternal benevolence and Mr. Rivers with a fussy irritability. But though Madame Louise might call them "dear," and though Mr. Rivers might dance up to them, jerking a fold into place or stepping back to admire the effect of an orchid held between finger and thumb against the shoulder, these young ladies reproduced with marked success the suberbly indifferent manner of their employers. They were bored, they were beautiful, they were scornful. They minced across the stretches of grey pile carpet as though the clothes they wore were their own. And indeed the clothes they wore suggested every varying hour in the life of a young lady of fashion, a débutante in the crowded and luxurious year of her first emancipation. She played tennis, she danced, she dined, she went to Scotland in tweeds and to Ascot in painted chiffon; she bathed, she went on the river; she was cool or cosy. But whatever she did she was exquisite, disdainful, and bored.

Evelyn watched this procession as she had watched it a hundred times before. Madame Louise and Mr. Rivers hovered over her, saying "Now there's a pretty little suit, Mrs. Jarrold,—just the thing for Luxor." Evelyn hesitated, playing with an idea. Should she go to Luxor when Dan had returned to Eton? There was nothing to prevent her.

But then another young woman crossed her vision, clad in a scarlet jersey and scarlet trousers. carrying a pair of skis over her shoulder, and she thought that she would like to go to Caux. Sun or snow, which should it be? But a strolling vision in white sauntered across the carpet, and she thought of Monte Carlo.

She was indeed terribly free.

Other women whom she knew came in, laughing, shaking the first flakes of snow from their furs, exclaiming about the weather,—though, to be sure, they had only run across the pavement from their car to the door. Mr. Rivers and Madame Louise were graciously pleased to welcome them. Chairs were brought. One of them was a Russian, Princess Charskaya, incomparably plain and chic, who had obviously come with the others in the hope that some pickings might fall to her lot. It was the only way she could manage to subsist. She had attached herself particularly to a rich, unpleasant widow, squat as a toad, whose personal vanity was as surprising as it was excessive, and whose capacity for flattery was as large as an elephant's capacity for buns. Mr. Rivers was grateful to Princess Charskaya for introducing Mrs. Denman to his shop, since her taste in clothes was expensive although juvenile. He expressed his gratitude in a manner both practical and discreet; he and the Princess had a private nod for one another behind Mrs. Denman's back.

Evelyn looked on at the comedy. They were all caricatures of people,—Martha Denman, Betsy Charskaya, Mr. Rivers, and Madame Louise. She wondered whether she herself were a caricature also. There was Julia Levison too, a hard, frizzed relic of Edwardian society, tacking herself on to Mrs. Denman, also for the sake of what she might get. She and Betsy Charskaya hated one another, under a great show of friendship, and yet at moments they almost enjoyed themselves together, seeing how far they could go with Mrs. Denman, and how many compliments they could get her to swallow without suspicion. It was not very pretty. Just now they were trying to persuade her to order a pale and evanescent ball-dress which a slim girl was parading before them. It would exactly match the colour of her eyes. . . . After a while, Evelyn got up and went away. Mr. Rivers accompanied her to the door. He winked at her as they went.

Five o'clock. She was going to a party that evening; she would go home and rest. (Rest from what?) Certainly she had no desire to see any more people. If she got bored between tea and dinner, if she couldn't concentrate her attention on a novel, she could telephone to someone or other and tell them to come round to her flat. But at present she felt that she wanted to be alone. There was no one she wanted to see except perhaps her niece Ruth, who was fresh and young, and who idolised her. She did not feel very much inclined to summon even Ruth. She would read,—if she could.

Evelyn lived at the top of a block of new flats in Portman Square. When she reached home, opening the door with her latch-key, she met Privett in the passage. Privett, as usual, wore an air of reproach.

"Miss Ruth is there, ma'am." She might as well have said straight out, "How late you are, and where have you been, I should like to know?"

"Oh, is she? Oh well. . . . Tell Mason to bring tea, will you, Privett."

"Mason's out. It's his Thursday."

"Tell Alice, then. Or bring it yourself.—Goodness," thought Evelyn, going towards the sitting-room, "haven't I got enough servants?—Ruth?" she said, opening the door.

"Evelyn, darling!" Ruth came to meet her and gazed at her with the generous admiration of a girl for an older woman. "How delicious you look, as usual. And yet you've come in straight out of a snow-storm. How do you manage it? I just missed you at Park Lane. I went there after luncheon with Daddy."

"Yes, I met him. He was with a man who wanted to talk to Papa, so I left."

"I know. Miles Vane-Merrick."

"Yes. Miles Vane-Merrick."

Evelyn knew suddenly that Ruth was interested in Miles Vane-Merrick. But of course she said nothing. She took off her coat and threw it on the sofa; took off her fur cap, and smoothed her thick hair. Then she smiled at Ruth.

"Come and sit down and tell me how you've been enjoying life."

Ruth enjoyed life frankly, making no bones about it. She was generally popular, because of her innocent assumption that everybody enjoyed thatt agreeable business equally. Some people found her innocent zest slightly exasperating,—Evelyn herself sometimes repressed a movement of irritation,—but as her contemporaries responded to her gaiety and as her elders usually smiled benignly, Ruth always had what she called a good time. Her grandfather especially liked to hear of her enjoying herself. Like other men who have risen from small beginnings, William Jarrold welcomed the idea that his descendants could afford to be idle; it flattered his vanity. And Ruth was not at all averse from taking full advantage of the Jarrold fortune; encouraged by her mother, a candid snob, she made use of it to frequent a society which was not really her own. Indirect use, of course; but it was certainly convenient to have motors which one could lend to one's friends and a country house where one could entertain them. Ruth Jarrold was very well pleased with matters as she had arranged them. All the Jarrolds were ambitious in one way or another, and Ruth's ambition took the form of a mild and harmless, though silly, worldliness.

Her devotion to Evelyn was genuine, and it was especially fortunate that the popular Mrs. Tommy Jarrold should be not only her aunt but a definite social asset.

She chattered. Evelyn lent herself amiably to the chatter; it seemed to her that she was always lending herself amiably to somebody or something, till she ceased to have any existence of her own at all. Would she ever turn round on the whole of her acquaintance, and in a moment of harshness send them all packing? She knew that the necessary harshness lurked somewhere within her; in fact, she was rather frightened of it. Once or twice in the past it had got the better of her; it might get the better of her again. She disliked it, thinking it ugly. But she felt sometimes that she could endure the emptiness of her friends and the conventionality of the Jarrolds no longer. The two old Jarrolds were real enough, in their separate ways, but the rest of them were puppets, manikins, and their acquired conventions were so much waste paper.

Fragments of Ruth's chatter reached her as though from afar. "And do tell me about Eton . . . was everybody

there? . . . did you watch the wall-game? . . . and how was
Dan? . . . I really must come down with you on the
Fourth next year. . . . it'll be Dan's last half, won't it? . . .
I always think the Fourth is such fun . . . everybody one
knows . . . as good as Ascot . . . and then the fireworks . . .
how I wish I had another cousin going to Eton! . . . or a
brother . . . but never mind, it'll be fun when Dan is up
at Oxford. I do think it so extraordinary, don't you, the
way one sometimes hears of a boy who doesn't like Eton?
I heard of one only the other day who actually asked to be
taken away, and he played for his House, too, and was
just going to be elected to Pop."

"And was he?" said Evelyn vaguely.

"Elected to Pop? No, of course not. Oh, taken away,
you mean. Yes, he was; he made such a fuss and said he'd
run away otherwise. His father had to pay for two full
halves, and as he wasn't at all rich he minded thatt much
more than taking his son away."

"And who was this?" asked Evelyn, busy making the tea.

"Well, as a matter-of-fact, it was Miles Vane-Merrick,"
Ruth paused. "Of course, he *is* very queer. He has all
kinds of extraordinary notions. He won't play cricket any
more, and he won't go to parties. . . ."

"Isn't he going to the dance to-night?" said Evelyn,
suddenly looking kindly at her young niece.

"Well, as a matter-of-fact, he is; I made him promise to.
I don't think it's good for a young man to shut himself
up in an old castle whenever he isn't in the slums of his
constituency, do you, Evelyn? With nothing but yokels?"

"Is thatt what he does?"

"Yes,—but don't let's talk about him, he isn't really
very interesting. Let's talk about you."

"I thought him very good-looking," said Evelyn carefully.

"Good-looking, yes, I suppose he is rather; like Sir Philip Sidney, I always think. Somebody once said he was very Elizabethan. He's very clever, you know," said Ruth; "he likes poetry, I believe he even writes it."

"What a pity," said Evelyn; "it would be so much better if he played cricket."

"Well, Daddy and I think so, but I shouldn't have expected you to think so. Evelyn; I always suspect you of being a bit of a highbrow." Ruth laughed affectionately. "But it *is* odd, isn't it, in a person like Miles Vane-Merrick? I mean, he's so good at everything, or might be, if he took the trouble; but he doesn't seem to care. Of course it doesn't matter quite so much, as he isn't the eldest son; I suppose he can do as he likes, but if he were the eldest son it would really be rather a pity."

"Sugar?"

"Yes, please, lots. And what about you, Evelyn? have you been enjoying yourself? Do you know, I haven't seen you for a week."

"Such a long time?" said Evelyn.

"I really miss you when I don't see you," said Ruth seriously, "though I don't suppose you would notice it if you didn't see me for a month. When you took Dan to Italy last summer I missed you dreadfully, and you only sent me a picture postcard. I am always terrified of something going wrong when you are away."

"Why, my dear child, what could possibly go wrong? Nothing ever goes wrong with you Jarrolds. You march from success to success; you're a lucky, prosperous family."

Even in the midst of her school-girlish admiration for Evelyn, Ruth thought it rather heartless of Evelyn to talk like thatt, considering that poor Uncle Tommy had been killed in the war.

"Things do go wrong sometimes, don't they?" she said. "And I always feel," she added, repairing her secretly disloyal criticism, "that you would be the only person to put them right. You can always get round Grandpapa. I'm sure," she went on, her enthusiasm gaining on her, "that you could get round anybody. You're wonderful, Evelyn; you're so quiet, and self-contained, and rather mocking, and yet perfectly human. I wonder what you really think about? When you're alone, I mean?"

"Clothes, mostly," said Evelyn, who disliked it when Ruth became intense, although her vanity made her jealously possessive of even this commonplace girl's devotion; "and of the next party."

"Thatt's the sort of thing you say, and I don't believe it's true a bit. You make me feel uneasy sometimes, Evelyn, much as I love you."

"But you do love me, don't you?"

"Oh, Evelyn, you know I do. Better than anybody, except of course Mummy and Daddy."

"Sure?" asked Evelyn, resenting the clause about Mummy and Daddy.

"Quite sure. But why do you want to know? You can't really mind whether I do or not."

"Doesn't everyone like to be loved?" said Evelyn. It was rather unfair, she thought, to play with the girl like this, but she must needs have all the Jarrolds at her feet, though she despised herself for it. It was a game, which she played when she had nothing better to do.

"Of course everyone likes to be loved, but I should have thought you got enough love without mine."

"One never gets enough love," said Evelyn, abruptly getting up. She had wrung the admission she wanted from the girl, as she might have wrung it from anybody else, and was suddenly bored. "You must run away now, my dear; I want to rest a bit before dressing for dinner."

"Oh, Evelyn, you are unkind. Can't I stay?"

"No, you can't. If you stayed, you might begin to love me less."

"You know I shouldn't; and if I did, you wouldn't care."

"Oh yes, I should," said Evelyn, taking the girl's face between her hands and laughing down into her eyes. Her expression as she did so was at one and the same time so gay, so mocking, and yet so tender that Ruth forgave her all her heartlessness and loved her the more. One could forgive Evelyn everything, when she looked at one like thatt. "All right, you brute," she said, "I'll go, and leave you to your rest. We meet tonight."

"If you call thatt a meeting. I shall see you in the distance, dancing with Miles Vane-Merrick. Your Elizabethan young man."

"Evelyn, don't tease."

"Mustn't I? All right, I won't."

Ruth was always strangely elated when she had been with Evelyn. She always came away, her head swimming with unusual, suggestive, dangerous notions. What was Evelyn's life, apart from what anybody could see of it? Outwardly, she led the ordinary, semi-decorous, semi-frivolous life of a woman dividing her time between her family connections and her personal amusement; she was a devoted mother to her son, an ideal daughter-in-law, sister-in-law, and aunt; once a week, at least, she lunched at Park Lane, leaving the old people in the best of moods after her departure; once a fortnight, at least, she dined with Ruth's parents, made Ruth's stiff and cautious mother unbend, and made Ruth's father say a number of things he would never have said but for her presence—daring things, even, which brought from his wife a secretly delighted "Really, Geoffrey! I'm surprised at you;" once a month, at least, she let Uncle Evan take her to a play, which could not be very amusing for an in-request woman like Evelyn, since Uncle Evan was habitually morose, occasionally uproarious in a disconcerting and unexpected way, but always stupid beyond even the Jarrold tolerance of empty-headedness. Ruth could not reconcile this ideally domesticated Evelyn with the spoilt, luxurious Evelyn who rang the bell fifty times a day for a patient though disagreeable Privett; who could get herself served first by all the head-waiters of London, Paris, and Berlin; who could accept your admiration as a joke, and yet make you feel that your admiration represented something of value to her; who gave you the impression of a life lived behind a life; who was, in short, apparently a model of the domestic virtues and who yet suggested all the chic of Vogue and all the passion of Shakespeare.

Ruth's mother and father were alone together when Ruth came in. Because they had nothing to say to one another, after twenty years of married life, her mother was doing a cross-word puzzle and her father was smoking his pipe over the evening paper. At the sight of their daughter they brightened a little.

"Hullo, Ruth, where have you been?"

"Darling child, you ought to go and rest before dinner."

Ruth had known exactly what they would both say. Far from irritating her, it soothed her to hear the expected phrases. It calmed her, after the inexplicable agitation of Evelyn.

"I went to see Evelyn," she replied to the one, certain that this reply would meet with approval; "Yes, Mummy, I think I'll go and rest for a bit," she replied to the other, glad of an excuse to escape immediately, since she had no more to say to her parents than they had to say to one another—except the things which could not be said, and which one did not say—and in the privacy of her own room she could at least telephone to one of her friends, even to Evelyn whom she had just left.

"You look tired, darling."

Another expected phrase. How comforting it was! though perhaps dull.

"Oh no, Mummy, I'm not tired a bit."

"What are you going to wear to-night? I should wear the blue if I were you."

"Oh, Mummy, I thought I'd wear my new red."

"Well, darling, if you like.—Geoffrey, what foreign word of six letters begins with p and ends with e and means attractive?"

"Piquante, I should think," said Geoffrey, who was reading the divorce court news.

"P-i-q-u-a-n-t-e,—no thatt won't do, thatt's got eight letters. Oh, Geoffrey, don't be such a broken reed. Do think of something else."

"Petite," said Ruth, inspired.

"Petite! I do believe you've got it, P-e-t-i-t-e. But does

thatt mean attractive? People have such odd ideas of attractiveness nowadays," said Ruth's mother, who stood five feet eleven in her stockings. "Anyway, there might be a t in the middle, fitting in with carrot,—a carrot *is* what one dangles in front of a donkey's nose, isn't it? I'll put it in, in pencil, so that I can rub it out if something better turns up. Darling, you've been so helpful, but do go and rest now. You look fagged out."

It made one sound interesting, to be told that one looked fagged out, although the effect might not be becoming. It was pleasant, to come home to one's family, and to be met by exactly the scene and the phrases that one expected. Ruth kissed her mother and went away upstairs. The house was warm, since it possessed the central heating which people less well-off could not afford,—or else despised, the English, among northern races, being the race which disregards its climate most in spite of its perennial, unique, and self-protective comments upon it. The house was warm, and full of hot-house flowers supplied weekly by a florist; flowers out of their season, tulips at Christmas, roses at the New Year, peach-blossom in January, spoiling the arrival of all such spontaneous and lovely things at the moment naturally ordained for them. But to Mrs. Geoffrey Jarrold and her daughter Ruth they represented no more than the necessary appurtenances of luxury; no more than the warmed rooms, the illustrated papers, and the lift which by the pressing of a little button spared one the effort of climbing two or three flights of stairs. Ruth felt sincerely grateful to her grandfather who entirely by his own efforts had ensured such comfortable circumstances for his descendants. Of course, she would have preferred to come of gentle stock, or, better still, of

an ancient aristocracy, but nowadays people soon forgot
that one's grandfather had been a self-made man, even a
man of the people: the new families quickly merged with
the genuine article. Nobody, to-day, could have told that
her own father was the son of such a man. Thus she reassured herself.—But, she thought, stretching herself out
luxuriously on the sofa in front of her sitting-room fire,
she really ought not to be so self-conscious about it all;
thatt was a slight give-away.

She wondered whether Evelyn ever troubled her head
about such things.

Deliciously vague day-dreams began to float through
her mind, so that she reached out a hand and turned out
the lamp, leaving the firelight to play alone over the room.
She would see Evelyn again thatt evening, and she would
see Miles Vane-Merrick, too; he would dance with her,
and she would chaff him about being at a party. Secretly
she hoped that he would ask her to stay at his old castle;
if she could secure thatt invitation she would be perfectly
satisfied with the success of the evening. She must make it
her goal. But of the two, she thought that she most wanted
to see Evelyn; her heart would turn over, as it always did,
when she first caught sight of Evelyn in the room. She
would be content, just to be in the same room with her.
Evelyn might make life seem more dangerous and more
exciting, but she also made it seem safer; she seemed to
have deep, strong resources within herself upon which one
could draw and rely. She made one feel that one must not
be frightened of life, not apprehensive of the perils which
might be lurking just round the corner; it was cowardly to
evade, cowardly to run away, even though one might
suffer. Evelyn, she divined, would suffer if she must, but

gallantly; she would take it all as a part of living, the rough with the smooth,—though Evelyn liked the smooth as well as anybody; she liked being an attractive woman, she liked tyrannising over people in her charming, half-kindly, half-cruel, way; she liked power, and, being very much a woman, used all her femininity to get it; she would, however, take the consequences bravely, even as she imposed them on other people. If she had certain standards, she was as prepared to live up to them herself as to exact them of others.

She would see Evelyn at the dance tonight. The danger, the reassurance, would all start into life again. And Miles Vane-Merrick would be there; he had said so. Her thoughts became hazy; she floated away; after a little while, she slept.

What a cold, rough night it was! so cold and rough that the usual little crowd of people had failed to collect on the pavement to see the Quality dashing out of its motors into Chevron House for the ball. Grosvenor Square was deserted, but for the procession of motors drawing up, one by one, depositing their loads, and gliding off again into the darkness against the railings, there to wait until the linkman bawled out the names at two or three o'clock in the morning. There was only one shivering old woman, trying to sell matches, by the steps of Chevron House. The very doors of the house had to be kept shut, opening as though by magic to admit each fresh arrival, and shutting again instantly, to exclude the wintry blast that otherwise would have rushed up the stairs, undoing the warm influence of the radiators, ruffling the women's hair, and disturbing the white lilies that stood so stately in their great golden wine-coolers at the corner of every step. Gentlemen's cloak-room to the right; ladies' cloak-room to the left; quantities of powdered footmen showing the way, contriving to be at the same time majestic and deferential; it was all very grand, all very much according to Ruth Jarrold's ideas of how things ought to be done. It was a pity that the eccentric duke, the master of the house, should be away on one of his inexplicable and unnecessary travels; but it really made very little difference, since he was still unmarried, and his mother gave the party in his absence,—a party which he would probably have vetoed had he been in England, for his disapproval of such extravagance was well known and, among his equals, richly derided. It was perhaps not a pity at all, but a good thing, that the duke should be somewhere in Asia instead of in London.

His mother stood at the top of the stairs, receiving her guests. She was somewhat wrinkled and withered, though it was evident that she had once been pretty,—Ruth recalled the words 'piquante' and 'petite' in her mother's cross-word puzzle,—and she carried on the traditions of her age gallantly into a changing world. She was still lively and voluble in the extreme; still had a word, a dozen words, a hundred words, for everybody as she shook hands, though her manner was flexible enough to admit many variations, so slight as to be imperceptible save to those who were very touchily on the look-out, such as Ruth Jarrold, for instance, who imagined that she detected a slight falling-off of the note of intimacy in the duchess' greeting compared with her greeting of Lord and Lady Roehampton who had immediately preceded the Jarrolds. "Sylvia, darling!" she had exclaimed; "dear

George!" but to Ruth's mother and father she had said only, "Oh, Hester, how nice to see you,—and Mr. Jarrold, too,—and dear little Ruth,—you'll find all your friends in there," indicating the ballroom. Her manner, though polite and even cordial, had implied a note of dismissal, whereas her manner towards the Roehamptons had implied only that she would fain detain them in conversation, but for her duties as a hostess and the press of other guests on the stairs. But perhaps Ruth was over-sensitive.

Once inside the ballroom, however, she had no cause for complaint. Young men by the dozen came up, asking her to dance. She had the pleasure of refusing several, either because she was genuinely engaged, or because she thought that a judicious procrastination would enable her to make a better choice later on. Ruth never lost her head, even when she was enjoying herself most.

She wondered, as she danced, turning rhythmically under the great chandeliers, what it would feel like to be the mistress of those sumptuous rooms. But it was no good thinking of thatt, for the duke, although a bachelor, was proverbially inaccessible.

Her cup of pleasure was not yet full: she had not yet discovered Evelyn. Evelyn would not take much notice of her. She never did at parties. Presumably she had something more amusing to do. She would just give Ruth a smile, and a word, before passing on. But the smile and the word would be so intimate, so caressing, that Ruth would be more enslaved than ever.

Ruth felt that life at such moments was too good to be true. She revelled in the lights, and the music, and in the privileged crowd of which she was one. Surely, she thought, the English upper classes (a horrid expression, but she must define them somehow) were the most decorative on earth. They looked as though for generations they had been well-fed, well-warmed, well-exercised, and nourished in the conviction that the world could not produce their peers. The standard of looks was amazing; they had the distinction and beauty of thoroughbred animals. The young men were as elegant as greyhounds, the young women coloured as a herbaceous border. What did it matter, Ruth would have added, had she thought of it, that those sleek heads contained no more brains than a greyhound's, since those slender bodies expressed an equal grace? What did it matter that their code should strangely enough involve a contempt for the intellectual advantages which might have been theirs? What did it matter that they should immure themselves within the double barricade of their class and their nationality? But Ruth had no such thoughts, being herself one of them, or, at any rate, so good an adaptation as to resemble them in almost every particular.

She was more definitely class-conscious than they, thatt was all. She could not quite take things for granted. She consciously enjoyed being Ruth Jarrold, dancing at Chevron House.

All the dance-tunes sounded much the same, and thatt, in itself, was reassuring. Faintly lascivious, faintly cacophonous; a young man's arm round one, a young man's body surprisingly close, his breath on one's hair, and yet a disharmony between oneself and him, or, at most, a fictitious temporary closeness which tumbled to pieces as soon as the music stopped. They were held together, she and the young men, only by their similar circumstances and their pleasure-loving frivolity. There were other things; such other things, for instance, as Evelyn by her personality suggested.

She looked across the room, over her partner's shoulder, and through the blaze of lights and the movement of enlaced couples saw Evelyn dancing with Miles Vane-Merrick.

She was glad, welcoming any link which might strengthen Vane-Merrick's friendship with her family. It even crossed her mind that Evelyn might be dancing with him for her, Ruth's, sake,—testing the young man in whom her niece had revealed an interest. Dear Evelyn, thatt was the kind of thing she would do, if only to indulge her weakness for having a finger in all the Jarrold pies. Ruth continued to dance, waiting for the moment when the turn of the dance would come, enabling her to observe once more the dark head and the fair, associated so harmoniously together. A disturbing tenderness overwhelmed her, seeing them thus unexpectedly combined, those two of whom she had hitherto thought quite separately: Evelyn whom she openly loved, and Miles whom she knew she could openly love at any moment, like an explosion produced by a touch on a prepared train of fire; indeed, she was not sure that the explosion had not been already produced by the mere sight of Evelyn in Miles' arms. Were they really dearer to her, those two, than anything else on earth, that the sight of them in alliance should move her to such a strong emotion?—It was surprising to see them together; so intimately and physically together as a dance necessitated. It was almost shocking. It was shocking that Evelyn's head should come so close to Miles' shoulder. She, Ruth, had never thought of them before as such vivid physical entities.

The music stopped and the illusion vanished; Ruth became once more a girl faced with the problem of talking to a young man she scarcely knew, between two dances. Fortunately the interval between two dances was a brief one, and those who had nothing to say to one another could then find other partners, and those who had everything to say could sit out. Ruth was one of those who found another partner. She carried a secret contentment within her, being sure that presently Miles Vane-Merrick would find her, and that in the delicious intimacy between two dances they would talk about Evelyn, and would agree.

Every moment which went by added something to her happy anticipation. It was an exquisite state of mind to be in, grown more exquisite since she had admitted to herself that she could love Miles Vane-Merrick. To admit that she could love him meant that she did love him. She took the plunge in her own mind, and then looked at him again, a new and rapturous terror possessing her, so that a physical uneasiness overcame her, her heart beat irregularly, her head swam slightly, a choking sensation rose in her throat, her head fell back a little, and her eyes closed even as her lips parted. It lasted for a second only; she came to herself almost instantly, and found herself still dancing with a young man whose arm was about her and who had noticed nothing wrong. The black cloth of his coat was very near her eyes, she could see the threads of the weaving. She went on dancing, but she was a different person: something of enormous importance had taken place.

When Miles came up to her, it was only by an effort that she could remember that he knew nothing of what

had happened. His manner was quite ordinary as he
asked her for a dance. The one after next, she answered,
wondering how she should survive until then, wondering
how she should endure it when it came. And to think
that it meant nothing to him at all! for having received
her answer he thanked her and turned away without even
an extra glance. Such ignorance on his part was un-
believable.

The music struck up again, but feeling that she must
be alone Ruth slipped out of the ballroom, jostled as she
went by the crowd of returning people. Noise and laughter
and music; lights and parquet floors and abounding flowers. A ball at Chevron House, with such hidden things
going on in one's heart. Men's voices saying, "Where are
you running away to, Ruth? Come and dance with me!"
But she disentangled herself from them all, saying that
she had torn her dress and must get a stitch put in it in
the cloak-room, saying anything, only to get away.

On her way down the stairs she met Evelyn coming up.
Evelyn was laughing with the man whom she was with.
She looked extraordinarily gay and mischievous, as though
she sparkled all over from some inner source of excitement
and happiness. With one hand she picked up her frock;
the other rested lightly on the banisters, a great fan made
of tortoise-shell and eagles' feathers dangling on a ribbon
from her wrist. A little diamond monogram twinkled as
it caught the light. Slender though she was, she looked
almost statuesque to-night, in the closely-swathed gown
of ivory satin reaching to the ground, and no colour on
her anywhere, nothing but the soft ivory which made her
rounded throat look whiter, and showed up the network
of blue veins on her breast. Her skin looked as cool as

marble, as warm as ivory. The only colour was in her mouth and in her cheeks, which were brightly flushed; in her dark blue eyes and short, curling hair. Ruth noticed how straight she held herself, although so flexible; how small her head was, and how delicately poised.

"Running away, Ruth?" she said, as the others had said.

Ruth gave her prepared excuse, then she felt that Evelyn was scrutinising her very closely. She was looking at her with a searching, mocking glance,—the expression she put on when she was about to make fun of somebody. The man, bored by this encounter, had gone up a step or two and was waiting for Evelyn, tapping his fingers rather impatiently on the banisters. Ruth had an impulse to say something; to release something of the turmoil pent-up within her. "Evelyn," she said, and stopped.

"What is it, then? Come, now! What is it?" Evelyn looked at her, sparkling with enquiry and mischief. She was radiant, quizzical, and animated. But she was unsafe. "Come, Ruth, what's in your mind?"

"Nothing," said Ruth. "Are you enjoying yourself?"

"Yes!—are you? A lovely party. Well, go and get yourself mended, since you won't say what you were going to say."

She doesn't know what I was going to say, thought Ruth; she wanted me to pay her a compliment, to tell her she was lovely tonight, to tell her I was glad to see her; thatt's all she wanted, and all that she expected. What was I going to say, anyhow? Nothing; there's nothing to say.

Coming upstairs again she met Evelyn coming down, accompanied this time by Miles Vane-Merrick. The strains of music floated out on to the landing above. They both smiled at her casually, but did not stop.

Ruth returned to the ballroom feeling as though something had happened to dim the lights. When the time came for Vane-Merrick's dance, she cut it.

Christmas at the Jarrolds' was always a very deliberate affair. William Jarrold believed in keeping up old English traditions, and since it was an old English tradition that the head of the house should keep Christmas with his family around him, to Newlands the family had to go, whether they would have preferred to be elsewhere or not. Then, the pervading theory that everyone should be festive amounted to a royal command. It was hard to see why a number of grown-up people should behave like a pack of children because the calendar indicated the twenty-fifth of December, but so it was. From earliest morning on Christmas-day, the house resounded with cries of delight and expressions of gratitude, and every room looked as though a waste-paper basket had been emptied over the floor. Then came church, and then luncheon, with the yearly argument as to whether one ought to blow out the brandy or not. In the afternoon the excitement subsided a little, and one went out for a walk. After dinner they had crackers, and everyone, from William Jarrold down to Minnie, Ruth's little sister, adorned their heads with paper caps and blew ear-splitting blasts on wooden whistles. Minnie went round the littered dinner-table, collecting the coloured crinkly paper off the crackers, the mottoes, and the pictures of black cats stuck on the outside. Then they went into the drawing-room and turned on the wireless, and had the usual difficulty in getting Minnie to go to bed. Next day all the writing-tables in the house were occupied by people writing to say thank you. Such was Christmas at Newlands, and there was no reason to suppose that it would be different this year from any other.

Evelyn was not looking forward to the prospect; this year even less than usual.

She had Dan to herself for two or three days first, in London. He had to be stowed away in the tiny spare-room at the flat. When he arrived she was lying in bed opening her letters and looking at the papers, for she had not expected him quite so early. She could scarcely believe that it was his voice she heard, as deep as a man's voice, saying "Hullo, Privett," in the passage, but next moment he came into her room. "Dan!" she cried, opening her arms to him. He bent down and kissed her, saying, "Hullo, Mummy," in his deep voice, as he had said it to Privett. She hugged him to her. He kissed her again.

Presently he sat eating his breakfast off a tray beside her bed, while, propped on her elbow, she regarded him with pride. At seventeen and a half, he was very large, sleek, and good-looking. Not spotty; she was thankful that he should not be spotty. In spite of his size,—his physique was really magnificent,—his face was perhaps rather too pretty for a boy. There was perhaps too much sensitiveness revealed by mouth and chin. But he had beautiful eyes, as brown as a fawn's, and a beautiful white brow, with dark hair growing thick and low. He was rather grave, taking some time to unbend from the sober and courteous manner habitual to him; immaculately and unostentatiously dressed, having inherited his mother's taste for clothes;

his hands were long and sensitive, but surprisingly dirty, which did not seem to go with the rest of him. A suggestion of some suppressed complexity, grinding at work behind the reticence of his manner, made grown-up people say, according to the degree of their own intelligence, either that Dan Jarrold was an interesting boy or that there was something wrong with him. Whatever they said, Dan Jarrold went quietly on his own way, taking very little notice of anybody.

He was happy now, sitting in his mother's room, letting his eyes rest on pretty and luxurious objects, and on his mother herself, lying among the soft feminine delicacies of her bed. He liked the thick carpet, the fire in the grate, the shagreen brushes and boxes on the dressing-table, the quiet, the pale colours, the silver on his breakfast-tray, and Privett moving about with clothes over her arm, at which he was just too shy to look. He was thankful to have escaped from his own bleak little room at Eton, and from the eternal clatter of boots on stone passages, and from the eternal irruption of other boys who upset one's ink or threw one's hat out of the window when one was trying to read.

"How was Eton, Dan?"

"Oh, all right, Mummy."

He said that he had a lot to do in London, and she smiled and let him go, knowing that "a lot to do" meant that he wanted to buy a Christmas present for her. Over his other presents he would ask her advice, producing grubbly little lists written on the back of a Latin exercise, but over his present for her he could consult nobody. It would be a lonely and worrying expedition; she imagined him gazing into shop-windows, then entering the shop, large and awkward, to be jostled by other shoppers and

thrown into confusion by assistants asking him what they
could show him, and finally leaving the shop again without
having bought anything. She thought with great tenderness of the pathetic bewilderment of the young,—not only
in shops, but among all the problems which they were so
ill-equipped to meet. But apart from his shopping she
would give him a good time; she would devote herself to
him entirely; she would make him escort her to theatres,
giving him the tickets to look after, making him find the
motor when they came out, all to give him a sense of
responsibility and competence,—things he shrank from,—
and she herself would enjoy going about with her tall son,
for she was more than a little in love with him, especially
when he wore his dinner-jacket. But she must make him
wash his hands; and she had forgotten to look at his ears.

The problem of Dan worried her a good deal. Not that
he was not a good boy, for she sometimes thought him
almost too good, and wondered uneasily whether he ought
not to give her more trouble; but that she felt ill-equipped
to deal with his perpetual doubts and conundrums. Too
loyal to criticise her, too immature to realise her inade-
quacy, he referred all his perplexities to her and expected
her to provide a satisfactory answer. Taking it for granted
that she also troubled about such things, he was always
confident that she could illuminate him on vital subjects
which, actually, she had never thought about. For Evelyn
Jarrold was not a woman who questioned the established
order of the civilised world. She was not stupid, but, in
such matters, simply acquiescent. Personal relationships
were more important to her than social or general con-
troversies. Where did Dan get his intensity from, she

wondered? Certainly not from his father, who had never worried about anything in his life beyond the cut of his riding breeches; not from robust old William Jarrold; no, she decided with a sigh, he owed it partly to his own temperament but chiefly to his own generation.

She dreaded the first open clash between Dan and his grandfather, or between Dan and the rest of the Jarrolds. Dan's ideas, so far as she could understand them, did not fit. This distressed her. Yet, although all her training was all on the side of the Jarrolds, she had a disturbing feeling that Dan, in his fumbling way, was following the better though not the clearer track.

She had the sense to realise that the one thing she must really dread in Dan, was a possible weakness in his own character. It was worse than useless to suffer the pains of such strong peculiarities without the courage or the determination to accept their consequences. She did not want Dan to grow up into a weakling with vaguely realised ideals.

Stock-phrases were useful and comforting to her; she applied one of them to her confused anxiety about, and appreciation of, Dan: "One must have," she thought, "the conviction of one's own opinions."

Her tyrannical instinct did not apply to Dan. She was genuinely unselfish about him. The maternal instinct in her, oddly enough, did not take the tyrannical form. She was quite willing to let the boy develop along his own lines; she wished only that she were better able to follow and to help him. She must make him talk to her, she thought; though she was alarmed by the depths into which his talk would plunge her, a bather who could not swim.

It was not easy to make him talk, though he would write

her letters of eight pages every other day from school when
his feelings became too much for him. She took out the
portfolio in which she kept them.

Eton College, Windsor, October 10, 1931

MY OWN DARLING MUMMY—You are so kind and sympathetic that I can't refrain from putting pen to paper and
writing "My own darling Mummy." But I will not write a
sorrowful letter (though, good God! I have reason to!) because I think it depresses you. But I love to get away in the
evening from the bloody crowd to whom I am continually,
inevitably condemned. It is really like a prison, this place;
I feel I could go and ride a horse (or even a bicycle) in
Windsor Park and breathe the soft cool air with its sense of
freedom and tranquillity. Anything to get away. But I have
begun in a different way to what I meant to. I meant to
begin with a happy phrase "how lovely the autumn yellow
of the trees looks against the dull red of the School Yard."
(I should be telling the naked truth if I said that,—they are
fantastically beautiful, and I long to go out of the house,
damn Lock-up! and see what they look like in semi-
darkness.) Do please come down one Sunday and see me.
It brings tears to my eyes when I think of you and the joy
of freedom, instead of being coped [*sic*] up in a prison.
Mummy, do *please* stop reading all this. You see it is rather
natural that I should like writing as I hate talking to
people here, but if you should get too bored of reading my
letters do say if you would like me to stop, and I will stop,
even though I should be done out of my sole remaining
occupation that I like. Oh if I could only get measles.
Do please write darling. What should I do without you?
I find it very hard to believe that you should think me

worth taking trouble about, as I don't work properly, I can't play games, I don't agree with anybody's ideas, I am difficult to satisfy, unpunctual, inefficient, and every defect. It is rather a mystery to me. Oh God, what must you think of me!—

Your loving DANIEL.

P. S.—Something compels me to go on writing. I know you don't mind if I go on writing. Perhaps I shan't send the letter. I wrote another letter the other day, but the boys have thrown away the key of my writing-case so could you please send the duplicate key which I left with you, to unlock my case. That is the worst of being as unpopular as I am. If only I was 19 years old! can't I skip 2 years?   DAN.

Eton College, Windsor, November 1, 1931

MY DARLING MUMMY—We had an O. T. C. field-day today, we just walked for miles and miles, and turned rattles and pointed wooden guns at the enemy when we came across him. It was all so silly and unreal, as all field-days are, and everybody was so serious and earnest about it. I was earnest too, I didn't want to get into a row again over something so unnecessary. I wish the people who think war uncivilised would hurry up and outnumber the people who say it is "human nature!" Or am I talking rot? I have no right to talk like that at 17, when learned men who do not get white tickets disagree entirely with me. I apparently know absolutely nothing about anything. I am quite prepared to believe that, because whenever I am with you I am getting information the whole time, and I am never told anything I already know, let alone me telling you anything you did not know already! I was so nearly beaten on Saturday, did I tell you in my last letter? We argued for ten minites [*sic*] and then he let me off. We had a row about me being slack in football. The same idiotic offence. I am not doing particularly badly in work this half though. I *do* hope you are not disappointed in me. —Your loving son,   DANIEL.

P. S.—They don't seem to want anything except everybody being like everybody else.

Evelyn put the letters away with a sigh. Full of blots and erasures, stumbling, confused, unhappy, they wrung her heart whenever she received them. Poor little Dan! so self-possessed apparently, so self-revealing in those pitiful letters! She had often wished for some friends who could interest and understand him, and on whom he could rely, more securely than he could rely on her,—it was not good for the boy to find his only outlet in his mother, especially a mother with such shortcomings,—but her friends were all of the conventional type who would never sympathise with any of his difficulties or ideals. They would say, behind her back, that Evelyn's boy was a poseur or a rotter. His father would have had no patience with him; his uncles, she knew, already despised him. But now, thank God, she could introduce him to Miles and Miles' influence.

Miles was not in London,—she had persuaded him that she must keep those few days entirely free for Dan,—but on the day before Christmas-eve he telephoned to her unexpectedly, saying that he had returned and hoped that she and Daniel would come to a play with him in the evening. Dan was in the room when the telephone rang, very carefully copying a water-colour of a bridge, on a corner of the table cleared for the purpose. He raised his head to listen to his mother talking.

"Who is it, Mummy?"

"Mr. Vane-Merrick," said Evelyn deliberately. "You don't know him.—Hold on a moment, Miles; Dan wants to know who I'm talking to.—Mr. Vane-Merrick wants us to go to a play with him tonight, Dan. Shall we?"

"I want to see *Earth,*" said Dan. "He won't want to go to thatt."

. "Darling, what on earth is *Earth?*"

"It's a Russian film," said Dan sulkily; "it's being given at Stratford,—not on-Avon; atte Bow. It's a very low place. You go to a play with Mr. Vane-Merrick, Mummy, and I'll go to Stratford by myself."

Evelyn was tempted; she had not seen Miles for over a week.

"No, no," she said; "I want you to meet Mr. Vane-Merrick. I'm sure he'll come to Stratford.—Miles," she said into the telephone, "Dan and I will come with you if you can bear to see a Russian film called *Earth* at Stratford-atte-Bow."

"One doesn't dress," said Dan hastily.

"One doesn't dress," said Evelyn into the telephone. "He says," she interpreted to Dan, "that it is the very thing he wants to see, but that he had supposed you would rather go to the Coliseum.—Will you come to dinner here first?" she asked. "Seven-thirty. All right. Good-bye."

"Mummy," said Dan, "thatt isn't *Miles* Vane-Merrick, is it?"

"Why, what do you **know** about Miles Vane-Merrick? Yes, it is."

"By Jove!" cried Dan. He jumped up in great excitement. "Mummy, you don't mean to say you know Miles Vane-Merrick? You've never mentioned him. I thought it must be a brother or something. I should have thought Miles Vane-Merrick was quite,—well, quite out of your beat," he said lamely.

"But, Dan, how do you know anything about him?"

"Oh, he came down to lecture to the Eton Political Society. He was quite a surprise to me. He said all the things I had always thought,—only, of course, much better. The Political Society simply hated him; hated his opinions, I mean; they couldn't hate *him*, he was so funny. Surely I wrote and told you about him?"

"I don't remember, Dan,—when was this?"

"Six months ago, I suppose,—in the summer half."

Six months ago, she would not have registered Miles Vane-Merrick's name, coming to her in Dan's handwriting. She must look up the letter. Strange!

"No, I don't remember. I hope you'll like him," she added, suddenly overcome by fearfulness. She had counted so much on Miles' help with Dan.

"But, Mummy, he's the one person I want to meet. But look here, Mummy, you must be tactful. You mustn't say, Dan wants to meet you. You mustn't say I heard him at the Political Society. You see, he couldn't have known I was there. Promise?"

"I promise." Evelyn knew how important it was, even for a person of Dan's independence, to keep school-life apart from home-life. "I won't put my foot into it."

"Mummy, darling, you never do." Remorseful, he came across and kissed her. She was extraordinarily moved by thatt caress, which expressed Dan's agitation at the

thought of meeting Miles Vane-Merrick. She could now
bring herself to utter the words she had been trying to utter
ever since Dan arrived. "As a matter of fact, he has asked
us both to stay with him during the Christmas holidays."

"Us both? But he doesn't know me."

"He knows me, though," said Evelyn.

"To stay with him? Where?"

"In Kent somewhere. He lives in an old castle. Would
you like to go?"

"Would I like to go! When, Mummy? New Year?"

"Just after New Year," said Evelyn, remembering the
surprise which William Jarrold had in store for his family
on New Year's Day.

"Oh, Mummy. What fun. How marvellous. Miles Vane-
Merrick! How incredibly marvellous!"

Evelyn and Dan and Privett travelled down to Newlands on Christmas-eve. They went first-class, and Privett
went third. The Rolls-Royce and a footman met them at
Leatherhead, also the Ford van for Privett and their luggage. (The Jarrold standard of luxury was high, if not
actually a little ostentatious. Evelyn wondered how much
harm it did to Dan, to climb into a Rolls-Royce and have
a grey squirrel rug put over his knees by a footman). He
sat back in the motor beside her, outwardly the very model
of a rich man's grandson. On the floor in front of him, however, instead of golf-clubs and a gun-case, lay his painting-
box and a rolled-up camp-stool.

"Are you looking forward to Christmas, Dan?"

"Yes, I suppose so, Mummy."

"No, tell me really."

"Well, I hate the Newlands part of it. I mean, I like

getting presents and all the rest of it, but I wish you and I could go away together somewhere, instead of having all this family business."

"Why, exactly?"

"Well, partly because I like being alone with you, and partly because I hate being expected to be all kinds of things I'm not. And then there's Robin,—I hate Robin,— little swine." He was more communicative than usual, because he was bothered and apprehensive, and had been repressing his anticipation for days. "By the way, did you say anything to Grandpapa about my hunting?" He had been longing to ask the question, but had shirked it.

"Yes, of course I did."

"Was he very cross?"

"He was, rather. I daresay he won't allude to it at all. If he does, you mustn't get frightened. I'll back you up."

"He'll catch me when you aren't there," muttered Dan.

"If he does, darling, you must be firm for yourself. You mustn't count entirely on me."

"I hate rows."

"Yes, I know, darling, but sometimes one is obliged to have a row."

"A matter of principle," said Dan.

She was surprised to hear the grown-up expression on his lips.

"How do you mean, a matter of principle?"

"Mr. Vane-Merrick said so."

"Dan! you're always quoting Mr. Vane-Merrick."

"Am I? Sorry. I won't if it bores you. But you must admit, Mummy, he is the most extraordinary person. I never met anybody so full of ideas. In fact I never met

anybody in the least like him. He seems to be everything
one is told not to be, and to believe in everything one is
taught not to believe in, and yet I can't imagine anybody
not being impressed and convinced by him,—even old
Marsham, or Latimer. They couldn't put him down as a
rotter, could :hey?"

"No, I don't think they could."

"The extraordinary thing about him," said the puzzled
Dan, "is that he is interested in general ideas. Now you
wouldn't believe it, Mummy, but at school I can't get
anybody to take an interest in general ideas."

Evelyn was distressed by this outburst, for it was one of
Dan's statements with which she felt herself unable to cope.
She really did not like disturbing and upsetting ideas any
more than Dan's schoolfellows or the Jarrolds liked them;
she preferred things to go on in their orderly way. Miles
in the short but overwhelming period of their acquaintance had already upset her quite sufficiently by his liveli-
ness and irreverence; he in no way resembled the people
she was accustomed to. Now she foresaw that he and Dan
were destined to an alliance. She sighed, telling herself
that it was healthy for the young to be dissatisfied, re-
bellious, inquisitive. She told herself this, not really believ-
ing it. Still, she loved Dan the more for his young eagerness
much as it disturbed her. She made an attempt to answer
his last remark as Miles would have answered it, wishing
meanwhile that Miles were there to catch Dan in this
mood and drop seeds of suggestion into him as the seeds
of flowers dropped into the soil made warm and open by
the rain.

"At school! but you won't find everybody so silly in life
as they are at school."

"Shan't I? But everybody I know is almost as silly,—
Uncle Geoffrey, and Uncle Evan, and all your friends,
Mummy, if you don't mind me saying so. They all slap
me on the back and ask how I'm getting on at cricket, or
how many days hunting I hope to get this season, or
whether I'm a corporal yet in the O. T. C. Thatt's what
I mean by saying I hate being expected to be all kinds of
things I'm not. And am I going into the Guards or into the
business? And am I in Pop? And if not, why not? And it
isn't because I'm a schoolboy, it's because those are the
things they really think important. They talk like thatt to
each other, with only a little difference. Nobody seems to
care about what you are, but only about what you do;
and it's the silliest things that you do that interest them
most. They don't care in the least what you are inside;
and what you are inside is a thing to be rather ashamed
of anyway."

This alarmed Evelyn again; she was being dragged out
of her depth; she felt that Dan was preternaturally ana-
lytical. She longed again for Miles to be there to help her;
Miles, who could have answered eloquently, convincingly,
and comprehensively. She had not expected to be dragged
into quite such deep waters, motoring through the dark
lanes of Surrey. It was different when she received Dan's
letters, and could take her time over the answers.

"I think, perhaps, Dan, that I've brought you into contact with the wrong sort of people. There are other people,
you know,—like Mr. Vane-Merrick,—who are just as
much interested in general ideas as you are yourself. You
mustn't think that the world is limited by Uncle Geoffrey
and Uncle Evan, who are just schoolboys grown up. A
great many Englishmen are just schoolboys grown up.

You may find people very different when you get to Oxford and can choose your own friends."

She was trying very hard to help him, although it went rather against the grain. There were moments when she really longed for him to be an ordinary boy,—a nice, ordinary boy. Yet she wondered whether she ought not to have cultivated some friends able to satisfy his needs. She could not keep him away from his relations, she could not take him away from school,—and indeed both suggestions would have horrified her,—but she might at least have given him some acquaintances outside the limits of his family and the circle of her own personal, futile friends. Miles had said that her friends were futile, and he had added that to remain contented with them was to acknowledge herself frightened of life. Frightened! the very thing she urged Dan not to be.

His next words came as an additional reproach.

"God, Mummy, what should I do without you? You always say the right thing. About encouraging me to believe that life at school is just life at school and so on. And thatt's all nonsense about bringing me into contact with the wrong sort of people. You can't help Uncle Geoffrey and Uncle Evan, and Robin and Ruth. (She would be the worst of the lot, but of course she's a woman.) Haven't you made me know Miles Vane-Merrick? But for you, I would never have known him. Do you know, Mummy, I feel I can hardly live till I see him again? I feel there are thousands and thousands of things I want to talk to him about, so many that I couldn't say them all in a thousand years?— But of course," he added despondently, "I can't, because he would only be bored of me."

"He didn't seem bored with you, Dan, did he, when we

went to see *Earth?* I don't believe he addressed one word
to me! He talked only to you, all through the evening."

"He was marvellous," said Dan,—'marvellous' was a
word that had caught his fancy. "I never understood
about Russia till he explained it. Mummy, I do think
Russia is one of the most important things, don't you?
The Five Years' Plan and all thatt. Of course one would
hate it in England. One couldn't plough up all the hedges
in England, could one? Mr. Vane-Merrick said he would
hate it if they did."

"Mr. Vane-Merrick," said Evelyn, laughing suddenly,
"belongs to the territorial aristocracy."

Dan did not understand; he, in his turn, was out of his
depth.

"He likes England," he said defiantly.

"Yes, of course he does.—Look, there's Newlands."

"Newlands isn't England," said Dan, looking with dis-
taste at his ancestral home.

"Oh yes, it is!" said Evelyn, suddenly becoming prim;
"a very big part of England, anyway."

Newlands could not be mistaken by anybody for anything but what it was,—the Surrey seat of a successful
business man. Acquired with gold, with gold it was maintained. Square, red, ornate, and comfortable, it dominated
the two hundred acres of Surrey that appertained to it,
whether fields, paddocks, or terraced gardens. The view
from its windows was in its way pleasant; unspoilt by town
or bungalow; but smug in the extreme. The smugness was
perhaps due to the excessive neatness and discipline of the
immediate Newlands property: not a paddock without
its white posts, not a drive without its iron railings, not a

road ungravelled, not an orchard planted in anything but regular lines. Everything within sight was the work of man, —rich man,—nothing the work of untidy Nature. A prosperous bourgeoisie was paramount. The hedges were clipped to perfection, the lawns always appeared to have been mown thatt very morning, the edges of the turf were drawn as by a line, the creepers on the house were trained so that not a strand wandered unruly in the breeze. Especially did the domestic purlieus of the house express this care for order, convenience, and propriety. A glimpse of the stables alone was enough to suggest the harness-room with its burnished leather, its shining bits, its serpentine reins looped over wooden pegs, its yellow horse-rugs, piped with scarlet, emblazoned with the initials W. J.; the rows of stalls, with their pipe-clayed halters and edgings of plaited straw, cobbles, and initialled buckets ranged beside the corn-bins. A glimpse of the garage suggested the concrete floors, the boarded-over pits, the taps in convenient places, the spoke-brushes, the chamois leathers. A glimpse of the servants' quarters suggested the pantry with its adjacent strong-room, the kitchen with its adjacent scullery, the lobby with its telephone box, the brushing-room with its broad deal tables and pots of blacking, dubbin, and Meltonian cream. A paradise for servants, who are well known to be snobs in such matters.

It was dark, after the short winter daylight, when Evelyn and Dan arrived. The lights of the car soared up the drive, illuminating the generous gravel sweep. The windows of the house glowed with a yellow welcome. Paterson, the butler, met them at the door, supported by two of his myrmidons in livery. Paterson liked Mrs. Tommy; she gave a good deal of extra trouble in the house, wanting telegrams and telephone messages sent at all hours or parcels fetched at the station. Moreover, she was apt to be late for meals, an indulgence permitted to nobody else; but he sized her up as a 'lady,' and added that the staff was large enough in all conscience to cope with her demands. Besides, she had a way of saying, "I'm afraid I'm giving you a lot of bother, Paterson," from time to time, just when Paterson was feeling that he would rather have twenty people staying in the house than Mrs. Tommy alone; and the way she said it made up for all the bother. He liked Mr. Dan, too, who in course of time would, be master of Newlands, even though Mr. Dan had a shy and stand-offish way with him, and was likely to forget to ask Paterson how he did, on arrival. On the whole, Paterson, who had not much reverence for the Jarrolds as a clan, satisfactory in some respects though they might be as employers, preferred Mrs. Tommy and Mr. Dan to the rest of them. They conformed more nearly to the type he had been accustomed to serve.

The outer doors were quickly shut, to exclude the icy air of the December night, and safe within a warm hall Paterson relieved them of their coats. Tea, he informed them, was going on in the library. And to the library he conducted them, after first delivering to Evelyn a packet of letters and parcels which were awaiting her, and one solitary letter with a halfpenny stamp to Dan. He led them through the hall and the morning-room to the library, where he opened the door and announced ceremoniously, "Mrs. Thomas Jarrold; Mr. Daniel Jarrold," and left them to the mercies of their relations.

The entire Jarrold family was assembled round the tea-table and rose in delight to welcome Evelyn. Dan stood aside, feeling a little out of it, thankful that he had pockets into which to put his hands. (Anticipating, however, that his grandfather would presently say, "Ha! the Eton slouch, m-m,—can't you hold yourself up, my boy?" he took his hands out of his pockets and tried to dispose of them rather awkwardly elsewhere.) They all seemed very much pleased to see his mother, and a place was created for her beside his grandmother at the tea-table. His grandfather fussed over her like an old bee over a rose, offering her scones, sandwiches, tea-cake, cracking a joke finally about being sure that she would prefer a cocktail. Uncle Geoffrey and Uncle Evan, from their usual lackadaisical manner, became quite animated; they passed their hands over their hair, and shot their cuffs, fiddling also with the set of their ties. Dan meanwhile continued to stand aside, glad that his mother's arrival should arouse so much attention, but not very sure how much he ought to thrust himself forward. Finally his grandmother patted a chair and made him sit beside her, on the other side.

It relieved him to find himself seated; he felt less large, less clumsy, less conspicuous.

The room was warm, ample, and brilliantly lit,—too brilliantly. It declared that the Jarrolds had no need to economise in electric light. A huge log fire blazed in the chimney, but thatt was largely for show; the true warmth of the room came from central heating. Enormous chintz-covered arm-chairs and sofas advertised the English sense of comfort, supplemented by the scones, the tea-cakes, and the steaming silver urn. Book-cases,—since the room was known as the library,—rose against the walls, behind the lattice of wire doors whose key hung on Mr. Jarrold's watch-chain, the master-key which also unlocked the cases

of the Museum in Park Lane. The library consisted entirely of collected editions of standard authors, from Spen-
ser down to Hardy, most of them uncut and few of them
read. The exceptions among the cut and read were Dick-
ens and—surprisingly—Swinburne, with whom Mr. Jarrold considered that English prose and English poetry
respectively had come to an end. The moderns, which
explained the presence of Hardy and Conrad, were represented by expensive editions ordered haphazard on the
advice of a friend by Mr. Jarrold whenever it occurred to
him that he ought to bring his library up to date. It was a
pleasant room, the library at Newlands, for anyone who
did not wish to read books.

Round the tea-table were seated William Jarrold;
Louisa, his wife; Geoffrey, his eldest surviving son, with
Hester, his wife, Robin, their son, and Ruth, their daughter; Evan, his second surviving son; and Catherine, his
spinster daughter. Minnie, the objectionable child, was
doubtless upstairs with Cocoa, the old nurse who had
brought all the Jarrold children up, and whose real name
everybody had long since forgotten.

A serene, typical, and harmonious family party, you
would have thought, held together by William Jarrold's
stubby hand. Yet there were discordant elements and
potential quarrels, as Evelyn was well aware. At any moment an explosion might occur between Evan and his
father. At any moment, another explosion between Dan
and his grandfather. And in Ruth's unhappy eyes she read
all the complication of the unspoken situation between
Ruth and herself; Ruth, and herself, and Miles Vane-
Merrick.

Dan was the first to rage. He raged in her room while

she was dressing for dinner. She had reproached him with
being so sulky and reticent at tea.

"The truth is, Mummy, I can't stand them. I like
Grandpapa and Granny all right enough, but I can't
stand the others. I feel stifled here. Why do they never talk
about anything worth hearing? Why do they sneer at all
the things I like? Why does Uncle Geoffrey pull my hair
and say, 'Going to be a poet, Dan?' just because I didn't
have time to get it cut? Why do they think it *funny* to like
poetry and pictures and music, and make jokes about
them, when they're so damned solemn themselves about
their golf or England's chances against Australia? Grandpapa's different somehow; it's true that he doesn't care a
hoot for the things I like either, but you do feel that he's
made something of his life, even though it is only business.
You do feel that he's been mixed up always with important things and that he could tell you a lot about running the world if only he took the trouble. One doesn't
mind his being a Philistine, exactly. But all the guts
seem to have gone into him and left none over for his
children."

"They're trying to conform to their conception of the
ideal Englishman," said Evelyn.

"Are you laughing at me, Mummy? You might be quoting Mr. Vane-Merrick. I say, what would they think of
him? I'd like to see him here amongst them!"

Evelyn knew precisely what they thought of him: A
traitor to his class. ("Can't make the chap out," Geoffrey
had said.) But she did not tell Dan.

"Cheer up, Dan; you'll be with him in little more than
a week."

"Thank God for thatt. Mummy,—this is something I've

never dared to ask you,—was my father like the uncles? Or was he like Mr. Vane-Merrick?"

"Your father was very like Uncle Geoffrey," said Evelyn after a pause. The question had given her a slight shock.

"But he had more character, surely, Mummy? (You know how they're always going on at us about character, at school.) I don't know so much about Uncle Geoffrey, but Uncle Evan strikes me as having no character at all. He's got all the right manner, but nothing behind it. Lots of people are like thatt. Was my father? I want to know,— I must know."

"Well, yes, Dan, since you want to know, he was. He was very charming and very popular and a very good all-round sportsman, but you couldn't describe him as a very strong man or as a very intelligent one. He didn't care about clever people, he mistrusted them. I suppose you would say he sneered at them. I know you will mind my saying this, Dan, but you know I always tell you the truth."

"Yes, Mummy. There's another thing about your ideal Englishman: he simply hates the truth. I've discovered thatt at school. If you say what you really think, or try to get at the truth, the real truth, people get uncomfortable as though you'd said something shocking."

Evelyn smiled at Dan's naïf discoveries; she was glad to be able to smile again, after the suddenly strenuous moment she had passed through. But what a problem he was! this young prophet crying in the wilderness. She wondered whether, for his own happiness, she ought to encourage him or not?

"You stick to your principles, Dan; never mind about other people. And now run away, or I shall be late for dinner."

At moments her love for him was greater than she could bear.

She was dreadfully bored at Newlands; not only bored but irritated. The irritation was new, and had come upon her since she had known Miles. The total absence of ideas among the younger Jarrolds, their perpetual heavy banter which passed for wit, the limitation of their interests, their intolerance, their narrow-mindedness, all appeared insufferable to her now in contrast with Miles' alertness and gaiety. She almost preferred the drunken Evan, whose weakness made him into something more nearly resembling a human being, to the wooden and self-righteous Geoffrey or Geoffrey's virtuously British wife. Mrs. Geoffrey could talk of nothing but her servants.

"Would you believe it, my dear, we can never have anyone to dinner on a Tuesday because the cook insists on going out. Do you think she would change her day to oblige us? not she! And the others are just the same. When I spoke about it to Baxendale the other day, do you know what she had the impudence to reply? 'Well, madam, everybody wants their little bit of pleasure.' Little bit of pleasure, indeed! And I'm told that the immorality among girls of thatt class is terrible. Look at the stories one hears about the parks, and have you ever walked down the front at Brighton in the evening?"

"Perhaps the poor things have nowhere else to go," said Evelyn.

"Really, Evelyn! you surprise me. It's quite clear that you never go to cinemas. Why, if you look round in the dark. . . ."

"Then why look round?" said Evelyn as her sister-in-law paused suggestively.

"Ha! ha! you *are* funny sometimes, Evelyn. Geoffrey, did you hear thatt? Thatt's really funny, I think. Isn't Evelyn clever, Geoffrey?"

"I always did say Evelyn was a bit of a highbrow," said Geoffrey from out of his arm-chair.

Mrs. Geoffrey screamed with delight.

"Yes, thatt's it: a bit of a highbrow. Advanced ideas, and all thatt. To think we should ever have had a highbrow in *our* family. And now Dan. . . ."

A little more chaff, and then:

"Seriously, Evelyn, we're all a bit worried about Dan. I hope you don't mind my saying so. But you know he wouldn't go out with the guns yesterday, he said he wanted to paint. Well, you know, thatt's not natural in a boy of his age, is it, Geoffrey? Do back me up."

"Would you think it more natural if he ran after the girls in the village?"

"Ha! ha!" said Geoffrey. "She's got you there, Hester."

"Evelyn dear, I do hope you won't say such things in front of Ruth."

"I sympathise with Dan, Hester, I'm afraid. I hate going out with the guns myself. I sometimes think that a man might be the worst cad on earth; if he were a good shot it would be forgiven him. And now I really must go and talk to Cocoa; I've scarcely seen her since I've been here and I don't want to hurt her feelings."

When Evelyn had left the room, Hester said, "I can't think what has come over Evelyn, Geoffrey. I believe somebody must have been getting hold of her. The things she says! Really I was quite shocked. What *would* poor

Tommy have thought? I think you ought to talk to Dan, Geoffrey, and try to take poor Tommy's place a little."

"The boy's a rotter," said Geoffrey gloomily.

"I'm afraid he is. Ruth says he has the oddest ideas."

"No decent boy ought to find it so difficult to get on at school. There must be something wrong with him. Boys always know."

"He ought to go into the Army."

"Yes, thatt would knock some of the nonsense out of him."

"I wonder what Papa thinks of him, Geoffrey?"

"I believe Papa rather likes him."

"Your father is so unaccountable, dear. What makes you think he likes him?"

"Well, I was ragging Dan yesterday about preferring his messy old paints to a day's shooting, when Papa came along and clapped Dan on the back and said, 'Stick to your guns, my boy.'"

"Was thatt a joke?"

"A pretty feeble joke," grumbled Geoffrey.

He was right, however. Mr. Jarrold did like Dan. He respected him, seeing that the boy was not a puppet as his own two sons were puppets.

"Catherine," said Hester, pursuing the subject later on, "what about Dan?"

"What about him, dear? You know I never like to say anything against anybody, especially the young. They are so touchingly unprotected, I always think."

This reply showed Hester that she might proceed. She proceeded. Catherine was an excellent audience. She had not preserved her virginity for forty-five years without revealing the fact in every phrase and gesture. A practising

Christian, she was packed with virtuous complacence and not one ounce of charity.

She was less interested in Dan than in Evelyn.

"Perhaps we ought not to blame the poor boy, Hester. You know the power of influence on a young mind, and perhaps Dan's home influence has not always been,—well, what it might have been had poor Tommy lived."

"You mean?"

"I think you understand what I mean. Don't oblige me to put censorious thoughts into words."

"You are so scrupulous, Catherine,—such a sweet trait in you, dearest. It's quite true, we know so little of Evelyn's life, apart from us. Her friends, for instance, she may have dozens of friends we have never heard of. Remember, Catherine, Evelyn is a pretty woman still."

"Yes, and she looks a great deal younger than she actually is. One must grant her thatt. It is not difficult, I believe, nowadays, if you like to spend your time and money in dressmakers' shops and beauty-parlours. Personally I can imagine a better use for my time."

"Well, then. You know how fond I am of Evelyn,—how fond we all are, in fact,—heaven forbid that I should say a word against her,—but she's a vain woman, Catherine, —oh, quite harmless vanity!—and, in short, what do you think?" Hester paused, expectant.

"I don't *like* to think," said Catherine, who liked it very much indeed.

"No, I thought you'd say thatt. Neither do I. But supposing there *should* be, well, somebody in her life? Somebody we know nothing of? Would thatt be a very good example for Dan? a very good way of teaching him to respect his father's memory?"

"Oh, Hester, I don't believe,—no, I can't believe,—I won't believe it."

"Mind you, Catherine, I'm not saying anything definite."

"Of course not,—but who could it be?"

"How can one tell? Evelyn goes about a lot,—and she has her own flat, after all."

"What a dreadful, dreadful idea," said Catherine, deliciously titillated. She thought it over, with all the details she could invent, while performing the Christian act of carrying a pot of jelly down to poor old Mrs. Moffat in the village. She looked at Evelyn with a fresh eye, noting her grace, her beauty, and imagining thatt grace, thatt beauty, taken into the arms of a man.

Then the two boys had an open row. Hester and Geoffrey, pacing up and down the garden together, heard angry voices coming from the gun-room. They heard Dan's voice saying, "You little skunk."

"Oh, Geoffrey, there's Dan upsetting Robin again."

They hurried towards the open door and found the two boys, Robin very flushed and defiant, Dan very scornful and superior.

"Now, then, you boys, what is it this time?"

"He said he'd thrash me," said Robin, relieved by the arrival of his parents.

"For shame, Dan,—and you twice his size! Is thatt the sort of thing they teach you at Eton?"

"What had you been doing, Robin?" Geoffrey asked, more sensibly.

"I did nothing at all, Daddy."

"Let Dan speak. Dan, what did he do?"

"Oh, nothing," said Dan, looking down and kicking his toe into the ground.

"Well, if neither of you will say, Robin had better come along with us and next time you meet try to behave yourselves properly.—Really, Geoffrey," said Hester as they walked away, "I think I must speak to Evelyn about the way Dan bullies Robin."

She spoke to Evelyn, and Evelyn lost her temper, and the whole family became involved. Everybody took Robin's part, and said that it was shameful that Dan should threaten a boy two years younger than himself. Everybody felt that Robin was a nice healthy normal boy, and that Dan was a freak, a pariah. Their manners were too good to allow them to say so openly, but the implication was not lost upon Evelyn.

She got Dan into her own room.

"Now, Dan, what was it all about?"

"I can't tell you, Mummy."

"I can't think why you and Robin don't get on better,—he's not very interesting, I admit, but he's quite a harmless little boy."

Thatt was almost too much for Dan, who was feeling very sore; he grunted. What would his mother think, he wondered, if she could overhear Robin's habitual conversation with one of the grooms? What would Aunt Hester think, or Uncle Geoffrey? They all approved of Robin's passion for the stables; his grandfather had said only yesterday, very pointedly, that he did like to see a boy who was fond of horses. If they only knew! But Dan wasn't going to tell them. Let them smile benevolently when Robin came back with bits of straw on his back. The only thing he, Dan, could do was to curse the little beast.

He would tell Mr. Vane-Merrick. He would put the ethics of the question to him without mentioning Robin's name.

"Mummy, how many more days have we got to stay here?"

"Five, Dan,—why?" Had she not been counting them, ticking them off, day by day!

"Oh, nothing."

"Do you want to go back to London?"

"No, I want to go to Mr. Vane-Merrick's. There's such a lot of humbug here,—I can't stand it."

There was even more humbug than Dan thought. Geoffrey had a pretty shrewd idea of his son's real character. But he only laughed to himself, in his easy-going way: Robin had something in him, not like thatt mealy-mouthed softy Dan. He felt a throb of pride whenever he watched his son taking his pony over the jumps in the paddock or bringing down a bird with the new gun his grandfather had given him for Christmas. If a boy of fifteen could do thatt, shaping towards the man he would eventually be, what did a bit of smut matter?

The boy would get his house-colours, too, before long. And they would never superannuate such a good cricketer! Geoffrey had had a conversation with Robin's house-master, who with a wink had reassured him on the point of Robin's superannuation. He wasn't much good at his books, certainly,—in fact, he had twice failed to pass in trials,—but he was the best fast-bowler in the house. These little difficulties could be got over. Robin was safe for his colours, eventually; and anyone who was safe for his colours was safe for Pop: not likely that they would superannuate anybody who was safe for Pop.

No, thought Geoffrey, Robin was all right; what a pity
he wasn't the heir. England would be safe, if boys like
Robin were always the heirs; not boys like Dan.

It was not a successful Christmas party; nobody could
pretend that it was. Evelyn had to spend all her time
steering them off the shoals. She had to be inexhaustibly
gay and inventive; and thatt was very hard, when she had
her own private preoccupations and, furthermore, was
herself involved in the family complications by her es-
trangement from Ruth. Ruth and she, at previous Christmas gatherings, had been accustomed to meet between
tea and dinner in their rooms and to compare notes idly
over the events of the day. She had drawn a certain satisfaction from Ruth's adoration; not that she cared particularly for Ruth, but to someone of her nature it was always
pleasant to hold another being in complete, uncritical
subjection. Ruth could be allowed to fill in the boredom
of her spare moments. She was quite cynically aware that
this wanton desire for domination sprang from the least
pleasant side of her nature. The most unworthy victim
was better than no victim at all. It irked her vanity now
to realise that she had lost her hold over Ruth; incident-
ally she was sorry for Ruth, but did not see what she could
do about it; and was additionally piqued by the irony of
Miles Vane-Merrick, of all people, defrauding her of a
slave.

Those evening meetings with Ruth were a thing of the
past. It was awkward for both of them. Ruth came once,
and tapped at Evelyn's door, but their conversation was
strained and brief; it had none of the silly, easy, friendly
flow of former days. It ended by both of them saying

simultaneously that they supposed they ought to write letters; both the simultaneity and the obviousness of the excuse made matters worse and more difficult. This was wounding and annoying. Then there was Ruth's manifest unhappiness; Evelyn had never realised that the superficial Ruth could be genuinely unhappy. Unreasonably, it irritated her that someone else should be unhappy, however mutely, when she herself was so terrifyingly, rapturously happy. Ruth's poor white face and pathetic efforts to appear normal were a reproach to her.

Ruth suffered acutely. The terrible verses ran in her head:

"For it is not an open enemy that hath done me this dishonour, for then I could have borne it.

"Neither was it mine adversary that did magnify himself against me, for then peradventure I would have hid myself from him.

"But it was even thou, my companion, my guide, and my own familiar friend."

Uncertainty tortured her further. Had she known for certain that Evelyn loved Miles Vane-Merrick, she could have borne it; but being a woman herself she had no illusions as to the depths of woman's cruelty where love or vanity were concerned. Evelyn, she knew, had a cruel and ugly side to her nature. She stated it in those terms, crudely, going no further, and not realising that in Evelyn she had to deal with an exceedingly complex and passionate temperament, quite beyond the limits of her understanding. She stopped short at the point where she realised that Evelyn might quite well be playing with Miles Vane-Merrick simply in order to humiliate her and bring her to heel, and also because she could not tolerate the spectacle of a man's interest going to another woman. Women, even the greatest of friends, did those things to one another. Ruth knew thatt. She took it so much as a matter of course that she would not have blamed anyone but Evelyn. But it hurt her to think that Evelyn, whom she had worshipped since childhood and who was already so rich in devotion of various kinds, should have wished to snatch her one poor treasure from her.

Perhaps Evelyn had no idea how bitterly she minded. But then why did Evelyn avoid her and make any excuse not to be left alone with her? No, Evelyn knew well enough what she was doing.

All doubt in the matter was removed from Ruth's mind on New Year's Eve, when, coming in from a walk, the party found their letters arranged in packets on the hall-table waiting for them. "Here are yours, Evelyn," Ruth said thoughtlessly, and saw that an envelope addressed in Miles' handwriting lay on the top of the pile.

Evelyn took the opportunity to say to Dan during the evening, in Ruth's presence, "I heard from Mr. Vane-Merrick to-day, Dan, saying that he expects us on the 2nd. Dan and I are going to stay with your friend Vane-Merrick, Ruth," she added turning to Ruth; "isn't thatt a joke? I believe he lives in the most hideous discomfort, but Dan wants to go, so I suppose I must sacrifice myself."

What on earth impelled her to make such an announcement? Neither Ruth nor Evelyn could have analyzed the impulse.

"I didn't know Dan had met him," said Ruth with a knife in her heart.

Dan was all eagerness at once.

"Do you know him too, Ruth?" He had not quite outgrown the naïf surprise of the young on discovering that someone they know is acquainted also with someone else whom they know. It is the second stage; after childhood which assumes that everybody in one's own little circle is familiar to everybody outside it. "Isn't he a marvellous person? He took us to a Russian film one night in London. I thought he was the most exciting person I had ever met. Mummy thinks so too,—don't you, Mummy? But she won't say so; I think she's afraid of my talking to him too much."

Dan suddenly stopped; he was not usually so expansive to Ruth. Only the reminder of Vane-Merrick had loosened his tongue. He felt snubbed when Ruth said casually, "Oh, is he so very marvellous? Quite a nice young man, I thought."

She knew the truth now. She was struck with pain at the thought that Evelyn would stay with him,—would see the queer half-ruined castle where he spent all his leisure alone,—would enter into his personal life, creating a fresh intimacy between herself and him, the intimacy of daily life shared without a cumbrous interrupting paraphernalia of servants; she imagined how Dan would be sent out to draw water from the well, while Miles coaxed the fire, and Evelyn called out to know whether the kettle was boiling yet. What fun they would have! and behind the fun would be the hidden, tremulous passion which must be concealed from the boy, but which would be the sweeter, perhaps, for its secrecy. The double pain hurt Ruth so much that she put her face into her hands with a little moan. She had not known until then how much life could hurt.

Evelyn shrugged her shoulders as she made her way towards the library. It had been an unpleasant little episode, and she was glad it was over. At least it had cleared things up between herself and Ruth; Evelyn had no relish for ambiguous positions.

As she neared the library door, Minnie ran out howling.

"Why, Minnie, what's the matter?"

"Grandpapa's so angry with Uncle Evan."

"In there?"

"Yes, in there. I'm going to Cocoa. I'm frightened."

"Are they alone?"

"Yes."

Evelyn hesitated. Should she go in and interfere? It might make things easier for Evan. But it was difficult, when one's head was full of one thing and one thing only, to throw oneself into the troubles of others. "Oh, Miles," she whispered, pressing her hands together in impatient exasperation, longing for the peace and happiness which would be hers next week.

She went in.

Mr. Jarrold was obviously very angry indeed. He was storming up and down the room, slapping his hands behind his back, as was his custom when in a rage. Evan stood by the fire looking very sheepish, a decanter of whisky and a siphon on the table near him.

Mr. Jarrold having lost all control of himself, turned instantly to Evelyn.

"Look at thatt, Evelyn, I ask you. Five o'clock in the afternoon, and he's at it already. Thought I was safely away at a board meeting. It's a disgrace. He hasn't been out all day,—he's just been swilling whisky in here, making a beast of himself. I tell him I won't stand it. I won't have a son of mine making a beast of himself in my house. If he wants to drink, let him go and do it elsewhere. But I'll alter my will, by God; not a penny of my money shall he touch, not a word shall he have to say in the running of my business. I've told him; now he can take his choice."

"And I've told Papa that it's unreasonable to curse a grown-up man for having a whisky and soda instead of tea on a cold afternoon," said Evan, very sulky.

"Damn you, sir, don't prevaricate," bellowed Mr. Jarrold. "You know very well why I curse you. You soak from morning to night behind my back. You're a useless, drunken, feeble, idle loafer. I'm ashamed of you. I've a good mind to turn you out of the house straight away. I don't know what's happened to all my children. Rotten fruit, thatt's what they are. Geoffrey's a nincompoop, you're a drunkard, Dan is a softy,—thatt's all the reward I get for raising a family and working all my life to give them the best of everything. And then you dare to talk to me about a whisky and soda instead of tea! By God, sir, I'd like to hit you, I'd like to bash in your silly face," and Mr. Jarrold, shaking with fury, advanced upon his son with a raised fist.

"My dear father," said Evan, taking refuge in a chilly superiority, and also edging away a little, "aren't you forgetting yourself? This isn't a collier's cottage, after all."

"No, it isn't," said Mr. Jarrold, "and sometimes I wish it were. I wish I'd never raised myself out of the class I was born in. Oh, I'm not ashamed of it, though you are. You're ashamed to remember that your father's father was a man of the people,—you, with your airs and graces, aping the gentleman, all so lardy-da. You're nothing,— you're neither one thing nor the other. I've made you into something false. Not a collier's cottage,—no. But I was born in a collier's cottage and I'm proud of it. My father had red blood in his veins instead of glucose. By God, England did produce men then."

He paused, forgot his personal grievance, and launched out upon the most illuminating discourse Evelyn had ever heard from his lips. Her respect for him increased; he might be crude, he might be rough, he might lack entirely the decorative charm of the gentlemanly Geoffrey and the contemptible Evan, he might lack the awaking sensibility of Dan, but he was as solid as an old bull in a field, and he had no fastidious artificial hesitation about saying what he thought. He was so vigorous, and withal so eloquent, that Evelyn understood at last how he had always been able to carry his board of directors with him. She was glad to see that Dan had crept into the room and was listening.

"I don't say that they didn't make mistakes. Many people think that it was a mistake ever to have turned England into an industrial country at all. But no man, in those days, could have been expected to have thatt degree of foresight. It was the great chance, and they took it. By God, they did take it! With both hands. They couldn't be expected to see that by nineteen thirty-one it would have become an unmanageable monster. Think of the excitement, the opportunity. My father told me what he felt when he set up his first workshops. A man like my father had had no chance till then; either one was a gentleman, or a peasant, or a small tradesman, or a working-man —big fry, or little fry, anyway. There wasn't any real midway class. It was all privilege on the one hand, and lack of opportunity on the other. Those who had the privilege took their rights rather than their advantage. Those who had no opportunity were obliged to go without

it. But then energetic men like my father grew up to make
the new England, and their sons carried it further,—I
carried it further myself. I say, we made something. It
might have been better unmade, but you can't go back
on the past; you can't go back on what has been done.
We created a new sort of Englishman, neither big fry,
nor little, but he was a real enough man in those days,
tough, outspoken, with no nonsense about him. Then
came the trouble: we weren't content to let our sons remain what we ourselves had been, plain men of business
who understood their job and were determined to get the
best out of it. We wanted our sons to become the very
thing that we had despised and envied. And now, by God,
we've got what we wanted. We've created a lot of good-for-
nothings who are damned careful of their manners and of
their manners only, because they know they're in a false
position. Give me a gentleman, give me a countryman,
give me a working-man, give me an honest-to-God middle-
class John Smith, but heaven save me from these pre-
tentious humbugs who imagine themselves the aristocracy
of the future.

"And let me tell you," he added fiercely, "you've got
even your imitation wrong. There was something to be said
for the Englishman of birth, once.—Oh, you may wince,
you may think me an old snob; I am.—He looked after
his lands and he wasn't ashamed either of his feelings or
his brains. Today he's been taught to repress his feelings
until he ceases to have any and the same is even truer of
his brains. He wasn't ashamed of his culture, once. Today
he is. And he hasn't replaced it by anything else. He keeps
his superior manner and his respect for good form, but
thatt's all he has inherited from his ancestors and thatt's

all that you and your like have imitated from him. He's a
fake himself, and you're doubly a fake. What use are you
in a world which wants living people and not waxworks
stuffed with straw?

"You may say that I'm talking against everything I seem
to have believed in. I daresay I am. I sent you and your
brothers to a public school, and I sent Dan to Eton; everything I complain of, I've brought upon myself. There's
worse to come, but you don't know it yet; you won't know
it until tomorrow. I thought I was doing the best by you
and by the family, and it's only when I see what a skunk
you are that I realise my mistake. I ought to have sent you
all into the shops. I've a good mind to do it even now."

Glaring round, he discovered the presence of Dan.

"So you're there, are you, boy? Well, and what about
you,—the third generation, eh? Come, now, are you a
softy or not? Your mother told me about your hunting and
I gave her a piece of my mind, but if you've anything to
say I'm prepared to hear it. It's something that you should
have a mind of your own, whether I approve of it or not.
It's something, that you shouldn't allow yourself to be
shaped altogether by Eton. I sent you there to be shaped,
but dammit, I like you for holding out. Well?"

He waited. Dan was speechless. He had no words to
answer this sudden challenge; besides, this was Uncle
Evan's row, not his.

"Tongue-tied, are you?" said Mr. Jarrold with surprising good humour. "Well, never mind. You're young. I
won't bully you. But look here, young man, you've got to
make good. Damned well got to make good. Skip thatt
generation,"—he indicated Evan with a jerk of his thumb,
—"pretend it hasn't been. Either go right back, or go for-

ward. There's a possibility in both. Come to me in a year and tell me what you mean to do."

"Yes, Grandpapa," said Dan, glad to take hold of something concrete; relieved; a year was something concrete.

"You can go to Oxford if you like, or else you can go into the shops. I won't make you a partner till you're twenty-five. No. I could make you a partner now, if I liked. But I won't. Not good for you. You'd better go into the shops when you leave Eton. Teach you things that Eton won't teach you. However, you must choose for yourself. But you must be something, boy; not an imitation of something."

"Yes, Grandpapa," said Dan, half understanding.

"As for you," said Mr. Jarrold, turning on Evan, "get out."

Evan went, thankfully; but he finished off his whisky and soda and strolled away with the air of one who remembers that it is time to have a bath before dinner.

He secured Evelyn later in the evening; Dan was playing chess with Mr. Jarrold; Mrs. Jarrold was studying a list of Japanese lilies while she knitted a jersey for the Waifs and Strays; Geoffrey, Mrs. Geoffrey, Ruth, and Catherine were playing bridge. Evelyn and Evan had cut temporarily out of the bridge, thus they were reduced to one another's society. Evan felt furious and humiliated at having been cursed like a schoolboy in Evelyn's presence, yet he was sure she would sympathise: she was such a good sort. In any case, it was impossible to let such a scene pass without assserting his own position.

His vocabulary was small; his training in the art of under-statement potent.

"Pretty outrageous, what?" he said.

"I shouldn't have come in, Evan. I thought I might help."

"I didn't mind your coming in," he said grandly. "One has to humour the old man. No good flying out at him. Much better to let him say what he likes. Words break no bones, after all.—What a pretty frock."

"Never mind my frock, for once, Evan. Don't waste time in pretence to me. What about this drinking? You've asked me to help you, before now. I thought you had made an effort?"

"It's hell," said Evan gloomily.

"My poor Evan, can't you do anything about it?"

"What, go into an inebriate's home, you mean? No, thanks. The worst of it is, that I don't really want to get the better of it. I only feel alive when I've got something in me. Otherwise things seem so flat. Why won't you marry me, Evelyn? It's legal, you know. I shouldn't want to drink if I had you."

"Evan, you've told me thatt a dozen times, and I've told you a dozen times that nothing would induce me to marry you. Do become my brother-in-law again, please. How tiresome and complicated you all are."

"Only because you make us all depend upon you."

"You mean, everyone is tiresome and complicated when you know them well enough?"

"Well, yes, I suppose so. Me and my drinking, for instance."

"It really worries you?"

"Worries me! I should think it did. I tell you, it's hell. I think about it first thing when I wake up in the morning. I try to hold out, but I've never yet got beyond half-past eleven. And once I start, I can't stop; I want more. And yet every morning when I wake up feeling like death, I make a resolution to drink nothing but water thatt day. And by half-past eleven I always break down."

"But, Evan," said Evelyn, seized by a sudden practical curiosity, "how do you get it, here? This isn't the sort of house where bottles stand about, handy on every table."

"Oh, Paterson is a good chap," said Evan carelessly.

"Then Paterson knows? Oh, Evan!"

"Don't you curse me too, for God's sake. It's quite bad enough without thatt. Yes, Paterson brings it to me in my room, if you want to know. I don't have to ask for it, he just brings it."

"Evan, I do feel so sorry for you,—I wish I could help."

"You could help, in the way I've told you."

"Thatt's out of the question. I'll do anything else."

"Anything?"

"Well, no, not quite anything. Anything within reason. I can see that you're wretched."

"Oh, no," said Evan, getting up, "I have a very good time. Look, they've finished the rubber."

Only one more day, thought Evelyn, waking on New Year's morning. She must go down to breakfast for once, to watch the effect of Mr. Jarrold's surprise on the assembled family. It would be amusing to see how he reconciled his attitude with his diatribes of the day before. Most probably, in a magnificently British way, he would conveniently forget that the diatribes had ever been uttered. He would sit there, modestly beaming and receiving congratulations, delighted at the success of the joke he had played on his family.

When Evelyn came into the dining-room he was already
in his place, a huge cup of tea steaming beside him. He
looked at her with a twinkle in his old eye.

"You don't usually honour us, my dear."

"Perhaps I've made a New Year resolution, always to
get up for breakfast."

"M-m-m, I don't think it. Come and sit here. Dan, get
your mother some coffee. What will you have to eat, my
dear? Sausage, egg, porridge, kidneys, haddock, kedgeree?
Or pie? Very good game pie over there."

"Nothing, thanks, Papa,—some coffee and an apple."

"Continental habits," said Mr. Jarrold disapprovingly.
"Very bad for you. Always start the day with a good
breakfast. Always make a good breakfast myself, even
abroad, where it's difficult."

He was in a serenely good humour as he sat stirring his
tea, looking down the length of his table towards his wife
at the farther end. The members of his family were ranged
down either side, not talking much, but eating. Knives and
forks were put down with a little clatter. Scones, rolls,
toast, jam, honey, marmalade, and fruit, covered the
white cloth. On the sideboard a row of silver dishes sizzled
over little lamps. Cups stood grouped round the teapot and
the urn. The long French windows revealed the Surrey
view in the bright, cold winter sunshine. Dogs lay stretched
in front of the fire. So the Jarrolds sat at breakfast, and
William Jarrold felt himself at peace with the world.

Paterson came in with the papers. It was a rule that the
papers should be laid beside the master of the house, who
could then distribute them, keeping back what he wanted
for himself. His eye met Evelyn's. Then he sorted the
papers out, pretending to be grumpy.

"*Daily Mirror*, Evelyn? Geoffrey, *The Express?* Dan, give your grandmother the *Morning Post*."

He buried himself behind the full width of *The Times*.

A moment later, the exclamations began. . . .

Evelyn had foreseen truly: no allusion was made to the day before. Mr. Jarrold himself seemed perfectly unconscious of any incongruity. He was bland and pleased, though he affected to treat the matter lightly. He grunted amiably when his wife came round and kissed him. He pretended not to look at the photograph of himself among the four new barons, but Evelyn caught him squinting sideways at the front page of the *Daily Mirror*. And when Paterson came back on some pretext, and paused to say respectfully, "May I be allowed to offer congratulations on behalf of the household to your lordship," William Jarrold was a very well pleased man indeed.

PART II

PORTRAIT OF MILES VANE-MERRICK

EVELYN found it hard to believe that such remote depths of country could still exist within fifty miles of London. She was better accustomed to Surrey than to Kent. She and Dan had changed at a junction, and now the little local train carried them between the woods and orchards of Kent. It stopped at every station, gathering no speed in the intervals, so that Evelyn had ample opportunity to look out of the window and to familiarise herself with Miles' country. She tried to imagine it under its spring aspect, when the orchards would float in low clouds of white and pink above the earth; when the woods would belly out into vast acres of green; when the travelling heaven would heap itself in white sails above the North Downs. Now, the orchards were ghostly under their winter wash; they stretched out their lime-whitened branches in little avenues as the train went by. The woods were brown wedges in the blue Weald. The long vistas of poles in the hop-gardens opened and shut in perspectives, bare of the bine. Winter brought its particular beauty, though it was perhaps not the beauty sentimentally and traditionally associated with Kent in spring.

No one, certainly, could deny the loveliness of this southern country. It owed its loveliness, in part, to the fact that it was so true to itself. The line of hills, the expanse of the Weald, the rosy cottages, the distant spires, the narrow lanes, composed themselves into a character belonging there and nowhere else. Anyone sensitive to the character of landscape would have said instantly that he looked out of the train windows on to Kent,—fruit-growing Kent, hop-growing Kent, Kent unreached by the tentacles of London. Miles had not said much about the place where he lived; he had said only that he wanted her to see it. Did she regret that she had not come there first in spring or summer? She hesitated, thinking of the Queen Anne's Lace in the lanes and the dog-roses along the hedgerows. On the whole she did not regret it. The trees were austere, the water in the pools was frozen; this severity imposed upon a subversive softness might help her, also, to the courage which she needed.

Meanwhile she was moved almost to the point of pain at the prospect of seeing Miles in his own home. She could form no idea of what it would be like; she knew only that she would see him striding about in surroundings, which to him were familiar, but whose geography to her would be entirely strange. She had never seen him anywhere but in London; she had never seen him in country clothes. It was even possible that she might suffer from a sense of exclusion, when she heard him talking to his people, saying that this field must be ploughed or thatt tree chopped down for firewood. Did he suffer from the same sense of exclusion when he heard her in her flat, answering the telephone to unknown friends, or giving an order to Mason or Privett? He had come to her, after all, as a completely isolated figure, simply himself, associated with no background, while she had continued to exist against the background which was her own. Now the position was reversed;

she was arriving into his life, instead of he into hers, bringing none of her own anchors with her; for even Privett had been left behind. She brought nothing with her out of her own life but Dan, who would be as strange and ignorant as she herself.

Strange? Ignorant? How much more strange! how much more ignorant! For she, at least, knew Miles and loved him; whereas Dan had seen him once only.

If she must lock away her agitation and apprehension, Dan needed no such caution. He was too much excited to read. He fidgeted up and down the compartment, and looked at his watch a dozen times in five minutes. He asked her repeatedly what time the train was due, and swore every time it stopped at a station. He examined the Southern Railway map over the seat.

"Two more stations now," he said.

He sat down again with his legs outstretched before him and stared at his mother. How composed she looked; flicking the ash off the cigarette in her long holder, her belongings disposed on the seat beside her,—for they had the carriage to themselves,—dressing case, travelling-rug, hand-bag, magazine. In order to pass the time he tried to imagine that he had never seen his mother before; that she was just a strange lady travelling in the same carriage as himself. He decided that everything about her was remarkably neat and right, from her close fur cap to the dressing-case with E. J. stamped upon it. She looked like a person who would never be in a scramble or a hurry, and would never have mislaid the thing she needed just at the moment she needed it. She looked quiet and composed, yet full of secrets and experience. It reassured Dan to look at her. She had fine, smooth hands which she used very well, and just the right number of rings. Dan remembered how, as a very little boy, he had amused himself with pulling off her rings and trying them on his own fingers. There was one in particular, a large cabochon sapphire, which reminded him now of the sky at Portofino at night. (They had gone to Portofino together, during the summer holidays.) She had always let him play with her hands and her rings.

Perhaps it was easy to be so composed when one was so well accustomed to going to stay with people.

He leant across the compartment and took her hand because he liked the big sapphire and the smooth whiteness of her hand.

"Hullo, Mummy, you've got a new ring."

"Oh, no, Dan; you've seen thatt before."

"Well, I don't remember it. Is thatt what they call an eternity ring? Stones all the way round?"

"I don't know, Dan; it may be."

"Mummy, do you suppose Mr. Vane-Merrick will meet us at the station?"

"Yes, darling, he said he would. He hasn't got a chauffeur."

"Is he poor?"

"Rather poor, I think. You mustn't expect a second Newlands."

"Good Lord, I don't. I'm sorry he's poor; what a bore for him."

"I don't think he minds." She thought privately that it would do Dan good to know someone who did not take wealth absolutely for granted.

"What sort of a car has he got?"

"A funny old car all tied up with dusters and bits of

string. He drives very fast, and you expect the car to come to pieces at any moment."

"Oh, you've been in it already?"

"Yes, I've been in it already."

"Another station!" cried Dan, jumping up again and rushing to the window. "It's the next station now, Mummy," he said, relapsing into his seat once more. "Aren't these stations like toys, set down at intervals? And listen to them banging the milk-cans. I do hope it won't be dark before we get there."

In the summer, Evelyn thought, these little platforms would be heaped with the round bushel-baskets of fruit, those lanes would be blocked by a great lorry lurching along under a load of hop-pockets; the hay-carts would pass, leaving their trail on the overhanging trees. She seemed to be sinking deeper and deeper towards the essential Miles. Terror overcame her; she felt herself committed to a danger beyond her strength. She felt suddenly convinced that something disastrous would be the outcome. The banging of the milk-cans reverberated down the platform; it was no longer a pleasant country noise, eloquent of pasture and dairy, but a daemonic din.

"Shut the windows again, Dan," she said, shrinking into her furs; "it's too cold."

The engine shrieked as the train moved on; it shrieked with a persistence that suggested a notice saying "Whistle for half a mile." Dan could think of nothing save that Mr. Vane-Merrick with his crazy car would be waiting for them at the next station. Several times he repeated "Dusters and bits of string!" and went off into fits of laughter every time he said it. Evelyn told herself that she ought to be delighted by the boy's excitement, but she could feel only that he was allied with everything that rushed her faster and faster towards collision.

The idea of collision made her think of railway accidents. The little train, however, pounded on its way with a leisureliness that turned such apprehensions into an absurdity. She was nervous, thatt was all; not unnaturally. This going to stay with Miles in his own home, taking Dan with her, was the most momentous thing she had ever done. For years, life was tame as a ball of wool unwinding; then suddenly a wild beast leaped upon one's shoulders with a roar.

"Oh, Mummy, look! look! he's running away!"

She joined Dan at the window, and in the fading daylight saw an old farmer trying in vain to hold a bolting horse. The cart rocked wildly down the lane, and the gallop of the terrified hoofs on the road echoed even through the shut windows of the passing train. Evelyn clutched Dan by the wrist. "Oh, Dan, don't look," she said, shutting her own eyes; "he'll upset in a moment,— and we can't do anything."

The train went over the level-crossing with a final triumphant shriek as the cart crashed into the gates, overturned, and left a ruin in the descending silence.

"Don't look, Dan, don't look," she said, covering his eyes with her hand.

A moment later, the train drew up at the station.

Miles was there, waiting, under the lights. The lights were yellow in the cold, blue evening. He was bareheaded, in an old leather jacket, riding-breeches, and leather gaiters. He looked vivid and eager, glancing impatiently up and down the train, with the station lights shining on his hair.

Evelyn had pictured their meeting exactly so, but the accident had flung her abruptly into a different region. There had been an accident, she said, clutching his arm. She did not know whether anyone else in the train had seen it. He must make enquiries; he must ask the guard. "Hurry, Miles; the man may be dreadfully hurt, he may be dying."

Dropping from his eagerness, Miles became grave at once. She and Dan must wait in the car, he said; they would find it in the yard outside.

He was away for what seemed to be a very long time. Dan and Evelyn huddled under the ramshackle old hood, while other motors drove away with their loads and the station yard became empty and silent. A goods train shunted in the distance. Darkness came quickly, and the signals sprang into green and ruby lights, high up. An express rushed through, screaming, and pouring out a long trail of smoke and flying sparks. Then silence again, while the signals clicked back with a little wooden sound.

Finally Miles came back.

"It was old Rowland," he said briefly. "He's all right. The man from the level-crossing box has just come down. There's nothing for you to worry about."

Evelyn knew from the way in which he said, "It was old Rowland" that he was not speaking the truth. But she asked no questions.

Miles drove off at a furious rate, his head-lights tearing down the road and rounding the hedges at the curves. By thatt, also, she knew that he was upset about something.

She trusted him absolutely as a driver. His car might be falling to pieces, but he hunted it along the road as though he were driving at Brooklands. He could extort an extraordinary response and speed from such an assemblage of scrap-iron.

The country was unknown to her. They flashed through villages and past cottages which she had never seen before. They swept down a hill and up the next slope before she had had time to record the incidents upon their course. The darkness added to the mystery into which Miles was driving her.

She began to think that Miles' castle was a surprisingly long way from the station.

At last they turned off the main road, down a rough little lane between hedges. A board at the turning said "Private road. No thoroughfare." For some reason the words startled her, as they sprang out in black lettering on the white board when the car lights swept across them. No thoroughfare. So this track led nowhere; nowhere but to Miles and his castle; one could not pass on and beyond, on the further side. One could of course turn round and come back, but in life there was no turning round and coming back. In her overwrought state of mind she nearly besought Miles to stop before it should be too late. But perhaps it was already too late, now that she had actually entered his domain,—for, knowing that the castle stood in the midst of a large farm, she assumed that the woods and fields on either side were his property.

She resigned herself to the symbolism. The old, rapturous happiness flooded over her again. Still, the shadow persisted, and she was afraid. She wished that the horse had not bolted with old Rowland; she wished that she could wipe the scene out of her memory. It had occurred so quickly; it had been so suddenly horrible.

The lane widened, and the fan of light showed up a group of oast-houses beside a great tiled barn; then it swung round on a long, low range of buildings with a pointed arch between two gables. Miles drove under the arch and pulled up. It was very dark and cold. The hard winter starlight revealed an untidy courtyard, enclosed by ruined walls, and, opposite, an arrowy tower springing up to a lovely height with glinting windows. Miles switched off,the engine and the lamps. In the ensuing quietness and darkness, the stars sparkled with redoubled brilliancy.

An old man came up with a lantern.

"Bring the luggage out, Munday, will you? Mind your head, Dan. I'm afraid there are a lot of nettles, Evelyn, but we've trodden a path across them. Anyway, they aren't up at this time of year. Can you see? Give me the lantern, Munday."

They crossed the courtyard, Miles going in front with the lantern swinging in his hand. They passed through an archway beneath the tower and came out on a cleared space with an old orchard beyond. The dark shape of a cottage rose up, and other walls, all of the same Tudor brick. Miles' castle seemed to consist of isolated buildings, connecting walls, and the dark background of the country lands. It was very lonely.

"This is where I live," said Miles, leading the way towards the cottage, which by its structure had evidently once formed part of the original castle. It was only a cottage, but in its mullioned windows it preserved traces of grandeur.

Evelyn now saw that the entire encampment, including

the orchard, must be enclosed by a moat. In spite of its untidiness, it had a symmetrical outline.

On the threshold of the cottage they were met by an old woman of surprising beauty, like a Roman peasant. She stood there, waiting, like eternal Ceres, ready to gather them to her breast. Her brows were wide over her grey eyes; her hair lay parted in two placid bands which reminded Evelyn of the wings of a bird.

"This is Mrs. Munday, Evelyn. Mrs. Munday, I know you'll do all you can to make Mrs. Jarrold comfortable, won't you? Come in; you must be cold. Come in, Dan "

He was nervous; the experience of seeing Evelyn in his home was almost as strange to him as the experience of coming there was to her.

"There's a cup of tea for the lady and the young gentleman," said Mrs. Munday. She had a rich, country accent. She looked at them in a motherly way, as though she were sorry for them after their long, cold drive, but also in an examining way, as though she were taking their measure as friends for Mr. Vane-Merrick.

A Great Dane got up from in front of the fire and came to Miles, nuzzling his hand.

The room was roughly panelled with dark boards from floor to ceiling. It was all rather rough, but comfortable. A glass of violets stood on the table. Books and newspapers lay about.

Evelyn thought of the library at Newlands.

Miles turned up the lamp under its green china shade; he took a wax taper from the fireplace and lighted the candles in the sconces. Evelyn realised that he was doing these small things to cover his embarrassment. Regaining her wits, she saw that she must make an effort.

"May I pour out the tea, Miles?—It's very exciting for Dan and me, arriving here after dark and not knowing what we shall see when we look out to-morrow morning. This place seems to be quite away from the world. I didn't know there were such uninhabited tracts in Kent."

She talked for the sake of talking, and Miles played up to her, but their usual spontaneity was absent; neither of them could think of anything but their desire to get Dan out of the way. Munday arriving with the luggage, created a diversion. Miles said that he would go and put the car away in the shed. The great black-and-white dog followed him out into the night.

Dan, who had been silent hitherto, burst out into chatter.

"Oh, Mummy, isn't it romantic here? Did you see thatt lovely tower, and all the buildings, and the oasts? What a queer place,—does he really live here all alone with those two old people? Do tell me more about it."

"I don't know any more, Dan, you must ask him yourself. Now would you do something for me? Would you go upstairs and show Munday which is your luggage and which is mine? And you'd better unpack your own. Put your things away tidily; don't hurry."

"Of course. I will, Mummy."

He sprang to his feet willingly; he was always so willing and charming when she asked him to do anything! Remorseful,—for had she not thought out this little plot against him?—she watched him as he moved with his young clumsy grace towards the door, stumbling over the leg of the table, dropping his camera with a clatter on the floor, knocking his head as he stooped to retrieve it. The pathos of his clumsiness, his ignorance, and his innocence tore her heart.

"Dan!" she said imperiously, "come here."

He came, surprised. She pulled him down on to the arm of her chair, held his hands tightly, and gazed searchingly up into his face.

"Dan, you love me, don't you? Say you do!"

"But Mummy, darling, of course I love you,—why? What's the matter? You aren't going to cry, are you? your eyes look so bright."

"I'm not going to cry," said Evelyn. "I just wanted you to tell me. I think perhaps the accident upset me," she said, feeling that she must give some explanation. "Dan. you must always love me,—promise,—whatever happens. Promise. Promise," she repeated urgently, pressing his hands till her rings hurt him.

He was frightened. Emotional himself, but outwardly controlled, except on paper, it frightened him to see this manifestation of emotion in a grown-up person. He felt as though he were looking down into a pit full of fire, such as he had once seen at Orlestone and from which, as a small boy, he had been carried away screaming. It was a force he feared and recognised, but could not wholly understand.

He divined, as from a great distance away, that his mother was shaken off her usual balance. The responsibility, the necessity, of reassuring her frightened him too. He could not cope with these intricate grown-up mysteries. He did not know what one ought to say. He wished he could escape, to help Munday,—nice, solid, grizzled old man,—with the luggage. But he must say something.

"Mummy,—of course,—I needn't promise,—I love you, —and there it is. For keeps."

"Whatever happens?" she repeated.

"Mummy, what *could* happen? Don't go on saying thatt. I expect the accident upset you,—I thought it was rather horrid myself,—but the man was all right, Mr. Vane-Merrick said so. Don't think about it any more."

"No, no, I won't think about it," said Evelyn. She let his hands go and gave him a little friendly push. "I was silly, darling, but I'm all right now. You go upstairs now and forget about it."

"Truly?" He kissed her, putting a special warmth into his kiss, but she knew that he was relieved by this return to the normal. She loved him for his sweetness to her, and for the childishness which had made him look at her so aghast, so bothered, and for the awkward, mistaken sympathy which had gratefully attributed everything to the accident.

He gave her a last, soft look; smiled; and was gone.

She was alone. She wandered to the door which opened straight on to the invisible garden, and stood on the threshold looking out into the night. She strained her ears for the sound of Miles' returning footsteps, or even for the sound of his car throbbing and rattling on its way to the shed, but could hear nothing in the black, frosty air; nothing but the cry of a wild duck coming from the south. The lake, she supposed, must lie in thatt direction. The lighted room lay behind her, but in front of her were darkness and shadow, which her eyes could not explore. The wild duck's cry heightened the loneliness.

Irresolute, she had almost determined to go and look for Miles, when the great dog came up the path, and the light streamed from the door on to his patches of black and white. Miles followed him, a quick step up the path; he almost collided with Evelyn standing at the door.

"Evelyn!—Where's Dan?"

"Upstairs unpacking, Miles, tell me quickly, before he comes back,—you weren't speaking the truth about the man in the cart? Old Rowland, I think you said. He was hurt? Killed?"

Miles frowned. He hoped her anxieties had been allayed. He persuaded her back into the room and shut the door.

"Miles?"

"Yes, he was killed. He was dead when they picked him up."

"I was sure of it. Who was it? Somebody you knew?"

"An old farmer,—he used to come to the market every Monday morning, driving thatt very cob, and he used to hunt it too. I hate hunting, but still, he was a splendid old fellow; we do get thatt type, round here. I was sorry you should have seen it happen. I wanted everything to be perfect for you, from start to finish."

Her heart rejoiced at the personal note: Miles was coming back to her. Even those few words began to disperse her gloom, such was the power of love over her.

"I wish I could decide what I really feel about these country people," Miles went on, "I see so many of them down here. They are dying out, of course, and with one half of myself I can't help regretting it. I see their sons going off to the towns, or grumbling about the dullness of life when they do stay on the farms, and for all their insolence and independence they seem to have lost the old people's real dignity. It was never undignified to be content with what you truly were. Pretension only makes for falseness and vulgarity. Yet one can't expect them to stand still. Instinct makes me reactionary, reason makes me progressive. I can't help feeling that if some of my constituents saw me here I should lose a good many votes at the next election."

What a way, thought Evelyn, to spend the few precious minutes while Dan was upstairs! She was too much of a woman to relish this impersonal tone. She was also too much in possession of her wits to protest against it, except inwardly. She had coached herself very severely into the resolution that she must make no mistakes with Miles but must let him follow the mood that took him. At the same time it was intolerable that he should greet her by talking like this.

He answered something of what was passing in her mind as he said "Thank goodness one can talk to you. I've been down here for ten days without speaking to a soul except the Mundays and the farm-hands."

"But you like it, Miles? Your letters sounded as though you were ideally happy."

"And you resented it!" he said laughing. "You wanted me to be miserable without you? Well, I wasn't. I was longing for this day, it's true, but I was living in such a state of exaltation that it carried me over. All day long I was busy, and the knowledge that you were coming warmed me like a secret fire. I almost wanted to put off the day, so that it should not be so quickly over. Even now, I want to put off, and put off, and delay. . . ."

He sat down on the floor at her feet, putting his head against her knee. "For shame, Miles! your pretty phrases!" But her happiness flowered to a sudden perfection. His change of mood, she thought, was like the swoop of a swallow: a moment ago, he was the serious young politician; now, the lover, with the rich, extravagant phrase at his command for her reassurance. It was his peculiarity to express himself extravagantly, picturesquely, and without false shame. In this he differed from the younger Jarrolds, who had been taught at school, and who had thoroughly absorbed the lesson, that understatement was the mark of a manly English reserve. Miles was less careful than they, less self-conscious. Indeed, he seemed to belong to an earlier generation altogether, earlier even that thatt of William Jarrold, who on occasion could be eloquent enough.

Irritated though she had been by his first detachment, Evelyn could appreciate the swoop of contrast. Exasperated she might be, but never bored, never secure. This richness and danger between them satisfied all her needs. She was more afraid of losing Miles than of coming to an end of his resources, but the possibility of losing him only added to his value. She prayed that she might manage him coolly; she had had experience of men; the only experience she had not had was of her own heart whose intemperance might betray her.

Dan thought that he would never get to sleep; he was much too excited, too much disturbed. Mr. Vane-Merrick's untidy room belonged to another world than Eton or Newlands or the flat in Portman Square or the houses of his mother's friends. Evidences of a dozen different kinds of activity lay carelessly about: periodicals of which Dan had never heard, books on such diverse subjects as Gerard Manley Hopkins and political economy, ledgers full of farm-accounts, the small blue of Hansard thrown down on the big brown of the *Architectural Review;* a gun stood in the corner, and a row of specimen potatoes lay ranged upon the oak beam of the mantelpiece. Dan had wandered round before dinner while Miles was away on some unspecified mission. His mother had reproved him, saying that she never knew he was so inquisitive. He knew that her reproof was not seriously meant.

"Look at the way he marks his books, Mummy! You always told me not to scribble in books, you said it spoilt them. But look here,—he's left a shoe-horn in this one, to mark the page, and he takes notes at the end,—*q.v.* page 44-46, Milton and Marvell. If I did thatt, there might be some chance of my remembering the books I read. Books aren't meant to be looked at, surely? And what a lot of different things he must be interested in! How does he find the time? Just think of Uncle Geoffrey and Uncle Evan, who never think of anything so far as I can make out, and do nothing, nothing, nothing all day long! But now look here, there's politics, poetry, farming, philosophy, architecture, music,—he's got a piano,—and books in French and German. And a Greek play,—Aristophanes,—why on earth should he want to read Aristophanes when he needn't? Grandpapa said he was a full man; I begin to see what he meant."

"Did Grandpapa say thatt?"

"One day when Uncle Geoffrey was running him down. Uncle Geoffrey said he posed. I nearly hit him. But Grandpapa said, 'No, my dear Geoffrey, m-m-m, he's a full man as you will never be.'" Dan could imitate his grandfather to perfection.

"Did they say anything else?"

"Yes. Grandpapa said something about his being a reversion to type. I didn't understand thatt. What did he mean?"

His mother had been unable to explain, because Mr.

Vane-Merrick had returned just as she seemed to be making up her mind what to say.

Then they had dined in the sitting-room. There was no dining-room, apparently, and both Mr. Vane-Merrick and Mrs. Munday had called it supper. Dan, who in spite of his independent spirit, was accustomed to the punctiliousness of Newlands, had been surprised. He was still childish enough to accept his family's standard of values in such minor matters. He was still more surprised to find that Mr. Vane-Merrick did not change for dinner, but contented himself with pulling on an old blue jersey instead of his leather jacket. Such unconventionality startled Dan, and caused him to lie awake trying to accommodate conflicting ideas in his mind. Uncle Geoffrey, who would have put on a boiled shirt in the middle of Arabia, would certainly have dismissed Mr. Vane-Merrick as an outsider. So would all 'Dan's acquaintances at Eton; including his adored Mr. Meiklejohn.

Dinner, or supper, had been a simple meal, cooked and brought in by Mrs. Munday. One could not pretend that it was well-cooked. The chicken, although nominally roasted, appeared to have been boiled in water, with a little flour and gelatine added to the sauce to give it a taste. The cabbage had undergone the same process. Dan had wondered whether he might refuse the chocolate-shape in favour of black currants ("bottled from the garden last year," said Mrs. Munday as she set them down) and cream, which at any rate was thick and plentiful; he had ended by eating both. The shape had been particularly nasty. But all that Mr. Vane-Merrick had said, smiling up at Mrs. Munday, was "Mrs. Munday is excelling herself. Usually she is only allowed to give me eggs and cheese for supper."

Mrs. Munday had stopped to talk to them whenever she came in. She volunteered information, such as that the wild geese had again been seen flying over the lake. She did like to see wild birds on a piece of water, she said, and Mr. Vane-Merrick must be careful not to scare them away with his gun. She stood talking comfortably and easily before saying that she must go and see that her saucepan wasn't boiling over. She said this with an air of polite excuse, as though they would be sorry to lose her but must really allow her to go. Her dallying, also, was a surprise to Dan. Mason at Portman Square or Paterson at Newlands would as soon have thought of taking off all their clothes in the dining-room as of entering into conversation after they had handed a dish. Dan, lying alone in bed, laughed aloud at the very idea.

Mrs. Munday reminded him of the *padrona* at the little restaurant at Portofino, where his mother and he had spent the summer holidays.

What did anything matter, though,—watery chicken or nasty shape,—when one had Mr. Vane-Merrick as a companion? Dan loved him to the further side of idolatry. He threw out sixty ideas a minute, all new, all disturbing; and although he seemed too quick and impatient to pause of his own accord, in order to enlarge and develop, he would linger willingly in response to Dan's questions, giving his whole attention, explaining, illuminating, taking trouble, so that the brilliant jet ceased to be a firework and became a fire; he could justify his aphorisms, in fact, by solid reasoning if he chose. Other people might shake their heads over Miles Vane-Merrick; Dan in his inexperience was dazzled.

Then after supper, when Mrs. Munday had cleared away, saying a great deal about hot-water bottles and enough blankets on the beds, Mr. Vane-Merrick had sat down at the piano. Dan hated music; he could make neither head nor tail of it. He liked tunes, but other sorts of music made him angry and argumentative. This evening, however, the music had pleased him, although he was longing to talk; he had sat on the floor by the fire, his mother had played with his ear, and the green lamp had made patterns in rings on the ceiling. It was very different from Newlands. Besides, the music had not gone on for very long; he had been almost sorry when Mr. Vane-Merrick got up from the piano, lit a cigarette over the green lamp, and dropped into the opposite arm-chair with his legs swinging. Then he had said that Dan was quite wrong about Aristophanes.

Dan was sure that he would never get to sleep. He recalled a phrase he had read in a novel, about "His brain was seething with ideas." Dan had a sense of words. Seethe: it meant boil and hiss and bubble. A cauldron; a frothy liquid; he had seen his Uncle Geoffrey beat up his champagne with a fork. It had seethed, then subsided; but he, Dan, would never subside so long as he knew Mr. Vane-Merrick. He had never known anyone before, not even Mr. Meiklejohn, who could stir one up and suggest a hundred things, without being for an instant didactic. Christ, thought Dan, applying his own limited experience, what a tutor he would have made!

He turned his pillow over and settled the bed-clothes more comfortably under his chin in the hope of coaxing sleep. He had pulled his curtains back, as he always did, and could see the stars outside his open window. The ducks cried, and an owl. This was the country, as Newlands was not the country. This was a strange little cottage to be in, alone with his mother,—for the Mundays slept in the long, half-ruined building and Mr. Vane-Merrick slept in the tower. He had said so. He had said, "Evelyn, I'm giving you my bedroom, do you mind? Mrs. Munday said it would be more comfortable for you. I've moved across to the tower, where I always sleep in summer." She had protested a little against the suggestion of turning him out. Dan, being in high spirits, had said, "I expect he likes the tower, Mummy,—it's so romantic," and then he had blushed miserably, thinking they would not see that he had intended a joke. It was perhaps not in good taste to make jokes about people's characters. But Mr. Vane-Merrick had said, "Quite right, Dan, you've put your finger on my weakness." He seemed amused, not offended.

The cooler side of the pillow became warm also, and still sleep did not come. Dan slipped from his bed and leant out of the window, breathing the cold air. A golden light was burning high up in the tower So Mr. Vane-Merrick was awake too? reading? working? Dan was curiously comforted by this evidence of another's wakefulness. As he gazed, the light went out. He could now see the tower very dimly drawn against the stars. He pattered back to bed, and fell instantly into his usual sleep.

It was "Miles, Miles! where are you?" all day long. Evelyn heard the boy calling, or, looking out of the window, saw him following Miles about everywhere, eager and devoted. This association produced mixed feelings in her: it lifted half the responsibility of Dan off her shoulders, it pleased her to see the boy's adoration of Miles, yet it filled her also with a double jealousy, and it complicated matters still further, in so far as she never got Miles to herself until Dan had gone to bed. And Dan was reluctant to go to bed. He and Miles always became involved in some discussion as they sat over supper, prolonging it into endless ramifications while Evelyn stirred restlessly with impatience as she lay in her arm-chair by the fire. It exasperated her the more, that Miles would not let the argument drop; would not create a pause in which she might say, "Now, Dan. . . ." Yet, the moment they were left alone together, he would come towards her saying "At last!" in a tone that repaired the hurt.

She was behaving with great circumspection; too great to allow her to expostulate with Miles. She must not make him feel bound in any way. He told her repeatedly that he loved the freedom she gave him; she never worried him; she was unlike other women. (Thatt phrase made her wince, but, true to her determination, she made no comment.)

Meanwhile, when she could control her exasperation enough to listen, instead of brooding silently over her very feminine grievance, she was astonished by the cataract of confidences that poured from Dan. The boy had thought more deeply than she had suspected. Ill-organised, childish, crude, his opinions might be, floating in the air, unrelated, without reasoned basis; but from them emerged a definite attitude which he had reached by some short-cut of his own. The originality was surprising, coming from a schoolboy. He might be alarmed by his grandfather, he might suffer unduly from the solecism of some unmanageable situation, but the mind that was in process of evolving so firm a doctrine was not the mind of a weakling. Miles said as much. "Thatt boy of yours," he said, "reacts violently against nearly everything he is taught at school. It takes some courage and initiative to do thatt."

"You encourage him, Miles. What about his after-life?"

"When he leaves school? Well, he must fight."

"You are permanently embattled yourself, I believe. If you had lived in the time when men wore swords, yours would never have been in its scabbard."

"Nonsense," said Miles laughing. "I'm a Tory squire."

It was hard indeed to visualise him as the young Labour member, when she saw him surveying his meadows or heard him talking to Munday. He loved the people, though he loathed and mistrusted democracy. With the people of the soil he was as much at his ease as they with him. He understood everything about them,—their sensibly practical outlook, their innate suspicion, their shrewdness, their limitations, their artfulness, their loyalty, and their endurance. He did not romanticise them in the least. "Munday is an old fox," he said, "so he thinks everybody else a fox too."

Evelyn would gladly have talked to Munday, if only in order to hear what he had to say about Miles, but owing to his strong accent she could not understand half he said. She therefore avoided his friendliness rather shyly. It was a new experience for her, to feel shy.

This country life was quite strange to her. She had scarcely realised that it still went on. "My dear!" said Miles when she told him this, "two-thirds of the population of this country is engaged in agriculture." Miles managed his own farm of a thousand acres (his father had made it

over to him during his life-time as the younger son's por-
tion, with the castle standing in the middle); but, he said,
he could not have run it without loss if he had had to
pay rent for it. Munday maintained that foreign grain
and butter were allowed to be dumped in England to the
ruin of English farmers because Members of Parliament
owned property abroad. "And Munday has a vote!" said
Miles, half in amusement, half in despair.

Evelyn had a great deal to put up with, for Miles still
assumed that her familiarity with country life was as
natural as his own. She wondered whether he assumed it
deliberately, in order to break and humiliate her,—for
he must surely realise, especially after what she had said,
that she was incorrigibly urban? The most that she could
muster, was a pair of crocodile shoes quite suitable to the
sedate afternoon walk on the gravelled drives at Newlands,
but wholly inadequate to the tramps over ploughed fields
which Miles expected her to undertake with him and Dan.
Considering her shoes in her austere bedroom, where she
could scarcely see her face in the mirror, she laughed
ruefully at this incongruous choice of a lover. What joke
of fate had thrown Miles across her path? He strode ahead,
leaving her to climb gates, to be scratched by brambles,
to extricate herself from mud,—she, the spoilt, the pam-
pered, the exquisite and yet the virtuous woman, who but
for Miles Vane-Merrick would shortly be at Luxor or at
Caux or on the Riviera, dressed in the appropriate creations of Messrs. Rivers & Roberts. He took it quite for
granted that she should dispense with the services of
Privett. Yet he was sensitive enough, in all conscience;
he was neither an oaf nor a bumpkin; his culture was
both wide and deep; his mind was lively and amusing.

Miles, ranging over a dozen topics as he drank his wine, was a different person from Miles ranging over his fields on a winter afternoon. Yet they were the same person really, and Evelyn, whose intellect might be under-developed but whose intelligence was acute though un-trained, recognised the truth of William Jarrold's epithet: a full man.

Thatt was what held her to Miles. He was vital; he grasped life. Whether he talked to Dan, or dragged Evelyn across the fields, or awaited her in his tower, he brought the same full energy into play. The sense of futility was unknown to him.

He was only twenty-five.

Love was a new discovery for him. He treated it as an enormous new region of life for him to explore, rushing into it with tremendous excitement. Yet he could keep it quite separate from other things; which annoyed Evelyn. She would have liked him to be aware of her all the time. As it was, he seemed capable of forgetting her for hours together, and she had to find what comfort she could in hearing him say that she was a good listener. When he did turn to her as a lover she had nothing to complain of, for he brought the same intensity and concentration to bear on love, as on other things. Her spirits went down and up, as she alternately believed that he cared for her not at all, or that she absorbed him to the exclusion of everything else. And she was persuaded of either with the greatest ease, one after the other.

She was unhappy at times. Passionately and exclusively as she loved Miles, both mentally and physically, she was aware of the gravest differences between them. She was full of premonitions which she tried to hide from herself.

She did succeed in hiding them. But they were there, like a black cloud at which she refused to look.

Miles himself was so youthfully light-hearted, so exultantly in love, that he lived only for the rapture of the moment. He had discovered Evelyn, he had got her for himself, and thatt was a miracle. In his exuberance he laughed from morning to night. It amused him to go away from her, to give his attention to other things, and then to come back to her, doubly ardent and refreshed. He was quite unaware how much she resented this system. He felt vaguely that love was cloying, unless one deliberately imposed periods of intermission. It amused him to pretend, for hours on end, that there were other things in life, equally important, even more important. Indeed, it was not wholly pretence. He was much too energetic to allow himself to be entirely absorbed by the Lethean sweets of love.

Besides, he was writing a book, a stiff book on the economic situation, and had no intention of allowing Evelyn to distract him from this. He very quickly saw that she would regard his work as her enemy, and would quite unscrupulously divert his attention to herself whenever she got the chance. She would do it subtly at first, but as time went on and as she grew less cautious, she would encroach more and more. The undeclared battle between them amused him; and he was determined to win.

Still, he had his sense of responsibility. He was young, and, under his gaiety, fundamentally serious. His seriousness seemed to Evelyn rather touching; it made her feel decades older than he. In some ways he was so entirely her master that she felt quite humble before him; in other ways he appeared to her as an inexperienced adolescent. She did not know which aspect made her love him the more.

He got it into his head that she would worry about their relationship. For his own part, he never cared in the least what people thought or said, but he was quite shrewd enough to know that Evelyn came of a different tradition. He teased her about it once or twice, and she admitted sadly that he was right.

"I can't help it, Miles; you may despise me if you like. But," she added rather pathetically, "you are doing a lot to startle me out of my old-fashioned ideas."

"It's an odd contrast, to look at you dressed in the height of fashion, and then to hear you talking about old-fashioned ideas! Thatt's what gives such a charming twist to your personality. The Victorian, and the chic. The quarrel between your inside and your outside. You ought to be dowdy. Thank God, you aren't."

Then he became more sober, stopped making phrases, and again asked her to marry him.

"You would be much happier. You wouldn't need to worry about the Jarrolds. You wouldn't need to worry about Dan. You know quite well that you live in terror of Dan finding out."

"Dan is a child, Miles; he can't judge the right or wrong of such things. Thatt is our business; not his."

"As a matter of fact, I don't believe that Dan would judge us harshly. Dan is a sensible boy,—but one never knows, with the very young. He might rake up some strange primitive feeling about his mother. Thatt's the worst of the conventions: they usually have their root in some useful, protective, racial taboo."

"I won't marry you, Miles."

"But why not?"

"Miles, I've told you already twice,—don't make me say it again. I don't enjoy saying it."

"What,—that I'm younger than you?"

"Fifteen years."

It always ended there. He expostulated, and she was adamant. He was really sincere in his expostulations, being so young that the thought of age could not trouble him. Besides, he could not think of Evelyn as much older than himself. She betrayed no signs of age; her hair was glossy, her skin clear, her body firm and white. True, 'forty' had an ominous sound, and she would be forty on her next birthday; if she had told him so once, she had told him twenty times. He set thatt aside. He was rash, impetuous, and unaccustomed to resistance. It angered him to be thwarted so calmly and consistently. He little knew what her firmness cost her.

She began to say that she and Dan must go back to London.

"We can't stay here indefinitely. We've been here for over a week."

"What does thatt matter? Aren't you happy here?"

"You know I'm happy here, only too happy. But what will people think?"

"People,—you mean the Jarrolds."

"They're very old-fashioned, you know, Miles; like me; very conventional."

"And you mind what they think?"

"Well, I have to consider Dan."

"Nonsense, Evelyn, thatt isn't true. I'll tell you what's

true, without humbug. You're old-fashioned; thatt's true. And, moreover, you're so vain that you hate the idea of forfeiting even a tittle of the Jarrolds' approval. You like having people, even the Jarrolds, completely under your charm. You resent criticism. What an odd mixture you are. You're so real, and yet so unreal in bits. I can't make you out."

"I'm afraid I don't share your fine aristocratic careless-ness, Miles, thatt's the long and short of it. I belong to a rather cautious and uneasy stock. You can afford to in-dulge yourself in this fine contempt; we can't. I hate my-self for it, but I remain a victim. You may be right about my personal failings too."

"I don't mind your personal failings. They amuse me. They charm me. I should rejoice if you applied them to myself. I think I will arouse your jealousy, just for fun."

"All right, Miles,—do, if it amuses you."

"No, thatt's silly. But what you say about a cautious and uneasy stock really interests me. You mean that you really care about what one calls your Reputation? Is it possible? Does anybody still think about such things? Aren't you being rather Victorian? even Edwardian?"

"Perhaps, but remember, Miles, families like the Jar-rolds are products of Victorianism."

"Yes, they are just the sort of people who opposed anaesthetics on the ground that if God had not intended man to suffer pain he would never have sent it into the world; the people who reconciled Genesis with geology by the theory that the earth was created complete with fossils buried in the rocks. Or that Adam was created com-plete with a navel although he had never had a mother."

"Did they say thatt?"

"Darling, you're so deliciously ignorant."

"I never pretended to be anything else, Miles. I know you always have illustrations ready to hand. I can't compete."

"You don't compete,—you're *hors concours*. You follow the short-cut of instinct. An unfair advantage—genius over talent."

"I wish you would be serious."

"I am serious. I'm a very serious young man. Most young men of my age concentrate on being Good Shots. I don't. I go in for social problems. I also go in for practical farming. What greater seriousness do you want than thatt? —Anyway, you are perfectly right about the Jarrolds being products of Victorianism. Of course they are, both by date and by temperament. You couldn't explain exactly why you said it,—probably you had some vague idea that Industry grew up in England during the reign of Victoria, —it was such a long reign, that one can afford to be a little vague about dates,—everything hides conveniently under those ample skirts,—like a lot of chickens under an old hen,—and you had a vague idea that the first machines were broken up by ignorant, angry people,—God, what foresight they showed!—and that people like the Jarrolds stood firm,—and Made England What She Is,—well, so they did, and made a nice packet out of it too from which they still benefit in their costive way,—but whyever you said it you were right. The Jarrolds are Victorians,— Victorians not only because they still believe in all the cant that goes with it. They believe in reputation and in respectability and in keeping up appearances. All those things. And in not allowing people to enjoy themselves on Sunday,—the only day in the week when they get a reprieve from a grinding life. And in condemning women to bear child after child, whether they can feed them adequately in their early years, educate them according to their talents, and settle them in after-life, or not,—all for the sake of keeping England What She Is. Give us emancipation from such ideas and from all that they carry with them, and we may begin to get somewhere. Your Jarrolds are anachronisms today. They ought to be stuffed and put under a glass case."

."You rather misjudge old Mr. Jarrold himself," said Evelyn, remembering Mr. Jarrold's outburst when he had been angry with Evan. "I daresay he would have equally harsh things to say about you and your like. I don't think he really approves of half the standards he tries to support."

"No, I like the old man," said Miles; "he's a fine old man in his own way, but he's an anachronism all the same."

"I see that you yourself don't intend to be an anachronism, nor Dan either if you can have any say in the matter."

"Dan is all right. Dan, I hope and pray, is young England. With a bold enquiring mind and a large pair of shears to clear away the brambles."

"Thatt's as it may be, Miles, but to go back to what we were saying: I can't stay here indefinitely."

Miles looked obstinate.

"You're doing no harm to anyone, and giving a great deal of pleasure to me."

"Am I really, Miles? Are you sure? Are you sure you want me? What about your work, which I interrupt? You know you care for your work more than. . . ."

("I mustn't say such things to him," she thought, "fool that I am. Besides, it isn't true,—or is it?")

("How impossibly feminine women are," he thought, but because he loved her he felt tenderly towards her.)

"Evelyn, don't be absurd. Well, I'll work for a couple of hours a day, if you want me to. Will thatt abolish your scruples?"

("Oh!" she thought, shot by a sudden pain, "he takes advantage of the opening I gave him.")

"What a good idea, Miles,—yes, work for two hours, a day, more if you like. Perhaps you can lend me some books to read while you're busy."

He was not deceived. Nor had he yet arrived at the stage of wanting to be deceived. He did not even want to pretend to misunderstand her. Even the most passionate lover of truth shuts his eyes to truth in the early stages of love. He came closer to her; took possession of her hand; fitted his fingers into hers. Physical contact, even the slightest, reassured him.

Any cloud between them could be dispelled when they reached out to one another again, physically. And half an hour's abstention amounted to half an hour's starvation.

Miles prolonged these abstentions, sometimes, deliberately. She was far cruder and more direct than he, underneath her surface of sophistication. Her feelings were too strong to allow her to practise deliberate tricks on them. It was all she could do to maintain a reasonable check on their inconvenient violence. Wisdom alone imposed such a check. She knew that she must make no mistakes in her relations with Miles. He was a difficult and dangerous colt to tame. Because he was a young and vigorous man, however, his hunger for her always ended by over-ruling his experimentalism. After he had pretended an impersonal indifference towards her for a time, his desire broke out again, flooding, irresistible.

Between the incertitude of the one and the persuasion of the other, he held her unhappy, happy, and enslaved.

She consented to stay on for a few days longer. The truth was, that she could not tear herself away from him. This late flowering of her heart and senses was altogether too sweet, too weakening. The world ceased to exist; she let it go; nothing remained but the enchanted square of Miles' castle. The tall, rosy walls shut them into a bewitched enclosure.

"Ah," he said when she told him this, "you must see it in the spring. Or on a summer evening."

They were walking in the walled garden, and the twin tops of the towers soared above them into the pale sky. The trees were winter-bare, and the sky full of rooks.

"I can hardly believe that it would ever seem more beautiful, Miles." She, who had never noticed such things before, and who had always demanded comfort rather than beauty, was really moved by this revelation of loveliness. Her perceptions were widening; she even liked Miles to read poetry to her. "I don't know what you are doing to me, Miles," she said, laughing; "you seem to be turning me into quite a different person."

At thatt moment she was happy. She took Miles' arm, and felt that she shared his life. She even listened patiently when Munday came up to speak to him about something he called dolly-wood. She had no idea what dolly-wood might be, but Miles seemed to know. Miles discussed gravely, and at some length, since length was inseparable from any subject opened by Munday, the advisability of cutting certain chestnut wood this year or of leaving it till next. She listened rather remotely, but with a new sense of the permanence of such arrangements. Miles and his forbears, Munday and his forbears, had been weighing such things for centuries. It seemed to her right that Miles and Munday should be weighing them today. Miles in his castle, managing his farm and his estate, talking to Munday, was the true, the traditional Miles.

When Munday had gone, clicking the garden gate behind him, she slipped her hand into Miles' arm again.

"I like you as a Tory squire."

"I apologise, darling. Munday has no tact. He pounces on me whenever he sees a chance."

"I tell you I like it. It's so new to me. I like you in thatt rôle.—Miles, look at those black woods. Look at thatt great sky. I don't believe it could be more beautiful, even on a summer evening."

An owl began to hoot, somewhere in the orchard.

"Oh, Miles,—promise to love me still, in the summer,— please, Miles."

For once he was not irritated by her demand; at thatt moment they were perfectly attuned. She felt the harmony, and was content. They continued to pace up and down the garden path, under the high wall, till dusk fell and other little owls took up the cry of the first owl in the orchard.

She was dismayed to find that Miles kept to his suggestion of working for two hours a day. She came into his room to discover him seated with another young man at a table heaped with papers. He looked up with a frown, but smiled when he saw her.

"I never thought you would be down so early. This is Mr. Bretton, who does his best to persuade my constituents that I am the only person fit to represent them. He has a hard job of it. Mrs. Jarrold, Bretton."

Bretton had flashing but rather small black eyes and tousled black hair. He shook hands awkwardly, as though he were not accustomed to social conventions. He was rather a stocky young man, ill-dressed, and Miles appeared more than usually graceful and at his ease beside him.

He said nothing, not even How-do-you-do? but Evelyn had the impression that it was not because he had nothing to say. He seemed on the contrary to be full of pent-up energy and resentments. She gave him her most charming smile, but felt that he disliked her at sight. They were antagonistic to one another.

"Don't let me interrupt you, Miles. I had no idea you were busy."

Miles opened the door for her. Bretton, who had sat down again, remained seated, fidgeting with a pencil. She smiled and nodded good-bye to him, and he replied by an embarrassed nod, obviously aware that he ought to get up, but unwilling to do so.

In the doorway she paused and looked at Miles. He looked back. They looked at each other for a second, straight into each other's eyes. Defiance and amusement were in his.

She went slowly down the corkscrew staircase of the tower, an angry woman. Miles was not treating her with even the common courtesy accorded to a guest. Because they were lovers he thought he could treat her in this casual manner. He should learn his lesson: she would return to London thatt same day.

She went up to her bedroom, avoiding Dan. Dan, she knew, was in the sitting-room, reading a pamphlet on economics which Miles had given him. She could not bear to face Dan's enthusiasm at thatt moment. She crept into the cottage by the back door; upstairs as silently as possible. It was cold in her bedroom. The fire was laid, indeed, but she was too proud and angry to light it. She remembered how Miles had run out into the orchard, last night, and had returned carrying a frosty log which he flung, laughing, on the fire. She moved about, putting her things into her trunk. Almost everything she handled awoke some association with Miles; the jerseys he liked, the shoes he had derided. She bundled them all in, regardless of Privett's disapproval when they would be unpacked. It would be a relief to get back to Privett, and to the warmth and compactness of her own flat. She must have been mad ever to think that she and Miles were intended for one another; that they could ever, possibly, have hit it off. Let Miles stick to his farming and his politics; let him find a woman more accommodating and slavish than she.

She had packed nearly everything when she heard Miles' voice downstairs. At the same time there came a scratch at the door and a low whimper. She opened, and Caesar, the Great Dane, lumbered in. He moved his tail so that it struck like a piece of wood against the furniture; he walked round nosing at her possessions, raising a puzzled head. "Dogs always know when one is going away,"—so Miles had said. "Yes, Caesar," she said, putting her arms round his big neck, "I'm going away."

Dan's steps bounded up the stair.

"Mummy! Mummy! where are you? Here's Miles."

She came out quickly on to the landing, shutting her bedroom door behind her. Miles appeared at the foot of the stair.

"Evelyn! Come out? I've got rid of Bretton."

She descended the stairs carefully; the steps were old and uneven. Miles was there, his hair shining under the window. Dan was there too, looking flushed and excited. They both seemed very young and guileless. She could not believe in the look Miles had given her when he opened the door for her to go out. She could not believe that he had really measured his strength against hers. He looked like a boy released from school.

"I must put on a hat, then," she said, "if you want me to come out."

She said nothing to him about her intention of leaving; she merely unpacked her things again, meekly, feeling half grim and half exultant as she recognised her submission to him. But she did ask him about Bretton.

"Bretton? He's my political agent. The son of the local blacksmith. A good boy, and a raging Communist."

"A Communist?" said Evelyn, as though Miles had said 'a lion.'

"Yes, poor boy, he has to water down his convictions for the sake of keeping his job with me. Bretton will go far, some day."

"He doesn't go in for good manners, in the meantime."

"No. Does thatt matter? It would be a sham on his part if he did. Would you like to undertake his training? If so, I'll ask him to luncheon tomorrow."

"For God's sake don't, Miles. He didn't like me, he didn't approve of me."

"Well, how could you expect him to approve of anybody with the value of three years' university education hanging in pearls round their neck?"

"I thought Communists didn't approve of university education any more than of pearls?"

"They don't,—but they envy it. They think it confers heaven knows what advantages. As a matter of fact, Bretton has a far fresher and more cutting mind than I have. He is quite free of sentiment and tradition and obscurantist handicaps of thatt sort. As for you, I don't suppose he ever saw anybody like you in his life before."

"Do *you* think me so contemptible, too, Miles?"

"I think you lovely, and decorative."

"But useless? idle?" she insisted.

"No," he said; "I like women to be idle and decorative. Life is quite ugly enough without women making themselves ugly too."

"Are you serious? or are you joking?"

"Both! You can take your choice."

She found herself alone with Bretton a day or two later. He had come to see Miles, but Miles had been fetched by Munday to look at a sick cow.

"Do come in, Mr. Bretton. Mr. Vane-Merrick will be back in a few minutes. Do warm yourself by the fire, it's a very cold day. Have you come far?" She was full of amiable chatter.

He was disconcerted by Evelyn; alarmed; mistrustful. He sat on the edge of a chair by the fire because she had told him to do so, but he was clearly independent of external comfort. The light which burnt behind his rather mean, vicious, intelligent eyes proclaimed him independent of such considerations. Evelyn, for all her worldly address, was not at ease with this young man. He presented her with a new experience, even as the Mundays had presented her with a new experience. But she was not angry with him now, she was interested. She was beginning to realise that England was not populated only by Jarrolds.

"You must have a very interesting job, working for Mr. Vane-Merrick?"

Still he would not thaw; he was sulky, but not unattractive. She was determined to charm him.

"I never realised, when I first knew Mr. Vane-Merrick, what a very active life he led. He seems to have so many different interests." ("Surely," she thought, "I am not spying on Miles in any unworthy way?") "I suppose," she went on, "he has a safe seat down here in his constituency?"

"So far as any seat is safe, Mrs. . . ." He stopped. He had forgotten her name. "I'm sorry," he said clumsily, "I'm afraid I've forgotten your name."

She liked him better and better; she was in a generous mood.

"Jarrold," she said, "but never mind about thatt. Do tell me what you do for Mr. Vane-Merrick. I am so ignorant about such things! Do you,—well, what do you do?"

He would not be drawn. He shuffled, and she felt that he was taking stock of her, unfavourably. At the same time she divined a loyal devotion to Miles.

"Mr. Vane-Merrick," she said impulsively, "strikes me as a very remarkable person."

"Oh yes," said Bretton; "yes." He seemed inclined to say more, but relapsed abruptly into the same reticence.

She was nonplussed.

"How stupid of me, Mr. Bretton,—won't you have a drink? I believe there's some whisky in the cupboard. No, don't move; let me get it for you."

She half expected him to say that he did not drink, but he let her go to the cupboard and find a glass, a syphon, and the bottle of whisky. She was relieved to see that he would accept a generous helping. He watched her pretty hands as she set down the bottle.

"Thanks," he said, and added "Here's luck."

"Luck to Mr. Vane-Merrick at the next election," she replied.

Bretton grunted. Then he drank.

"Has he a great future, do you think?"

"A great future, Mrs. Jarrold? Will he have a seat in the next Cabinet, do you mean?" His tone was full of scorn.

"I suppose I do mean thatt,—I don't know much about it."

"He might have," said Bretton, "under a Tory government."

He stopped again, with the same air of leaving things unsaid.

"But he isn't a Tory."

"No."

She refilled his glass.

"Mr. Bretton,—forgive my ignorance,—but isn't it rather remarkable that he shouldn't be a Tory."

"Given his birth, you mean?" said Bretton, looking at her with a contempt that made her wince.

"Well. . . ." said Evelyn. Any comment on this remark could only have been couched in terms which she could not bring herself to pronounce. She let it go, rather lamely, saying, "Well, one would expect to find someone of his sort on the safe side."

"Of his sort, yes, but not him."

For the first time, Bretton's appreciation peeped out.

"Thatt's all the more to his credit, Mr. Bretton."

"Yes."

She had said the wrong thing; she had implied patronage. She tried an extreme simplicity, which was not wholly insincere.

"Mr. Bretton, I do believe very truly in Mr. Vane-Merrick's ability. Thatt's why I started talking to you about him, in this rather impertinent way. I hope you won't resent it."

"Ability,—he's got plenty of ability."

"Perhaps his views aren't extreme enough to please you?" said Evelyn, smiling.

Bretton did not answer; he only emptied his glass. Evelyn could not flatter herself that she had made much headway. She was relieved when Miles came in with Caesar and Dan at his heels, and a blast of cold air.

Bretton was not sulky with Miles. He relaxed at once. He was reserved still, but not sulky. Miles chaffed him, and he consented to grin. Evelyn felt that he was won over by Miles even against what he might consider to be his better judgment. She liked Bretton now, but he still made her acutely uncomfortable. She was thankful when he—somewhat ungraciously—declined Miles' invitation to stay to luncheon.

Dan burst out in indignation.

"What a horrible man, Miles! I nearly hit him for being so rude to you."

"He hasn't got your Eton manners, Dan."

Dan looked taken aback.

"I don't understand. Surely manners matter? You've got good manners yourself."

"So has your uncle Geoffrey."

"And you mean,—give you Bretton every time?"

"Yes, give me Bretton every time. Though he may cut my throat before he's done with me."

Evelyn got a letter from Ruth. It was written on New-lands writing-paper, and there was a coronet now instead of a crest on the flap of the envelope.

Jan. 10th, 1932.

DEAREST EVELYN—I don't know where you are, so I send this letter to your flat to be forwarded. We are still here. Uncle Evan has left. We think he had a row with Grandpapa, but we don't quite know. Anyhow he has left, and we don't mention his name. We think better not. Grandpapa says sarcastic things about him from time to time. Grandpapa is very sarcastic altogether. He says what a look-out for the country when a lot of ignorant young men think they can run it. Such as Miles Vane-Merrick. He says there is no sense left anywhere. It is rather dull here. The Beckwiths came to tea. What lovely weather. It doesn't look as though Dan would get any skating. I hope you are both in the country, enjoying yourselves. Everybody seems to be out of London, so I don't suppose London would be much fun just now. I suppose you will be going back there before long. Let me know when you do. In the meantime I send my love, as Mother would if she were in the room.—Your loving

RUTH.

P.S.—When you were staying with Miles Vane-Merrick (I think you said you and Dan were going to his old castle) was Princess Charskaya there? I am told that she and M. V.-M. have been having an affair for years!!!

P.S.S.—Minnie has been simply *unbearable*. She put a mouse into Cocoa's bed (a live one) and two hairbrushes into mine.

Evelyn was not unduly upset by this letter. When she first read it, she smiled compassionately and thought "Poor little Ruth." Ruth was no stylist, and her methods were crude. She was sorry for Ruth, but Ruth was really so crude and raw as to be negligible. Ruth had no importance at all. She was sorry for Ruth, but really one must be ruthless. She made the pun deliberately. It seemed to absolve her from any responsibility towards Ruth.

Why should she feel any responsibility towards Ruth? Miles was fair game; and if she had snared Miles when Ruth had failed to snare him, thatt was Ruth's funeral. They had started at scratch; Ruth, even, had known him first. She could absolve herself from any feeling of guilt towards Ruth.

Then Ruth's letter began to fester. Not very seriously. She scoffed at herself for remembering it even after it was thrown into the fire. Betsy Charskaya. . . .

"Miles," she said, "you know Betsy Charskaya?"

He looked up from his book.

"Betsy Charskaya?" he said, "Yes. of course I do. Why?"

"What do you think of her?"

"I don't think anything. A parasite. I suppose circumstances have driven her."

"How well do you know her?"

"Well, I suppose I've played bridge with her three or four times. Why? What made you think of her?"

"I met her the other day in a dressmaker's shop. You don't know her at all intimately?"

"God forbid."

No, Miles thought very little about women. Thatt seemed certain. It was bad enough to have to compete against his book, and against Bretton and all that Bretton stood for,—a much more serious rivalry. A rivalry, indeed, against which she could not and must not compete. She must be content to absorb one half of his life, and must count herself lucky in the apportionment. It was hard for her to compromise, with her domineering temperament and the excess of her love for Miles, but she was determined to be wise. Miles had to be ridden with a light rein.

He seemed to know something of the struggle in her mind and to take a wicked pleasure in testing and humiliating her. Exasperated, she accused him of sadistic qualities. He laughed and said that she had them too. He looked at her with a hard, mocking gleam in his eyes. She was frightened of him when he looked at her like thatt, seeing how pitiless he might be if he chose. Then at other times he would be so charming, so tender, and so boyishly simple, that she forgot her fears.

She wondered, however, whether she would be able to control herself if he displayed any interest in another woman.

He surprised her by asking her what she thought their future would be. At thatt, she turned on him a look so anguished that even he was touched.

"I don't know, Miles. You are perfectly free, you know,

—I have no hold over you except love. I don't wish to have. If thatt isn't enough, I prefer to let you go."

"You say thatt, knowing quite well that it is enough."

"For the moment, yes. But . . . oh well, never mind."

"Tell me, Evelyn, could you be jealous?"

"Atrociously," she said in a low voice.

"Yes, I need not have asked. I see that I must be careful, or the mutilated body of a young man will be found under a hedge in Kent."

"Don't tease me, Miles."

• "But I like teasing you."

"Yes, I know you do. Tease me about something else. It's only too horribly probable that you will make me jealous before you've done with me. I don't want to anticipate it. I want to live in the present."

"Wise woman."

"No, Miles, I'm afraid I'm not very wise."

He let her go back to London finally, because he was obliged to go there himself. Dan insisted that he should come frequently to the flat. He pressed invitations upon Miles while Evelyn silently listened, feeling that fate in this respect was kind to her. In spite of Miles' sarcasm, she still shrank from the Jarrolds' inquisitive criticism of her sudden intimacy with this young man. They would be bound to find it out sooner or later, even if Ruth did not make it her business to tell them,—and Evelyn had a shrewd suspicion that Ruth, for sore and private reasons, would keep her own counsel,—they would be bound to find it out, because in the close family circle which the Jarrolds traced round all their members nothing could long remain hidden; the connexion was too well main-

tained, too constant. If Mrs. Jarrold,—Lady Orlestone!—
or Mrs. Geoffrey, or Evan, should come to the flat at
tea-time three times in the week, as they were apt severally
to do, having the true bourgeois conception of a nice,
smug, cosy, family life within the clan, and if one of them
were to coincide with Miles on each occasion, then it
would not be long before they began to compare notes
and to draw the inevitable conclusion. Hitherto Evelyn,
beyond a vague boredom, had never questioned their
right to arrive unannounced at her flat at all hours of the
day. She herself sprang from the same bourgeois tradition.
She had accepted, as a matter of course, the theory that
one was fond of one's relations because they were one's
relations. But now Miles' influence was stretching her
ideas to a greater elasticity; his unconventionality was
contagious; she grew impatient of this assumption of family
rights over her privacy.

She chose to put it in those terms in her own mind; she
chose to tell herself that these incursions into her private
life were intolerable. In truth, she was discovering only
that love brings its peculiar complications. She wanted
to be free for her lover.

She despised herself for considering the opinion of the
Jarrolds, yet so strong was her training that she could not
help considering it. Thatt was what made Miles' renewed
suggestion of marriage so especially tempting. Absurdly,
she did not want the old Jarrolds to criticise Miles for
compromising her in the eyes of the world. Yet she knew
she must never consent to marry him. It would not be fair.
She clung to thatt, as a principle.

But if she could put half the responsibility on to Dan,
she was saved. If she could represent Miles as Dan's friend,

philosopher, and guide, she might hoodwink the old Jarrolds. They were simple and unsuspicious souls; or, if not simple and unsuspicious, they were at least self-deceiving enough to seize on any pretext to excuse their daughter-in-law in their own eyes.

Whether they would approve of Miles as friend, philosopher, and guide to Dan, was another matter.

Then there were her own servants. She was even more ashamed of shrinking before the scrutiny of her servants than of shrinking before the scrutiny of the Jarrolds. She knew that she ought to be above such things. Yet she foresaw with dread the sly and sneering expression with which Mason, or Privett,—especially Privett, since she was probably committed to Privett for life, whereas Mason might leave at any moment,—would open the door to announce "Mr. Vane-Merrick!" and would shut it again, retiring to the kitchen to make furtive jokes at her expense.

She hated herself for this timorousness. She knew only too well that it had never crossed Miles' mind that the Mundays might speculate as to their relationship. Anyway, the Mundays probably hadn't. Or, if they had, they had accepted it in a straightforward country way. They had probably said, at most, that it was a pity their young master hadn't taken up with a lady nearer his own age; that he might have married and begotten an heir. Several heirs. Sons and daughters. (She wished now that she had taken more trouble to win over the Mundays.) But Mason and Privett were London servants. Mason would snigger; and Privett would sourly disapprove.

But if she could say to Privett, "Mr. Vane-Merrick is coming this evening to see Mr. Dan,"—then, again, she would be saved.

Dan would go back to school at the end of January.
But by thatt time Miles would be established as a constant
visitor. She knew the value of an established habit to
minds like Privett's.

"By the way, Privett," she said, "Mr. Vane-Merrick
may be coming this evening to see Mr. Dan. I may be
out when he comes."

"Will they want dinner?" Privett was always grumpy.

"Dinner? Oh, no.—Oh, well, yes, perhaps it would be
just as well to provide dinner. Mr. Dan may persuade
Mr. Vane-Merrick to stay for dinner,—you know what
Mr. Dan is. He doesn't realise that shops shut at six.
Boys don't. Order a grouse, will you, Privett? And some
oysters. And tell Mason to lay three places."

She stayed out late, deliberately, in order to keep Miles
waiting. With her return to London she had regained
something of her feminine self-assurance. She was no
longer so much at Miles' mercy that he could make her
tramp in his wake across muddy fields. It was a cold,
snowy evening, and she longed for nothing so much as
for the comfort of her own warm room and Miles' presence
there. Well, Miles might solace himself with Dan. She
would not trot to Miles' beck and call. Snug in her own
car, she had herself driven to Rivers and Roberts'.

She did not want in the least to go to Rivers and Roberts'. She wanted to be at home with Miles. She really
hated, now, the luxury and extravagance of Rivers and
Roberts'. She compared the mincing obsequiousness of
Mr. Rivers with the sullen reticence of Bretton. Disquieted,
she was more than usually charming to Mr. Rivers; more
than usually discerning about the creations he paraded

for her benefit. He decided that Mrs. Tommy Jarrold was really, from every point of view, one of his most satisfactory clients. She was a charming woman and she did credit to his clothes.

"We haven't seen you for some time, Mrs. Jarrold. We've missed you,—yes, I declare we have."

"I've been in the country, Mr. Rivers."

"In the country? At this time of year? Surely thatt's very unlike you, Mrs. Jarrold? Now, the country in summer . . . well, one can put up with it. But in January!"

· She remembered walking with Miles up and down the garden path, with the tower pricking up into a clean sky.

"Dreadfully cold and muddy, Mr. Rivers! But one can't always do what one likes."

He bowed.

"I quite appreciate thatt, Mrs. Jarrold.—I hope Lord Orlestone is well?"

So he thought she had been at Newlands.

"Very well indeed, thank you. He is really wonderful for his age."

"Seventy, is it?"

"Seventy-five."

"Dear me!—And thatt handsome boy of yours, Mrs. Jarrold? Let me see, he must be the heir? Fourteen, is he?"

"Nearly eighteen, I'm afraid."

"Dear me! How time does fly. Nearly eighteen! No one could believe it, to look at his mother,—if I may say so without impertinence. Nearly eighteen! Tut, tut!—And will he be going back to Eton,—he *is* at Eton, of course?— or is he leaving?"

"No, he goes back at the end of this month."

"And then what will you be doing, Mrs. Jarrold? Not staying in this horribly damp island, of course? Oh dear me, no! The sun,—the sun calls us at this time of year, does it not? The Riviera, perhaps? Or Egypt? But not England,—oh dear me, no! One must get away, must one not, if only for the sake of one's health?"

"Are you going away, Mr. Rivers?"

He sighed and displayed the palms of his hands.

"Alas, Mrs. Jarrold! Business obligations, you know. Perhaps a little later on. . . . A brief little dash down to Cannes."

"Indeed, I can't imagine what Madame Louise would do without you."

"You are too kind, Mrs. Jarrold. You flatter me. Madame Louise is not here today, I fear; a slight chill. . . . Oh, nothing at all. I have sent one of our young ladies with some grapes. And a spray of gardenias. A very chaste perfume, I always think, do you not agree? I see you have a spray of rosemary pinned into your coat. Very original, —very becoming. Not orchids,—no. Rosemary. *Far* more subtle. There are so few flowers at this time of year, are there not? Nothing but orchids and gardenias. And lilac of course; but thatt is scarcely for the buttonhole. Rosemary,—yes, I must remember thatt. Rosemary for remembrance, I think? Ah, very subtle, very charming. We all have something we would like to remember, have we not? —Now come, Mrs. Jarrold, I mustn't waste your time talking about the things we would all like to remember. Where are my young ladies? I must clap my hands. . . ."

He clapped them.

All the time, she had been thinking only of what

clothes she could buy to please Miles. She knew his tastes by now. She would go home with something new and exquisite to wear at dinner.

Mr. Rivers, an impatient little autocrat in his own domain, clapped his hands again.

She came home to find Dan alone.

"At last, Mummy! Miles was here,—he's gone."

"Gone?"

"Yes, he said he couldn't wait. Granny came too."

"Did she find you with Miles?"

"Yes. Why were you so late, Mummy? Did you forget Miles was coming? He stayed for about an hour,—of course poor Granny was terribly in the way,—we couldn't talk about anything,—such a bore. Miles talked to her about rhododendrons. Miles seems to know something about everything. Granny was delighted, I thought she'd never go away. You might have remembered, Mummy."

"Did Miles leave any message?"

"Oh yes, I forgot, he said you could ring him up if you liked. He said he was dining with Princess somebody or other. I forget. Some Russian name."

She did not ring him up.

But she was glad that old Mrs. Jarrold,—Lady Orlestone,—had liked Miles.

Life in London was more complicated than life at Miles' castle. Miles was much in request in London. She soon realised that if she played these tricks on him, she would not see him at all. Yet, perversely, she continued to play them. He was not patient under such treatment. He retaliated always and instantly. People ran after him, and if

Evelyn chose to leave him to his own devices he had plenty
of devices to be left to. He made this unambiguously clear.
Battle was joined between them. She would not yield;
neither would he.

In the end she yielded.

She looked back on the days spent at his castle. Occasional and very significant battles they had had, but, in
the main, every day had drawn to its proper conclusion.
Though they might have quarrelled as lovers during the
day, every night had joined them as lovers again. Viewed
in retrospect, the days at Miles' castle were idyllic, perfect.
She had never been so happy as at Miles' castle. She was
wise enough to recognise that upon her and upon her
alone depended the continuance of their happiness trans-
ferred to London.

She must make concessions. Miles was proud and restive.
She herself was vain and spoilt. But her vanity and her
spoiltness were of a cheap and superficial kind. She was
insignificant, compared with Miles. She must buckle
under. He was a full man, and she but an empty woman,—
empty of all save the power to please him in his leisure
hours. She must make concessions, she must subordinate
her own vanities to his needs.

She no longer minded about the Jarrolds' criticism.
She was determined only to recapture the days when she
and Miles had been so happy.

He was happy too,—she could see it. He expanded and
flowered; he no longer tormented her, when she no longer
tormented him. She told Mason quite frankly to say that
she was not at home, when Mr. Vane-Merrick was there.
They heard the door-bell ring, and laughed together to
hear Mason shut the door behind the intruder. They were

happier, shut into Evelyn's flat, even than they had been at his castle.

It was warm; it was private. Dan had gone back to school. Evelyn had suffered torments of conscience when she saw him go off; and not of conscience only, which is a jejune thing, but also torments of love. She loved Dan. She loved him in an animal way. His young and adolescent beauty moved her; his young, perplexed mind moved her; he was her own creation. The fact that his father was dead made him more exclusively hers; the fact that his father had had no part at all in the making of Dan, save for a short, distasteful and essentially uncontributive episode. Dan was no Jarrold.

All the evening she and Dan had watched the clock. They had had buttered toast for tea. Dan, like Miles, liked buttered toast, and, though Evelyn might forget, Privett always remembered. There was always buttered toast for tea on the day that Dan went back to Eton. (Privett was annoyed when Mr. Vane-Merrick brought a toasting-fork with him one day.) And there were always two jars of honey and two pots of jam packed up ready in the hall, for him to take back. They were packed up by Privett, in neat parcels of stiff brown paper.

Dan and his mother watched the clock, each pretending that they were not watching it. They made conversation; they talked about Newlands; they did not talk about Miles or Miles' castle or any of the things that interested them most. They avoided such things. They did not even talk about Dan's next half at Eton or Dan's unhappiness there. They were both feeling too keenly to mention the things that had real importance for them.

At seven o'clock Evelyn stirred.

"Dan, darling, I think you ought to start."

She had ordered the motor for him. He was going in the most luxurious way possible to the most luxurious school in England. Yet she pitied him. Miles had said that Dan at school was like a bird of Paradise in an aviary full of sparrows.

"Dan, darling, I hope you have a good half. This is a short half, remember. The Easter holidays come quite soon."

"Will we go to stay with Miles again in the Easter holidays, Mummy?"

"Yes, I expect so. Bless you, Dan. Bless you. Have you got all your things? Your paint box? Your suit-case? Your overcoat?"

"Yes, Mummy, I put them all ready for Mason to take down.—Oh, Mummy, my skates!"

"Well, where are they, darling? It's getting late,—you ought to go."

"I left them at Miles' castle. Would you,—could you,— ask Miles to tell Mrs. Munday to send them? You'll be seeing Miles, won't you?—You see, I thought the lake would freeze.— I'm so sorry to be such a bore."

"Darling, you aren't being a bore." She was well-accustomed to such last-minute forgetfulness.

"Mummy,—promise to arrange with Miles for us to go there again for Easter."

"Yes, darling, yes,—but now you must go."

"I'll get into a row if I don't go."

Still he lingered.

"Dan, it's silly to be unnecessarily late,—isn't it?"

"Mummy,—come down in the motor with me to Eton?"

She was torn in half: Miles was coming to dinner with her. For the first time since the beginning of the holidays, they would be alone.

"Darling! three-quarters of an hour more?"

"Oh, yes, it's silly, I know. Well, good-bye, Mummy. See you at Long Leave, anyhow.—What the hell has Mason done with my things? Mummy, you ought to sack thatt man.—Oh, there you are, Mason. Where's my coat? Well, good-bye, Mummy. See you at Long Leave. Good-bye!"

• He went, tumbling hurriedly down the stairs.

Evelyn turned back into the flat, alone. These partings with Dan always shook her. She felt that she was condemning him to another three months of unnecessary and yet necessary suffering. She felt especially guilty towards him this time, because for the past three weeks she had been using him as an unconscious shield against the world. Poor little Dan, so generous, so naïf, so excitable, so affectionate! Her heart followed him, as the motor carried him through the dark streets of Hammersmith and along the Great West Road.

But it was warm and private in the flat. Miles and she were alone. She had resolved privately that Miles should stay in London thatt night. She would make him stay. She told Mason that he might go to bed.

Dan, meanwhile, having arrived at Eton, hauled his paint-box up the wooden stairs and flung it down in his bleak little room.

After dinner, she thought that Miles was in a propitious mood. He had seemed glad to find her alone, after the long interruption of the holidays, and although her heart still ached for Dan she was happy to find that Miles shared her relief in their solitude. "I thought you enjoyed talking to Dan," she said, jealously, wanting to hear his contradiction. "I do enjoy talking to Dan," he said instantly and honestly, "but I prefer being alone with you." She was satisfied by thatt. She let Miles sit at her feet, and, while she rested her hand on his hair, she laid her schemes for keeping him in London for the night. She knew that he had his book to write; she knew that he was working hard; but she could not see that twenty-four hours made much difference.

"Miles, stay with me; stay with me just this once. Give me this evening; it can't make much difference if you get back to your work tonight or tomorrow morning! You won't do any work tonight; you'll reach the castle much too late."

"But I shall start working tomorrow morning directly after breakfast."

"Yes, I know, but if you take the nine-fifteen tomorrow morning you'll be home by a quarter to eleven. You'll lose only an hour or so. Miles, please! just this once."

He could hardly resist her pleading eyes. Yet he said, "But it isn't just this once. It's nine times out of ten,—no, thatt isn't fair,—it's three times out of ten."

"If you count the hours against me like thatt," she said, releasing him, "you had better go."

Then, of course, he stayed.

But he loved her the less for it. He liked to organise his life according to time-table: a time for work, a time for walks, a time for reading, a time for love. Evelyn interfered with this system; to her, all times were the time for love.

She, unlike him, had nothing to do with her time except
to wring pleasure out of it. Moreover, she was very violently and painfully in love, never having been really in
love before. When she had married Tommy Jarrold she
had believed herself to be in love, because it was the
orthodox thing to be when one became engaged; but she
now discovered the difference. The difference was so
great, that she must needs make herself a nuisance to
Miles, who was an active man; and the more she saw that
she was making herself a nuisance, the more of a nuisance
she made herself. The more he resisted, the more she insisted. Her motives were mixed: partly, she wanted to
defeat him; partly, she genuinely craved for his presence.
Vanity and passion, between them, wrecked Miles' time-
table and led to countless quarrels and reconciliations,—
the quarrels of opposed wills, the reconciliations of passionate lovers. It was all very destructive, although when once
she had gained her point she made him feel that his lost
time was well lost in her arms. But he knew that these
temporary intoxications, however persuasive, bore very
little relation to reality. Reality was a different thing: it
was represented by his castle, his farm, his new gates;
by his ideas, by the book he was writing, by Bretton, even
by the House of Commons; by his interchange with the
various people he knew; by his books, by poetry, by his
love of music, by his interest in a hundred things,—not
solely by Evelyn and love. Love and the woman were insufficient for an active mind. Love and the man, however,
were all-too-sufficient for a starved heart and unoccupied
mind. Miles learnt it, to his cost; Evelyn never learnt it,
to hers.

He stayed, but to stay resentfully is worse than not staying at all.

Then there were other ways in which she irritated him. She expected him to write to her every day, when they were not together, but at the same time she shrank from her servants seeing his letters arrive every morning by the early post. They must know his handwriting, she said; they must recognise it; and they must draw their own conclusions. Well, said Miles patiently, I'll type my envelopes. This satisfied her for a time; then she suggested he should vary the pattern of his envelopes. "Really," he said, "one would think you were spied on by a jealous husband," and although he laughed as he said it, he would not give in to her, but continued to enclose his letters in the blue envelopes he used at his castle. "My dear," he said sensibly, when she reproached him with having no care for her feelings, "Mason and Privett can see the post-mark, whatever the colour of the envelope." "But they wouldn't always look at the postmark," she objected, "and thatt bright blue paper of yours can be recognised a mile off." "Yes," he said; "the colour of a summer sky."

Thatt was always the end of her arguments with Miles: he worsted her by a phrase.

He was irritated, but he was enamoured enough to persuade himself that her absurd qualms were charming. They were part of her make-up, and he would not have her otherwise,—so he told himself. His regard for truth was obscured by this new experience of being in love. He had always thought that he valued clear-thinking above all things; now he perceived that love was its very enemy. Either he must resist, or he must allow himself to be defeated. Up to a point, he would allow himself to be defeated. But only up to a point.

Dan came back from Eton before Long Leave. He came back, because his grandfather died. A very strong man, William Jarrold went suddenly. On the tenth of February he caught a chill, and by the twenty-fifth he was dead. Evelyn was sent for, and witnessed his last hours. He put up a strong fight, against double pneumonia. Dr. Gregory was hopeful, Dr. Gregory, the family doctor, who had been summoned from London because the old man was accustomed to him and would take his physic when he refused to take anyone else's. But then Dr. Gregory was always hopeful; listening to Dr. Gregory, you might believe that there were no such things as death and danger in the world. The other doctor, a stranger, from London also, was less hopeful; he said quite frankly that when people of Lord Orlestone's age got double pneumonia there was no denying that it became a serious matter. In short, the other doctor, the stranger, gave him twenty-four hours, but William Jarrold defeated him by nearly a week.

To the last moment of consciousness he insisted on signing his letters. Evelyn respected the old man for his tenacity, though she could not quite understand her respect for such physical tenacity and vigour. It seemed to be an adventitious blessing, conferred at birth by some fairy god-father, irrespective of the personality thus blessed. There was no real reason why she should respect her father-in-law more for refusing (for a week) to die. The only explanation she could give to herself, was a respect for the life-force that kept him going. A week more or less in seventy-five years, was a detail. But she had always loved Mr. Jarrold, and her love for him was increased by his refusal to die. Bretton might have sneered, but she felt that a bit of Victorian England died with him, and died hard.

The normally cheerful atmosphere of Newlands underwent a change as soon as it was recognised that its master lay within the shadow of death. The belief in a passing indisposition soon gave way to a more disturbing anxiety. The spirit of danger suddenly walked into a stronghold. Death,—the thing which one pretended would never happen,—had suddenly become a presence. Hester telephoned to Evelyn and suggested that she might come down for the week-end, "just to cheer us up." So far, no admission that her presence was urgently required. Evelyn went, of course, by the next train, and found them all maintaining the fiction that everything was as it should be. The library was as bright as ever, under the remorseless electric light; they sat round the tea-table, and chaffed and bantered as usual; only, every now and then glances were exchanged, and some member of the family rose and slipped out of the room, to be absent ten minutes or more, and then returned to resume the vacated place, and after a moment someone would say "Well?" and the reply came, "Nurse doesn't seem quite so satisfied tonight . . . he's rather restless"; and then would come questions about temperature and pulse, uttered in a different voice.

There was some discussion as to whether Evelyn should be allowed to see him or not. On the one hand her arrival might distress him; might suggest to him that he was iller than he knew; on the other hand Evelyn had always had a good effect upon him: the sight of her might cheer him up. One day he seemed slightly better, and spirits revived; next morning he seemed definitely better, and the doctor gave his opinion that she might with advantage be admitted to his room. Only for a moment, though. She was taken upstairs by Hester, although she knew the way perfectly; Hester turned the door-handle, holding it tight and pulling the door towards her as she turned, then gave the door a quick little push so that it opened three or four inches without a sound. "Go in," she whispered to Evelyn; "I'll shut it behind you."

The room was in semi-darkness; an uncertain pink light came through the drawn curtains. There was a screen round the fire, and within the cubicle thus created was the nurse in her arm-chair and a little table on which stood some bottles, jugs, a drinking-cup, a fountain-pen, and a medical chart lying open. Evelyn could see the zig-zag of the temperature record, going up and down into peaks and chasms, like the geographical elevation of a mountain range. Beyond the screen was the bed, with someone lying very quiet in it. The nurse got up quickly and quietly, laying down the novel she was reading. She smiled at Evelyn, and nodded in a silent conspiratorial way.

"Lord Orlestone," she said in a clear voice, going over to the bed, "here's Mrs. Jarrold come to see you." And she motioned to Evelyn to come forward.

"Papa?" said Evelyn, going right up to the bed, in the brave way one uses towards those who are very ill.

She could hardly see him, in the pink half-light. She could just see his head denting the pillow and his hands lying out on the folded sheet.

"Papa," she said again, "I'm so glad you're better."

"Who's thatt?" he said, stirring a little; "Evelyn? You all right, my dear? Nice of you to come. Dan here too, eh?"

"No, Papa, Dan isn't here, Dan's at school."

"Not sent for the heir yet, then, haven't they?" He cackled a little, very feebly, at his own joke. "Well, they don't tell me much, my dear,—thatt damned nurse, eh?— but so long as they don't send for the heir,—what?"

He was very weak, but quite in his right mind, Evelyn thought.

"You'll be downstairs again in a fortnight, Papa."

He tried to wag his finger at her, but the effort to raise his arm was too much for him, and his hand fell back upon the sheet.

"Nice to see you, my dear," he murmured; "nice of you to come."

The nurse beckoned her away.

The funeral took place at Orlestone, not at Newlands. The old man had left a letter, clearly stating his wishes as they were to be carried out. On no account, he said, was his body to be burned. He did not hold with such new-fangled ideas. Buried he would be, and decently, near the pits which had made the fortune of his family. He would be buried near his father and his grandfather, and he hoped that his grandson (though of course he could lay no obligation on him) would when his time came be buried in the same place and in like fashion.

The whole family came to see him buried. Distant cousins, of whom Evelyn had scarcely heard, turned up, proud of their association with the Jarrolds. They gave their names distinctly to the representatives of the Press, hoping to read them next day in *The Times*, the *Morning Post*, or the *Daily Telegraph.* (Actually, the Press reported: Lady Orlestone, widow; Mr. Daniel Jarrold, grandson; Mr. Geoffrey Jarrold, son, and Mrs. Geoffrey Jarrold; Mr. Evan Jarrold, son; Mrs. Thomas Jarrold, daughter-in-law; Miss Ruth and Miss Minnie Jarrold, granddaughters; Mr. Robin Jarrold, grandson.)

Dan was terribly upset by both the death and the funeral. He stayed the night in his mother's flat, having got special leave from Eton. He was upset too by his vision of the Midlands, lying under a fog of smoke when he had left Windsor in a haze of February sunshine. He was upset by the streams of pit-workers and factory-hands who had followed his grandfather's coffin. He was not upset, as yet, by the sudden responsibility which had devolved upon him; he was too young, and too diffident, for thatt. He did not, as yet, realise the power which had come into his hands. He was simply upset by death, with which he was not familiar, and by the smoky Midland background of his grandfather's life. It was so different from the pleasant luxury of Newlands! Yet Newlands had grown out of it; the laburnums and rhododendrons of Newlands had grown out of the coal of Orlestone, even as the coal of Orlestone had come from the rotting, primeval forest. He sat over the fire in his mother's flat, holding his head, unable to understand death.

Evelyn tried to comfort him. His grandfather, she said, was an old man; it was quite natural that he should go. But it was not his going that distressed Dan; it was the thought of his grandfather rotting underground.

"He wouldn't be burned, Mummy,—why not?"

"Darling, Grandpapa believed in the Resurrection of the Body."

"But if the body can resurrect from a skeleton, it can resurrect from ashes. Either it can, or it can't. Surely? The one is just as reasonable, or as unreasonable, as the other?"

Evelyn found no answer. Hers was no logical mind. Even as she believed in the force of human passion, and lived up to thatt belief, so had she an instinctive and un-analytical belief in the dogmas of the Church. In the last resort, she followed her instinct, not her reason. She could sympathise with a person who did not go to church every Sunday, but she was secretly shocked when Dan questioned the ordinary procedure of Christian burial. She belonged to the tradition of the family vault.

"Surely, Mummy, it's much more hygienic to be burned?"

"Dan, you ought not to think of such things."

"But, Mummy, it is. One doesn't take up so much room. And one doesn't run down into other people's water-supply."

"Dan! What do you mean?"

"Well, the cemetery at Orlestone stands immediately above the waterworks. Surely you must have noticed thatt? Grandpapa will trickle down the taps of his colliers, for years and years . . . ten years . . . till he becomes a skeleton. It takes ten years to become a skeleton, especially when you are buried in an expensive coffin."

"Dan! You mustn't say such things. Dan! it's horrible, it's morbid."

"No, Mummy, it's the truth."

"Dan, stop. A boy of your age oughtn't to have such ideas. You make me want to put my hands over my ears. Your poor grandfather,—can't he have peace in his grave?"

"He won't have peace, Mummy. I read a sermon by Donne. . . ."

"Donne? Who was Donne?"

"He was a poet in the seventeenth century whom nobody took any notice of until now. And he was a clergyman too."

"Miles told you all thatt."

"No, Miles didn't,—so there. I found it out for myself. And Donne preached a sermon on being eaten by worms, —I'll quote it to you. I learnt it by heart. "This posthume death, this death after death, nay, this death after burial, this dissolution after dissolution, this death of corruption and putrefaction, of vermiculation and incineration, of dissolution and dispersion in and from the grave. Miserable riddle, when the same worm must be my mother and my sister. Miserable incest, when I must be married to my own mother and my sister, and the worm shall feed, and feed sweetly upon me. . . ."

"Dan, please stop; I can't stand it."

"No, the people he preached to couldn't stand it either. They were carried out, fainting. But it was true,—you can't say it wasn't true. Donne was a realist."

"He was a blasphemer," said Evelyn with angry energy.

"All realists are called blasphemers," said Dan.

He was growing up. The young had strange, shocking ideas.

"Miles told you thatt," said Evelyn again.

"Yes," said Dan this time, serenely "he did."

Dan went back to Eton, the owner of Newlands and of the Orlestone mines and works. Evelyn was worried. They were richer than ever, but she dreaded the responsibility in Dan's young hands. With her strong Conservative tendencies, she dreaded the use he would make of it. She thought him too young, too Utopian, and too wild. She had been well trained in the theory of "keeping those people in their place." She had a traditional, prosperous attitude towards the unwashed poor. She was vaguely sorry for them, but she did not like them, and quieted her conscience by saying that they would not appreciate altered conditions. "You know," she was accustomed to say, and to hear her friends say, "if you give them decent clothes they only pawn them, and if you give them a bath they only keep the coals in it." This settled a disquieting matter. So long as one did not visit the slums at Orlestone, one could forget about them; or could reassure oneself by thinking that the people who lived in them had a different standard from one's own. But she had an uneasy feeling that Dan would not take the same view, once he woke up to his new position, and that Miles would be on his side, not on hers. Not that she wanted people to live in slums. She was only afraid that Dan might explode suddenly into something altogether too revolutionary and tiresome. It would be so much quieter and pleasanter and less strenuous if only he would conduct himself for a few years in the normal fashion. When he had reached the age of twenty-five he might begin to take himself seriously, if he liked.

She did not dare say these things to Miles.

Miles was half derisive and half delighted.

"At last I've got what I wanted,—a young capitalist wholly in my power."

"Miles, what are you going to do to thatt boy?"

Genuinely anxious, she secretly delighted in his influence over Dan.

"Use him, of course, my dear. Use his money, and use his very conveniently secure position in the House of Lords. Exploit him, in fact."

"Miles! It's monstrous."

"What's monstrous? To get the best out of the boy and his chances because he happens to pay some attention to what I say? Is thatt monstrous?"

"No,—but because his mother happens to be your mistress."

A sensuous shiver went down her as she said it.

"Thatt's neither here nor there,—I might have known Dan even if you and I had never seen each other. I might have met him at the Eton Political Society."

"How cold you are, Miles."

"No. Not cold. Sensible."

"I hate sense."

"Most women do."

"Thatt's why women bore men, I suppose, except when they lie in their arms, and sense ceases to count."

"Yes, I expect it is."

"Miles, we're quarrelling now."

"Are we? I thought we were merely having an argument."

"Arguments are always quarrels."

"Yes, perhaps,—for women."

"Miles, you hate me sometimes, don't you?"

"No,—only when you say that I hate you."

"I'm a fool, Miles. I won't do it again."

Miles asked her to come out to dinner with some friends of his whom he wanted her to meet,—Viola and Leonard Anquetil. Her conventionality at first rebelled.

"I can't go to dinner with people I don't know!"

"But they've asked you."

"How do they know about me? What have you told them?"

"I told them the truth, ages ago. Do you mind? I dined with them a few nights after the ball at Chevron House and I couldn't keep it to myself."

These words gave her a pang of such extreme pleasure that her alarm and mistrust vanished.

"Of course I'll come if you want me to. Will anyone else be there?"

"A couple of men perhaps. I'll tell Viola not to ask any other women, because I want you to make friends with her. Don't put on an evening dress,—they never dress."

This struck Evelyn as very odd; everybody she knew dressed for dinner, the Jarrolds and the people to whom Miles sarcastically referred as her smart friends, the bridge-playing crew of Betsy Charskaya and her like. She decided that these Anquetils must be Bohemians. She had heard of them before; Leonard Anquetil was known as a traveller and explorer who had married the only daughter of Chevron House.

"Bretton may be there," said Miles.

"Bretton?" He was not at all the kind of person whom Evelyn associated with Chevron House.

"They have all kinds of friends," said Miles, and gave no further explanations.

She felt curiously shy, as though she were a young girl, engaged to Miles, and about to be taken by him for inspection by his friends. Don't put on an evening dress, he had said, so she wondered what she should wear, feeling slightly irritated by this dispensation with the ordinary conventions. Evening dress was a formula, a safeguard, like good manners; it was a part of all those things which greased the wheels of life. Evelyn appreciated such things; she was self-conscious about them, and it always made her a little uneasy to observe Miles' utter disregard. She felt jealous of these friends, who, apparently, were equally indifferent to the things she still thought important. They were better attuned to Miles than she was. She disliked them in advance, with instinctive hostility, deciding in her own mind that they posed.

She put on a black silk shirt with a loosely knotted scarlet handkerchief. It looked careless, but was in fact extremely expensive and studied,—one of Mr. Rivers' more picturesque creations. Mr. Rivers was in the habit of saying that few of his clients could afford to look both picturesque and chic, but that Mrs. Tommy Jarrold was one of the exceptions. Sitting before her mirror, Evelyn was pleased with her appearance. The red handkerchief suited her small head and dark curling hair. She was glad to be the kind of woman who looked well in any clothes, whether in the country, or in a ballroom, or in the street, or dressed as she was to-night. She wished only that her heart were as smoothly finished as her exterior: these tortures that she endured since Miles had entered her life were not consistent, and she was frightened of her own violence even as she sat polishing her nails.

Miles came to fetch her. He was especially gay. What fun, he said in his most boyish way; and looking her over from head to foot he said that she was lovely and filled him with pride. She smiled rather sadly, being suddenly aware again of the discrepancy in their ages. For how many years

longer would he want to show her off to his friends? It was
ridiculous to have thought of herself as a young girl,
engaged to Miles. Those were the visions that floated into
the mind, under the kind seduction of the shaded electric
light.

He was in one of his charming moods. She wondered
why, and became suspicious.

"Miles," she said, as they stayed in her sitting-room
drinking each a glass of sherry, "do tell me more about
these mysterious friends of yours."

"Potted biography?" he said, looking at her, his eyes
shining and full of laughter.

"Of course I know the obvious facts about them. Tell
me something more. What age are they, for instance, and
are they very alarming?"

"Age, Viola must be forty-two or three, Leonard about
ten years older. Alarming,—you must judge for yourself.
Some people find them alarming. I know them too well."

"Are you very fond of them, Miles?"

"I adore them both; but if you mean, have I ever been
in love with Viola, I haven't. There now, you see I am
shrewd sometimes. That was what you meant, wasn't it?
Now don't you think we ought to start?"

He was mocking her, but he put his arm round her and
kissed her. She mistrusted him, but could not resist him.
It was in a mood of exultant happiness that she preceded
him downstairs.

Her mood changed when they reached the Anquetils'
house, for she felt instantly that Miles was completely at
his ease. He was at home in thatt house. Anquetil himself
opened the door,—a lean, grey-haired man with a scarred
face and an uncommunicative manner, untidily dressed

in an old jacket and grey flannel trousers. He nodded to Miles and shook hands rather reluctantly with Evelyn, as though he considered such a concession to ordinary manners as a waste of energy and time. "Come in," he said, taking the pipe from his mouth in the dark passage.

The drawing-room was a studio on the ground floor. It was large and shadowy and ill-defined. Several people stood round the fire; two or three men, a girl, and a woman. Evelyn recognised Bretton, who, like Anquetil, was smoking a pipe. The girl was pretty and impudent looking, with short golden curls. She wore a blue Chinese coat and black satin trousers. Evelyn knew at once that all these people were very intimate; and that Miles was very intimate with them too. Feeling completely out of it, she was angry with Miles for having brought her there. This was not at all the kind of world to which she was accustomed, and she resented the fact that Miles should have been for years an intimate of this world so unfamiliar to her. Even her pleasure in the fact that he had revealed their true relationship to these people, the Anquetils, turned to resentment when she came face to face with them, though she could not have explained why.

Yet she liked Viola Anquetil, in spite of herself. Viola Anquetil came forward to greet her, a calm, tall, self-possessed woman in a dress of Venetian red. She was a beautiful woman in early middle-age, statuesque, her dark hair lying sleekly in two bands above her brows, and gathered into a knot at the back. Her hand, when she gave it, was cool and slender; her manner peaceful. Evelyn, who had heard that she was alarming, realised that this woman had a very deep life of her own. She realised that the stream of life in this house flowed very deep and strong and intense, and that its serenity proceeded entirely from the woman. It certainly did not proceed from the man; any man with thatt queer scarred face was by nature a stranger to serenity. Serenity had been the woman's gift to him, and their understanding enveloped them as with a radiance. Not that they spoke to one another, or even glanced; thatt was unnecessary. But it was clear that they were absolutely united.

Everything was very informal. Viola introduced her son, a coltish boy of about Dan's age. She introduced the girl as Inez Marston; the other young man as Mr. Allen. Neither of these names conveyed any meaning to Evelyn. No one took any further notice of her or made any fuss about her, but returned to their interrupted conversation. The girl and Bretton sat on a divan talking very earnestly; the girl was talking, and Bretton, listening intently, nodded from time to time as the girl drove home her points. Evelyn remembered with resentment how she herself had been unable to capture his attention or his approval for a moment.

There appeared to be no dining-room in the house, for they dined at a table in a corner of the studio. There were no servants visible either, but Anquetil and his son cleared away the plates and brought fresh supplies from a sideboard. Evelyn felt completely out of her element. The conversation disconcerted her too, for there was none of the small-talk to which she was accustomed; if these people had nothing particular to say they merely remained silent. They did not seem to think it worth while talking for the sake of talking. Neither gossip nor personalities interested them, but only ideas, in complete contrast to both the world of the Jarrolds and the world of Betsy Charskaya.

Yet they were not solemn. They flashed and laughed, and
were eager and argumentative. Only Anquetil was a little
grim and unbending. An austere man, with the highest
possible standards, he never allowed himself to be anything but rather grimly amused.

Evelyn tried at first to talk to him, but found that she
got no more response from him that she had got from
Bretton. It was clear that the men, in this universe, would
not put themselves out to be conventionally civil to women.
Perhaps thatt was partly responsible for the atmosphere of
steady reality. These people were real; Evelyn owned it,
much as she hated them. She fought against them; tried
to impose her standards on them by making conversation
to Leonard Anquetil; failed; retired into an angry silence.
Nobody noticed; nobody cared.

She observed Miles. He was talking to the man Allen,
not to his hostess who sat neglected and absorbed in her
own thoughts. This, again, enraged Evelyn. It enraged
her that Miles should adapt himself so naturally to the
manners of these disconcerting people. Viola Anquetil was
a rare woman,—she had guessed thatt,—and Miles was
treating her with no more courtesy than he would have
accorded to a man. All Evelyn's feminine solidarity was
aroused. Then she grew doubly enraged on discovering
that the other woman did not resent Miles' detachment in
the least.

The conversation quickened every now and then into
the tempo of a row. Reality was it?—these people felt
passionately on the subjects that interested them. Evelyn,
nurtured in her own good careful middle-class traditions,
was genuinely horrified by the subjects they discussed.
She looked at the coltish son, and at the girl Inez, with an

inborn veneration for their youth. The boy was not eighteen, the girl not twenty, yet they took things lightly for granted which would have puzzled Evelyn rather than interested her, at their age. They took them for granted, with an intelligent and ardent interest which showed that they had already thought over them and had come to some conclusion in their minds. And it was not only that they discussed such subjects as the necessity for easier divorce,—Sweden, they said, was a sensible country,— Evelyn could swallow thatt, knowing that the young were no longer so ignorant as they ought be to,—but their frankness horrified her,—their frankness about incomes, other people's and their own,—their frankness about their feelings. Such things were taboo in the Jarrolds' world; and even in the world of Betsy Charskaya, a decent reserve was maintained. But here in the Anquetils' house, there was no reserve. There was a desire for truth; thatt was the best that could be said for it.

She hated them, but she must admit that they were frank and fresh and gay. She compared their dragon-fly chatter with the empty banter of the Jarrolds. This was a different England. They were frank, and even coarse, but they were real. They were clever, but they couldn't help thatt,—the girl, especially, was horribly clever,—but through all their cleverness they wanted to arrive at something they really meant. They belonged, irrespective of age, to a generation living in a difficult world: the Anquetils, the girl, the young men, all of them. The security of the Jarrolds was entirely absent; and, with it was absent the pretence that the Jarrolds put up of all being right in a world ordained for Jarrolds. Evelyn felt that they would have liked the old man, but would have no use whatever for the old man's children. And what would they have thought of Robin? Evelyn suddenly softened towards them, as she realised how violently they would dislike Robin, and how much they would like Dan. Then she became afraid that Miles would introduce Dan to the Anquetils, and that he would become absorbed by them.

After dinner the women moved towards the fire. The studio was large enough for the two groups to be quite separate. Viola Anquetil sat on a low stool, stirring the fire with a poker; the firelight fell on her red dress and on her face with its curiously spiritual, unorthodox beauty.

"Inez, you must play the piano because I want to talk to Mrs. Jarrold."

A Jarrold woman would never have said thatt. Evelyn could not imagine Hester or Catherine saying it. She was alarmed, being unused to frankness between women. Women played a game of their own, in both the worlds to which she was accustomed. She was afraid of Viola pulling out her heart, as it were, with a corkscrew. She stiffened as the girl went towards the piano and struck a few soft chords in the shadows of the room.

"I am so glad Miles persuaded you to come, Mrs. Jarrold. He told me you might be reluctant,—and I don't blame you,—it is very trying being introduced to the friends of one's friends."

"It was charming of you to ask me."

"Now, shall we drop all thatt? It wasn't charming of me; I was curious. You see, I have known Miles ever since he was a little boy; well, seventeen. Your own boy is seventeen, isn't he? So naturally I take an interest in Miles' concerns, and when he first talked to me about you, and when I first saw how important you were to him, I thought, I must see Evelyn Jarrold for myself. I hope you don't mind? We are both very fond of Miles."

"Both?"

"Leonard and myself."

"Oh,—yes, of course. And he is very fond of you."

Evelyn had to make an effort of generosity, to say thatt.

"Miles is rather an exceptional person, Mrs. Jarrold,—but of course I needn't tell you so. Exceptional,—and consequently, difficult; not nearly so amenable as he appears on the surface. He's very amiable, but he has a rough, determined side to his nature. He's very ambitious, of course."

("Aha!" thought Evelyn, "she is telling me that I mustn't hamper Miles,—mustn't try to interfere with his career. Damn his career," she thought, glancing across to the dinner-table where Miles was deep in talk with Leonard Anquetil, his head shining in the light of the four candles; "damn his career, why can't he be mine, mine, mine?")

"I'm sure he has a great future," she said aloud.

"I don't know about a great future," said Viola; "thatt's such a relative term anyway, isn't it? But I do know that Miles is very energetic and lively. He will never keep quiet. And indeed one would never wish him to keep quiet, wasting himself.—I've sometimes thought," she said, "that he was a little too detached to satisfy his friends. He hurts one, sometimes. One has to be patient with him. It takes years to understand him fully."

("How transparent you are," thought Evelyn; "transparent and rather impertinent." But she could not really think Viola Anquetil impertinent, when she looked into those serene and level eyes.)

"I think Miles is such an interesting study," said Viola,

and the tone in which she spoke redeemed the words from any suspicion of heaviness. "He really is, you know, Mrs. Jarrold. He's a perpetual source of amusement to me. I don't think you know his family, do you?"

"Tell me about them," said Evelyn. She was profoundly resentful, but she capitulated, partly because Viola charmed her and partly because she greedily welcomed any sidelight on Miles. It was an odd experience, this unforeseen discussion of Miles with another woman, while Miles sat in the same room, and the piano accompanied the two separate groups of talk with its unobtrusive chords. The girl Inez played well; her hands strayed idly on the keyboard. The evening was full of reality and of unreality mixed.

"Well, he has several brothers and an old father," began Viola as though she were telling a story to a small child. "His father was a governor of some colony, once,—several colonies,—I forget which. He sacrificed himself to the public service because he conceived it to be his duty, when what he really enjoyed was tramping about after partridges on his estates at home. He had the colonising spirit, you see,—a real old Empire-builder in the old tradition that believes in governing reluctant people who can't peaceably govern themselves. A dear old man, on the whole, according to his own lights, just as I imagine your father-in-law, Mrs. Jarrold, to have been a dear old man? Miles has told me about him."

"Yes," said Evelyn, "he was a dear old man."

"They belonged to the same generation," said Viola, "only their activities happened to lie in different spheres. Your father-in-law built up a business; Miles' father helped to go on building up an Empire. Both very honourable.

Both strictly limited by their own boundaries. Now, what happens to their descendants? I don't know your relations-in-law, Mrs. Jarrold, but I know enough about them to imagine them. They haven't advanced at all. They have merely fulfilled the cosy comfortable ideal that was expected of them, as the prosperous descendants of the people who did the work. They reap the benefit, if benefit it is. So do Miles' brothers. Miles' brothers, today, grumble about the taxes they have to pay,—but they worry about very little else. They grumble about the world that has gone, and they cling on to its poor remnants while they may. I dare say the remnants may last out their lifetime. Miles, on the other hand, looks forward.—His father doesn't approve of him."

"But I should have thought, Miles in the country. . . ."

"Oh, Mrs. Jarrold, I've seen Miles in the country! At his castle, you mean. Yes, of course, Miles at his castle is all that his father would most approve. Miles the squire, Miles the farmer. But what about Miles in his constituency? Would his father approve of thatt?"

"I've never seen him in his constituency," said Evelyn coldly.

"I have. I went down to canvass for him at the last election.—But this is taking us away from what we were talking about: Miles and his family. Miles comes from the sort of family which is very difficult to break away from. ("Yes," thought Evelyn, "you know it, because you come from the same sort of family yourself.") Miles, you know, was sent to Eton. You can imagine the future his father foresaw for him,—the future of a younger son,—Miles was his favourite son too,—Miles should have the ruined castle and the big farm,—Miles should run the farm and be a landlord,—he showed no inclination for the Army or the Foreign Office or the Indian Civil Service, or, heaven help him, the Church, so the land remained, and the family estates could provide: Miles should go on the land. Well, Miles likes being on the land. There's a good landlordly Tory tradition in Miles. But it isn't enough. He disputes; he questions. He breaks away from the public school tradition. He goes back to what England used to be."

"How do you mean," said Evelyn, "what England used to be?" She was interested in spite of herself. She wanted tó dislike Viola Anquetil, but she could not dislike her.

"I have a theory," said Viola, as though amused at her own thoughts; "I don't know if you'd like to hear it?"

"Please."

"It may be all wrong."

"Never mind. Please tell me."

"Well, I have a theory that Miles is a reversion to type. Your Englishman of birth and education wasn't always the cautious, repressed creature he is today. There was a time when he was ashamed neither of his feelings nor of his culture. He was cruder and coarser then, in some ways,— less gentlemanly, according to modern ideas, but *more* gentlemanly, as I see it.—I don't know if you've ever studied the Italian Renaissance?"

"I'm afraid not," said Evelyn, with vague ideas of Leonardo da Vinci.

"Miles would have fitted into the Italian Renaissance. He would have been quite happy at Urbino. He would have appreciated a great doorway with swags of marble fruit and flowers, yet at the same time he would have enjoyed hours spent in empirical argument and he would have liked Alberti who could build a temple at Rimini or

jump into the saddle without putting a hand on his horse.
Do you see what I mean? The imaginary Miles of the
sixteenth century, whether in Italy or in England, had no
limitations. He drank life greedily. He would have been
happy at Urbino, at Rimini, or in Elizabethan England.
He was a cosmopolitan then, a citizen of the world, he
wasn't merely and dully an Englishman. But now something has gone wrong."

"What went wrong, according to you?"

"I don't quite know," said Viola; "I fancy it was a
mixture of Dr. Arnold and Victorianism. Anyhow, the
better bred you were, and the more expensively educated,
the tighter you learnt to shut your mind. You were taught
to be less and less of an individual, and more and more of a
type. And our extraordinary theory about Character came
in, as though character and brain and imagination were
incompatible. The only kind of brain we tolerate at all,
in this country, is the political brain or the administrative
brain. We don't jeer at our statesmen or at our administra-
tors as we jeer at our artists. Our statesmen are even
allowed to wear their hair rather long, without any comment being made in *Punch* or the popular press."

"How pleased my boy would be to hear you say thatt."

"You must bring him here one day; will you? Miles says
he is delightful. He is at Eton still, isn't he?"

"Yes," said Evelyn, feeling, for the first time in her life,
slightly ashamed that Dan should be at Eton.

"I am afraid that you would think that we gave Paul,—
my boy,—rather a freak education. We sent him to Ger-
many instead of sending him to a public school. You see,
he is a musician and we thought it better for him to be
happy at Munich than wretched at Eton. Both Leonard

and my brother were very much against sending him to a public school. My brother was at Eton himself, but in spite of Eton he managed to grow up into quite a definite character," said Viola smiling, "and as for Miles, you must have heard of his Eton career. His brothers were so scandalised, they would hardly speak to him for five years. They tried to explain it away by saying that Miles was hopelessly affected. His father was much more sympathetic about it, but even his father has found it hard to swallow Miles' political views, nor can he bear his son being a prominent pacifist. The old man still believes that all foreigners are rogues and that most non-Europeans are niggers. And as such, of course, they ought to be shot down. —I'm talking too much," said Viola, and seeing that the men were moving she called out to Inez to come across to the fire.

Miles tried to meet Evelyn's eyes, but she would not look at him; she knew that he was full of an anxious curiosity, but she would not own to him even by a glance that she liked Viola Anquetil.

He took her home, rather late, and they quarrelled. It was the first time they had ever quarrelled openly. She had always foreseen and dreaded their first quarrel, but had staved it off by strangling her own feelings or her own temper,—but now perversely, it was she who provoked it. Thus, when emotions run too high, do things happen. Miles himself was in a good mood; he was always in a good mood when he had been with the Anquetils, and this evening his cup of pleasure had been especially full, because of Evelyn's presence. He had enjoyed seeing her sitting amongst his friends. He was rather touchingly naïf about it, but although she was touched somewhere in her heart that loved him, she remained on the surface disagreeably obdurate and sarcastic.

He came upstairs to the flat with her. In the motor, on the way, he had ventured nothing more than "Doesn't Paul play well?" Paul had played after dinner.

"I suppose so, Miles, but then I am no judge of music."

It was a chilling answer, promising badly.

But in the flat, flinging off his overcoat, he plunged recklessly.

"Well, how did you like them?"

"Is it really necessary to be so dirty or so boorish as Mr. Anquetil?"

Miles laughed.

"Oh, didn't you like Leonard? Most women find him very attractive. Wouldn't he respond? I admit, he's not at his best with strangers. But Viola,—how did you get on with her?"

"I don't think she liked me much, Miles,—I'm not nearly clever enough for her."

"Damn cleverness,—Viola isn't clever, she's only intelligent. I hate clever women."

"I don't see much difference, I'm afraid."

"Don't you? So much the worse for you." A note of irritation was coming into his voice. He was not a long-suffering or patient person. He blundered on. "Very beautiful, anyhow, don't you think?"

"In her own untidy way, yes. I suppose so."

"Untidy? Oh, I suppose you mean she's not dressed in the latest fashion, nor made up with the latest Dover Street cosmetics. No, she isn't. She doesn't go to race-meetings, to be photographed sitting on a shooting-stick, 'with friend,' whether the friend be a man or a Pekingese. Neither she nor Sebastian ever lent themselves to thatt kind of thing."

"Sebastian?"

"Her brother."

"Yes, of course. She mentioned him."

"She adores him. But he spends only half the year in England, and when he is here he buries himself in the country."

"At Chevron?"

"Yes, at Chevron. Do you blame him? It isn't his fault that he's an English duke, and he takes the line that the best he can do is to be a good landlord on his estates. He's an unhappy man."

"I suppose he would rather be like Bretton."

"The son of a greengrocer in Rotherham? I dare say he thinks so. But you know, Evelyn, all thatt is rather rot: anybody would rather be born an English duke than the son of a greengrocer in Rotherham."

"You surprise me, Miles; I thought you hated privilege."

"I do hate it,—theoretically,—but I enjoy it, and so does Sebastian. Let's be honest."

"Honest,—honest,—you talk a lot of rubbish about being honest. Bretton. . . ."

"How you hate Bretton!"

"He's so rude, Miles."

"Rude,—you mean he doesn't pick up your handkerchief when you drop it. No, he's thinking of other things. And if you women want equality, you can't have it both ways."

"But you, Miles, would pick up my handkerchief, or any other woman's."

"Thatt's because I was partially educated at Eton. I wasn't taught to pick up women's handkerchiefs there, but I *was* taught to cap my tutor.—This is a silly discussion. The long and short of it is, you didn't like the Anquetils."

"I didn't dislike Viola," said Evelyn after a pause.

"Thatt means that you disliked everybody else."

"Well, take them separately, Miles. Leonard Anquetil has no manners at all. Bretton,—you've guessed what I think about Bretton. The boy Paul,—although I dare say he played well,—seemed to me uncouth and odd. Thatt young man,—was Allen his name?—talked too much, and about things he shouldn't have mentioned in front of a girl. . . ."

Miles laughed uproariously.

"Do you mean Inez? My dear, she's been Allen's mistress for years."

"Indeed? I thought she might possibly be Bretton's."

"Why? because she was talking to him on the sofa? No, Bretton holds quite different views.—I'm sorry. I shouldn't have taken you to the Anquetils."

"I go back to what I said, Miles: I'm not clever enough. You'd better take Dan there instead."

She turned away, and he saw that she was trying to swallow her tears.

"Evelyn, darling!"

"For God's sake, leave me alone. Keep your friends, and leave me to mine. I'm too old for you, I belong to a different generation, I belong to the Jarrolds."

"Viola is years older than you."

"Well, then, she's more adaptable than I am. I don't know. I'm out of the picture, Miles, and the sooner you realise it the better. She talked a lot about you, and I realised how far you and I were apart. I expect she did it on purpose."

"Viola? Never! She's not thatt kind of woman."

"All women are thatt kind of woman."

"There's another of your traditional ideas. Can't you discard them and start with a fresh mind? Those ideas are so hampering, if only you'd admit it."

"Some things remain true, however much other things change and shift."

"Well, I suppose you know more about women than I do, but I protest that you misjudge Viola."

"Why not go to your friends, then? They're far better suited to you than I. Why did you ever come, Miles, to upset my life, and Dan's? I was quite happy before I knew you."

"Were you? Playing bridge, playing up to the Jarrolds, wasting yourself. . . ."

"I've nothing to waste, and you know it. Go back to your friends, and leave me to myself. Leave Dan alone, too. Dan worries me enough, God knows, without you. And now, if he gets into the hands of the Anquetils. . . ."

"Do him good," said Miles firmly.

"Oh, Miles, Miles, you're a stranger to me! You're so hard, I don't understand you. Thatt woman understands you. I can't compete. I'm not jealous of her as a woman; don't misunderstand. But one day you'll meet a woman of whom I shall be jealous, a woman like thatt girl Inez perhaps; I don't know. I know only that we're bound for disaster. I love you to the last drop of my blood, but you don't love me in the same way, and we ought never to have come together."

PART III

PORTRAIT OF LESLEY ANQUETIL

THEY had quarrelled. It was a landmark in their relationship. Having once lost control of herself, Evelyn could not regain it. All the feelings which she had repressed rose to the surface. Everything which had charmed her about Miles began now to arouse her opposition. She nagged at him about his work, his politics, his manners, his friends, even his clothes.

"Miles, I do wish you wouldn't wear thatt black hat. It makes you look like a conspirator, or an organ-grinder."

"But I don't in the least mind looking like a conspirator or an organ-grinder."

He took it good-humouredly, and thatt irritated her too. If she could goad him into a rage, she felt, she would be satisfied. She interpreted his good-humour as a sign of indifference; she was always on the look-out, now, for signs of indifference.

"He can't love me for ever," so she argued miserably to herself. "The day will come when he turns naturally to a younger woman,—it *must* come,—he *must* begin to fall out of love with me. The sooner I make up my mind to it the better. Haven't I always foreseen it? Oh, if only I could go back to those first few weeks, when I refused to think of it,—when loving him and being loved by him was enough! And if I go on as I do at present, I shall only drive him away from me before I need. What a fool I am! I must stop myself, I must, I must."

So she walked up and down her room, pressing her hands together, unhappy and tortured, after every fresh lapse.

To make matters worse, the Jarrolds had found out her liaison with Miles. They did not say so openly, but they made it clear to her. Hester's innuendoes were unmistakable. Evelyn minded terribly. She despised herself for minding, but her training and traditions were too strong for her. She determined not to tell Miles, and of course told him next time she saw him.

He laughed.

"Dear old frumps! are they shocked? What does it matter?"

"It may not matter to you, Miles,—you're a man, and you're different anyway. But they're my only family."

"I thought they bored you?"

"They do bore me,—but I don't want them to think ill of me."

Miles was incapable of understanding this point of view. He had nothing of the bourgeois in the whole of his composition.

"The remedy lies in your own hands," he said, as patiently as he could; "I've suggested over and over again that you should marry me."

"I know you have, and the very way in which you put it shows me what you really feel about it. 'I've suggested over and over again!' You know quite well that you suggest it only in order to please me. You don't really want it. Naturally, I don't blame you for not wanting to tie yourself to a woman fifteen years older than yourself. Indeed, it's very nice and chivalrous of you to suggest it at all.

But you needn't be afraid, Miles: I shan't take you at your word."

"Evelyn, don't be so unreasonable; I do want it; I admit I hate the idea of marriage as an institution,—it always makes me think of Mr. and Mrs. Noah and the animals went in two by two,—but if ever I wanted to marry anybody it would be you. Why not? we could always divorce, if it wasn't a success."

"Miles, please stop joking."

"I'm not joking. I'll get a special licence tomorrow, and it'll be a smack in the eye for your precious sanctimonious Jarrolds. I'll even buy a bowler for the ceremony. Or would you prefer a top-hat? And where shall we go for our honeymoon?"

His flippancy jarred on her.

"You don't understand, Miles. Nothing would induce me to spoil your life."

"Oh, for God's sake don't start bringing out the big phrases. And do try to regard the Jarrolds with the contempt they deserve."

He saw then that she was really distressed, and coming over to her he sat on the arm of her chair.

"Darling, I'm sorry if I can't take the Jarrold prejudices as seriously as you do. I can't stand people with severely admirable precepts and no charity in their souls. Pharisees! That thatt stick of a Hester should dare to criticise you, or thatt dried-up old virgin Catherine! It would do Catherine all the good in the world to be raped, and as for Hester I don't suppose she ever knew a moment's honest pleasure in all her life. Of course they envy us, and whisper about us, and stick darts into you whenever they can. Well, let us shut their mouths for them."

"Never, never, Miles; I never will; you mustn't ask me, because it's so hard for me to say no."

"Listen, you know you hate the irregularity of our relationship; you hate it right inside yourself, not only on account of the Jarrolds. You know it worries you and makes you unhappy; you think that Dan would criticise you if he knew,—as he very soon will know, he's not a child any longer; I believe you even mind *vis-à-vis* Privett. You try to pretend to me that you don't mind, and all the time it gnaws at you and makes you uncomfortable. Whenever we squabble, I believe that thatt is at the rôot of it,—not only my book! When I ask you to come down to the castle, your pleasure in coming is entirely spoilt by the fear that people will find out where you are. You resort to all kinds of subterfuges, and being very aboveboard by nature you find subterfuges irksome. Yet out of sheer obstinacy you won't accept the remedy I offer you. I believe that at the back of your head you think I ought to marry a Nice Girl, and say good-bye to you for ever."

"It's only too true, Miles; I don't deny a word of it. I shan't urge you to marry your nice girl, because I simply haven't the strength or the courage, but I shall and do refuse to marry you myself."

"Then at least be consistent, and forget your qualms and hesitations, and let us be as happy as we may."

"I will, Miles, I really will." She looked at him and smiled, trying to banish the cloud and to prevent him from guessing the force of the temptation to which he exposed her.

She was grateful to him for having understood her so well, and to show her gratitude she not only refrained from sharp and nagging remarks, but allowed him to take her

out to places where they would be sure to meet their
friends and invite comment on their constant appearance
together. The Easter holidays were over, and she could
no longer plead mourning for old Mr. Jarrold. For Miles'
sake and in order not to incur his contempt, she discarded
her instinctive discretion. It was a form of martyrisation
for her, and she tried to pretend to herself that she liked
it, but actually she endured the greatest discomfort; and
looking at herself in the glass one evening when Miles was
coming to fetch her, she wondered why her inner feelings
could not accord better with her outward semblance.

"I ought to be dowdy," she said to herself; "Miles was
quite right." His phrase had stuck in her mind. "I ought
to wear grey voile and an amethyst cross; I ought to look
like the bourgeoise I really am."

Did she regret having met Miles? Did she regret having
been swept away from the virtuous path she had always
followed? Did she regret the smug and comfortable position she had always held, ensconced in the heart of the
Jarrolds? those bolsters and pillows of family affection
and respectability, sheltering her in the world to which she
belonged? They had never had cause to criticise her before.
Even when she went with friends to the Riviera, a district
of which Jarrolds disapproved, they knew that her conduct
remained impeccable, and the most they could say was
that if dear Evelyn wanted a little sun in the winter why
didn't she go to some Swiss resort, or even to Rapallo,
where they understood one met very nice people?

Well, those days were over now; she had valued her
reputation and she had lost it. She was ashamed of her pre-
occupation over something which Miles regarded as so petty, but it lay deep, deep within her, as deep as her bones.

"Forget it," she kept saying to herself; "forget it, and keep Miles happy. Then he won't turn away from me to somebody else quite so soon." And she ordered more clothes, and went out dancing with Miles, and boldly met the amused glances of other women, and let other men talk to her in a way they would not have ventured on before.

She saw less and less of the Jarrolds now, and in a way, although they had bored her, she missed them. She missed her occasional week-ends of Newlands, where old Mr. Jarrold had kept the family together. They were dispersed; the old lady was living in the dower-house, quite happy with her rhododendrons; Newlands was more or less shut up, and Evelyn suspected that Dan, when he came of age, would decide to sell it. She met Evan sometimes, at a night-club, and from the look in his eye she could tell that he had as yet set no restrictions upon his brandy. She went to dinner once or twice with Geoffrey and Hester, but noticed that Ruth always contrived to be out. She supposed that she ought to feel relief at the close family life having come to an end.

At Long Leave, at the beginning of July, resisting the united appeals of Miles and Dan, she firmly took Dan down to stay with her own father at Biggleswade, saying that it was right and proper that he should visit his surviving grandfather. It gave her a good deal of satisfaction to say this, since the argument was unanswerable. Even Miles could not and did not sneer. Dan could and did grumble, but she remained virtuously obstinate.

It gave her a curious satisfaction, also, to reënter an atmosphere to which she had nearly become a stranger.

Her father's house, in its modest way, was the counterpart of Newlands; her father's creed was, tacitly, the creed of the Jarrolds. Mr. Wilson, a retired solicitor living on an adequate income behind the oak paling of his two acres of grounds, gave a reassuring impression of well-invested stability. His house, which was of red brick discordantly covered by Virginia creeper, was comfortable though not luxurious; he believed in cutting his coat according to his cloth. He prided himself on his cigars and on his cellar, whose key, more from convention than from mistrust of his elderly parlour-maid, he kept on his watch-chain. Before each meal he would descend ceremoniously to the cellar with an electric torch, and would himself select the bottle he wanted. A good deal of his conversation revolved round various wines and their years of vintage, with appropriate anedcotes reminiscent of the Inner Temple. He habitually ate rather too much, without noticeably impairing his constitution, and in his own way was a gourmet, though it was not in the French way; he liked to have egg-sauce with his fish, horse-radish with his roast beef on Sunday, Lea and Perrin with his cold roast beef next day, mashed potatoes with almost everything, except pheasant which demanded chips; a dinner of less than five courses would have seemed to him a lapse from good breeding; and his luncheon was always rounded off by a savoury. He prided himself, moreover, on being a man of culture; his views on these subjects were immovable, and seemed to have come to a standstill at whatever point where they happened to have stuck; he considered Mr. Galsworthy supreme among English novelists, but set his mind resolutely against the novels he received twice a week from his lending library,—the list compiled from the more reputable

of the weekly and Sunday papers;—read them with a
certain amount of pleasure and a certain amount of dis-
quiet; and returned them hoping for something better
attuned to his own ideas next time. Among his water-
colours, however, he felt quite safe; he liked to wander
round his sitting-room, when he had nothing better to
do, and to look at those pretty, comforting sketches of
children in sun-bonnets among corn-fields and red pop-
pies; Evelyn liked them too,—so he told himself, for he
sometimes felt lonely, and the thought of Evelyn was a
solace,—Evelyn liked them, and Evelyn's boy would
have them all when he died; it was nothing compared
with the wealth his other grandfather had been able to
leave him, but still perhaps Evelyn's boy would find a
place for the water-colours in his own particular study.

Evelyn was bringing the boy down for Long Leave.
Nice of her. He ordered a specially good dinner, and a
specially large one, thinking of a schoolboy's appetite.
His little household was all in a fluster. Ellen, the parlour-
maid, asked if she should buy a hot-water bottle for Mrs.
Jarrold's bed.

"Won't Mrs. Jarrold bring her own, Ellen?"

"A stone one, I thought, sir, for the feet, you know,
sir, just to warm the bed."

"But the beds are aired, Ellen?"

"Oh, sir!"

"Yes, of course, Ellen, I knew they were.—I was just
thinking, this is July.—Well, buy a stone bottle if you
think right. Yes, I dare say it would be a good thing—
please Mrs. Jarrold, you know,—and a bottle always
comes in useful, I dare say?"

"Yes, indeed, sir, even though you won't never have one yourself. And what about his lordship, sir?"

"Boys don't need hot-water bottles," said Mr. Wilson severely, "and if they do, they shouldn't. Especially in July."

He had not seen Evelyn for some months and was enchanted by her when he did see her. He could scarcely believe that so delightful a woman was his own daughter. All his old gallantry rose up in him,—and in his earlier years he had appreciated women,—so that he felt he must exert himself for her entertainment. As he dressed for dinner, he thought out his best stories, but was afraid she had already heard them all. It was a little confusing: he felt as though he had a stranger under his roof, a pretty bewildering stranger, yet thatt stranger was his own daughter, the same Evelyn he had known as a little girl in pinafores. A good girl; she had always been a good girl; any other woman would have married again, after poor Tommy's death, but she, Evelyn, had devoted herself to Dan. Not many women of Evelyn's attractions would have done thatt. Thank God, Evelyn had been well brought up; well grounded; she had had a good mother, although her mother had died when Evelyn was but nine years old. (The first seven years of a child's life were the most important; so he had heard.) Thatt good grounding was bearing its fruits. As Evelyn had had a good mother then, so had Dan a good mother now. Mr. Wilson felt obscurely that the whole credit reverted to him. In an exceedingly good mood he descended his Turkey-carpeted stairs to dinner, to the chimes of a punctual gong.

Evelyn was happy too. She was seldom wholly happy nowadays, even in her most delirious moments, and it was a relief to let herself relax. She almost forgot Miles. Miles faded and receded, for the first time in seven months. She was happy, sitting between her father and her son. It was safe here, safe and continuous; there was no danger, no need to adjust oneself to a swiftly moving current. She could rest. The boat was anchored.

"I'm afraid, my dear, that you may find it rather dull."

"Oh, Father, if only you knew how I enjoy getting away from London!"

"Very good of you to say so, my dear. And what about Dan? Doesn't he want parties? theatres? I did, at his age. . . ."

Dan answered politely; he made his answer quite convincing, but Evelyn knew that he longed to be with Miles. She resented this reminder of Miles. She looked from Dan to his grandfather: Dan so handsome in his adolescence, his grandfather so handsome in his old age, with his white curls and rosy beaming face, looking floury, as though he smelt good. She knew that his grandfather was proud of Dan, assuming, as a matter of course, that the boy was 'a good boy'; knowing nothing of the gulf which separated Dan from his own ways of thinking.

Ellen put the port on the table and left the room.

"A glass of port, my boy? No? Quite right, quite right, —but wait till you get to Oxford! And see here, I'll tell you something: when you were born I laid down a pipe of port, and one day you'll thank me,—don't forget. Eh? Now tell me, what are you going to do with yourself, eh? When you leave Oxford, I mean?"

Dan answered evasively. He had the tact which springs

from a kind and sensitive heart. He hadn't made up his mind, he said; and then, at the end of his resources, looked at his mother to help him out.

"I think Dan ought to travel, Father, don't you? before settling down?"

"There's nothing like travel for broadening the mind," said Mr. Wilson, who disliked nothing on earth so much as a broadened mind, although he would have denied it hotly, "and nothing like travel, I always say, for showing one that one's own country is the best. Splendid idea, Evelyn! It isn't everybody that can afford it, these days. Dan's lucky. And then what'll you do? Get down to work as a hereditary legislator?"

Mr. Wilson laughed at his own phrase. He belonged to the school that thought polysyllables funny. He laughed so innocently and simply that Evelyn was filled with tenderness for him. Besides, Evelyn, when she was away from Miles, still thought polysyllables rather funny too.

Then Mr. Wilson grew curious, as though he had just remembered something.

"How is it you aren't at Lord's, Dan? You mustn't stay down here just to please an old man, you know. Like to go up tomorrow for the day with your mother?"

"Oh no, Grandpapa, thanks, I'd rather stay here."

"I might come with you, if you asked me, who knows?" said Mr. Wilson, twinkling; "I've only been once to Lord's in my life,—it would be quite a jaunt for me."

"They talked of abolishing Lord's, I believe," said Dan hurriedly, to divert Mr. Wilson from this dangerous idea; "for the sake of economy, you know."

"Abolish Lord's!" cried Mr. Wilson in consternation; "bless my soul, they'll abolish the Constitution next."

He was shaken; his vision of himself, strolling on the grass
with an elegant young grandson, which had become quite
vivid for a moment, was unkindly shattered. "Bless my
soul," he said again.

Dan wanted to argue. He looked at his mother, but she
winked him into silence. She would have been ruffled by
an argument between Dan and his grandfather,—an
argument leading nowhere but to mutual irritation and
misunderstanding. Better to let things slide; better to let
Mr. Wilson and his generation slip undisturbed into their
graves. There was enough to disturb them without carrying the disturbance into the heart of their own families.
Poor old men, let them go in peace. Dan agreed, when
she put it to him later in the seclusion of her bedroom.
She was grateful to him for his agreement, for she wanted
no echoes of Miles and his subversive doctrines among the
water-colours of Biggleswade.

The July weather was against her, in her rejection of
Miles, for it spoke to her of the softness of love. She knew
that Miles was at his castle, and, walking between the
rose-beds of her father's little garden, the insufferable
ache for Miles returned. She sent him a telegram, when
Dan had gone back to Eton, saying that she would come
down to stay with him.

"Miles," she said, when he met her at the station and
they racketed off in the same old motor down the lanes
now rich with summer, "do you remember the first time
you met me here, me and Dan, on a winter's night, and
the old man was killed at the level-crossing?"

"Don't think of thatt."

"I don't want to think of it. Thatt's why I spoke of it.

I felt superstitious about it, as though it were an ill-omen haunting me ever since. If I tell you so, perhaps the shadow will go. I always avoided speaking of it before. I want us to be completely happy now, without a cloud." She looked at him with a frank and confident smile. She felt happier and more light-hearted, suddenly, then she had felt for weeks.

"Don't drive quite so fast; let's dawdle a little; I want to look at the country, so green after London. I like the waste ground along the hedgerows, encroaching on the width of the road with all kinds of flowers whose names I don't know. I like the wild roses waving their sprays above the hedges. I feel like a Fresh Air Fund child from the slums, released out of London into the country. I like the tall grass, and the fields where the hay has been cut. Will you take me out into the fields, to-morrow? every day?"

"How many days are you going to stay with me, then?" He was amused by her enthusiasm; amused, delighted, and puzzled.

"For as many days as you want me. Something has happened, something has come right. I don't know what it is; I only know that while I was with my father I tried to forget you, and then wanted you so urgently that nothing else mattered. Miles, drive even a little slower. Let me enjoy this summer drive, and let it wipe out thatt winter evening. Do you remember, you said you wanted me to see your castle in the summer? and I said, it couldn't be more lovely than on thatt winter day? I think I really meant that our love was independent of the seasons. It was so perfect then, that I didn't believe it could last; I certainly didn't believe it could grow. But it has grown, hasn't it? I love you now even more than I did then. You disturb me, you upset me, but I love you more; I'm less able to escape from you. I've no desire to do so."

She murmured to him, sitting close beside him as he drove. She stooped swiftly, and her lips touched his hand as it lay on the driving-wheel. Responsive, he caught her exaltation, slackened his speed, and they lingered between the July hedges as people in a trance. He had not expected her to come, and her telegram had brought him to the station in a mood divided between apprehension and excitement. But when they met, the apprehension vanished; their moods rushed together; fused; found perfection in the microcosm of love. She, alone, existed for him, and he for her. The summer and the country lanes existed for them both.

"You didn't enjoy coming to night-clubs with me," he said, confessing to an unkindness which he had imposed upon her.

"I hated it, Miles; it wasn't you, it wasn't me. Or, if it was me, it was a contemptible me. This is better. Let's stay here, buried, lost.—Look, here we are at the turning to your castle. There's the board which says 'Private road, no thoroughfare.' Do you know, I was frightened when I first saw thatt board. It was the first time I came here, and the lights of your car swept across it, and I knew I had committed myself to a road without retreat. Stop for a minute; pull up."

He stopped the car by the side of the road, shut off the engine, and she lay against him, so close that she could feel the beating of his heart.

"Can you feel my heart, too, Miles? no, of course you can't, I'm on the wrong side. Darling, drive on very slowly.

This is your own rough lane. These are your own fields on either side. This is the real you, I think,—more real than the you of night-clubs, or even than the you of the House of Commons. Bretton doesn't really know this side of you, nor do the Anquetils. Nor do I," she added humbly; "I've never been a country person, and I can't understand a word that Munday says. And I was very indignant—though you didn't know it—when you dragged me across your ploughed fields. Still, I can feel your castle and your fields as a back-ground to you and to our love. Do you look on me altogether as an interloper?"

The motor slipped down the steep approach to Miles' lane, a lane so roughly kept that the Queen Anne's Lace and flowering grasses brushed the mudguards as they passed. He put his arm round her shoulders and drove with one hand, scaring a brood of young partridges into the ditch.

"I want nothing but this," he said, and, at the moment, believed it.

The heavy golden sunshine enriched the old brick with a kind of patina, and made the tower cast a long shadow across the grass, like the finger of a gigantic sun-dial veering slowly with the sun. Everything was hushed and drowsy and silent, but for the coo of the white pigeons sitting close together on the roof. Miles said that he really preferred the spring, when the green was fresher, the trees less dark and heavy, the year less full-blown, but Evelyn forbade him to find any fault with such perfection.

"Even if we die tomorrow, Miles, today will have been flawless."

He teased her, saying that she and he and the castle
between them made a picture like Marcus Stone, and
that thatt was what she liked; and she grew momentarily
a little sad, not because he had teased her, but because
she knew that Marcus Stone painted only young lovers.
She refrained, however, from explaining the reason of the
tiny cloud crossing her. There were no other clouds; she
was determined that there should not be. She even made
him talk to her about his book, the bugbear subject which
even in their happier moments was taboo. He had just
finished it, he said; had, indeed, written to tell her so three
days ago; and was now making the final corrections.
Well, she said, he should work at it tomorrow morning,
but not this evening, Miles, please; let this evening be
mine. At which he laughed, but fondly, and said that she
was no wife for an author or for a politician.

They wandered under the high brick walls after dinner
in a perfect communion. The evening was absolutely still;
the tower sprang like a bewitched and rosy fountain
towards the sky. Evelyn looked up at its windows, and
her clasp tightened on Miles' fingers. She remembered
the first night when she had gone across crisp, frozen
grass, to find Miles in his tower, while Dan lay innocently
asleep in the cottage a hundred yards away. Then, it had
been cold, and she had come shivering and unaccustomed
into Miles' arms. Now, it was warm, and they were ex-
quisitely familiar to one another.

"Miles," she said, "are you sleeping in the cottage or
in the tower?"

They laughed over the question. Of course he was sleeping in the tower. What would Mrs. Munday think, if he slept in the cottage alone with Mrs. Jarrold? They laughed happily, as lovers laugh, who share a secret.

"I shall come to you this time, Evelyn, and leave you with the dawn."

They strolled up and down the path under the wall. They forgot the world, and broke off little branches of southern-wood to crush between their fingers. The pansies and the white lilies stood out startlingly in the half light. It was a dream, a suspension, a trance.

Later, they climbed the seventy-five steps of the tower and stood on the leaden flat, leaning their elbows on the parapet, and looking out in silence over the fields, the woods, the hop-gardens, and the lake down in the hollow from which a faint mist was rising. The moon was full in a light sky; few stars were visible, by reason of the brightness of the moon; only stars of the first magnitude, and one or two steady planets. Evelyn asked Miles which they were, and he immediately named them; it was the sort of thing he always knew, and, although such things were alien to her, she always delighted in his knowledge. She took a pride in making him show off; in testing his superior information. Nor did he ever fail her. Other people might say that young Vane-Merrick was a bit glib, a bit shallow,—though in some directions he was serious enough, they said; even weighty;—Evelyn, at any rate, was infallibly impressed by the catholicity of his knowledge, especially when it interfered in no way between himself and her. If he had been engaged on serious astronomical studies, she would have resented a night spent at the telescope; as it was, she liked to point to a bright star and say, "What's thatt one, Miles?" and to receive his answer, meaningless to her though it might be, "Arcturus,—you can find him always by following a half-circle down from the Plough." It was elementary, but Evelyn did not know it. She did not discriminate between the things which Miles really knew about, and the things which he scarcely knew about at all. She knew only that some things bored her and others did not; politics bored her, and his book bored her, and astronomy bored her, but it did not bore her when Miles named Venus to her in the evening sky, and told her that this was the planet consecrated to lovers. She looked at Venus, after thatt, with an added respect.

They came down again, and wandered away from the tower, the garden, and the moat.

Down in the wood, by the lake, they sat on a fallen tree among the tall bracken. The lake glimmered through a clearing. The oaks above them blotted out half the sky. It was still and warm,—so still, that they heard a rustle in the leaves; so warm, that Evelyn threw back her cloak and Miles let his hand fall across her bare throat. It was a real, warm summer night, rare in England. They scarcely spoke.

They sighed at last, and, rising, wandered across the meadows back towards the tower. Some belated grass had been cut, and they walked between the ridges of the fresh swathes. Once, they sank down into the scented hay and stayed there for a space, silent but for the eloquent touch of love. Then they rose again, as by common consent, and, looking at one another,—though by now the night had fallen, and they could scarcely see one another

—pursued their way, hand in hand, across the meadow towards the tower.

Next morning Evelyn awoke still filled with the same sense of supreme happiness. Their absolute seclusion at the castle, in the middle of Miles' thousand acres, invested their secret love with idyllic colours. Far away was the censure of the Jarrolds and the threat of the discrepancy of age. They were purely lovers, united by the ever-young, lyrical bond of love. She sprang from her bed and began to dress, joyful in the thought that she would go down to meet Miles at breakfast, and that another day would unroll itself for their delectation, with another sinking of the summer evening, and another coming of the summer night, and the moon shining through the latticed windows of the tower. The anticipation of such renewed joy weakened her as she dressed, and made her sit swooning for a moment in the chair beside the vast, unlit fireplace of her bedroom. Swallows were nesting in the chimney; they swooped down the chimney, out into the room, perched briefly on the bar of the open window, then swept out into the garden, and returned, regardless of the room's other inhabitant, with nourishment for their cheeping, invisible brood. Evelyn watched them go and come. She would never have believed that she,—she of all people!—she, so urban,—could enter into a communion with swallows; but love worked strange miracles. She watched the little creatures at their parental business, and forgave them the messes they made over her hairbrushes and dressing-table. They were occupied solely in fulfilling the demands of nature. How natural, simple, and inevitable their creed! So natural, that it seemed to her divine. To pair; to nest;

to hatch out a brood; to seek food for their young; to bring food, whether down the chimney or through the window; to spill their little innocent dung on the way; to pause in confabulation on the top of her mirror; to feel nothing but the urgency of begetting and upbringing in the brief months before the inexplicable necessity of migration began; to have such confidence in man's benevolence as to nest under his roof or in his very chimney! those fragile, vulnerable birds, destined to the long mysterious journey after the simplicity of their English summer! Sunk into the chair before the fireplace, she watched them on their restless flight; and found no strength to go on with her dressing, so absorbed was she in the tiny drama of the swallows, so envious of their simplicity, so envious of the babies they reared up there in the darkness of the chimney. Half-dressed, in her shift, she went down on her knees and peered up the chimney; and there, on the edge of the nest, she saw two hesitating, bunched, half-fledged forms, almost ready to fly; and, drawing back, she pressed her fingers into her eyes so that the eye-balls hurt, thinking of the children that she and Miles might have begotten; and then she thought of Dan, who was not Miles' son; but the summer morning was so sweet, outside the window, and the memory of the night so fresh, and the anticipation of the days so clear, that she took her fingers away and roused herself, and put on a summer frock to go down and meet Miles who was, after all, her lover.

He had been swimming in the lake before breakfast and came in, sleeking back his wet hair. Mrs. Munday was in the room, putting down a large dish of eggs and bacon; she wore her usual air of wide serenity and perfect understanding. The door stood open on to the garden and bright flowers; sunlight poured into the room.

"I hope you slept well?"

She answered him with a quick and meaning smile.

"Perfectly, thank you. Am I late! I dawdled, watching a pair of swallows fly up and down my chimney."

"I should have warned you that they were there,— why, you might have lit the fire last night! Mrs. Munday doesn't like them, but I intercede for them and she spares their lives."

"You wouldn't like them either, sir, if you had to clean up after them."

"I dare say not, but you know you wouldn't hurt them even if I let you. In Greece, Mrs. Munday, it is considered the luckiest thing in the world if swallows nest in the house."

"Indeed, sir? I learn a lot from Mr. Vane-Merrick, don't I?" she said, turning humorously to Evelyn. "Now I hope the coffee is as you like it, and is there anything else I can get you?"

"We have everything we could possibly want in the world, Mrs. Munday."

When Mrs. Munday had gone, Evelyn stretched out her hand to him.

"Did you really mean thatt? About having everything we wanted in the world? Do you feel like thatt too, Miles? I felt so happy when I woke this morning that I thought I should die of it. Come to the door just a moment before we have our breakfast. Oh, Miles, the warmth of the sun! Lay your hand on the brick,—it's quite hot. I never saw flowers look so brilliant before; it seems as though they had doubled themselves during the night, and every separate petal shines. Is it possible that you and I are here together? alone? and in love?"

She leant up against the doorway in the sunlight in her summer frock, excited, radiant, incredulous, looking now at Miles and his sleeked and shining hair, now out at the garden brilliant with flowers and sun. She crushed his fingers between her own. The knuckles hurt, bone against bone. The memory of the night was alive within her, an ideal night succeeded by so ideal a day.

"Now we'll have breakfast," she said, releasing his hand, and going to the table she poured out his coffee and gave him his eggs and bacon on a plate. Their intimacy rejoiced her. After such a night, she could help him to eggs and bacon.

"Why are you smiling, Miles?"

"I'm smiling at your domesticity."

They breakfasted in perfect union. "I never knew," she felt but did not say, "that breakfast could be so romantic a meal." She was in so good a mood that after breakfast she asked him what he was going to do, instead of assuming that he would stay idling with her. "I'm sure you ought to see Munday, Miles. I'm sure a cow has calved during the night. Something of the sort always seems to happen in the country. Or, even if no cow has calved, you ought to correct your book. I shall go and stroll across the fields, and you can come and join me. Don't hurry." Privately she thought that the ecstasy of the moment when he re-joined her would be enhanced by their brief separation. She felt full of virtue, too, for suggesting that he should correct his book.

He let her go, watching her muslin figure under a parasol recede down the long colonnade of cobnuts. The Great

Dane stood by his side, waiting patiently. He saw her pass out from the shade of the nuts, unlatch the little gate, and walk out into the sunshine of the field beyond. She turned and waved to him. He waved back. She was as brightly coloured as the flowers in his garden. He fancied, indeed, as he watched her with the eyes of love, that she was just a flower blown out of his garden, blown down the avenue of the nut-trees, passing through shadow as a petal might go whirling, recovering its colour as it came again into the sunlight. She could be darkened by shadow, or lit up by the sun. He preferred her lit up by the sun. Shadow made him impatient and irritable. His life was too full and virile to admit her purely feminine problems. He loved her, but she represented his diversion; not his whole life. He loved her, certainly. But he loved her especially when she was as gay, as happy, as simple, as easy, as decorative as the flowers in his garden this morning through the open door. What he could not endure was when she was difficult and strenuous and jealous. Then he felt that he wanted to break away from her for ever, and be rid of love and all its wearisome and feminine complications, but when she was gay and easy, and as pretty as she had looked in her muslin frock leaning up against the door-jamb in the sun, then he felt that he would keep to her for ever.

He was especially grateful to her for sending him back to his book. Time and his publishers were pressing, and in the last few months he had lost many days on Evelyn's demand. Why could she not always be reasonable as she was this morning? Then, no trouble would ever arise between them.

He went back into the cottage and began turning over

the papers on his desk. At the back of his mind he kept the vision of her passing down the nuttery, unlatching the gate, and walking out into the sunlight of the field beyond; he knew that in an hour's time, two hours' time, he would go out and find her, and that their relation would be as idyllically resumed. But in the meantime, he was detached enough to be grateful to her for her hour of concession to his ordinary life.

So grateful was he, and so unusually relieved,—for he had prepared a solid revision of his book in advance, and Evelyn's unexpected advent had made him fear that he must delay its execution,—that he became absorbed in his writing and forgot all about the time.

He wrote better than usual, and his mind worked more clearly, because of his consciousness that she was out somewhere in his fields, waiting for him.

Evelyn crossed the fields till she came to the lake in the hollow, when she sat down on a tree-stump and gazed across the shimmering water. She thought of nothing consciously; her being was simply lapped in a sensuous warmth, compounded partly of love and partly of the summer day. Presently Miles would come back to her. Nothing else mattered. She knew that he had his book to write; let him write it! His book was important; yet unimportant. He might even ring up Bretton at Maidstone, and have a long conversation with him, a voice interrupting every now and then to say "Six minutes,—nine minutes, —twelve minutes," but all those minutes would be as nothing compared with the minute when she would see him coming down the field towards the lake to join her. It's a terrible thing, a divine thing, she thought, pressing her fingers again into her eyeballs as when she had watched the swallows, to be a woman and so much in love. One must keep the poignancy of it even from one's lover; and thatt constitutes the loneliness of love, for a woman. However much in love he, and I, may be, there is a difference: the world remains with him, and the world vanishes for me. The masculine world remains quite separate from the world of love. So,—the logical sequence followed in her mind,—I must not bother him. I must fit in with the mood that moves him, and be grateful for what I can get. He is a man, and I am a woman. His life is full, and mine is empty, except in so far as he fills it.

But it was hard for her to school herself, sitting beside the lake, waiting for Miles to join her. Twenty hours with him had unfitted her for rational argument. She was his; therefore he must be hers. His book, and his telephone calls to Bretton, were insignificant. "I, thy God, am a jealous god," when the god is the god of love.

She waited for so long that her reasonableness began to evaporate and her temper to rise. Really, she must mean very little to him, if he could waste so many hours when they might be together! She pulled up a little tuft of grass and nibbled the stalks crossly, making a valiant effort to control herself. She was determined not to receive him sharply, when he did consent to arrive. It was her own fault: she had told him to work at his book and not to hurry. He was not to blame for taking her at her word. Thus she admonished herself. Still, her temper began to rise at his assumption that she could happily and patiently watch wild-ducks on the lake for an indefinite time.

Then she saw him coming towards her across the fields. Her indignation dissolved. The fields, and the summer, and love, and Miles, were again blended in her mind.

They were all part of the same thing. She forgot that he
had kept her waiting.

She would not rise to meet him. She would delay the
moment when he would take her hand and say that his
writing was over and done with, and that he was free to
be with her for the rest of the day. A physical tremor ran
over her at his approaching nearness. "Seven months!" she
thought, "and still so idiotically in love!"

He came up to her and threw himself down on the
grass at her side.

"Finished your writing, Miles? What shall we do? Shall
we go for a walk in the wood, or would you like to take
me out in the boat? Whatever you like. I'm perfectly
happy so long as we are alone."

"We aren't going to be alone, I'm afraid."

"Not alone? What do you mean?" She sat up straight,
then she relaxed again, as she guessed what he might
mean. "You've got to see Bretton or someone," she said,
determined to be reasonable.

"The Anquetils telephoned," he said deliberately;
"they want to motor down for the day."

"Miles, you didn't say they could come?"

"Of course I did,—they haven't been here since last
year. You don't mind, do you?"

"Not mind! Oh, Miles, you knew I should mind. How
could you do anything so inconsiderate and so cruel?
You did it on purpose, I believe, to spite me, to provoke
a quarrel. Or did you really think I should not mind?
Are you just obtuse, or most ingeniously cruel? Whichever
it is, I don't understand you, I don't understand."

All her serenity and happiness were piteously dispelled;
she was hurt, angry, and astonished. She looked at him

as though trying to penetrate into his motives. He returned her gaze with the hard eyes she had learnt to dread. As a matter of fact, he felt guilty, and the sense of guilt made him defiant. It was not true that he had intended to spite and provoke her; but it was true that he had intended to humble what he considered as her unreasonableness. Even as he had answered the telephone, he had smiled wickedly at the thought of her indignation. Now he was sorry, when he saw her disappointment and distress; still, he would not give way.

"How you exaggerate! They will go back to London this evening, leaving us alone,—if thatt is really what you like."

"You're a brute, Miles,—a cold brute. Very well: if they come, I go."

"Aren't you rather losing your sense of proportion?"

"I don't think so. If you are capable of doing something which you know will hurt me, it means only one thing, doesn't it? That you don't care about me as I tried to persuade myself that you cared. You have left me alone the whole morning, anyhow. You are either a brute, indifferent, or a bully. Whichever it is, makes very little difference. I won't accept you on such terms. I prefer to leave you now, at once, and for good. You can go on with your book in peace, and you can keep your friends."

She got up.

"You needn't lie there sneering at me, Miles. I mean it. You know that we have each always wanted the upper hand,—oh, I'll admit, if you like, that neither of us has a very nice character. We're both vain and domineering. Well, you haven't won. You've won in a way, because I loved you far more than you ever loved me; you can count thatt as a triumph if you like. Now it's over, and I daresay you will be thankful to be rid of me."

"Evelyn, you're saying all the things that people say on these occasions. One after the other, they're inevitably trotted out."

"My dear Miles, you're welcome to your superiority. Keep it for the Anquetils,—perhaps it will impress them. It doesn't impress me. I'm an ordinary human woman, not clever, not intellectual,—I always told you so. I never tried to keep you on false pretences. But at least let me say this to you, I gave up things for you that I never thought to give up. . . ."

"Your respectability, I suppose you mean?"

"Yes, I do mean thatt. You may sneer. It meant something to me.—And there again," she added, reminded of another grievance, "you never gave me a thought when you asked the Anquetils down here. What would they think if they found me here, alone with you! You know how much I risk by coming at all, without publishing it to all the world."

"The Anquetils aren't all the world; besides, they know about us already."

"Yes,—you told them. Without asking my leave, you told them." She chose to forget the pleasure she had experienced on hearing that he had been unable to disguise his new happiness from his best friends. "Never for one moment have you stopped to think how much you might be compromising me. Dan,—my servants,—my relations, —have you ever thought of them?"

"Good Lord, that you should reckon with such contemptible things!"

"They may seem contemptible to you. To me, they

aren't. Yet I have sacrificed them all to you, Miles. Do you imagine that the sacrifice meant nothing to me?— No, I won't reproach you. I've suffered on your account, —more than you know,—but I've been happy with you, too, at moments,—no, I won't reproach you.—I'm going now, Miles. Don't tell the Anquetils I was here, will you?"

Alarmed and irritated, he caught her by the skirt as she moved away.

"Evelyn, don't be so ridiculous. There are other things in life than lovers' quarrels. The quarrel and the reconciliation,—it's a convention of fiction."

"Miles, let go of my skirt, please. It is you who look ridiculous sprawling on the grass, clutching at me.— Anyhow, what do you mean by saying the quarrel and the reconciliation are a convention of fiction? Get fiction out of your head, and you'll be a wiser man."

"Get sense into yours," he grumbled, releasing her, "and you'll be a wiser woman."

"We're both right," she said, looking at him very sadly; and although at thatt moment he could have recaptured her easily, since she was unhappy and temporarily softened, he missed his opportunity, and she went away from him across the field, in the pretty frock he had liked so much before breakfast.

Cross, he watched her go; then jumped up and went after her.

"Evelyn!"

She stopped and turned to him, but she was very cold.

"I don't think there's any more to be said, is there?"

"These quarrels are so silly. We were so happy."

"Yes, we were, but you've spoilt it."

"Can't we put it right?"

"If you want to put it right, Miles, telephone to the Anquetils and stop them from coming."

"No," he said, after a pause.

"You won't?"

"I won't.—The issue is an absurd one. And it's too late anyway."

"I see: you prefer your friends to me. Well, let us leave it at thatt."

She walked on.

"I don't prefer my friends to you," he said, following her, "but I do prefer a peaceful life to a life full of wasteful and unnecessary emotion." His moment of remorse had gone; he was very angry and resentful.

"Is it unnecessary emotion," she said, stopping, "when I sit for hours waiting for you and thinking to myself that at last,—at last!—I shall have you to myself all day, yes, and all night too, Miles, and then you come and say calmly that other people are coming to spoil our solitude, and seem not to care that those other people should rob us of what is so precious to me if not to you? And indeed invite them deliberately, knowing full well that you destroy all my pleasure: meaning, indeed, to destroy my pleasure because you think me unreasonable. Have you no imagination, you who pride yourself on your intelligence?—Oh yes, Miles! you have imagination; you have enough imagination to know quite clearly what you were doing, and thatt's what I can't forgive. I could forgive your stupidity,—you're only a man after all,—but I can't forgive your deliberation. You meant to hurt me; well, you've succeeded, but you've lost me in doing it."

"What a speech!" he said to himself, enraged that she should make this fuss over nothing, but at the same time he knew somewhere in his heart that her resentment was justified according to her own lights; he knew that she had tried to be good about his book; he knew that the Anquetils symbolised some essential rift between himself and her. The fuss she made was unjustifiable in the letter of the law, but in the spirit of the law something could be said on her side. "Damn love, damn women," he said to himself, watching her cross the field. He was upset and sorry; still, he was not willing to give way. "Why shouldn't Viola and Leonard come just for the day?" he said to himself, watching her go; and he wondered if she would really go for ever, but having a tyrannical nature himself he reckoned on her not breaking so easily away from him, and was pleased rather than otherwise at the test he had imposed upon her. "Another tiff," he said to himself, strolling after her. He hoped only that she would not be rude to the Anquetils. Rudeness was a thing he could not tolerate, unless it sprang flaming from the furnace of some conviction,—Bretton's rudeness, for instance, always gained his sympathy, and Leonard Anquetil's gruffness merely amused him. The bad manners of ill-temper, however, he found displeasing and embarrassing.

He decided that he could trust Evelyn: she was too conventional to be rude.

When the Anquetils arrived, she was nowhere to be seen. He felt a little uneasy. Was she really packing, up-stairs? Had he really lost her? His mind was divided between pleasure at the Anquetils' arrival and anxiety as to the black cloud that had obscured Evelyn's heaven. He knew,—no one better,—how acutely she suffered from these storms of feeling; he knew too, doing her justice, that she usually tried to disguise her feelings from him, unless they overcame her beyond the point of prudence and wisdom. On this occasion they had overcome her; and on this occasion he was entirely to blame. She was right: he had known full well that he would destroy all her pleasure. He hated himself for his wanton unkindness; yet at the same time he was angry with her for her resentment. It was in no good mood that he went out to meet the Anquetils.

Their charming simplicity at once reversed his mood. They were frankly delighted to see him, and frankly delighted with their jaunt into the country. He felt instantly, as he always felt in their company, that no petty misunderstandings could possibly arise amongst them. Here was real friendship, both between Viola and Leonard, and between Viola, Leonard, and himself. They had brought their boy Paul with them, and Lesley their daughter; and they had brought a lobster too, bought on the way through Tonbridge, fearing that Mrs. Munday's catering might prove inadequate for so large an invasion. "Hermits like you, Miles, live for a week on a leaf of green salad, I know," said Viola, as she gave him the lobster wrapped up in a bit of newspaper.

"Not at all," he said, thinking that he might as well get the announcement over at once; "I am entertaining a party, which means that I live in luxury. Evelyn Jarrold is staying with me,—you remember, Viola, I brought her to dine with you."

"Oh, what fun," said Viola instantly, "I shall enjoy seeing her again. I don't think you were there thatt evening, Lesley? No, of course, you were in Paris.—Lesley insisted on going to the Sorbonne, you know, Miles, and

we were thankful to let her go, rather than to see her fly
off to Australia. She had to have some outlet for her
energies, and of the two the Sorbonne alarmed us less.—
My dear Miles, how lovely your castle is looking. You've
abolished all the nettles since last year. And as we drove
through your broad acres, Leonard remarked that you
had put up several new gates. You remember, last year
they were all broken down and off their hinges."

"One does these things little by little," said Miles,
smiling. He was grateful to her for skating so delicately
over the announcement of Evelyn's presence, and he was
grateful to Leonard for noticing his new gates. Evelyn
had not noticed them. "Lord!" he said, suddenly expressing a secret thought, "I wish I could afford to be a really
good landlord."

"You ought to hob-nob with my brother-in-law," said
Anquetil in his gruff way; he was always gruff, but never
disagreeable. "You're both of you old Tories at heart.
The only difference is, that Sebastian can afford to be an
old Tory, and a good landlord, and all the rest of it, and
you can't."

"Never mind," said Miles; "I do my best and I get a
lot of pleasure out of it. My new gates give me quite as
much satisfaction as all his model dairies give Sebastian.
But now come along," he said, "and forget your sneers at
landlords,—whom you confuse with capitalists, which
God knows they aren't,—come along and give the lobster
to Mrs. Munday, and then we may get some luncheon."

He took them down the garden path, happy and soothed
by their presence. They walked with him, stopping to
appreciate his flowers, chaffing him on his country habits.
Their appreciation was genuine, and so was their chaff.

All the time he was wondering when Evelyn would appear. Surely it was not possible that she should play him a trick by remaining in her room until they had gone, or, worse, by telephoning for a taxi to take her to the station. Knowing how violent she was, he could not be sure of her.— There she was, coming in her light frock through the gateway at the end of the path.

She behaved, of course, perfectly. Nobody but Miles could have detected the slight chill in her manner. Outwardly she struck exactly the right note, assuming neither the prerogative of a hostess nor the detachment of a stranger. So perfectly did she play her part that even Miles might have deluded himself into the belief that she welcomed the Anquetils as cordially as himself. Miles, however, knowing her so well, saw through her graciousness; his knowledge of her was like a foot stamping on a thin film of ice. He knew, moreover, that she was tempted to like the Anquetils in spite of herself. Thatt made it all the more difficult for her. It was so difficult to hate people whom one really liked! The situation was consequently rich with complications.

It was even richer than Miles knew, for he forgot that Evelyn had never seen the girl Lesley,—had never previously heard of her existence. From the first moment Evelyn regarded the girl Lesley with suspicion; nay, with terror. She made up her mind instantly that the daughter of the Anquetils was the ordained wife for Miles, and having made up her mind she sat down to luncheon with death in her heart. Miles, who had never given a thought to Lesley Anquetil, beyond noticing her as a particularly unschoolgirlish schoolgirl, was unaware of all this. He was aware only,—which was also true,—that Evelyn was divided between a longing to loathe the Anquetils and a strong inclination to like them. Who, indeed, could fail to like them, he thought? so friendly, so easy, so intelligent? His affection for them was warm, as he surveyed them sitting at his luncheon-table. He was glad that they should be there, and he wished only that Evelyn could freely share his pleasure. There were other things in life, as he had said, than lovers' quarrels. Lovers' quarrels bored him; he liked the flowers of love, but not its thorns. There were other things: friendships, interests, conversation. . . .

Lesley Anquetil was very quiet; she never spoke much. Miles, glancing at her, supposed idly that she must reflect almost exactly what her mother was at her age: calm, self-contained, and full of unspoken criticism. Only, Viola in her luxurious unbringing had had much to criticise; Lesley could have had very little. She had grown up in a rational and enlightened atmosphere. Yet she remained detached and critical. Well, thought Miles,—who was only six years older than Lesley,—it is right that the young should criticise. The criticism of the young is what keeps things on the move,—so thought Miles, young himself, but just old enough and wise enough to add that the older generation could dump a corrective and steadying weight into the scales. Miles, of course, being a man, was far in advance of Lesley. In spite of the Sorbonne, he had seen more of the world. In spite of the House of Commons, he had contrived to see more of the world. He knew all sorts of people,—the variety of his acquaintance had sometimes come as a shock to Evelyn. Lesley was necessarily limited, yet she preserved somewhere within herself the same sense of values as Viola, at the same age, must have imposed upon the standards of her ancestral home. In her quiet way, she would take nothing for granted,—not even the advanced views prevalent in her parents' house. She would think everything out for herself. But she had the good sense to keep quiet about it. Miles liked her; he liked her smooth brow, her reticence, the intelligence of the few remarks she made.

"You've grown up in the last year, Lesley," he said as they walked down to the lake after luncheon.

Evelyn and Viola were together; the boy Paul and his father were looking for moorhens' nests among the reeds. Miles wondered rather grimly how Evelyn and Viola were getting on. He wished that they might make friends. It would do Evelyn good for Viola to poke a little fun at her.

Viola, however, could not win Evelyn's confidence. She was polite, but formal. Viola, divining very well that Evelyn under her conventional exterior was a woman of passionate feeling, wondered whether she dared be bold and say outright some of the things in her mind, but decided that she had better be prudent. It was usually best to be prudent with women; they were secretive, suspicious, and apt to misunderstand. Her instinct told her that Evelyn Jarrold was a very feminine woman, in some ways quite unworthy of Miles, though in other ways singularly well suited to him. She was sorry for Evelyn Jarrold. She knew Miles well, and knew that he was not the man to deal with an exacting and passionate woman: he might be patient for a time, but in the long run he would revolt. Thatt kind of love was a tyranny, and Miles was not made to be its slave. She sympathised with Miles, yet she could not help being sorry for Evelyn Jarrold. Evelyn would end by having a bad time at Miles' hands; and though she would have brought her trouble on herself, she would not have been to blame,—except in so far as anyone is to blame for the frailties of his own nature.

She sighed, thinking how well Lesley could have managed Miles.

Later on, she confided some of her thoughts to Leonard.

"Thatt affair, Leonard, will end badly. I wish I could do something about it. I really feel worried, both for Miles' sake and Evelyn Jarrold's."

"The sooner he gets rid of Evelyn Jarrold the better," said Leonard who had no patience with very feminine women, however pretty.

"I agree, but I think you judge her too harshly. You think her simply empty-headed and vain. There's more in her than thatt. For instance, she's passionately in love with Miles."

"You can be passionately in love, and yet be empty-headed and vain."

"Of course you can, but I think she is capable of loving exceptionally deeply, and thatt softens me towards her. She loves in a way that will make her suffer horribly, and if she suffers horribly she might do anything desperate. I am really anxious, Leonard. Evelyn Jarrold, whom you think such a fribble, is the sort of woman who commits murder or suicide."

"My dear, what has happened to your imagination? She is merely the sort of woman who loves selfishly, sensually, and acquisitively. She has no respect for Miles as an individual; she is the sort of woman who wants a lover to be a slave."

"You're right about thatt, but I am right too. And,

what makes it more serious, is that Miles is the last person to allow himself to be made into a slave. You know, Miles is a hard man."

"Well, we shall see," said Leonard, who was nearer to agreeing with Viola than he wished to admit.

The next thing they heard was that Evelyn had broken with Miles. Viola heard it from Miles himself. He appeared unexpectedly one evening, and Viola, divining that he had something on his mind which he wanted to say and could not, asked him point-blank what was the matter. Then it came out: Evelyn had refused to see him for three weeks. He was very worried and unhappy, but also obstinate and angry.

"It was becoming intolerable, Viola; we quarrelled all the time. Nearly all the time. When we didn't quarrel it was perfect. I blame myself, of course; I wasn't amenable enough; she said I put other interests before her, and I daresay I sometimes did. I knew, you see, that if I wasn't firm she would absorb me entirely, and I could never stand thatt."

"What did you quarrel about mostly?"

"Oh, ridiculous things,—my work, my book, my engagements. . . ."

"Other women?"

"I never gave her cause to quarrel about any other women," said Miles after a pause.

"Still, you did quarrel?"

"Viola, you're very shrewd, aren't you? Well, yes, we did. Any women I saw or spoke to."

"She spied on you? Suspected your engagements?"

"Viola, please don't make me say things I don't want to say."

"I'm sorry, I oughtn't to have asked. Please believe that I'm not prejudiced against her. On the contrary, I'm very, very sorry for her, and I think I can understand both her point of view and yours. Would she consent to see me, do you think?"

"How can I tell? I haven't heard a word from her for three weeks. When I go to her flat, I'm told she's out. When I telephone, a servant answers and says Mrs. Jarrold is out. When I write she doesn't answer my letters. The boy must be home for his holidays by this time, too, but I haven't heard a word from him either. She must have forbidden him to write to me. I wonder what reason she gave him? She'll probably take him down to the country for his holidays, and then she'll be more than ever out of my reach. What on earth am I to do? I could waylay her on her doorstep, of course, but I'm damned if I'll do thatt."

"You want her back, Miles?"

"Good God, of course I do."

She wondered if he was being quite sincere, even to himself.

"You're quite, quite sure, Miles, that in the end you won't be happier without her than with her? Don't be angry with me. You see, I never thought it was a very happy affair. You didn't seem to understand each other very well. Besides, think of the future. You're a young man, a very young man." She paused.

"I want her back," said Miles obstinately, as she had foreseen. She thought she had said enough. She had annoyed him, thereby arousing his loyalty, but thatt would not prevent her words from dropping fertile seeds. She was sorry for the woman, but her first interest must be for Miles.

"Well, if you think it will do any good, I will go and see her."

"You're an angel, Viola. I knew you would offer to do thatt, and honestly I can think of no one but yourself. Her own friends are all such ninnies, and besides one can't trust most women. What worries me, is that she must be making herself unhappy. She does, you know. Perhaps you won't believe me, but she really has an unhappy nature."

"I believe you entirely."

She spoke so gravely that he gave her a look. She saw that he was deeply troubled.

"Don't worry too much, Miles; I'll see what I can do."

They sat silent for a time, the same thought in the minds of both.

"Miles," she said then, "will you tell me something? Has she ever wanted to marry you? or perhaps I should say, have you ever wanted to marry her?"

"She won't," he replied.

"Thatt's to her credit."

"Yes, thatt's to her credit. There's a lot to her credit," he said with a sigh.

Presently he got up and went away. Viola pitied him as she let him out into the warm and empty street, he looked so perplexed and forlorn.

"Come and see me whenever you like, my dear. In the meantime I'll let you know the result of my interview."

Turning back into the house she took up the telephone

and asked for Evelyn's number. As Miles had said, a servant answered it.

"Could I speak to Mrs. Jarrold, please?"

"What name?"

She hesitated. Should she lay a trap for Evelyn? No; it would be unfair.

"Lady Viola Anquetil."

"Now she'll refuse to speak to me," she thought, wondering whether her scruples had perhaps been foolish, but then to her surprise she heard Evelyn's voice.

"Is thatt you, Mrs. Jarrold? Viola Anquetil,—yes. We haven't seen you for such a long time, could I persuade you to come and dine with us? We should be quite alone. Any night, this week or next."

Thatt would show. If Evelyn meant to avoid her, she would make some excuse, and then more direct methods must be tried.

Evelyn made the excuse; she said she was going out of London. Her regrets were civil, but her voice was icy. "This," thought Viola, "is a very unhappy woman," and the relief she had involuntarily experienced on hearing that Miles' release had entered on its first stage turned to pure anxiety on behalf of the unseen and lonely offender. When matters became serious, discretion became a farce; she threw discretion aside.

"Listen: asking you to dinner was a pretext. I want very particularly to see you. If you are really going out of London tomorrow as you say, may I see you this evening? I would come to your flat now, at once."

"I'm so dreadfully sorry, Lady Viola, I'm just going out to dinner and I'm late already. I do so wish I could wait . . . how awful London is, isn't it? . . . never a moment to oneself . . . but perhaps I may let you know when I come back from Newlands? I have to go down there with Dan tomorrow, but when I come back I'd love to see you. . . . I don't quite know when thatt will be . . . some time towards the end of September, I expect . . . so dreadfully sorry. . . . I'm afraid I must go now . . . do forgive me. . . ." The voice trailed off, and Viola could hear the receiver being put down.

"Poor Miles!" she thought; and then she thought, "Poor Evelyn!" and then she thought, "What am I to do next?"

When Leonard came in, five minutes later, she went up to him and took his hand. They were an undemonstrative couple, as a rule, and he wondered what had happened to move her.

"Leonard, our relationship has never been complicated, has it?"

"I should have left you long ago, if it had," he replied, taking his pipe out of his mouth and then putting it back again.

Miles came frequently to their house; he turned to them in his distress. Summer was at its height, and officially he was supposed to be living at his castle, but his restlessness brought him constantly up to London. The Anquetils were oddly perverse people: they liked remaining in London through July and August, when most people who could afford it went to the country, to the sea, or abroad. Miles teased them, saying that they were born Cockneys; but even as he teased them he remembered Viola's upbringing at Chevron and Leonard's adventurous youth, both so different from the life they led now, both so ludi-

crously different from a Cockney birth. Their house was
the meeting-place of young men like Bretton and Allen;
a stream flowed through it, a stream of activity, of enter-
prise, of people engaged in some idea or other, a young
painter, a young politician, or whatever it might be.
Miles came there now, feeling that he came under false
pretences. Ostensibly he appeared as the young politician,
but really he came as an unhappy young man seeking
Viola's support. At dinner, and after, he might talk with
his usual brilliance; but all the while he knew that Viola
observed him, guessing that his heart yearned after his
castle and the summer country and after a peaceful life
with Evelyn who was lost to him and whose state of mind
he could not gauge. He and Viola seldom talked privately
together. She was not one to insist on the almost accidental
privilege of intimacy. But her presence was encouraging
to him; reassuring. Her standards were the standards by
which he could measure everything: not only his disasters
of the heart, but also his more permanent ideals. He found
comparative peace in her house; elsewhere, he was tormented by his heart, his senses, and his conscience.

Evelyn had vanished out of his life. Her disappearance
had been so complete and so sudden, that he could not
yet take it in. It was as though he had had a limb lopped
off,—a right hand that he had been accustomed to use,
and must now do without. His feelings were exceedingly
complex. Sometimes he longed for her so intolerably that
he had to restrain himself from rushing off to Newlands.
At other times he realised with shame that his freedom
gave him a certain sense of relief. His innate honesty
alone compelled him to make this admission to himself.
He hated it, but he faced it. It was a relief, definitely, not

to be rung up by Evelyn at all hours of the day, not to be questioned as to his appointments,—for her earlier good resolutions had broken down lamentably of late and she no longer tried to disguise her querulous curiosity,—not to be criticised and discouraged and rebuked, not to be reproached for some fancied neglect. Then again his mood would turn to sorrow as he remembered how exquisite she had been in the early days; how unhesitatingly she had surrendered herself, after the ball at Chevron House, when he came to her flat and told her that he loved her; how light-hearted and happy, in spite of her occasional qualms; how she had thought of nothing but pleasing him, making herself lovely for his delight, coming into his arms when he arrived, greeting him with such warmth and tenderness and passion that his rapture was wholly compounded of joy and gratitude, ecstasy and security. He could not endure to recollect those days, but, calling Caesar to follow him, would stride off across the fields in the hope of tiring himself out so that he might sleep through the night and not dream,—not dream! But the summer fields gave him an added anguish, for they reminded him of the day when she had come down in July and had asked him to dawdle as they drove through the lanes, and had said that she loved him more with the passing of the months. They had walked under the brick walls in the evening, crushing a sprig of southernwood between their fingers, and once, when unthinkingly he broke off a grey-green tip and its bitter smell reached him, he flung it from him and deliberately struck his knuckles against the rough brick as a corrective to his pain.

Still, he could not quite understand why he had let her go so easily. They had parted in anger, after a terrible scene; he had made no effort to stop her then, but had said the cruellest things he could think of,—their cruelty towards one another had indeed been well matched. All the day, after she had gone, he had raged; next morning only, when he came across her forgotten handkerchief, small and scented, had he begun to feel remorseful. Perhaps, even in anger, he should not have said the things he had said. He should not have told her that she complicated and hampered his life. He should not have taunted her with her limited outlook, her vanity, her lack of true companionship. He should not have told her that her love for him was destructive, not creative. (Thank God he had not added that perhaps the difference of generation accounted for many of their misunderstandings. It had come into his mind, as he searched round for things to wound her; but, angry as he was and violent as was his temper when he lost it, he had at least foreborne from saying thatt.) Yes, it had been a terrible scene, ugly, shocking, and quite naturally he had let her go; had even persuaded himself that he was thankful to be rid of her. He had driven her to the station at a speed reckless enough to terrify her; she had not said a word, but he saw how white she was when they arrived at the station. He had seen that her hand was shaking as she bought her ticket; still he had remained hard. He hated her; they hated each other. But with the softening that came to him next day, he began to suppose that even such terrible scenes as this could be forgotten; he began to suppose that a reconciliation would take place, as it had always taken place before, and stitting down at his table with her handkerchief in his pocket he had written to her, asking that his words might be wiped out and that they might make a fresh start on a better basis of understanding. He had purposely made the letter rather cold and sensible. When no reply came, for the first time he became seriously anxious. Up till then, he had felt no more than a little uneasy. They had had so many rows, and they had always blown over! She had always been so generously penitent, —even though within twenty-four hours the rows might begin again. Surely this time also she would return to him? and perhaps the quarrel might even be proved to have cleared the air?

Then as she remained silent, he took other steps. He wrote again; he telephoned. His temper rose after repeated rebuffs; he decided that if she wanted to sulk, he would let her sulk. And so, almost before he realised it, many days went by, and the gulf between them widened until it began to seem improbable that it would ever close up.

Why, then, had he not taken some really drastic measure? This was what, looking back, he could not explain to himself. Why had he not forced himself into her presence? A truly desperate lover would have found some means. Was it possible that, in spite of his pain and his remorse and his regrets, he was not a truly desperate lover?

He was unhappy enough to roam restlessly up to London; unhappy enough to confide in Viola; but somehow the ultimate urge to take violent action was lacking. It was as though something held him back. And whenever he was with the Anquetils he came near to admitting what thatt something was: Evelyn had never been meant for him.

In this way the Anquetils were Evelyn's worst enemies. The contrast was too great. Viola herself was well aware of what was happening. She wondered where her duty lay.

"Miles," she said, "have you still heard nothing from Evelyn?"

"Not a word, not a sign."

"How long is it now?"

"Two months, nearly."

"It looks as though she meant it to be final. Why don't you do something, Miles? I confess, I am puzzled by the way you have allowed things to slip."

"What more can I do?" he said with the irritability of an unquiet conscience. "I've written, I've telephoned, I've tried to see her; I've even asked you to see her. She won't have anything to do with either you or me. I can do nothing more."

"Lesley thinks you ought to force her to see you."

"Lesley? What does she know about it?"

"Don't be an ostrich, Miles; everybody knows about it. People talk, you know."

"The devil they do. What does Lesley say, then?"

"She says you have no right to let anyone make themselves as wretched as Evelyn must be making herself."

"Look here, Viola, why are you taking Evelyn's part suddenly? Even though you may deny it, and even though you never said so in so many words to me, you know you were relieved on the whole when we quarrelled."

"I don't deny it. I was relieved. I always thought her unsuited to you. But thatt doesn't prevent me from listening to Lesley when she comes to me very solemnly and says you ought not to leave Evelyn quite alone to bear the consequences of what, after all, was a very heroic action."

Miles stared at her, amazed.

"An heroic action?"

"Oh, Miles, don't be so stupid! Really I have no patience with men sometimes. Don't you see that Evelyn left you entirely because she thought she was destroying you?"

"She left me for my good, I suppose?" said Miles bitterly.

"You may be sarcastic, but thatt is what it amounts to. I've had time to think it over, and I see the whole thing quite clearly. So does Lesley."

"Lesley must be possessed of powers of divination. Or is it what you call feminine intuition?"

"I don't mind how disagreeable you are. Have I at any rate made you see the situation in a new light?"

"You've appalled me," said Miles. "I never thought," he added naïvely, "that Evelyn was capable of anything like thatt. Now I believe that you must be right. Oh, God, I told her something of the sort! I said she was spoiling my life. I said so during thatt last quarrel we had, the day she left me. I'll go to her at once, Viola; I'll go down to Newlands. Bless you for having opened my eyes. Now if she comes back to me," he said with a smile, "you'll only have yourself to thank," but already he was on his feet and his face was irradiated with happiness and expectancy.

"He loves her still," thought Viola, and she wondered whether her sympathy for Evelyn had not led her into a great foolishness. "One moment, Miles," she said, detaining him; "you jump to the conclusion that I want you to get her back. I don't mean that you should try to do thatt. Only make her believe that you understand her motives; that you appreciate them. I think, if I have any knowledge of your Evelyn, that you'll find she will stick to her decision. Well, don't make it too hard for her. If you will use your reason for a minute, instead of rushing off in this hot-headed way, you will see that you are both really much better apart. Look forward, Miles. You know the quarrels would surely begin again. Don't, don't try to get her back! If you try hard enough, you may succeed, when she actually sees you. You can be very eloquent when you choose, and you may convince her. Don't try. Try only to remove all the bitterness and the soreness, and let her feel that what she has done hasn't been done in vain."

She spoke very urgently, saying exactly what she thought, for the energy of his response had alarmed her. She should have remembered how impetuous he was, and she foresaw what might happen if they came face to face.

"Couldn't you write, instead of going to see her?" she suggested.

"Too late, Viola! you've done the mischief now." He was as gay and excited as a schoolboy. "Bless you, and bless Lesley. May we both come to dinner with you one day next week? And may we bring Dan? He must have left Eton at the end of the summer half. You'd like Dan,— and who knows? he might fall in love with Lesley. He's a very good match, you know."

"You won't listen to me, then?"

"No, darling Viola, I won't listen to you. I'll kiss your hand instead,—*ich küsse Ihre Hand, madame*. And I'll ring you up tomorrow morning."

He had never been to Newlands before, but he reached it faster than William Jarrold's Rolls-Royce had ever reached it, only to be told by Paterson that Mrs. Jarrold had left England thatt morning with Lord Orlestone. They had gone on a motoring trip to Spain; had left no address; and would be away for about a month.

"So you see, there's nothing to be done," he concluded despondently to Lesley.

It astonished him to find that he had talked to Lesley. He could not think how it had come about. It was not his habit to scatter his confidences broadcast to all and sundry. He had, however, gone to see Viola, and, finding her out, sat down to wait for her in such obvious dejection that Lesley finally asked him what was the matter. The conventional denial rose to his lips, but he had no use for such a farce. So he looked at her and said, "I think you know."

Thus, he remembered, had it come about. He had found himself talking quite naturally and simply to Lesley. She was easy to talk to, because she just listened and nodded and said something from time to time,—not something sympathetic,—he was in no mood for sympathy,—but something firm and, usually, severe. He accepted her severity; it stung him, but it braced him. It was, indeed, a relief for him to be subjected to criticism by a person he scarcely knew, but who through a chance of circumstances possessed a knowledge of his most intimate affairs, and whose judgment remained entirely without bias. Lesley was neither on his side, nor on Evelyn's. To her, they were just protagonists, like people in a play. If she judged him severely, it was because he deserved a severe judgment. She did not spare him, and he respected her for her candour.

Only afterwards did it strike him as rather out-of-the-way, this discussion of his mistress with a girl of nineteen. He grinned. "How horrified the Jarrolds would be!" he thought.

It was difficult to regard Lesley as a girl of nineteen. She had nothing of the fabled innocence of adolescence. It seemed that she had already made her mind up on such problems of life as are fundamental and yet elementary.

Miles thought again how much she must resemble her mother when her mother had been nineteen, both of them remaining faithful to their own standard of values. Viola in the luxurious surroundings of Chevron. Lesley in the austere yet stimulating atmosphere of her parents' house. He liked Lesley very much indeed, partly because he was so fond of Viola and because it amused him to fancy that he was talking to the Viola of twenty-odd years ago, but also for her own sake. When he had finished pouring out his rage, disappointment, and frustration, emptying himself of these things until there was no more emotion of any sort left in him, he suggested to Lesley that they should spend the rest of the evening together. A surprising change came over her then. She ceased to be the severe young mentor, and became merely the play-fellow ready for an evening's fun. He had been inclined to think her if anything a trifle solemn; the revelation came to him as a welcome and amusing surprise. He liked people who could change their mood more rapidly than they could change their clothes; he was like thatt, himself. So they went out together. They did not mention Evelyn again thatt evening, but simply enjoyed themselves according to the ideas of people of their age. If recollection stabbed Miles every now and then when the band played some tune he had been accustomed to dance to with Evelyn, he consoled himself rather angrily by thinking that she was now happy without him, drinking coffee with Dan—and with whom else?—on some warm, flat roof overlooking Seville. Their explanations could be deferred.

He went out again with Lesley. They fell into the habit of going out together. He would arrive at the Anquetils' house and would ask Viola quite naturally for the loan of Lesley, much as he might have asked for the loan of a handkerchief. There were no complications of emotional feelings; simply a comfortable companionship. Viola, a wise but prophetic woman, knew this and contemplated the possible results. Miles and Lesley? well, she knew Miles' faults, as she knew Lesley's faults, and came to the conclusion that they might make a good mixture. There would be the right degree of antagonism and understanding. Viola was no believer in smug matrimony; she believed in sparks of disagreement struck every now and then, with a basis of common concord.

She foresaw, too, that Miles would soon begin to draw comparisons between Lesley and Evelyn. They would not be quite fair comparisons; in fact, they would not be fair at all, in one sense, and yet in another sense they would be sound enough. He would contrast their behaviour, and in such measure as he found Lesley easy-going he would find Evelyn proportionately difficult and tiresome. She observed, for instance, that he had no hesitation in telephoning at the last minute to cancel an engagement with Lesley, confident that she would understand and that there would be no fuss. Viola could well imagine the fuss there would be if he treated Evelyn in the same way,—as he probably often had. (It was part of Miles' make-up to be rather insolently casual about such things; he could no more help it than he could help the colour of his hair; but Viola could imagine the effect on a woman violently in love.) Lesley made no fuss, partly because she was casual herself and wholly free from feminine vanity, partly because she was not in love with Miles. Thatt made all the difference. It was easy not to make a fuss when one did not mind very much one way or the other; difficult to refrain from making a fuss when one minded vitally. Still, even after making thatt allowance, a fundamental difference remained between Lesley and Evelyn. Viola conceded it, and knew that Miles sooner or later would begin to notice.

Then, in a purely maternal way, which surprised and interested her by its novelty, she began to wonder what Lesley would be like, in love.

PART IV

OBITUARY NOTICE OF EVELYN JARROLD

AUTUMNAL Spain was hot and parched in the north, hot and scented in the south. Dan and Evelyn lingered at ·Granada, for Granada pleased them, and there was no reason why they should hasten to one place rather than remain content in another. Neither of them had any ties or obligations: Dan had left Eton, and Evelyn had left Miles. ·They were both therefore quite free to follow their inclinations in each other's company, with this difference,—and it was an important one,—that Dan would presently resume his life, going to spend six months with a French family before he went up to Oxford, and that Evelyn felt her life to be at an end. There was no sense or meaning in a life without Miles. Dan, in leaving Eton, had merely left something behind him which would lead on in natural consequence to other things; Evelyn, in leaving Miles, had cut life short. She looked forward to nothing. She desired nothing,—nothing could replace Miles, and indeed a strange and unexpected loyalty (or was it sentimentality?) prevented her from wishing anything to replace him. She felt only, that she would wish to consecrate the rest of her life to the memory of her few months' happiness, though, at the same time, she wished nothing more ardently than that she might forget him. Whichever wish should find its fulfilment, her life was

ended and empty. Miles had filled her life richly; she realised now that he had been like the sun and the breeze and
the thunder-storm and the rainbow and all the colours of
the flowers in his garden; she reproached herself with not
having truly appreciated him while she possessed him.
She saw him now, in retrospect, as a person who could
give, and who gave, so much. Cruel at times, even deliberately cruel, at other times he gave so generously out
of the riches of his nature that it made up for all the
cruelty and harshness of his more irritable moments.
She thought, at times, humbly, that she had been fortunate
to know Miles as intimately as she had known him. For
indeed, in her own poor judgment, she estimated him as
a remarkable young man; and stray observations from
other people confirmed her estimate. This induced an
absurd pride in her. She knew, herself, that it was absurd.
It was not for her intellectual companionship that Miles
had chosen her; far from it! She had never been his companion, but only his mistress, and any effect she had ever
had on his work was to interfere with it: thus did she now
abase herself in her own mind. Well, it was over; Miles
should never be worried or hampered by her again.

She bore him no grudge, only loved him more deeply
than before. The pain of loving him was so great that at
moments she longed to die and be finished with it, but
it was a different pain from the miserable pain of their
recurrent quarrels and of her incessant jealousies; thatt
had been sordid, degrading; this had a certain nobility,
like fire. It seared, but it purified.

She had hoped to escape it in some degree by leaving
England and dashing off to Spain. Idle hope! she learnt
only the bitter experience that one's inward self goes

with one, take the body where one will. She remained the same woman, leaning over the parapet of the Generalife, looking out over the *vega* of Granada, as leaning over the balustrade at Newlands looking out over the trim paddocks of Surrey. Personality could not be shed, and the same thoughts, the same memories, accompanied her through the changing landscape. She might writhe, but she could not escape.

At least she was no longer pursued by Miles' letters; she no longer started and turned faint at the ring of a telephone or a door-bell. Thatt, in itself, was a relief; thatt, and the knowledge that she could not possibly run into Miles at a street-corner or see him appear suddenly at Newlands, so familiar, so dear, with his shining head, slim body, and beautiful hands. How wise she had been to seek this relief by simply leaving England! Flight? yes, it was a flight, but it would give her a respite, it would give her time to gather her forces. She would not think of the day when she must go back to England, and court again the risk of colliding with Miles at a street-corner.

But for Dan she would have gone off on a long journey. She could not leave the boy, however,—for towards him, at least, her love had never been selfish, and moreover she had learnt the lesson now that selfish love brings its own worst reward. She recognised the difference in herself; one does not pass through such an experience as she had undergone without emerging altered on the other side. Nor would she appeal to Dan to let her go; it would not be fair. He had developed astonishingly, ceasing suddenly to be a child; he no longer seemed tentative and perplexed, but firm and decided. He had at last re: lised himself as master of Newlands and the Orlestone works. Newlands, indeed, with its parks and paddocks, counted for nothing in his estimation; Orlestone with its slums and collieries counted a great deal. Dan now held very definite opinions. Orlestone made him rich, but he had no intention of remaining rich at the expense of Orlestone. He had no desire for personal riches. On the other hand, he had a great desire for the Orlestone miners to benefit out of his profits. He had discovered that his income exceeded his needs, to an extent that seemed shocking and excessive to his democratic views; he wanted neither grouse-moors nor yachts; he wanted only to establish a fair understanding between his colliers and himself. What else could he do, he said, worried by the injustice of the whole system? what could he do, short of treating his people as decently as possible? He would be damned sooner than grind them down to a minimum wage; he would pay them the maximum and let Newlands grow grass on its gravel drives if need be. Evelyn listened, and, in her new-found wisdom, approved. Then Dan, encouraged by her approval, went on. He would make the Orlestone works into a model community. He would institute special schools, scholarships, a theatre, a picture gallery, a racquet-court, and a swimming bath. . . . Schemes bubbled in his head, and he poured them all out to his mother looking towards the sunset over the *vega* of Granada. He would go to France for a bit, if it pleased her, but he would come over to England often, for the week-end, to see how things were getting on. She must promise to take his part against Uncle Geoffrey, who would be certain to disagree with all his ideas. Uncle Evan, thank goodness, had been left without any voice in the matter, but Uncle Geoffrey would be a difficulty.

Dan was tactful enough not to say, "If only I had Miles to help me!"

The necessity of mentioning Miles to Dan had been one of Evelyn's incidental problems. She had no idea what Dan thought of their relationship; she knew only that he would begin to clamour for Miles directly he returned from school. She dreaded the moment, and, when it came, tried partially to shirk it.

"And what about Miles, Mummy? Where is he? When are we going to see him? He hasn't answered my last two letters, which is very unlike him. I thought perhaps he had gone abroad? I didn't worry, because I was sure you would know."

"No, he hasn't gone abroad." Now that she must speak, she hesitated, with a feeling almost of suffocation.

"Well, then? Is anything wrong? Is he ill?"

"No, he isn't ill. At least, I don't think so. Dan, I may as well tell you: I've quarrelled with Miles. We shan't be seeing him again, ever."

"Quarrelled? seriously? for good? Oh, Mummy, no! Not with Miles? But why? what about?"

"I can't tell you thatt, Dan; you mustn't ask. I'm very sorry,—for you, I mean, because I know how much you will miss him. You must just believe that I couldn't help it; just take my word for it; just take it on trust. Perhaps some day you can be friends with him again, but for the moment I think it's better that you shouldn't try to see him. And you must understand that I can never see him; even if you and he are friends later on. I don't want to prevent your friendship, but you must never try to reconcile Miles and me; you must never bring him here: all thatt is quite finished,—done with."

She had half intended to tell him the whole truth, but could not force herself to it; it cost her enough to say what she had already said. Besides, Dan might be shocked; horrified. Her ideas on some subjects were too old-fashioned and conventional, when it came to the point, to admit the possibility of telling a boy that his mother had a lover.

"But surely," said Dan, greatly distressed, "people often quarrel when they are in love and then they make it up again? Is there *no* hope, Mummy? Can't you possibly reconsider it? Poor Miles! he must be so unhappy. And so must you."

"Dan, what are you saying?"

"Well, Mummy, you didn't suppose that I didn't know?"

"You knew?"

"Of course. Not quite at first,—not the first time we went to the castle, perhaps, or then only subconsciously, —but soon afterwards."

"How did you know? who told you?"

"Nobody told me. I guessed. I put two and two together. It was obvious, surely? I couldn't help noticing the excuses that you both made to get me out of the way. I couldn't help noticing the disguised jokes you had together. At first I knew only that you were alluding to something I couldn't understand, and I thought it was something grown-up that a person of my age couldn't understand anyway; you see, at my age one is rather humble and rather easily snubbed. Then I realised that your jokes were something quite special to yourselves; private jokes; and thatt made me think. They were recurrent jokes,— little phrases that made you both laugh in a secret way

every time you uttered them. You laughed; and then you
looked at each other; and then you both looked at me to
see if I had noticed; and you thought I hadn't; but I had.
—I'm sorry, now, if I was so obtuse at first. I must have
been a bore. But then, you see, I didn't know. I was more
tactful later on, surely? Or wasn't I? I tried to be. I meant
to be. Yes, of course I knew. I wasn't surprised; I mean,
I could understand anybody falling in love with Miles.
Or with you. He was so terribly attractive,—I don't quite
know why I say 'was,' as though he were dead. He isn't
dead; he's alive. Or isn't he? Mummy, you aren't trying
to break to me that Miles is dead? No, he can't be; I should
have seen it in the papers. Mummy, please?"

"No, Dan, no: he isn't dead; we've only quarrelled,
thatt's all; I'm telling you the truth."

"Yes, Mummy, I'm sure you are. You always told me
the truth; you told me the truth when you said that my
father was like Uncle Geoffrey. Thatt was a shock; but
you were quite right to tell me, when I asked you.—But
about Miles, now. I mind too much to leave it alone. I
can't bear to think that Miles has gone out of our lives,
yours and mine, for ever. He was so valuable to both of
us, in different ways! Are you sure, Mummy, that you
haven't made a horrible mistake?"

"Oh, Dan, don't torture me,—yes, I'm sure, I'm sure."

"Well, if you're so sure, Mummy, I expect you're right.
I don't know about these things.—But what was it, anyhow, that went wrong? If you were thinking of me, you
know I would have adored Miles as a stepfather. No fairy-
story jokes about Miles as a stepfather! and fairy-story
jokes are about stepmothers anyway, not about step-
fathers,—I wonder why? Why didn't you marry Miles,

Mummy? You were both free to marry, and I would have been delighted,—so why not? Why not, even now? Look here, is it too late? I'm sure he wanted to marry you. . . . Can't we send him a telegram? Look here, I'll send it myself; I'll say 'Please come quickly and marry my mother.' Will thatt do? And then everything will be all right, and we can all three be happy together for ever after. Wouldn't thatt make it all right? And then Miles could help me about Orlestone. He would be in a position of authority against Uncle Geoffrey. Uncle Geoffrey would be frightened of Miles; he'd be over-awed, especially if Miles were my stepfather. And then I could carry out all my schemes and everyone would be happy except Uncle Geoffrey, who doesn't matter. You would be happy, Mummy, and so would Miles, and so would I. Look here, can't I make it all right just by sending a telegram? It seems so simple. Quarrels are so silly, such a waste of time, between people who really love each other. I'm sure they are; it's as though you and I were to quarrel. Let me send thatt telegram to Miles! Damn the man, I've forgotten his telephone number at his castle, and he forbids the exchange to give it."

"No, Dan, leave things as they are; don't send any telegrams; I know that you mean it all for the best, but there comes a point where one must judge things for oneself and nobody can help.—I would rather not talk any more about it just now, please, Dan. Let us talk about your holiday plans instead."

Dan had given her a look then, and she had wondered how much he exactly knew. His matter-of-fact acceptance of her relationship with Miles had staggered her; then this childishly simple solution of the problem had staggered her afresh. Had he meant it seriously? Had he been joking? Did he really believe that all love-affairs ended in marriage? His realisation of their relationship had been so surprising; his urgent little speech no less surprising in contrast. At one moment he seemed so calmly adult; at another moment, so naïf and direct.

She was glad that he knew; knew, and did not mind.

They referred no more to Miles. Evelyn noticed how Dan would give a quick turn to his sentence whenever the forbidden name threatened to arise. By this she knew that he gauged the pain of her feelings, and when she suggested to him that they should go abroad together there was no necessity for her to explain her desire to escape: he was aware of it already.

They could not remain abroad for ever. She must screw up her courage to return. How she dreaded the winter, with its cycle of dates that would all be anniversaries! There would be the date when she had first seen Miles at Park Lane; the date of the Chevron House ball; the date, —next day,—when he had come to her flat to say that he loved her. What a state of mind she had been in during those twenty-four hours, between the ball and his arrival! for she had recognised well enough the catastrophe which had overtaken her. Had it overtaken him too, she had wondered, pacing her room in an anguish of uncertainty, anxiety, apprehension, and indecision? If it had,—and she had little doubt of it, remembering his ardent eyes and his manner that suggested his wish to speak, but for an effort of restraint,—if it had, what should she do? Virtuous and self-disciplined, she wondered if she could resist temptation. Then he had suddenly telephoned and asked to see her; "I must see you today if possible," he had said, and all her indecision had vanished like a dream. She could only sit then and await his coming.

Now she must live through all those dates again, and through the ensuing months with their mixture of retrospective ecstasy, dissatisfaction, and misery. She supposed wearily that she would survive it. If only Miles would leave her alone, would not try to weaken her, then she might get through. She *must* get through. Some day he would be grateful to her. Meanwhile the pain that she must suffer was her own affair.

It was raining in England when they landed at Dover. It was raining in London,—long, wet streets, dreary and deserted under the watery shine of the lamps. But it was warm in the flat, and Privett, who had disapproved strongly of Spain, for once looked pleased as she unpacked Evelyn's things and rearranged her bedroom as it had always been. There were piles and piles of letters, however; Evelyn eyed them with a shrinking heart: would she come across thatt familiar writing? She would not look through them until after dinner.

Then turning away she went idly to smell the great white lilies standing on the piano, supposing that they had been sent up from Newlands, but tied on to them she found a card: From M. There was a branch of southernwood amongst them. So he had found out when she was coming back! He had no intention of leaving her alone. "Oh God," she murmured in an access of despair, feeling that she had no strength for this long and torturing struggle.

It had begun already, ten minutes after she had entered the house. Fortunately Dan was out of the room, or she must have betrayed her weakness and lassitude at thatt moment. She must pull herself together before he came back. Her life, henceforth, would consist of the frightful loneliness of pulling herself together always and concealing her secret thoughts from other people.

Mason came in, and found her with her hand still on the lilies. She had never liked Mason: he was respectful but furtive.

"I forgot to tell you, madam: Mr. Vane-Merrick brought those."

"Thank you, Mason; I found the card."

"He brought them this morning, madam. Mr. Vane-Merrick telephoned several times, madam, to know when you would be back. He telephoned again yesterday evening."

"Thank you, Mason."

"I don't know whether I did right in telling him, madam; I had had no instructions to the contrary."

"Quite right, Mason."

"Lady Viola Anquetil also telephoned, madam; she was anxious that you and his lordship should go to dinner. The message was, would you ring her ladyship up. I have the number written down."

"Thank you, Mason; please put the number on my writing-table and I'll ring up tomorrow."

"Mrs. Geoffrey Jarrold also rang up, madam. There was no message; only to ask when you would be back, and whether you and his lordship would be staying here or going to Newlands. I replied that I was unable to inform her."

"Thank you, Mason; if Mrs. Jarrold or Mr. Vane-Merrick should telephone again, please say that I am going down to Newlands with his lordship early tomorrow morning. In fact, if anybody telephones, you had better say that I am out. I have a good deal to do before going to Newlands."

"Very good, madam."

Mason withdrew. No other word could express his removal of himself from the room. Evelyn hated him; she was sure that he knew everything, from beginning to end. Privett probably knew too, but she minded Privett less,—good, staunch, disagreeable old Privett, sour as a lemon and solid as a turnip. It was Mason's spying on her that she hated.

She detached Miles' card from the lilies with meticulous care and threw it into the fire. She watched the brief message shrivel; the "From M." blacken and go up in a smoky twist.

Privett came in, carrying Evelyn's attaché-case to set down beside the writing-table.

"Privett, could you put those flowers outside, do you think? They smell too strong in here, they give me a headache."

"In the bathroom shall I put them?" said Privett regarding the heavy vase with disfavour.

"No, put them in the passage. Take them into your own room if you like; I don't want them."

Would Mason tell Privett that they had come from Mr. Vane-Merrick? She must risk thatt. Anything to get them out of her sight.

Privett took them away, and came back with the branch of southernwood.

"I know you always liked thatt stuff, to burn," she said gruffly, giving it to Evelyn.

Evelyn threw it on to the fire. It flared aromatically, and its scent filled the room.

Dan came in, washed and clean.

"Hullo, what a good smell."

"Dan, tell Mason we'll have dinner, will you? Tell him to hurry—tell him we're hungry. Tell him we'll have some champagne."

She could bear no more. The smell of the southernwood was the last straw.

The champagne did her good; it strengthened her. She had never been accustomed to drink much wine, and two glasses affected her instantly. She remembered poor Evan's words; he never felt alive, he had said, unless he had something in him. With a grim sense of humour, induced by the champagne, she reflected that she must not take to drink as a remedy for a broken heart; it would really be too trite, too well-precedented. Nevertheless, she felt better; Miles seemed a long way off; detached; her anxieties decreased; she began even to think with amusement of how easily she would greet him, were he to be ushered in suddenly by Mason. And, getting up, she said to Dan, "Come on, Dan; let's dance."

They went into the sitting-room and turned on the wireless. The sitting-room was not a good room to dance in; it had a thick pile carpet and far too much furniture. But it amused Evelyn, this evening, to dance under difficulties and to steer her way among the many obstacles of chairs and tables. It amused Dan too, for he also had had some champagne; just enough, not too much. He, like his mother, was an instinctive and beautiful dancer. They both had enough recklessness and rhythm in their blood.

They had often danced together before, but the same
current had never run in quite the same way between
them. Dan was excited, without knowing exactly why; he
supposed that it must be the champagne and the strange-
ness of finding himself back in the flat after the distant
loveliness of Spain and the long motor-run home, with
their stops for the night in little Spanish and French
towns, sitting out on the pavement drinking *sirop* or ver-
mouth in the evening, while the local population passed
up and down wearing un-English boots, and stiff black
clothes, and he and his mother made silly jokes and were
happy together, and warm, and care-free.

Care-free? Had she really been care-free, even for a
moment? He remembered then with a pang of remorse
the sorrow that must have accompanied her all the time
like a shadow cast by the sun. She had concealed it from
him,—she had been unselfish enough to conceal it. She
had never referred again, even obliquely, to Miles. Yet
she must have been thinking of him all the time. Evelyn
felt Dan's hold on her tighten as they danced. She wondered why, but responded by giving herself even more
softly into his arms. And he, for his part, felt her yield;
and felt the softness of her woman's body in her silken
clothes; and knew how much Miles must have loved her,
and how much she must have loved Miles.

At half-past eleven the telephone-bell rang.

"Answer it, Dan. Mason must have gone to bed.—
Dan! If it's Miles, say I've gone to bed."

"All right, Mummy."

He took up the receiver; said "Hullo!"; and listened.

"No, Mummy, it isn't Miles; it's Uncle Evan." He had covered the mouthpiece with his hand.

"What does he want?"

"He wants to come round."

"All right, tell him to come round."

"But, Mummy, aren't you tired?"

"No, tell him to come round."

"Uncle Evan, Mummy says yes, do please come."

"And now, Dan, you go to bed. You must be tired."

"But so must you."

"No, I'm not. And anyway it wouldn't matter if I were. You go to bed, Dan. Good night, my sweet; sleep well."

"Can't I have another glass of champagne, Mummy? before I go?"

"No, you can't. Go to bed, darling; it's late."

"Good night then, Mummy; sleep well."

"Sleep well, my sweet."

Evan came; she opened the door to him. He was not very drunk; only just drunk enough to welcome the champagne she offered him. He had had just thatt amount of drink to make him want a little more.

"By Jove, Evelyn, you look lovelier than ever."

"Do I, Evan?"

"Yes, by Jove you do. How do you manage it, after a long journey in the train?—oh no, I forgot,—you went by motor, didn't you?"

"Yes, we went by motor."

"You and Dan?"

"Yes, I and Dan."

"Oh yeah? Tell me another, Evelyn. You and Dan,—going off to Spain alone together? And who went with you, eh?"

"Nobody went with us, Evan,—unless you count Privett. Privett didn't like Spain. She found a flea in her bed, several fleas."

"And what did you find in your bed? Not a flea, I bet. Something better than a flea,—what?"

"Evan, if you are in the mood to be so vulgar, I think you had better go away."

"Nah, Evelyn, don't be cross. Remember, I haven't seen you for months. Tell me some more. How have you been getting on? There's been all sorts of talk about you in the family." He had not meant to say this, but a third glass had made him indiscreet.

Evelyn winced; she regretted having allowed him to come. The mood was passing off in which she had felt that anybody's company, even Evan's, would be preferable to her own. She was now just very tired; very tired and very sad; too tired to feel anything acutely any more.

"I hate gossip, Evan; please don't repeat unkind things to me."

"I don't wonder you hate gossip, especially when it's true. Of course *I* knew all about you, but don't imagine that I gave you away; it was old Hester and Catherine, nosing about. I knew what they were after when Hester asked me casually one day if I knew a certain young man."

"Oh, Evan, do leave it alone, please. I really don't care what you think, or what Hester thinks, or what Catherine thinks. I should have cared, once, but I'm past caring now. Just leave it alone."

He looked at her with a sudden sympathy; it was unlike Evelyn not to care what the family thought.

"I say," he said, "have things gone wrong, then? I'm sorry."

"Thank you, Evan, but I really don't want sympathy. I don't want the subject ever mentioned again. If you want to do me a good turn, tell Hester and Catherine that whatever might have been true once is true no longer. And now you must go away, and I must go to bed."

She had only one desire, to get rid of him. It seemed that whatever she did, whichever way she turned, she was fated to be persecuted by reminders of Miles; even Evan, who was not ill-natured but merely a sot, could not leave her in peace. She had let him come, thinking that he would divert her for a quarter of an hour with his usual silly chatter and his latest Stock Exchange stories; partly also to provide herself with an excuse for not looking at her letters; but all she got was Miles again,—Miles! Would it always be like this?

He was reluctant to go; she edged him towards the door, but he lingered and tried to put his arm round her. He was dreadful in this mood, and she hated him.

"No, Evan, please don't; please. Can't you see that I'm worn out? I can't struggle with you this evening; don't be a cad."

Pity for her sent a vague message through his fuddled brain, and he let her go. He was swaying slightly.

"All right, I won't bother you. But can I come down to Newlands?"

"Yes, if you behave."

"I'm so damned fond of you, Evelyn; thatt's the trouble. Never cared for anybody else."

"Rubbish, Evan; you make love to every woman you meet."

"Not every woman," said Evan, with a slight return of humour; "only the pretty ones."

She had been feeling that she should scream if Evan or any other man ever tried to make love to her again, but his reply made her laugh quite naturally.

"Thatt's honest, anyway. Now go, and come down to Newlands whenever you like." She pushed him out and shut the door behind him.

He had gone at last and she was alone; alone in the small warm flat with Dan sleeping peacefully next door. She tried to tell herself that here were safety and comfort. But there could be neither safety nor comfort for her anywhere.

An idle rhyme came into her head:

> *When lovely woman stoops to folly, and*
> *Paces about the room again, alone,*
> *She smooths her hair with automatic hand*
> *And puts a record on the gramophone.*

Miles had read that to her, once, at his castle. He and Dan had been caught by the jingle, and had, ridiculously, marched up and down the room declaiming it, taking a line each. She remembered how Miles had taken the first line and had come to a full stop after the deliberately misplaced "and." It was like the piano stopping suddenly in "musical chairs."

> *When lovely woman stoops to folly, and.*

He and Dan had laughed like silly children, shouting
the lines louder and louder, several times over. She had
smiled at them, loving them both. Then she had said
that the lines reminded her of something else, though they
seemed somehow to have gone wrong. And Miles, who was
in his highest spirits, had pointed a finger at Dan, chal-
lenging him. "Now, Dan, give your mother the right
quotation," and Dan had said, solemnly:

> *When lovely woman stoops to folly,*
> *And finds, too late, that men betray,*
> *What charm shall soothe her melancholy,*
> *What art can wash her tears away?*

Then Miles had snatched a book out of his shelves, and
had said, "Now you must listen to this." Evelyn could
not remember what he had read; she remembered only
the last line, which had frightened and impressed her.
He had read:

> *Come into the shadow of this red rock,*
> *And I will show you something different from either*
> *Your shadow at morning striding behind you*
> *Or your shadow at evening rising to meet you;*
> *I will show you fear in a handful of dust.*

She had remembered thatt last line, though at the time
it had held little significance for her, so happy was she,
so gay, with nothing but the slight worry of gossiping
tongues, whether the Jarrolds' or the world's. How petty
those worries seemed now! How gladly would she face
them now, had they but still occasion to wag! Now, gossip

mattered not at all to her,—had she not told Evan, truth-fully, that she did not care what Hester thought, or what Catherine thought, or what anybody thought?—all thatt had receded into its proper place, and nothing but reality remained, the reality of:

I will show you fear in a handful of dust.

She could see fear, now, in the handful of dust that was her own flesh. She began to understand what people who liked poetry found in poetry. They found the things that held significance when the terror and the danger of life became imminent. She had never cared for poetry; she had thought it only an unnecessarily complicated way of saying things which could just as well be said in ordi-nary language. She had liked poetry only when Miles read it to her,—and thatt was because she watched the sunlight on his hair and listened, sensuously, to the tones of his voice rather than to the sense of what he was reading. But certain phrases came back to her now, though she had not consciously registered them at the time:

Now more than ever seems it rich to die,
To cease upon the midnight with no pain.

Miles' deep voice had made those lines sound like music; she preferred music to poetry; music made appeal to her emotions, which were responsive always; poetry to her intellect, which was weak and reluctant. Now she per-ceived that the two were closely allied.

To cease upon the midnight with no pain.

It was midnight,—it was after midnight. She tried to turn on the wireless, and the bathos of its silence convinced her that midnight had already struck. She must go to bed,—go to bed in the old, usual, dreary way; undress; wash; brush her teeth; brush her hair. How meaningless! How much better, to cease upon the midnight with no pain.

The pile of her letters caught her eye. She must face them sometime,—or should she take them down, unopened, to Newlands? No, thatt was cowardly. She sat down before the dying fire and turned them over, five weeks' accumulation. One, two, three, four, five, six,—nothing from Miles. But the seventh was his. How often had she seen thatt writing, and had set it aside to open the envelope last! Now she trembled as she held it in her hand. Then she got up quickly and locked it away unopened with his other unopened letters.

She went down to Newlands early next morning; early, according to her standards; thatt is to say, she ordered the motor to be at the door at ten, and came down to it shortly after eleven, accompanied by Dan and Privett. She regarded Newlands as a place of escape, much as she had regarded Spain. She was frightened of being in London, since Miles might arrive at any moment. At Newlands she would feel comparatively safe.

She had not telephoned to Viola Anquetil. Viola Anquetil was Miles' confederate, and any contact with her would mean contact with Miles.

Still Miles pursued her, although he had not telephoned or arrived in person. He pursued her in a way which could not have been intentional, but which was yet extremely painful. His book had been published on the day she returned to England,—the book of which she had always been jealous and whose composition she had always tried to interrupt. She could not open a newspaper without seeing some reference to it. *The Economic Situation of the Post-War World.* The title could hardly be more severe; yet the book, according to the reviews, might be read by the ignoramus and the professional economist alike. There had been no book like it since J. M. Keynes' *Economic Consequences of the Peace.* It was both intelligible and technical, both practical and imaginative,—an almost impossible combination; but Miles, apparently, had achieved it. He had written a stiff book which was yet a readable book. Serious papers took it seriously. They referred to Miles as "one of our younger politicians who will be heard of." The yellow press took it as news; the serious press took it as a serious contribution to political and economic literature. The newspapers were suddenly full of Miles' name. Miles had become important, suddenly, between a Thursday and a Friday; he had become a person to be reckoned with. *The Times* went so far as to hint that the next Government would not be able to ignore the claims of Mr. Vane-Merrick.

Evelyn remembered that he had wanted to dedicate the book to her, and that she had dissuaded him, saying that it would 'make people talk.' She remembered the look he had then given her, and the faint smile of amusement; but he had not argued. He had not even teased her, as he usually did, about her timidity.

She began to dread that he would send her a copy of the book, and that she would unsuspectingly open the parcel with the bookseller's label. She had looked over his shoulder once while he corrected his typescript, and though the sight of figures had alarmed her, a sudden picturesque phrase had caught her eye and had made her laugh. She had read on, over his shoulder, while he turned the sheets for her. It was good, very good; Evelyn could see thatt, although she was no reader and although statistics were abhorrent to her. Even so, she had not read very far. She had soon said, "Now you've spent quite enough time over this; come out and pay a little attention to me."

No parcel came, and although she had dreaded its arrival she grew disappointed when it failed to arrive. Miles, also, had ceased to write to her. No letters followed her to Newlands. "Thank heaven," she said; but more inwardly she thought, "He is beginning to forget me."

Yet she knew thatt could not be true. No one, not even Miles, forgot so quickly. No, it was far more likely that pride was keeping him silent after her consistent refusal to answer him. Was not thatt exactly the consummation she had desired? She had prayed only that he might leave her in peace to bear the burden of suffering which was her own choice and her own decision, but now that her prayer appeared to be granted a new bitterness was added to her sacrifice: Miles had allowed himself, very easily, to be discarded.

Horrible suspicions came into her mind. Had his efforts to get at her been perfunctory? Those letters which she had refused to open, but which she still possessed,—had they been perfunctory too? She unlocked the box in which she kept them, and hesitated, with the point of a paper-cutter ready slipped into the first envelope. She looked at

the postmarks; they went right back into July; the first
one bore the date of the day after the day she had left
him. It came from his castle,—the familiar blue envelope.
What had he said when she tried to persuade him to
change it because Mason and Privett could recognise the
colour of it a mile off? "Yes," he had said," the colour of
a summer sky." The next had been written from London,
—the almost equally familiar white envelope of his club.
(But he had never written to her very often from his club,
because when he was in London they saw each other every
day, and the notes she had had from him from his club
had been written always just after they had parted; at
midnight sometimes, to say how lovely she had been to
him and how much he loved her, and that she must have
a note on her breakfast-tray to tell her so; only the last
collection, damn it, was taken at twelve o'clock, and so
he supposed that he had missed it. Still, he said, he must
write; never mind when the letter arrived.) The third
from his castle again,—she could trace his movements
by the post marks and the envelopes. Then several from
London—so he had been in London in August? why?
Was it because he feared to remain alone at his castle?
Was it because unhappiness chased him away? This reflection gave her a momentary comfort. It was unlike
him to be in London in August. She knew how much he
loved his castle, and the country. He must have come to
London on her account. She was revengefully glad of
thatt.

Still the contents of those envelopes tormented and
tantalised her, and still she hesitated, fingering the paper-
cutter. She had had the strength of mind not to open a
single one. At first, she had refused to open them lest their

urgent pleading should weaken her resolve. Now, she feared to open them, lest she should find a less urgent pleading than she desired. If they were really perfunctory, she felt that she would die of it. No, no, she thought: and put the packet away again, and threw the paper-cutter across the room as though it were a dagger.

Then she discovered that Dan had got Miles' book, for she came into his room one day and found him reading it. The gesture he made to hide it, and his blush, told her instantly what it was. And, seeing that she had guessed, he mumbled something about being sorry, and not having meant her to see it. It was the first reference that either of them had made.

She took the book from him with such naturalness as she could command. There was his name on the title-page, —*The Economic Situation of the Post-War World*, by M. Vane-Merrick. She pretended to turn over the pages indifferently, but really she was looking to see if he had dedicated it to anyone,—yes, there it was: "To Viola and Leonard Anquetil, in friendship." Well, thatt was not so bad, and she had only herself to blame if the dedication was not to her.

She gave it back to Dan. He was touched to the heart by the peculiar smile with which she handed it to him.

People came to stay at Newlands; a stray succession of boys of Dan's own age, Eton friends, for he had made some friends after all, during his last year; relations; and some former friends of Evelyn. She cared little who came, and who went. On the whole she was glad to have people in the house; she was glad enough of any distraction, however futile. *Tête-à-tête* with Dan was too much of an effort; besides, it was unfair on the boy. She could not ask him to be alone with her, evening after evening, when she knew herself to be no fit company. It had been different in Spain, where everything was unfamiliar; but here, at Newlands, what could they do but sit either side of the fire pretending to read and longing each in their separate way that Miles might be with them? It was much better to fill the house with people, and to dance after dinner or play fives on the billiard-table, and pretend that no such thing as sorrow had ever entered an excellent and careless world.

Evelyn's friends, who naturally discussed her amongst themselves, said that she was a little too excitable; they wondered, even, if she was not drinking a little too much. But they supposed that she would be all right. She had taken a knock, thatt was all; it happened to everybody sooner or later, especially to women who were so irrational as to fall in love with men fifteen years younger than themselves. It amused them to think that Evelyn Jarrold should have done such a thing; she, so circumspect always, so correct, so careful! And, in spite of the concern they expressed to one another,—poor Evelyn, they hoped she had not taken really too hard a knock?—they were maliciously rather pleased that she should have gathered the inevitable fruits of her folly.

It was said, too, openly, though not in Evelyn's hearing, that Miles Vane-Merrick was always about with Lesley Anquetil.

No one knew the secret things Evelyn kept to herself. They did not know that she slept badly; woke at four and could not sleep again until seven; slept fitfully then, and half-woke a dozen times to the flooding remembrance of

who she was and of what ailed her. They did not know
that she rose in the morning with shaking hand and
jumping heart, a dizzy head and cold sweats unexpectedly
breaking over her body. They did not know that until the
afternoon she could not so much as sign a cheque, because
the pen between her trembling fingers traced a writing
like the writing of an old woman. The first part of the
day was in fact intolerable to her. Thatt waking remembrance of everything, thatt physical and uncontrollable
weakness, poisoned the daily return to consciousness.
Sometimes, when she escaped to her sitting-room and
waited in real, physical, involuntary alarm with her hand
pressed against her heart until the sweat, the faintness,
and the nausea diminished, she wondered whether she
should not welcome death rather than fear it. "Am I going
to die?" she wondered, half-convinced that thatt strange,
invisible, and vital organ, her heart, would cease to beat,
and that in a few hours' time she would be found by some
searching servant, inert and sunken in her chair. She
wondered, with a detached curiosity, what the actual
moment of passing would be like. Would there be a
struggle for breath? a gasping? a clutching? or would the
faintness merely increase, until it became an enveloping
night from which, simply, one did not waken?

Ten minutes later she would be downstairs, watching
Dan play squash-racquets with one of his friends.

Ruth came to stay, self-invited. Ruth, who, having lost
Miles herself, had avoided Evelyn during all those months,
being unable to endure the sight of her grace and beauty,
came now that she believed him to be safely lost to both
of them. Her love for Miles,—if love it could be esteemed,

—had never gone very deep; certainly no deeper than her love for Evelyn; only, the two in conjunction had upset her and had made her imagine herself, for a brief period, far unhappier than she really was. She had now forgotten Miles and his attraction for her, and was only glad to think that she might have Evelyn to herself again. Ruth was not one of those who are likely to be broken by life.

It was not entirely out of malice that she took the first opportunity of mentioning Miles' name. She had an idea, bred of library fiction, that when people minded about something, they blenched when thatt something was mentioned. She was not quite sure how people set about blenching, but imagined vaguely that it must be some definite and recognisable manifestation. She had no conscious desire to hurt Evelyn; merely a desire to find out whether Evelyn still minded. Evelyn, however, failed to blench when Ruth asked her whether the rumour was true, that Miles Vane-Merrick was engaged to Lesley Anquetil. She did not even look startled; she simply smiled and said she hoped so, for she could imagine nothing more suitable.

So thatt was the explanation of Miles' silence! How crude, how commonplace, how cheap! And Ruth, who was crude and commonplace and cheap herself, had been chosen as the instrument to break this news to her! She supposed that everyone else had known it long since, but, being less crude than Ruth, had had the decency to conceal it from her. For a whole day she was too angry and humiliated to be conscious of any pain at all. For two days after thatt she suffered all the terrible pangs of imaginative jealousy. Then even jealousy left her, and she knew nothing but an utter and final despair, which taught her that until thatt moment she had really been living on a thread of hope.

For days she was unable to rouse herself out of her apathy; she could scarcely even make the effort to play her part of hostess. Finally, restless and tormented, she asked Dan if he would very much mind her going up to London for a few days. He said of course he would not mind; looked as though he wanted to say something more; but held his tongue. He was worried about his mother; she looked ill and feverish, and her eyes were not right. He was, however, too shy to make the first move.

Evelyn went, not knowing exactly why she was going. In her mind there was no consciously formulated intention of seeing Miles, yet, looking back on it afterwards, she supposed that she had really gone with the idea already teasing at her. If not Miles, then Viola Anquetil; but in some way or other she must get nearer to Miles, and at all costs she must know the truth. At first she took no steps; she remained in her own flat nearly all the time, doing nothing, walking up and down, swaying from indecision to indecision. Then, scarcely knowing what she did, she went out and drove to the Anquetils' house.

Viola was alone in the big studio. She was horrified by Evelyn's appearance. The woman looked as though she had not slept for weeks. "My dear," she said, hastily getting up and dropping her embroidery, "this is a very great pleasure. Do sit down. I must just go and say something to the servant, and I'll be back in a moment."

"No, don't," said Evelyn. She sat down weakly. "I

know what you want to say to the servant," she said; "you're afraid lest Miles should come. Well, if he must come, let him. Perhaps it would be better. If I must see him at all, I'd rather see him in your house. I promise you I won't make him a scene."

She smiled so pitifully that Viola was deeply moved, and wondered wildly what to do for the best.

"I had better tell you at once," she said then; "I think it very likely that he will be coming."

She thought Evelyn was going to faint, for she put her hand over her eyes and remained silent.

"Listen," she said gently, "at least let me tell the servant not to let anyone else in. About Miles, I will do as you like. Which is it to be?"

"Let him come," said Evelyn in a whisper.

Viola got up and went out of the room; when she came back Evelyn had picked up a copy of Miles' book from off the table. She put it down again.

"Is he likely to come soon?" she asked.

"No,—certainly not for another half-hour."

"Then may I talk to you for a little first? There is just one question I want to ask you. On your answer depends whether I go or stay."

"Ask me anything you like."

Evelyn seemed unable to speak; she got up and walked over to the fireplace. She picked up a little ornament, looked closely at it, and set it down.

"Is it true," she asked, turning round, "that Miles is engaged to your daughter?"

"Engaged to Lesley? no, it is not true; who has been telling you thatt? They are very good friends, even very great friends, but they are not engaged; I am sure they

are not; Lesley would have told me. Now do sit down,—
you look absolutely worn out,—and let us talk about what
can be done."

"One more question, and I will. Are they in love with
one another?"

"You ask me a more difficult question there, but,—no,
I don't think so. I am almost sure that they are not."

"Almost sure? not quite sure?"

"How can one be quite sure? I don't want to mislead
you. They have much in common, they are constantly
together. . . ."

"And they are much the same age," Evelyn finished
the sentence for her.

"You know," said Viola, "thatt has not really much to
do with the matter. Whether one falls in love or not, has
nothing to do with reason."

"You needn't try to spare me," said Evelyn, "although
it is kind of you. I assure you that I have learnt neither
to spare myself nor to deceive myself. It is true that falling
in love has nothing to do with reason, but remaining in
love has to do with a great many things."

"I think you are deceiving yourself after all; the trouble
between you and Miles did not arise because of the difference in your ages."

"Then why, according to you, did it arise?"

"Do you want me to be frank? Because of the difference
in your temperaments."

"But you don't, forgive me, know anything of my
temperament."

"One guesses," said Viola, "and I know Miles pretty
well. I will tell you honestly, I am sorry for any woman
who loves Miles."

"Your own daughter, though. . . ."

"I have told you already that I do not believe Lesley to be in love with Miles. Of course, one never knows. People are secretive about these things, and sometimes even unaware themselves until the moment of revelation. It is quite possible that Miles and Lesley might come together suddenly. I don't think you could blame Miles. He has been very unhappy."

"It is not a question of blaming him.—But has he been so very unhappy? I don't believe it. When one is very unhappy, desperately unhappy, one does something drastic about it."

"But Miles has written to you, tried to see you. . . ."

"Oh, Viola! Is thatt enough? Is thatt all one does? Look, I am speaking to you without vanity. You know yourself that Miles is hot-headed and impulsive enough not to hesitate when he wants something. He wrote to me, yes; he tried to see me, yes,—for a time. He could scarcely do less, and I dare say he was genuine about it. But now what has happened? He no longer tries to see me, he no longer writes; quite clearly, he has accepted my decision."

"Miles is proud, you know,—and you withdrew yourself very abruptly and thoroughly."

"I had no choice; it had to be one thing or the other; half-measures weren't possible."

"Couldn't you perhaps have adapted yourself to him a little more? I don't want to preach to you, but couldn't you have spared yourself and Miles a great deal of misery? Couldn't you, even now?"

"Viola, I am sure you are arguing against your own convictions; I am sure you would be sorry to see me and

Miles together again. You know quite well how it would end; in a repetition of the whole miserable business. Admit that you know I have been right."

"Then, tell me, why do you want to see him today?"

Evelyn looked at her, startled.

"I don't know," she said.

"You have been firm for all these months, right or wrong. Personally, so far as I can judge, I think you were probably right. I know at any rate that you did it from the best motives. Miles knows it too."

"Miles?"

"I told him. But what I don't quite understand is why you weaken now. Is anything to be gained by seeing him?"

"I didn't come here with the intention of seeing him, remember."

"But when you heard he might be coming the temptation was too strong for you?"

"You can put it thatt way, if you like.—No, I don't think it was entirely for thatt reason. I think I want to be quite quite certain that I ought to give him up. I want to be quite certain that he himself would prefer it. I shall be able to tell in an instant from his manner. I almost hoped that you would confirm the rumour about him and Lesley. . . . It would make it much easier for me. At present I wonder sometimes whether I am not making a horrible and unnecessary mistake. If Miles really wants me . . . but, no, he doesn't, he doesn't. You said yourself that you thought I was probably right."

"It seems a harsh thing to say. . . ."

"No, you must be truthful. The whole thing matters so seriously,—to me, at least,—that you must be truthful at all costs. Never mind how much it may hurt me. It is too important for there to be any room for kindness. Tell me again, you really think I was right?"

"If you couldn't adapt yourself to Miles,—if you couldn't make him happy in the way he wanted,—if you believe that you never could,—then I am sure you were right."

"I did try, Viola; at first I tried very hard, and at first I think I succeeded. But once things began to go wrong, some cussedness forced me always to make them worse. If I saw that I was annoying Miles, I wanted to annoy him more. Can you possibly understand?"

"I understand so well, that I wish you would stop lacerating yourself in this way. You need not tell me; I know already."

"I was even jealous of him."

"I am sure you never had any reason to be thatt."

"Not by his fault, perhaps. But Miles is very popular . . . and rather vain; women ran after him, and he didn't dislike it, and I never knew when he would meet some woman who would take him away from me. . . ."

Viola smiled.

"Thatt was scarcely the best way to keep him, perhaps."

"I know, I know! I was insane. I couldn't stop myself. He was very patient on the whole.—What's the good of talking? I see how things are. I had much better go away, now, at once, before he comes."

She got up, collecting her bag, and her gloves, as she did so.

"But where are you going?" said Viola, getting up also. She could not bear the idea of Evelyn's loneliness; indeed, she was afraid of what she might do.

"Oh, back to Newlands, I suppose"; said Evelyn; "where else can I go? Any place is the same to me, anyhow, and I have Dan to look after. Let me go, Viola, and thank you for being so good to me. I shall always be grateful to you, always."

She looked so white and tired that Viola nearly took her into her arms, but she knew that Evelyn would break down.

"Listen," she began, but at thatt moment Miles came into the room.

Viola never knew exactly what happened between them. After the first moment in which they all three paused in equal consternation, she decided that she had better leave them together; circumstances had forced it. She went upstairs, after telling the servant that Mrs. Jarrold and Mr. Vane-Merrick had business to discuss and must not be disturbed. Business! yes, of a vital sort. She went upstairs to her bedroom, and there spent two of the most anxious and unpleasant hours of her life. In the middle she remembered that both Leonard and Lesley were out, and would probably let themselves in by their latch-keys and burst happily into the studio. So she crept down to leave a note for both of them in the place where they always put notes. Then she went upstairs again, and spent another hour looking out of the window, thinking about the two downstairs, and wondering which of the two would remain behind to tell her what had taken place, or whether she would see them both leaving together, thoughtless in a taxi. Then she saw Evelyn come out of the house, hail a taxi, and drive away. Miles, then, was left? But before she could go down to him, he, also, came out of the house and walked away, hatless, at an angry pace down the street.

Evelyn went back to Newlands and found Dan with a party of young people playing poker. They were all very pleased to see her; rose politely, abandoning their game; and said that they had missed her a great deal. Dan was especially affectionate, taking her arm and pressing it against his side. "Darling Mummy," he said, "how lovely to have you back." For a moment she felt that here she was really wanted. For a moment she felt that this could suffice her. Dan, at least, was her own.—But Dan would go away from her in time; Dan would have his own loves and his own ideas.

His own ideas he had already, and they were not hers: they were Miles'.

Still, in a stupor, she held on. She entertained Dan's friends and her own, and even went up to Orlestone with Dan to open a new hostel organised by a young man who reminded her of Bretton. There seemed to be many young men of thatt type among Dan's acquaintance; uncivil, fierce young men; and she resented it. Dan, at least, had perfect manners; she supposed that thatt was because he had gone to Eton. She thought that old William Jarrold might have been right after all.

Dan was upset again by Orlestone. He brought the young man like Bretton back to the hotel with him, and they sat up talking till three o'clock in the morning. Dan said that something must be done; that he was willing to sacrifice the whole of his personal fortune, but that thatt was not enough; it might relieve the misery in Orlestone, but it would not help the problem as a whole. Evelyn left them to it, but as Dan shut the door behind her she heard him saying, "Now Miles Vane-Merrick. . . ."

Always Miles. She could not escape from him, either in talk or in the newspapers; least of all, in her own thoughts.

They came back to Newlands. Dan hated Newlands, now, and wanted to rid himself of it as quickly as possible. Newlands was in the market as a desirable residence not desired by its young owner. Evelyn's father, who had seen the advertisements in *The Times* and in *Country Life*, wrote a distressed letter to Evelyn saying what a pity it was that Dan should wish to part with such a nice place. Geoffrey Jarrold could not understand why Dan should wish to sell Newlands. What nicer place could the boy want? unless, indeed, he wanted a better sporting centre, —but then, he understaod that Dan didn't care much for shooting or hunting, so what the devil was the boy after? Evelyn showed this letter to Dan, asking him what reply she should give? "Tell him," said Dan, "that I hate the white posts, and the chains, and the paddocks, and the gravel drives, and the whole of Surrey."

Evelyn did not entirely grasp his meaning. But she came nearer to grasping it than she would have come, twelve months ago. And thatt, again, was due to Miles.

Dan must go to France. He protested vigorously, though without giving his true reason: his reluctance to leave his mother. Evelyn, however, was firm. She was surprised, herself, at how firm she could now be; adversity seemed to have called out all the latent strength of her character. Much as she wanted to keep Dan, she was determined always to consider his good before her own; she had had enough of selfish love.

Protesting to the last, he went, and she was left alone in England. Alone, in spite of the people who surrounded her, for Dan was now the only person in the world who held any significance for her. The rest of life was nothing but a thin shadow.

She tried to interest herself in other things, but since all zest was lacking she felt as one who would attempt to lift heavy weights without the necessary muscles. It was love that she wanted, having once known it. She supposed that some women were like thatt, and that she was certainly one of them. It was a tragedy, to be made thatt way.

Viola Anquetil was the only other person she wanted to see. She could have found a little temporary peace, sitting quietly in Viola's cool presence, even without speaking. Diffidence kept her away; she had no right to impose her troubles upon Viola. Viola telephoned several times, and wrote, but she always replied that she was away at Newlands.

There, again, she was firm.

This firmness was mysterious, even to her. It seemed to be the reverse of the medal. The medal was stamped on the other side with self-indulgence, softness, luxury, egotism; now she had turned it over and found a certain austerity, pride, and self-sacrifice.

All the same, she thought, what did the future hold? She had perhaps thirty to forty years of life left to her. Would this sense of having done the best thing for Miles be sufficient to sustain her? Or was it but a temporary exaltation? When it failed her, when the spirit sagged, would she fall broken to the ground, as an acrobat who topples from his tight-rope?

The interview with Miles had been final. She had

known it, even while he besought her. He might storm, rave, appeal, implore: the genuine accent was missing. She was intuitive enough to know the difference; besides, she knew him so well! Emotional, eloquent, and unafraid of expressing his feelings, he was capable of working himself up into a state of agitation which deceived himself and would have deceived anybody but her. (Though, God knows, she had desired ardently enough to allow herself to be deceived.) On the point of yielding, she had looked at him sardonically, and had said "Tub-thumping as usual, Miles?" Then, taken up short, he had shot her a look of real hatred and all their past differences leapt suddenly into life again. "Tub-thumping"—what perverse ingenuity had led her to choose that word? It involved the whole of his public career,—their principal enemy in the days when they had been lovers. "Well, if you think thatt . . ." he had said, striding away to the opposite end of the room. She had watched him go, torn by his agitation and by the familiar grace of his movements. How near she had been to calling him back at thatt moment! He had stood silhouetted against the big window of Viola's studio,—silhouetted, but with his hair shining;—angry, his hands in his pockets, and she had nearly gone up to him, saying, "Miles?" in the voice which she knew would swing him round to her and make him take her, then and there, into his arms. Once again she would have known thatt physical contact which meant so much and yet so little; for the moment they would have melted together, come back to one another; for an hour, for a night, for a week, their union might have touched perfection again. She had resisted the temptation,—at what cost!—and was glad. She had remained by the fire, while he stood over by the window, and had driven her points home. "There's your natural platform, Miles," she had said, "the tub, or the orange box. You stick to it, and let me go."

It was difficult for him to answer,—almost as difficult as to answer an American who says "pleased to meet you, Mr. Vane-Merrick"; his heart was not in the answer; there was the truth of it. He began then to doubt whether he had a heart at all. Emotion he had in plenty; eloquence at his command; but—heart? What did heart mean, anyhow? Compassion? Lust? Were those the ingredients of love? Not of love, as he understood it. Still less of love as Evelyn understood it. Love as Evelyn understood it was an entire absorption of one lover into the other. He could not see love in thatt light. He wanted to retain his individuality, his activity, his time-table. He wanted to lead his own life, parallel with the life of love, separate, independent. So he had turned upon Evelyn, and had tried to explain, but he had explained in an exasperated voice and she had seen the exasperation behind the explanation. "Don't worry, Miles," she had said. "We had seven lovely months, and one can't expect these things to last for ever."

She hoped thereby to convey the impression that the affair had come to an end for her as well as for him. She wanted him to take it lightly. She wanted him to believe that she herself took it lightly. She did not want him to be distressed,—thatt was part of her exaltation. If she must sacrifice herself for him, then she would do it as thoroughly and as graciously as possible.

He had retaliated on her for the phrase about tub-thumping. As she knew, he was readily stung to retaliation, but on this occasion he hurt her bitterly, though she concealed it. What did an extra hurt matter, when the heart was already one vast wound? He said, "I dare say you were glad to be rid of me. You always worried about what the Jarrolds might say." She smiled at thatt, and said, "Yes, Miles, I'm afraid I did."

She went back to London after Dan had gone. December in the country was not to her taste; besides, she could not easily get people to stay at Newlands in December. And she must have people with her always, meaningless to her though they might be, for she feared her own company. She must have people from morning till night,— or, rather, from morning till morning, for she seldom went to bed now till two or three o'clock. When she did go to bed, she could not sleep; and dreaded those small, weak hours when all the ills of life swelled to the size of the globe and crushed her on her pillow. At six or seven she would fall asleep; would sleep till nine or ten; then, waking, would reach for the telephone and command Ruth or some other adorer to come round instantly. She took some pleasure in bullying Ruth, and having sent for her, would keep her waiting indefinitely while she had her bath. It was a petty revenge to take, on so petty an object; but her smarting soul sought any relief.

Evan, too, was constant in his attendance. She despised and disliked Evan with his maundering and sentimental ways, but at all events he was always available. She could ring him up at a moment's notice and say that she wanted to go to a theatre or a night-club. She preferred him, really, to the young men who were always ready to take her out. Although he made most distasteful love to her, he was still her brother-in-law, and she could be on easy terms with him; they could talk about Tommy or about Lady Orlestone and her rhododendrons; she could snub him as much as she liked, and he never took offence. They could maintain an endless and effortless chatter about their common family. She could scold him about his excessive drinking, and, seeing him look down his nose, could feel that she had done him a little good, besides giving him sympathy. Relations with Evan were quite easy, especially in a public place, where he could not try to put his arm round her shoulders.

She avoided seeing him alone in the flat.

Evan had, too, a sort of clumsy tact. He never mentioned Miles. But the sense that he knew about her and Miles gave her a curious comfort and support.

She was with Evan when she first saw Miles and Lesley Anquetil together.

They were dining at the same restaurant and did not catch sight of her for some time. Indeed, it was in a mirror that she herself saw them. The familiar image struck her suddenly as she raised her eyes to the mirror on the wall, and turning round she assured herself that the minute reflection had not misled her. They were laughing and talking confidentially, leaning their elbows on the small table, both looking very young and remarkable. Yes, they were striking, Miles so fair and Lesley so dark and sleek. They looked distinguished and intelligent,—absurd words, with which to describe the pang Evelyn felt as she observed how they complemented one another. She could not continue to stare at them over her shoulder, but, turning back, saw them again in the mirror. What a strange thing a mirror was! It gave the colour of life, the size of life, the gesture, yet offered nothing but a remote unreality. Thatt was not Miles, his hair shining above the dark suit and the white cloth; reaching out his hand to take bread; pouring red wine from a dark bottle. Yet it was Miles; she had but to turn round, and the reality was close behind her.

"Evan," she said, "has anyone ever invented a spectroscopic mirror?"

Evan stared. He had been talking, and she had evidently not been listening.

"Eh?"

"I was just thinking, a mirror shows everything flat, doesn't it? Not really in the round? I mean, you don't feel as though you could put your hand behind anything reflected in a mirror? It's so life-like, and yet not life-like at all. Rather frightening, I think."

Evan not unnaturally looked up into the mirror just behind his head. Then he saw.

"Would you like to go away?" he asked, having seen.

She was grateful to him,—poor Evan! But she shook her head and smiled.

"No, Evan dear, it's no good running away."

"It was bound to happen sooner or later," he said.

"Yes, it was bound to happen sooner or later."

"Is this the first time?"

"Yes, it's the first time."

"Then you've been lucky."

"Yes, I've been lucky."

"Have they seen you?"

"No, I don't think so,—not yet."

"They will."

"Yes, of course they will."

He could not know what pain thatt pronoun "they" gave her.

"They'll come up and speak to you, Evelyn."

"Yes, I expect they will. They'll feel bound to. It's awkward for them, isn't it?"

"Evelyn, don't look like thatt."

"Like what?"

"Well,—I don't know."

She laughed.

"Well done, my inarticulate Evan!"

"What does thatt mean, exactly?"

"It means that you aren't very good at expressing what you mean."

"Well," said Evan uncomfortably, "one isn't."

No, Evan and his sort were not good at expressing what they meant. Miles, on the other hand, had been extremely good at it. Perhaps thatt was partly what Viola had in mind when she called Miles an Elizabethan Englishman. . . . Still, Evan was a kindly soul, and she was glad to be with him rather than with a stranger.

Half-way through dinner, Miles saw her. Their eyes met in the mirror. He had looked up just at the moment when she was again looking into it,—for she could not keep her eyes away. It was a curious experience. She saw his startled look in the glass; she saw him drop his eyes and seek her out,—the real her, in the flesh. Seeing his reflected self do this, she refrained from turning round. Unless she turned round, their eyes could not meet. So she went on eating her dinner and talking to Evan, although she knew that Miles was looking at her.

She tried to keep her eyes away from the mirror, and succeeded but for one glance. The one glance showed her again Miles talking to Lesley. It told her that Lesley was still unconscious of her presence. Miles betrayed himself by an over-nervous animation. The girl was serene as ever; interested in her companion and in what he was saying. They were again leaning their elbows on the small table, talking. Miles betrayed his nervousness only by the rapidity with which he crumbled his bread.

Evelyn did not know what she said to Evan. She had only the comforting sense that Evan understood, and forgave her all her lapses.

She became aware that either she and Evan, or Miles and Lesley, must leave the restaurant first. Some movement had to be made, so she rose gallantly, and passed between the tables. She paused to speak to Miles and Lesley. Lesley looked up, surprised; then, recognising her, was all friendly smiles. Evelyn wondered how much she knew. Miles got up, embarrassed. He dropped his napkin, and had to grope for it under the table,—a ridiculous attitude for any man to take, but because she loved him it endeared him to her all the more. She was sorry for him, because she had inadvertently spoilt his evening. Yet she was glad to have spoilt it.

The encounter passed off in the most civilised way.

She had come home late, the fog being thick over London. (She hoped that Dan, in France, would escape the fog.) It was thick, it was horrible. It was the kind of fog in which women had their earrings torn through their ears by an unseen assailant. Evan brought her home late thatt night, or, rather, early next morning, for they had gone on to dance, and having got rid of Evan with some difficulty, she paused alone in the flat before going to bed.

Evan, growing more and more sentimental as the night wore on, had again besought her to marry him. "It's allowed, you know,—Act of Parliament," he had said for the twentieth time; and for the twentieth time she had chaffed him, saying, that proposal of matrimony was a bad habit growing upon him. He didn't propose matrimony to anyone but her, he said; and poor Tommy would have approved. She said she was tired of hearing poor Tommy's posthumous views quoted. Evan boggled at that; he was alarmed by words such as posthumous; he said she must have picked them up from young Vane-Merrick,—having by then at two in the morning lost his natural tact. Young Vane-Merrick was a damned highbrow, he said; look at that girl he was dining with, dressed in a shirt made of some green silk Indian stuff. Some Chelsea model he had picked up. Not at all, said Evelyn coldly; Viola Anquetil's girl, I know her well. She tried to make it sound as though Viola Anquetil's girl were her best friend; almost her god-daughter. Well, said Evan, she's not the marrying sort; anything else you like, but not marriage. Evelyn did not know whether to be pleased or not by thatt remark. She did not relish the allusion to "anything else you like." At the same time, she preferred it to a marriage in St. George's, Hanover Square, or St. Margaret's, Westminster, whereby Miles would be advertised to the world as the official and authorised lover of Lesley Anquetil, or another. Vanity took strange forms,— vanity and jealousy, too. She had come to the point of scarcely minding what Miles did with his private life; he was a young man after all, and must have his relaxations, she could understand and tolerate thatt, but she did mind passionately about his being advertised publicly in connection with another woman. It was an absurd form for jealousy to take, no doubt; but jealousy took it.

She opened the window and leant her elbows on the sill, thinking of Miles and Lesley together. She was sure that one day soon she would read an announcement in the *Times:* The Hon. M. Vane-Merrick and Miss L. Anquetil. Would Miles warn her in advance? would Viola? Viola surely would; she understood the workings of the heart. Miles did not understand them at all. He grew worried and bothered about them only when other people's feelings became inconveniently acute. His own feelings were kept for public affairs. Lesley would never bother him. It was as impossible to imagine that her feelings would ever overcome her to the point of inconvenience, as to imagine that those two swallows' wings of hair on her forehead would ever become tousled and disordered. Certainly, she was the perfect wife for Miles,—if a wife he must have.

Evelyn continued to lean her elbows on the sill, though the December night was cold and the fog was deep: she remembered the way Miles had leant his elbows on the small table, before he became aware of her presence. Just in such a way did she lean her elbows on the sill now, but whereas Miles had talked across the table to Lesley, so did she now breathe the cold solitary air, with no one to talk to but only her own thoughts to keep her company. She had had a bath and was warm; too warm, she knew, for the chill deadly air that crept in through the open window. These fogs of London, how strange they were, turning everything into unreality; as strange as the mirror reflecting Miles. She would never again be able to look into a mirror in a public place without a feeling of dread.

She ought to go to bed. But she had fallen into the habit of delaying the hour when she must turn out the lights and lie sleepless in the darkness. To-night she would take a sleeping-draught; it was a luxury she allowed herself as seldom as possible. To-night she thought she deserved it. She felt so wretchedly lonely, and the fog seemed to increase her loneliness. Leaning out of the window, she could see the flares at the street corner making a lurid orange patch in the fog. Had Miles made his way home safely, she wondered, as a solitary taxi passed, hooting carefully?

She realised then that she was very cold indeed, and after measuring out her chloral she lay awake for some time with her teeth chattering, in spite of the warmth of her bed.

Horrible dreams assailed her; she dreamt that she stood on a cold night with Miles on the top of his tower, and that he refused to let her go down into warmth and safety. When she urged him, he sprang upon the parapet and leaped over; she heard the thud of his body on the flagstones below. She awoke sweating and trembling, unable to convince herself that it had been only a dream. At first she thought that the sweating and trembling were due to the dream; then she realised that she could not regain control of her limbs, and passing her hand over her forehead she discovered that it remained wet. The room was dark; no transparency of light was visible behind the curtains. She turned on the lamp, and saw to her astonishment that it was eleven o'clock. The chloral, she supposed, had made her sleep so long. She ought to feel refreshed, but, on the contrary, she felt tired and heavy; her head was aching and so were her limbs.

She rang for Privett, who came with a disapproving air.

"You've been taking thatt stuff again," she said, as she saw the empty glass beside the bottle.

"Privett, is it really eleven?"

"Yes, it is, and after. What can you expect if you take thatt stuff?"

"But the room was quite dark."

"There's a fog so thick you could throw it about in handfuls."

Privett drew back the curtains and revealed a solid brown wall beyond the windows. The room remained lit by the electric light; a bright cell scooped out of the darkness. She turned on the electric fire.

"Only half the fire, Privett, please, I'm so hot."

"Hot? Why? It's cold and raw." Privett came over and looked at her. "You're flushed. Not feverish, are you?" She put her hand on Evelyn's forehead. "I'll take your temperature," she said firmly.

Evelyn really felt too ill to resist. Privett's rough kindliness and concern were a comfort; she allowed herself to be taken in charge.

"Well?" she said, when Privett, having assumed her spectacles, studied the thermometer under the light.

"Over a hundred," Privett announced finally. It was actually a hundred and two, and she was alarmed.

"A hundred's nothing," Evelyn murmured. "I must have got a chill last night."

"You'll stop where you are."

Evelyn smiled.

"All right, Nannie. I haven't much inclination to do anything else."

"I don't expect you have," said Privett grimly as she went out of the room.

She wondered what she ought to do. A hundred and two was not a good temperature to have early in the morning. Send for the doctor? Ring up Mrs. Geoffrey? "There's no one to look after the poor lamb," she muttered, and for the thousandth time she cursed thatt young Vane-Merrick. If Mrs. Jarrold had got a chill it was Vane-Merrick's fault.

She rang up Mrs. Geoffrey.

"Of course, Privett, quite right; send for the doctor at once. Dr. Gregory, of course. I'll come round myself, if I can get there through this fog."

The doctor came first. He said that Evelyn had undoubtedly got a chill, and a severe one; prescribed aspirin, and nothing but soup for luncheon; and informed her cheerily that bed was the best place on a day like this.

"You aren't missing much," he said, rubbing his hands together and looking with appreciation round the pretty room. He was an elderly doctor with a fashionable practice, and did not at all object to visiting pretty women with insignificant complaints and agreeable surroundings. Mrs. Jarrold, he thought, looked very lovely lying there in bed, as soft as a fallen petal, flushed, her curly head dark on the pillow, very quiet and rather sorry for herself. He wondered why she had never married again.—"You'll be all right in a day or two," he said, "I'll look in again this evening. But now tell me," he added, "what have you been doing to land yourself with a chill like this? Going about late at night in a thin frock, eh? Oh, you frivolous young women!"

"No," said Evelyn, "I stood by an open window last night after a hot bath."

"Admiring the fog, I suppose? Well, if people like you didn't do these crazy things, I suppose we doctors would starve. Or were you trying to commit suicide?" He laughed; a fat, comfortable laugh at his own joke. "Now don't get up to admire the fog today," he said, wagging his finger at her.

On his way out he met Mrs. Geoffrey and Ruth. They were old friends; he had, in fact, received Ruth as she made her entry into the world.

When they had exchanged their views as to the state of the weather, they referred to the patient.

"Just a chill, Mrs. Geoffrey; she'll be all right in a couple of days."

"Privett quite frightened me: a hundred and two, you know . . . nothing for a child, of course, but quite a high temperature for a grown up person."

"Oh, servants are always alarmists. You'll see, her temperature will be down by tonight."

"But temperatures always go up at night."

He laughed in a kindly and superior way and patted her arm. "I think you'll find it has gone down. I'm going to send her something which will bring it down."

"There's nothing to worry about, then?"

"Oh dear me, no; nothing to worry about. Go in and see her, but don't let her talk too much. The quieter she remains today the better."

The doctor was right; her temperature did go down. Her sister-in-law came again in the evening and chaffed her about the fright she had given them. Evan sent some flowers with a sympathetic note. She lay in bed, feeling rather weak but peaceful. She was too tired to think about Miles. Her limbs and head ached too much for her to think about the ache in her heart. She noted with a cynical amusement that physical ills could obliterate the ills of the mind, and, noting it, wished fancifully that she might permanently suffer this slight discomfort in exchange for the other. It was not unpleasant to be slightly ill; even the pains in one's joints were interesting rather than inconvenient. It was interesting to move one's foot and to feel the remote, indefinable pain in one's ankle. It was difficult to say where the pain exactly was; difficult to pin it down. She knew only that it spread itself almost sensuously over her whole body; it was just enough to make her aware of her body, like a caress. Shut away in her room, a compulsory prisoner, she felt more at peace than she had felt for months. Privett was kind, and the necessity of asking Privett to attend to her small physical needs came as a curious relief to the personal loneliness she had recently endured. It was a relief to ask Privett for another glass of milk and soda; a relief to say that she was thirsty; almost equivalent to saying that she was unhappy. Illness, even a trivial illness, so rapidly became important! The sickroom, so rapidly, became the center of the world.

Privett was very kind. Twice during the night she stole into Evelyn's room on tiptoe in slippers,—which was remarkable for Privett, who usually tramped about defiantly in noisy boots. Hester and Ruth and Evan were kind too; they came to see her, bringing flowers and grapes. Her room was soon heaped with the things that people send or bring when one is ill. Knowing Miles, she could imagine how he would let loose his scorn on such conventional expressions of sympathy. But from Miles she had had no word at all. She could not blame him, for how could he know that she was ill? Only the unreasonable petulance of the invalid made her resent his silence; and once, as she lay alone staring at the fire, she felt a tear trickle down her cheek.

The fever appeared to pass, but she developed a cough which troubled her more, for it shook her and made her head ache again. The doctor forbade her to get up until it should be better. "We don't want you down with bronchitis," he said, and he came to see her every day. She had already lost count of time, and was astonished to find that she had been in bed for a week. It was surprising how one could lie doing nothing for most of the day, and yet not feel that time dragged with intolerable slowness; the small routine of the sick-room punctuated the day, dividing it up and making it pass. She would have been quite content, but for the cough that worried her perpetually and hurt her chest.

"Yes," said the doctor in reply to Hester's question. "there is certainly a touch of bronchitis. A mere touch. If we keep her warm, it should soon go off."

It showed no signs of going off, however, and a small array of remedies began to appear in Evelyn's room: inhalers, and a kettle that had to be kept steaming day and night. Hester expressed anxiety to the doctor. Surely this bronchitis should be better by now?

"What can you expect in this weather?" he said. "These fogs and damp don't give anybody a chance. We can't even open the window to air the room without being half choked."

They heard Evelyn coughing next door, and stopped to listen.

"Poor thing, she must be racked by it. It's so tiring, and it keeps her awake at night."

"Thatt reticent maid of hers seems very devoted."

"Thatt reminds me, Doctor Gregory: Evelyn worries because Privett goes in constantly to attend to her in the night. It didn't matter when we thought she would be up in a few days, but, after all, she has been in bed now for over a week and it begins to look as though she would be there for another week."

"She certainly will," said the doctor.

"Well, then, do you think we should get a nurse? It seems absurd to suggest a nurse for such a slight illness, but it would spare Privett and I think Evelyn would prefer it. She could sleep in Dan's room, and Evelyn could have a bell."

The doctor thought it a good idea, and the nurse was installed, though everyone was very careful to insist that it was in order to spare Privett, and not because Evelyn really needed nursing.

Hester and the doctor agreed privately that when she was well enough to travel she should go away to a warm climate for a few weeks,—the South of France, perhaps, or even Egypt.

Meanwhile there could be no question of it, for her temperature, which had gone up again when the bronchitis began, remained up obstinately. The nurse kept a temperature chart, at which Hester glanced always on the sitting-room desk before going through into Evelyn's room. Evelyn was not allowed to talk much, nor had she any desire to do so, for talking made her cough. She just smiled when Hester came in, and patted her hand as it lay on the eiderdown. Hester thought she looked very ill, so flushed, and her eyes large and bright; and she could see by Evelyn's hands how thin she had become. She had now been ill for ten days; yes, ten days; it was the sixteenth of December.

Hester asked the doctor for his opinion.

"She doesn't seem so well today, certainly. The cough wears her out, and I am afraid there is a slight congestion. Don't be alarmed, Mrs. Geoffrey; I assure you that I am not seriously worried."

"Congestion of the lungs, do you mean?"

"Yes, congestion of the lungs."

"Doctor Gregory, you are not afraid of pneumonia, are you?"

"Well, of course in these cases one always has to bear the possibility in mind; no more."

"Is there nothing more we can do?"

"For the moment I don't think there is; she is receiving good nursing; no, I think we can only wait and see. Don't, I beg you, mention this to your sister-in-law. I would not have mentioned it to you, but you asked me."

"You really think the chance of pneumonia is a remote one?"

"Oh, very remote, I hope; oh dear me, yes, very remote. Tell me, Mrs. Geoffrey,—I don't want to be indiscreet, but I have known you all for a long time,—has your sister-in-law anything on her mind, do you know?"

Hester paused before answering.

"What makes you ask?"

"Frankly, when I went in this evening, I thought Mrs. Jarrold had been crying."

"Frankly, then, I think she may have had reason to be unhappy lately. I am not in her confidence, so I cannot say for certain, but one hears things, you know."

The doctor nodded.

"I understand. You don't think there is anyone she would like to see for a moment? It is very important to keep her mind at rest while she is still so feverish."

"I don't know, but I can ask her."

"I wish you would, but they must not stay for more than five minutes, and she must talk as little as possible."

Hester tried to put the question tactfully, for at heart she was not an unkind woman, and though she had disapproved rigidly of Evelyn's affair with Vane-Merrick she was really touched now by Evelyn's frailty and appearance of suffering exhaustion. So she leant over her and said gently, "You must be so bored, my dear, lying here. The doctor says you may see any one of your friends, if you like, for just a few minutes."

Evelyn looked up at her in surprise, and Hester saw her eyes suddenly fill with tears. But then she turned her head away, and shook it without speaking.

It was the anniversary of the Chevron House ball, but of course Hester could not know thatt; neither could the doctor.

Hester went out and had a few words with the nurse. They spoke in low voices now, and everything was very hushed and silent in the flat. The nurse, true to the manner of her kind, was extremely non-committal, though she admitted that Mrs. Jarrold did not seem "quite so well tonight as usual." What a strange way the medical profession have of putting things, thought Hester, going back into Evelyn's room to say good-bye.

She found that Evelyn had written something for her on a slip of paper; it was the means of communication they used sometimes to spare Evelyn's voice. She had written: "I should like to see Viola Anquetil; Mason knows the telephone number."

Hester, after reading, said she would see to it. She was a little surprised, for she had no idea that Evelyn knew thatt eccentric Viola Anquetil; but then she had known sδ little of Evelyn's life. It had always been a grievance amongst the Jarrolds. They imagined that Evelyn spent her time with smart friends who played bridge and went racing.

Evelyn caught her hand as she was about to turn away, and beckoned her down to whisper. "Tonight," she said.

"Yes, yes, I promise; I'll see about it tonight. I'll telephone to her myself."

The weak irritability of the invalid overcame Evelyn at Hester's inability to understand at once what she meant. If Hester only knew what it cost her to speak and give explanations!

"I mean, will she come tonight?"

"Oh, Evelyn dear, isn't it rather late? Very well," she added hastily, seeing Evelyn's instant look of distress; "if the nurse allows it, she shall come tonight. There, are you pleased?"

She smiled with bright reassurance; stooped to kiss the curly head, and went to telephone.

Viola said of course she would come immediately. No one had told her that Evelyn was ill.

Curiosity kept Hester in the flat until Viola arrived.

She wanted to see this woman whom everyone knew by repute, although she deliberately shunned all forms of publicity, and who now turned out so unexpectedly to be a friend of Evelyn's,—the one friend, in fact, whom she had asked to see. Viola arrived within twenty minutes, calm and beautiful. Hester recognised her beauty, although it was not of the obvious sort and although she thought Viola's clothes very odd indeed, Viola on the other hand thought Hester exactly what she had imagined the Jarrold women to be; a rather hard face, sensible tweed coat and skirt, and large feet with low-heeled shoes. The kind of woman who would be intolerant and critical in ordinary life, but reliable and kindly in an emergency,—if it were an emergency she could understand, such as physical illness. The illness of the heart or soul would leave her baffled.

Hester took her into Evelyn's room and left them together.

She waited for Viola to come out, having told her to remain for not more than five minutes. She employed those five minutes in talking to the nurse,—a common but efficient little thing, very much on her dignity always, devoting herself conscientiously to her patients and making herself objectionable to her patients' servants in the background, when she imagined that they slighted her or did not serve her meals properly. It was part of her dignity, also, to preserve a reticent hostility towards the friends and relations of her patients; those tiresome anxious people who asked questions that nurses were not allowed to answer. She knew quite well that Mrs. Jarrold was in for pneumonia. She had seen many such cases. But she was not going to say so; thatt was the doctor's business. She quite liked Mrs. Jarrold, who apologised always when she rang the bell in the middle of the night and who had such lovely pyjamas and lovely things on her dressing-table. But her patients were so many ciphers to her, really, although she did her best by them and could send a little money home to her mother in Yorkshire. She had learnt to adopt a manner towards the friends and relations of her patients; a nurse was compelled to do thatt, in self-defence. They were all ciphers; the patient who was just 'a case,' aħd the friends and relations who besieged her with anxious questions that she either might not or could not answer—although by virtue of her uniform they appeared to think her omniscient. The only person who was not a cipher was the young medical student who took her out to a cinema on her free evenings; when they never talked shop.

Viola came out of Evelyn's room after the prescribed five minutes. She went up to Hester and the nurse, and said: "Look here, she is very ill indeed." For some reason, neither Hester nor the nurse resented this statement. They merely looked at her as she voiced what they already knew and felt. The nurse knew it, and Hester felt it. "Oh no," said Hester, "the doctor says he is not seriously worried."

The nurse just looked at Viola, knowing that this was not a person who would bother her by questions, but who would call in a specialist regardless of Doctor Gregory. Dr. Gregory, in the nurse's private opinion, was competent to deal with measles or influenza, but not with a case of double pneumonia. She, the nurse, had no special interest in Mrs. Jarrold, but her professional vanity minded seeing a case die under her hands. This Lady Anquetil was the sort of person who would insist on a consultation. Mrs. Geoffrey Jarrold was the sort of person who came most assiduously every morning and every evening, and was quite sensible on the whole,—compared with some relations,—but who respected the doctor too much and accepted his too optimistic view. Lady Anquetil formed her own judgment, and was prepared to tackle the matter with her own hands. The nurse was pleased when she heard Lady Anquetil say that a specialist ought to see Mrs. Jarrold. Lady Anquetil—what an odd name!—said that it was rubbish, the doctor saying he was not seriously worried. If he was not seriously worried, then he ought to be. In her opinion, Evelyn was very ill indeed. If Mrs. Geoffrey Jarrold agreed, she said, deferring to her as a person having the rights of a relation, a lung specialist should be called in without delay. She would see about it, if Mrs. Geoffrey Jarrold agreed.

Hester agreed. She was surprised, and resentful, but on the whole grateful to this unknown woman who had come to take all responsibility for Evelyn. They would ask Dr. Gregory to call in a lung specialist next morning, she said, reasserting herself as the person who would be there in charge when Dr. Gregory came. But Viola said, quietly, that she would be back by ten in the morning; she would like to see the doctor, and hear the specialist's report.

Evelyn spent a bad night. She coughed a great deal, and could not sleep in the intervals, because she was thinking of the ball a year ago at Chevron House. Next morning the nurse had to trace a bigger peak than usual upon her temperature chart. She drew it with her pen, automatically and meticulously, stopping at precisely the accurate line. Then she sat back in her chair—Evelyn's chair at Evelyn's desk—and looked at the chart. It went up and down like an outline map of the Himalayas. The nurse was well accustomed to such charts but still she shook her head doubtfully. She was glad that Lady Anquetil had insisted on calling in a specialist.

The specialist was not very comforting, and Dr. Gregory resented his presence in a deferential way. The specialist said that both lungs were affected, but that he hoped the mischief would not spread. He said that one must await developments and that he would return next day. He altered Dr. Gregory's prescriptions just enough to annoy Dr. Gregory, but not enough to produce any noticeable effect on the patient. The nurse treated him with a shade more respect than she accorded to Dr. Gregory. Then he went away, driving off in a long, grey, Rolls-Royce coupé to his next rich patient.

Evelyn appeared to take very little interest in the sudden introduction of a specialist. Hester, who was growing really anxious, asked the nurse whether this indifference were not a bad sign? No, said the nurse, they were always like thatt. Hester resented the pronoun 'they'; it indicated that Evelyn had entered into the generalised class of people who were ill. It made Hester feel suddenly fonder of, and more protective towards, Evelyn. She began to dislike the nurse, although she knew that the nurse was doing her best by Evelyn. She experienced all the helpless antagonism of the flustered ignorant towards the cool professional.

But the person who really took charge was Viola An-

quetil. Viola allowed no conventional considerations such
as the rights of relationship to stand in her way. She was
civil and even friendly towards Hester, but she made it
quite clear that although merely a friend, she intended
to see Evelyn safely through this illness. Both the nurse
and Dr. Gregory, in whom she obviously had no confidence at all, recognised her power of authority. Their
manner was quite different, as they spoke to Viola or as
they spoke to Hester. Viola could make suggestions, and
Dr. Gregory would accept them. He dared not do otherwise. Hester herself, managing and masculine woman
though she was, found herself submitting to Viola's de-
crees. They were proffered with so much knowledge and
experience behind them, so much cold sense, and yet
without any offensive air of superiority. Viola held both
Dr. Gregory and Hester completely in control. The nurse,
too, knew that she would not ask questions, but would
simply give orders.

She came every morning, and stayed at the flat all day.
She was the only person whom Evelyn wanted to see.
Evelyn was very quiet now, except when she coughed.
She lay in her bed, but when Viola came in she smiled
and reached out her hand. Viola took it, but not sentimentally. She had to be practical, not sentimental. It was
important that Evelyn should not know how ill she was.
Viola alone knew how ill she was. Dr. Gregory kept up
his pretence that she would be all right in a week's time.
The specialist, too, was optimistic. The nurse, whose judgment was probably the best, expressed no opinion; it was
not her place to do so. Hester, of course, was negligible.
But Viola knew that Evelyn was very seriously ill.

Every day she noticed a slight change in the patient.

She noticed the definite withdrawal that accompanies serious illness. Evelyn would lie silent hour after hour. At first, she had written little notes on her block of paper. "Please, will you thank Evan for his flowers?" "Please, will you send Dan a postcard and tell him I'll write next week?" Now, even these pathetic messages had stopped. She appeared to be quite indifferent to anything going on outside. Viola could not tell what she was thinking about, —if, indeed, she thought at all. She just lay in bed, and allowed anything to be done to her, without protest, without interest.

On the twentieth day they shifted her on to a water-bed, fearing that she might get bed-sores. To do this, they had to lift her off her bed on her mattress, so that for a while she lay on the floor on her mattress while they heaved the water-bed into place. They had spent some time filling it with water from the bath-room tap. It was an unwieldy object, it leapt about convulsively, as the water swelled up into its various compartments. Then they lifted her up, Viola at her head and the nurse at her feet, and laid her on the strange new balloon of a mattress. She was exhausted by the process, but smiled at them and said that she felt far more comfortable. Viola went away into the next room, trying to forget the fragility and thinness of the shoulders she had lifted, and the way she had had to support the head.

She stayed at the flat thatt night.

Next day Evelyn was definitely better. Her temperature had gone down and her cough had decreased. Doctor Gregory came out cheerful from the sick room. "We've turned the corner, I do believe," he said, rubbing his hands together. Viola, who was tired, listened without conviction. Still, when she went in to see Evelyn, she observed a real difference, and sent a comforting letter to Dan—Dan whom she had never seen, but to whom she had written every day for a week, in France. Although she had never seen the boy, she was prejudiced in his favour by what Miles had told her of him, and by the letters she had received from him since she had started writing to him about his mother. He reminded her, in some way, of her own brother at the same age.

Next day, again, the improvement was maintained, as Dr. Gregory put it. Thatt meant that for the first time, Evelyn asked to see the paper, and asked whether any letters had come which she ought to answer. She asked weakly; but still, she asked. It was a good sign. She was told not to worry; there were no letters to speak of, only circulars. She easily and gratefully accepted this untrue assurance.

Hopes were held out to Dan that he might be allowed to come home for Christmas after all. He sent a telegram in eager response, saying that he would start at a moment's notice. But Viola, still cautious, wrote to tell him that his room in the flat was still occupied by the nurse and that although his mother was now practically out of danger, mere considerations of accommodation might make it advisable for him not to come. Dan telegraphed again, impatiently, saying, "But I can stay at an hotel."

Viola had not thought of thatt.—She laid Dan's telegram aside, to be answered next day. Next day, Evelyn was not so well. She had coughed a great deal during the night, was weak and tired by the morning, and complained of the pain in her chest. Even the cheerful Dr. Gregory did not like this relapse. He pretended, however, that it was just temporary. "In a week or two, she'll be as right as rain," he said, looking out of the window at the streaming rain which had replaced the fog.

Viola wrote to tell Dan that he had better make up his mind to spending his Christmas at Blois. His mother was much better, she said, but she still coughed when she tried to talk, and excitement was bad for her. Dan's arrival would be an excitement. So Dan must be unselfish, and stay away for Christmas. Perhaps by the New Year he might come home. . . . In the meantime, he must not worry about her. She was really much better, but it was essential that she should be kept quiet.

Dan sent another telegram saying, "Quite understand give her my love and tell her to keep quiet will spend Christmas here and hope to come home for New Year."

Next day, again, Evelyn was not so well. She lay very silent, but, when asked, said that her chest and her back hurt her. The nurse put it down coldly in her notebook: "5.30: complained of pain in the lumbar region." Viola read the comments each time she passed through the sitting-room. Her breathing became more difficult, and it was obvious that she drew every breath with pain. The atmosphere of anxiety which had lightened over the flat during the forty-eight hours, now deepened again, and all the little jokes were stilled, which cluster gallantly about a sick-room and about such ludicrous objects as bed-pans and water-beds,—the little jokes pretending that life goes on as an absurdity without death and danger standing just outside the door.

Evelyn herself scarcely wondered what was happening to her. All her instinct and effort were concentrated on sparing herself as much as possible. She wished only that they would leave her alone, instead of constantly washing her and rubbing her back with whisky and changing her sheets. She dreaded the nurse's approach, fearing that she would be required to move, sit up, or eat something, or speak. She spoke only when compelled to do so, for with every breath she took she felt as though the corselet of her ribs deepened into her body like the closing jaws of a shark.

There were two nurses now, a day and a night nurse. The night nurse sat near the fire, with a screen round her, and played Patience or read a novel throughout the night. She was very quiet, but Evelyn would lie listening for the tiny rustle of the page being turned over, or for the click of the falling cards. Every now and then the nurse would make up the fire,—for the electric fire had been condemned as drying the atmosphere too much; every now and then she would come warily over to the bed, to see if Evelyn slept or if she wanted anything. Watch in hand, at intervals, she would take her pulse. It was a curious intimacy, with a woman of whom she knew nothing, and who knew nothing of her beyond the secrets of her suffering body.

The nights were the worst time of all, interminable without the small diversions of the day. At night, indeed, everyone seemed to have abandoned her and to have gone away back into normal life, leaving her to this strange concentrated existence which was the epitome of loneliness. Normal life was resumed for them, the moment they left her room; but for her there was no possibility of escaping into a saner air. They could forget; the burden of going on with it was left to her.

Hearing her moan, the nurse rose and came over to her. "Feeling uncomfortable?" she asked, and, slipping her arm under Evelyn's shoulders, she deftly turned the pillow. She brought a sponge, and wiped Evelyn's forehead, which was damp with sweat. "Is the pain bad?" she asked, bending down, for the doctor had left a piqûre of morphia with her in case it should be needed.

Evelyn nodded without speaking.

"Worse than usual?"

Evelyn nodded again. There were tears in her eyes, from the pain.

"Wait a minute," said the nurse, making her decision, —for if Mrs. Jarrold did not sleep all night, she would be exhausted by the morning. "I'll give you something to take it away, and then you'll have a lovely sleep."

Evelyn looked up at her gratefully, and tried to smile.

Such a relief had never occurred to her as a possibility. She started a little as the needle went into her arm, and as the nurse pressed it home with its merciful charge, and dabbed the puncture with iodine. The tiny, localised pain distracted her attention for an instant from the vast, general pain. She wondered vaguely what the nurse had done to her. Then everything in the room began to float, and the familiar sensation of falling through the bed became pleasurable instead of terrifying. She began to speculate with amusement on what the couple in the flat below would say if she gradually descended through their ceiling. The pain receded to a huge distance,—though it was still there, somewhere. But although the pain receded everything else took on an exaggerated significance,—the handkerchief under her pillow, the texture of the sheet under her chin, the proportions of the room, its height, its curtained windows, its white ceiling, —what an expanse! —she wished the room were more brightly lit, so that she might observe it better; it was like the full moon, only oblong instead of round,—how wrong, that the ceiling should not conform to the shape of the moon!—the screen round the fire,—all became immensely important and amusing. She remembered Miles. But Miles did not matter. He was a long way off. Miles? Who was Miles? Someone she had seen in a mirror. "Give me a looking-glass," she said in a strong voice.

"There, there," said the nurse, sponging her forehead. "You go off to sleep."

"Give me my looking-glass," she said again, and tried to sit up. The pain was quite unimportant now, but it was extremely important that she should see Miles in a mirror.

The nurse knew well enough that morphia excited some patients before sending them off, and that it was better to humour them. In a few minutes Mrs. Jarrold would be asleep. By the next morning she would have forgotten what she looked like in the mirror, and no harm would be done. She would not remember enough to be alarmed by her own feverish and emaciated appearance. So she fetched the hand-glass off the dressing-table and gave it into the hand that had only just enough strength to hold it.

Evelyn looked into the mirror and saw Miles. He was laughing and gay and fair. His hair shone. He was alone. No woman was beside him. He looked at her and laughed.

The mirror dropped from her hand, and she slept. The nurse restored the mirror to the dressing-table and went back to tiptoe to her novel beside the fire. The patient slept till nine o'clock next morning.

When the doctor came, the nurse told him that she had administered the morphia. He said she had done rightly, but it must be saved up as far as possible. Mrs. Jarrold would of course ask for it, now that she had discovered what it could do for her. But it must be kept from her till the last possible moment, and used only to give her a night's rest.

Evelyn did ask for it; she knew now that something could give her release from the pain she had thought herself compelled to endure. The hour when they gave it to her became the one hour for which she lived through the day. She started to beg for it at least an hour before it was due, and, realising dimly that for some reason they were reluctant to give it to her, appealed to Viola. Viola was terribly distressed. She went to the doctor and said, "Can it really make so very much difference, one way or the other?"

"How do you mean, Lady Viola? Of course it makes a difference, it relieves her discomfort and sends her to sleep."

"I don't mean that, Dr. Gregory. Bluntly, I mean, how much chance do you think she has of recovery?"

"We are all in the hands of God, Lady Viola."

"Leaving God aside for the moment, if you don't mind, she is in your hands. More immediately than in God's. And since I can't ask God,—I only wish I could,—I ask you. How much chance has she? You see, I have made myself responsible to a certain extent, as well as her sister-in-law, of course. It may become necessary to send for Mrs. Jarrold's son, who, as you know, is in France. It will take him a day to get here. If you think we ought to send for him, you must give me due warning."

Dr. Gregory hated being pushed into a corner, and Viola was always pushing him into one. He said cautiously, "Lord Orlestone would no doubt like to spend Christmas in England. One enjoys being with one's family at a time like Christmas. I think it might possibly cheer his mother up to feel that he was in the house."

"In other words, you think he ought to be sent for."

"I wouldn't go so far as to say that, Lady Viola."

"But thatt is what you mean, isn't it?"

"Well, if you put it like thatt, I think Lord Orlestone might advisably be nearer at hand, certainly."

"I will telegraph tonight."

"Oh, no need to telegraph. I should write, if I were you. The posts to France are very good."

"No, I will telegraph. But then, to return, if you take so serious a view, can the morphia make so very much difference?"

"I never said I took so serious a view."

"Dr. Gregory, please! If you are thinking of my feelings, I assure you that you need not spare them. I only want the truth. I want you to spare Mrs. Jarrold as much suffering as possible. I cannot bear to hear her moan hour after hour, knowing that the morphia would relieve her, if she is going to die in the end. Surely you don't want to prolong life by twenty-four hours, at the cost of forty-eight hours of agony? If she is going to die, then let us make her last hours as easy as possible. Surely?"

Dr. Gregory was shocked. He was not accustomed to such plain speaking. Usually, the family of his patients asked for reassurance, the reassurance which he was always ready to give. This Lady Viola seemed to charge straight ahead to the worst. But then, of course, she was only a friend, not a relation.

He asserted his dignity.

"I am afraid Mrs. Jarrold can have the morphia only once a day, and it is better that she should have it at night."

"Well, Dr. Gregory, will you promise me this at least: if the case, in your view, becomes hopeless, you will keep her under morphia all the time?"

• "We must wait and see, Lady Viola; wait and see. Meanwhile we mustn't lose heart."

"There is another thing, Dr. Gregory. I don't, of course, know exactly how these illnesses go. But supposing she were to ask to see a friend? What should I say?"

"She is not very likely to ask to see anyone, in her present state."

"No, I know. But it is possible. Supposing it occurs to her that she is dying, there is one person, I think, whom she might wish to see."

"Had we not better wait until the occasion arises?"

"Certainly, if you think so," said Viola, tired of talking to Dr. Gregroy and resolving to tackle the specialist, who was a shade more prepared to face facts, although he was always in a hurry and managed to convey the impression that his appointments with his patients were a nuisance. She had not dared to mention Miles to Evelyn, though she felt some surprise that Evelyn herself had never mentioned him. She had not asked once whether he knew of her illness; whether he had enquired; whether he had called at the flat. In point of fact, Miles was beside himself with anxiety, and Viola could keep him away only by saying that she was sure Evelyn would not like the Jarrolds to know he was always in the sitting-room. He wanted to remain there all day, to be within call in case she asked for him. He said the Jarrolds could go to blazes.

"Yes, Miles, but Evelyn really would mind when she found out afterwards."

Now that there was not likely to be any afterwards, and seeing Miles really distraught, she relented and told him that he might come if he were very careful not to allow Evelyn to hear his voice. She then hit on an ingenious way of explaining his presence to Hester.

"Mrs. Jarrold, Dan may be arriving at any moment, and I have asked Miles Vane-Merrick to be here when he arrives. Dan is very devoted to him, and I think it will make things easier for the boy."

She hated herself for the hypocrisy, but she knew that Evelyn would be grateful,—afterwards.

Hester had to swallow it. She drew herself up stiffly for a moment, then, remembering that it was not a time to stand upon one's dignity or to consult one's prejudices, she relaxed and assented. Still, she thought it very odd. She was shocked, too, that Dan should be devoted to his mother's lover. But no doubt the poor innocent boy did not know.

She took her departure before Vane-Merrick could arrive, saying that she would return later in the day. Inwardly, she was very resentful of this invasion of strangers, —Viola with her high-handed methods, and now this young man who had no right whatsoever to be there; whose presence was indeed indecorous. In her view, the only people who had a right to look after an invalid were the invalid's immediate relations; and they had been ousted, simply ousted, by this total stranger, who took it upon herself to bring Evelyn's lover into the flat! Hester, although she had tried to behave well when Viola made the suggestion, snorted as she drove away from the door. It was really going a little too far.

Miles came at once. He was pathetically anxious to obey Viola's injunction; entered the flat on tip-toe, and spoke to Mason in a whisper. The familiar sitting-room looked strange; the arm-chairs had been pushed aside into different positions, and beside the door leading into Evelyn's bedroom stood a kitchen table covered with a white cloth and a cluster of white jugs, cups, and basins, an unopened bottle of champagne, and a pine-apple. He glanced at them shyly and obliquely. Beyond thatt door lay Evelyn, how changed? how different? What did they do to her? What did she think about? Did she suffer too much to think? Would he be allowed to see her, or would she be kept away from him, behind this mysterious veil of danger and pain? He felt horribly excluded, from an Evelyn submitted to the ministrations of strange hands.

The bedroom door opened and Viola came out, shutting it very quietly behind her. She looked tired and strained, but smiled on seeing him, and put her finger to her lips. They went over to the further side of the room, where they could talk.

"How is she?"

"Quiet for the moment,—dozing. The effect of the morphia hasn't quite worn off. Dan is coming."

"Is it as bad as all thatt?"

"I hope not, but I couldn't take the risk."

"You hope not, but you think so?"

"Yes, Miles, I think so."

"The doctor . . ."

"The doctor never says anything he can avoid saying, but he didn't dissuade me from sending for Dan."

"The specialist?"

"Not very hopeful. Miles, what do you think I ought to do about her father? He's an old man, and I cannot see any point in dragging him up to London. Yet Hester seems to think he ought to be here. You know what the Jarrolds are like: family, family, family. People's private emotions don't seem to count for them at all. Hester was obviously horrified at the idea of your coming here,—I had to say it was on account of Dan; forgive me—but she is quite prepared to drag a poor old man up from Biggleswade because she thinks it the right thing to do. He would only be in the way; it would distress him; and Evelyn wouldn't ask to see him. Isn't it better and kinder to leave him where he is, even at the risk of giving him a shock if she dies?"

"Unfortunately, Hester, as you call her, is Evelyn's sister-in-law and you aren't, so if she wants to send for Evelyn's father she will probably do so without consulting you."

"How silly it all is, isn't it, Miles, this idea of family? You and I know far more about Evelyn—though heaven knows I know her little enough, as time goes,—than all the Jarrolds put together."

"Don't send for her father. If Hester likes to send for him, then it's her responsibility. I agree with you, that it would be simply unkind and unnecessary to introduce the old man here."

"He may blame us afterwards."

"Still, you will have done the kindest thing. He may

not realise it, but in your own mind you will know that you did right."

They were silent for a space.

"What about her temperature?"

"Thatt doesn't seem to count very much. It has never been very high. The pulse seems to count much more, and the strain upon her heart."

"What about the pain?"

"The morphia relieves it, but she is allowed only one injection a day. The hours in between are pretty trying.— Miles, I must go back, in case she wakes up."

"If Dan arrives, what am I to say?"

"Say that she is bad, but that we have hope. Whatever you do, don't let him burst into her room. I shall leave you here on guard."

"One has one's uses," said Miles bitterly.

"You will be a great comfort to Dan."

"Does she know he is coming?"

"No, of course not. He won't be allowed to see her, unless she gets better, or unless she doesn't."

"Shall I?"

"Miles, dear, you must be patient; we must all be patient. You shall see her if it can do her no harm. What are you going to do? Will you read?"

"I'll find a book if I want one," said Miles, looking at Evelyn's bookcase. How often he had teased her about the well-bound books her friends gave her for Christmas! He knew the room so well, and every object in it, except those alien introductions on the white-clothed table. Everything was associated with Evelyn and his memories: there was the writing-desk at which he had so often found her sitting; the arm-chair in which she had always sat, while he sat at her feet; the toasting-fork which he had given her because he liked making his own toast for tea. He missed various other things he had given her, and supposed that she must have put them away; this hurt him quite unreasonably. He wondered if she had taken off the ring he had given her? He went over to the writing-desk, and found there the exercise-book in which the nurse kept her notes of the case; he opened it idly without realising what he was doing, but the few words he read caused him such anguish that he hastily put it down again.

It was no good straying about the room, being so restless: He might be left alone there for hours; he must try to concentrate on something, must try to keep some grasp on life which became so insanely hideous the moment he let his imagination get possession of him. Looking about for a book, he found one which he himself had given Evelyn, a translation of *Du côté de chez Swann;* he had given it to her, he remembered, after one of their quarrels, saying, in the restored good-humour of their reconciliation, that herein she would find the passion of jealousy depicted in all its aspects. And then, when he asked her repeatedly if she had yet read it, she always replied that she hadn't had time . . . that it was so long . . . that its unbroken pages frightened her . . . that she thought she liked books with more conversation in them. And then he had grown annoyed again, and had said that she was really hopeless. What did she mean, by saying that she hadn't had time? What else had she to do?

Looking back, it seemed that he had always scolded her.

Dan arrived unexpectedly early, at four o'clock, having travelled from Blois to Paris by a night train, and flown from Paris by the first available aeroplane. Bad weather had delayed him. He arrived in an agony of impatience and anxiety, and seemed scarcely surprised to find Miles waiting for him in the flat. He took Miles' presence for granted, and greeted him at once with the inevitable question: How is she? And added immediately, making for the door, "I must go in and see her."

Miles stopped him.

"No, Dan, I'm afraid you can't."

"Can't? But why? Why, else, should I have been sent for? Why can't I go in? You've seen her, haven't you?"

"No, Dan, I haven't. And you mustn't talk so loud; she might hear your voice. She doesn't know that you are here."

"Doesn't know? Miles! Then she really is so very ill?"

"They still have hope," said Miles, as he had been told to say.

Before Dan could speak, Viola came out from Evelyn's room. She saw Dan, went up to him, and took him into the passage outside.

"You are Dan, I know. I'm Viola Anquetil. Look here, you must be very quiet; your mother doesn't know that you have arrived."

She saw that the boy was completely bewildered.

"She is very ill, I'm afraid," she said.

"Can I see her?"

"Not now,—later on, perhaps. You must be patient and wait with Miles."

"She isn't dying, is she?"

Viola respected him for the direct question. Here was a boy to whom one could tell the truth. She had always recognised the difference between the people to whom

one could tell the truth,—even in insignificant matters,—
and those to whom one could not tell it, but during the
last few days she had recognised it more deeply, more
acutely.

"She is very gravely ill this evening," she replied, meeting his level eyes.

"Is the doctor here?"

"He is coming back at any moment. The specialist too.
We have telephoned for them. You shall see them when
they come."

After all, Dan was nineteen. It was right that he should
bear part of the responsibility; right, though hard. She
could see how childish he still was, though outwardly so
grown-up.

She went back into Evelyn's room. It was quiet in there,
but for the faint moan that came regularly from the bed.
Viola went over to the fire and talked with the nurse in
whispers. They need have no fear of disturbing Evelyn
who was half unconscious.

"Her son has arrived."

"Thatt's good."

Their voices ceased, they sat listening to Evelyn moaning
in pain.

"Can't you give her the morphia now, Sister?"

"Not till eight o'clock, I'm afraid."

"Or when the doctor comes?"

"Yes, if he allows it."

Evelyn called feebly from the bed. Viola went across.
She bent down, and caught the one word, "Morphia."

"Quite soon, darling. The doctor is on his way here,
and he'll give you some."

She would rather have morphia, Viola thought, than be told that Miles is in the next room. How strange and terrible it was, this body, which could obliterate everything from the mind and heart and soul! What was the meaning of it? Was it on Miles' account that she was dying? And, if so, the long laborious process of death meant more to her, just now, than Miles himself.

What a horrible muddle she had made of her relationship with Miles! and how she was paying for it!

The doctor and the specialist arrived together. They went straight into Evelyn's room without seeing Dan. The specialist immediately ordered a saline injection, for the heart was very weak. It was given, and she revived slightly and asked for the morphia again. The specialist took Viola aside. He no longer had the air of being in a hurry, or of considering his patients a nuisance.

"We may as well give it, Lady Viola. But she will not wake from it again."

"Should she see her son for a moment, before you give it?"

"Yes, and anyone else you think she would like to see."

Viola perceived that the specialist knew everything and understood. He had noticed Miles' presence in the next room. Still, she felt bound to say, "Should I telephone for her sister-in-law and brother-in-law?"

The specialist hesitated. Then, being a man who by reason of his profession had a wide knowledge of human life, and who observed more than he appeared to observe, but who released his observations only at the last moment, he said, "We can telephone for them after she has had the injection."

"Then I had better call the boy in at once?"

"Yes, there is no reason for delay."

Viola went into the sitting-room and spoke to Dan. He and Miles were sitting there, on either side of the fire, in the dark. They had restored the two arm-chairs to their original positions.

"Dan, would you like to come and say good night to your mother?"

He rose immediately.

"Just go up to the bed and say good night. Don't be alarmed if she doesn't answer you. She is very tired and half asleep. She may not recognise you. Just say good night and come away quickly. Miles and I will wait for you."

He went, after a scared glance at Viola.

"You must go in next, Miles. They are going to give her a *piqûre*, after this."

Miles knew quite well what she meant.

"This is the end, then?"

"They seem to think so."

It was surprising, how calm and remote everything seemed, almost as though nothing really mattered.

Dan came back.

"She knew me. She said she was glad I was home."

"Now, Miles, go and say good night to her."

Miles went into the familiar bedroom. It was dark but for a shaded lamp burning near the fire. The nurse rose as he came in, with a glimmer of white uniform, and slipped from the room. He was alone with the shadow on the bed, the shadow that was Evelyn. He could see nothing, at first, in the half light, but the darkness of her head on the pillow.

"Evelyn?" he said. "It's Miles."

He sat down beside her and took the hand which he found lying out on the sheet. He noticed that she was still wearing the ring he had given her, but that it was now very loose on her finger. This small fact touched him inexpressibly.

"Miles?" she said. She said no more, but lay contentedly with her hand in his. He did not know whether to speak or not, so sat there in silence, expecting that at any moment Viola would come to take him away. In all the hours of his intimacy with Evelyn, he had never been so completely alone with her as this. It was strange and terrifying, and yet comforting. It seemed to be the complete purification and consummation of all that had gone before.

Viola did not come to take him away. He sat on, having lost all count of time. Evelyn neither stirred nor moaned, but every now and then she pressed his hand, so that he knew she still lived. Once, as she pressed his hand, he whispered, "Do you want the morphia?" and she whispered back "I shall presently." By thatt he knew she was temporarily out of pain.

So long a period of time seemed to pass, that he began to wonder whether she slept or had died. But when he tried to withdraw his hand, she kept it and whispered, "Don't go." So he stayed on for an indefinite period again. He thought of nothing, not even of how often he had scolded her. He was simply merged with her in the dark room, with no physical contact between them except her hand lying in his.

THE END

The first Virago Modern Classic was published in London in 1978, launching a list dedicated to the celebration of women writers and to the rediscovery and reprinting of their works. While the series is called "Modern Classics" it is not true that these works of fiction are universally and equally considered "great," although that is often the case. Published with new critical and biographical introductions, books appear in the series for different reasons: sometimes for their importance in literary history; sometimes because they illuminate particular aspects of women's lives, both personal and public. They may be classics of comedy or storytelling; their interest can be historical, feminist, political, or literary. In any case, in their variety and richness they promise to confuse forever the question of what women's fiction is about, while at the same time affirming a true female tradition in literature.

Initially, the Virago Modern Classics concentrated on English novels and short stories published in the early decades of the century. As the series has grown, it has broadened to include works of fiction from different centuries and from different countries, cultures, and literary traditions; there are books written by black women, by Catholic and Jewish women, by women of almost every English-speaking country, and there are several relevant novels by men.

Nearly 200 Virago Modern Classics will have been published in England by the end of 1985. During that same year, Penguin Books began to publish Virago Modern Classics in the United States, with the expectation of having some 40 titles from the series available by the end of 1986. Some of the earlier books in the series were published in the United States by The Dial Press.